Dance with the Devil

BOOK 2 in the Dance series

By

Ren'e Fedyna

This book is dedicated to my husband George, who despite my whining and bouts of frustration, motivated me to fulfill my long-awaited dream to write. Thank you for your patience and support.

Cover design by Swift House Press

WHAT PEOPLE ARE SAYING ABOUT
DANCE WITH THE DEVIL ~

"This is a much-anticipated sequel to book #1: "Dance of the Restless Soul." I became invested in the lives of these characters and am excited to find out what fate and the future have in store for all of them!" – *Brenda Schancer*

"This book is a real page-turner. I couldn't put it down! I loved the first book in the series, "Dance of the Restless Soul" and now that I've read book 2, I can't wait for book 3." – *Jackie Kaperick*

"Rita is my favorite character -I felt like l really knew her and understood her. I cared what happened to her. I also felt like each of her adventures could be a book in itself." - *Suzanne Ward*

"I was immediately drawn into Lola's story in book one and so I looked forward to book two and was not disappointed. The author has a way of taking us on a non-stop journey of her characters, each so different and each so interesting. I'm looking forward to the next book with eager anticipation." – *Claire Middleton*

After reading the first book, I anxiously awaited the next book in the series and it certainly didn't disappoint. I am totally invested in the lives of the characters and look forward to the next book in the series. So get to writing Ren'e! – *Pat Simmons*

Chapter 1

Émile La Fontaine, former minister to the French government had just won a great deal of money at the Hippodrome, the racetrack at the elite Bois de Boulogne gardens. He returned to his sprawling townhouse on Faubourg Saint-Germain, in the 7th arrondissement of Paris, an area known as the preferred home of French high nobility.

At the entry door, Émile handed his top hat, walking stick and gloves to his long-time footman, Joseph.

"Did you have a good day Monsieur le Ministre?"

Émile smiled. "*Oui*, thank you, Joseph. A very good day!"

With a bounce in his step, Émile entered his study and headed to his liquor cabinet. He selected a bottle of Courvoisier L'Esprit de Cognac, the liquor he saved for special occasions. Seated at his heirloom Louis XV style kingwood desk, he poured himself a celebratory drink. He sipped his cognac. *It was brilliant of me to disregard the advice of my friends. I showed them I know winning horseflesh when I see it!* A light tap on the door caught his attention.

"Your mail has arrived, Monsieur le Ministre. Shall I bring it to you?" Joseph asked.

"*Oui, merci.*"

Joseph laid the mail on his master's desk.

Émile wrinkled his nose. "Joseph, have you taken to wearing perfume?"

The old man frowned, "Perfume? Oh no, Monsieur! It is something in the mail."

Émile flipped through the stack in search of the cause of the offensive scent. He pulled out an envelope that smelled like a whore's cheap cologne. He knew of no lady who would wear such a repulsive scent. Émile was curious, yet he feared he might know who sent it. He took a sip of courage and tore open the envelope. His face twisted into a mask of fury when he read:

My Dear Monsieur La Fontaine,

You are cordially invited to attend the grand opening of my bordello,
La Fontaine du Plaisir. Named in your honor, The Fountain of Pleasure
is the finest bordello in Paris. It exists because of the money you gave me. You have made me so very happy and now I wish to return the favor. Please come to 12 Rue de Richelieu at Ten O'clock on the evening of April 22, 1907. I will make sure you will have the best of everything!

Fondly,
Madame Sophie

Émile slammed his glass onto the desk. The liquid shot out, spilled onto the desk and splashed his clothing. He shouted, *"Putain!"*

Chapter 2

Sophie Décharde was the happiest she had ever been. As a child living on the streets of Paris, she had dreamed of this day. She stood in the private dressing room of her living quarters and admired herself in the full-length mirror. A proud smile spread across her lips. Her maid had just finished dressing her in preparation for the debut of her bordello, *La Fontaine du Plaisir*.

As the maid left, Roccu Faucheur, better known as Apash entered. He carried a bottle of Cristal Champagne and two newly purchased crystal glasses. Apash, originally from Corsica, had been a thug who became Sophie's pimp, business partner and lover.

Sophie had been a Parisian streetwalker when they met. She didn't believe in love, but when Apash took her hard in an alley, he set her world on fire. She feared his dangerous temper and had been a victim of his abuse. But when she looked at his swarthy face, black curly hair and large, obsidian eyes, the danger added to her excitement. For her, Apash was more addictive than opium.

"Monsieur Apash, I must say you look quite dashing in your tailcoat." Sophie winked at him. "I do believe this is the first time I've seen you with your hair combed. I think this is a good look for you."

He growled, "I don't like it. I'm very uncomfortable. The waistcoat is too tight and these fancy shoes hurt my feet."

Seated at her dressing table, Sophie laughed. "Poor Apash!" She pointed to her tiny waist. "How would you like to be laced into a bone and metal corset? It's impossible to breathe in this straitjacket!"

"If you're so uncomfortable, I'd be very happy to rip your clothes off!" Apash gave her a lascivious smile. "I guarantee you'll feel much better!"

"Oh no! This is not the cheap clothing I used to wear. I would have to lie on my back for six months, day and night, to pay for it!" Sophie lifted her glass. "Isn't it time we had some champagne?"

Apash popped the cork, poured champagne into Sophie's glass and filled a glass for himself. "There's a crowd of hungry-looking *fornicateurs* at your front door. I think we'll have tremendous success tonight." They clinked and he toasted. "Here's to the unwilling generosity of Émile La Fontaine!"

The bubbles fizzled as they quaffed their champagne. Sophie filled each glass and said, "Here's to the stupidity of Lola La Fontaine, and of course, to the brilliance of our very profitable scheme!"

She rested an elbow on the dressing table. With her chin in her hand, Sophie said, "I'm grateful that Lola is such a fool, but I can't understand her. Born to the best of everything, she's a woman of exquisite beauty, she had the love of her father and the opportunity to marry one of the richest men in France. Any woman would give everything for that life. But not Lola, she sacrificed it all to be a performer. To dance and sing. What nonsense!"

"Why do you complain?" Apach poured them another glassful. "It's because she and her father fell for our scheme that we can enjoy all the things in life that little tart chose to forfeit."

"You're right! Too bad you couldn't see the expression on Émile's face when I convinced him that Lola committed suicide. But the most delicious moment was when he paid us ransom for his granddaughter!"

He nodded, "It's true, I would love to have seen his face at that moment."

Sophie smiled, "I invited him to come to the opening tonight. Imagine Émile's expression when I tell him Lola is alive and well and living in America."

Apash's face turned dark. He moved so close to Sophie she could feel his hot breath. He gripped her throat. "You'll do no such thing!"

Sophie pushed his hand away and rubbed her neck. "Of course not! Do you think I want to lose my head in the guillotine?"

At a knock on the door, Sophie called out, "*Entrez.*"

The maid announced, "Madame Sophie, many gentlemen are asking to see you."

Her eyes bright with excitement, Sophie gazed at Apash. "The best part of our life is about to begin!" She gathered her skirts and left the room. As she strode to the balustrade, she thought, *Who would have believed one day, Sophie Décharde, the dirty little urchin, would be the madam of the most luxurious bordello in Paris?*

She peered at the crowd of men milling around on the floor below. *Bankers, politicians, and captains of industry. When I approached them to invest in my dream, they got their pound of flesh from me! They believe they're*

13

better than I am, but their appetites are the same as the lowest peasant. They're no different from animals in heat! How I hate them, with their pompous self-importance and their hypocritical morals. They lie and cheat and treat their dogs and horses with more respect than they treat women. But these men will make me very rich. And one day I will have everything—everything I deserve!

Sophie heard shouts from the men below. "You've kept us waiting long enough! Come down and join us!"

She blew them a kiss and sauntered to the winding marble staircase crafted with wrought iron handrails in the latest Art Nouveau design. Sophie stopped at the top of the stairs and waited until all eyes were on her. She felt like a queen.

Designed by the famous House of Worth, her gown of royal blue velvet had a pattern of curlicues embossed in black with a long matching train. The neckline plunged dramatically, exposing the swell of her bosom. Bell sleeves came down to her elbow-length black kid gloves.

To impress her audience, her hair had been combed into a Pompadour style, with crisp little waves high above her forehead, from which ringlets cascaded to her temples. Two strategically placed diamond-studded combs enhanced her hairstyle. Her necklace held a large heart-shaped sapphire surrounded by a filigree of tiny diamonds and she wore matching pendant earrings.

To be sure everyone had time to admire her, Sophie descended each step slowly and with purpose. Her long train flowed behind her, enhancing the drama, and pooled around her as she reached the stairway bottom.

The patrons surrounded her and asked questions about the special delights they could expect at *La Fontaine du Plaisir*.

Sophie gestured with a raised hand. "Patience my dears, your *plaisir* will be unlimited here. But first, I must give you a tour. I'm sure you've noticed our fountain, for which this establishment is named." She brought them to the spectacular fountain situated in the center of a grandiose foyer.

An immense crystal chandelier hung from the cupola centered above the fountain. "Observe this beautiful sculpture. This stunning enchantress waits serenely by the waterside, her naked beauty captured forever within elegant white marble. As she gracefully reclines, champagne flows from her overturned vase and rests in the pool below."

One of the men shouted, "That body looks familiar. Is that you pouring the champagne?"

Sophie smirked. "A lady never tells."

She pointed to an open area nestled below the staircase. "I turn your attention to the alcove. Excellent musicians are performing the music you hear. The music they're playing has been written to correspond with the melodious splash of champagne."

Sophie sensed Apash behind her. His lips touched her ear. "I think I should take you right here, in front of all these men and show them how to do it right. What do you think?"

She flushed with arousal but continued as if she hadn't heard him and directed her audience, "Follow me please."

The patrons trailed Sophie as she glided through a corridor of marble floors and columns. On either side of the corridor sat an elegantly adorned table covered with linen tablecloths, sterling candelabra, stacked crystal champagne glasses and a variety of beautifully displayed hors d'œuvres. A smartly dressed wait staff attended the tables.

Sophie opened the door to several rooms and explained, "Every chamber is designed for comfort and contains devices and costumes to satisfy your predilections. You will have a choice of many *cocottes*. Each is a sorceress schooled in providing gentlemen with exquisite pleasure."

Sophie brought them back to the main lobby, where many well-proportioned young men and dozens of stunning young women posed in a variety of costumes and various stages of undress, including a belly dancer, an Egyptian goddess, and an Amazon. Her patrons quickly moved toward the *cocottes*, leaving Sophie to stand alone.

Apash approached her. "It looks like it will be a successful night."

She said, "*Oui, mon amour.* I will remember this night for as long as I live."

Chapter 3

Regardless of the weather, every Monday at exactly two in the afternoon, Émile sat on the same bench within the expansive park grounds of the Augustine Convent Grandchamp and stared at the heavy wooden entry doors.

This had become his standard routine for about a year, but today would be different. Sitting on the bench with his hands resting on his walking stick, he waited impatiently.

Émile felt ashamed and relieved as he saw her approach through the street gate. He smiled and rose. They embrace and he kissed the old woman on each cheek. "Teresa, I'm so happy to see you."

He guided her to sit beside him on the bench. Teresa said, "Monsieur La Fontaine, it's so good to see you too. It's been a very long time. How are you?"

Émile hesitated. "Not well, I'm afraid."

Teresa looked concerned. "You are ill?"

"No, my health is good. But I have a heavy heart."

"I'm sorry to hear that. Can I help you in some way?"

"Yes, that's why I've asked you to meet with me."

"I wondered why you asked to meet me at this convent. This is the place I last saw Lola. It's been so many years. She must be grown by now." Teresa raised her eyes to the sky in thought. "She's at least…twenty-four years of age?" She looked to Émile for confirmation.

Barely above a whisper, he said, "Twenty-five."

"She's still here? Has she taken vows?"

Émile looked at his feet and shook his head slowly. "No, Teresa."

"Is there another reason why you asked me here?"

"Teresa, I've been a prideful and selfish man. I've done many things that I regret. Because of my stubbornness, I'm lonely and unhappy. My conscience weighs heavily on me."

"Does this have to do with Mademoiselle Lola? How is she?"

"Lola is…my dear Lola is dead. And it's my fault."

"Dead?" Teresa's face went pale. She crossed herself. "Lola is dead? No, that's not possible! What happened?"

Émile inhaled a deep breath. "I let my pride come between us. You may remember, I betrothed her at birth to Marquis Bouton. At sixteen, I told her she must marry him. Not only did she refuse my wishes to marry, but she sneaked off to perform at a cabaret! Humiliated and possessed by anger, I thought sending her to this convent would bring her to her senses. But after you delivered her here, she escaped."

"Escaped! But how?"

"It doesn't matter. She wanted to be an entertainer at any cost. I told her that she must return to the convent or I would disinherit her. I said she would no longer be a member of my family and I demanded that she change her name."

Teresa gasped, "Oh, no! What did she do?"

"I hadn't seen Lola for several years. Then one day she came to my home. She told me she was pregnant."

Teresa's mouth dropped. "Pregnant! Had she been married?"

"No. The sight of her so disgusted me I almost struck her face. I called her a *putain* and insisted she leave my house and never return. I told her she was dead to me."

"Oh, Monsieur La Fontaine, what a terrible nightmare!" Teresa exclaimed. How did Mademoiselle Lola die?"

"She committed suicide!"

"Suicide! *Mon Dieu!*" Teresa crossed herself again. "Lola was so full of life! Why would she do such a thing?"

Émile said, "What I'm about to show you will explain everything. It's very difficult for me, but I feel you should know what happened." He reached into his pocket and removed a letter. "This is the last communication I had from Lola."

My dearest Papá,

All my life I have loved you and never meant to hurt you. But I was a foolish girl, and I have made many mistakes. Mistakes I can never undo. I can no longer live in a world without your love, and I cannot live with the shame I have caused you. The only way I can end your pain and mine is to end my miserable life and start a new life through my little one. The baby that I am giving birth to, even as I write this letter. My dear friend Sophie will bring this innocent child for you to raise after I am gone. I pray you raise my baby to be a better person than I have been. I will love you through my child better in death than I have ever been able to love you in life.

19

Pray for me and please, please forgive me.
Your loving daughter,
Lola

Teresa returned the letter to Émile. Tears slid down her cheeks. She pulled a handkerchief from her purse. Her shoulders quaked as she softly sobbed. After a few moments, she wiped her tears. Her voice thick with emotion, she asked, "She died after giving birth?" Teresa thought for a moment. "If she committed suicide, it is not possible to be buried in this convent, but—?"

"No, she is not buried here. I sent André, my manservant, to the Exhibition Room of the Morgue every day for months. Every day he looked through the window at the bodies on display, but Lola never appeared." He cleared his throat. "Her body has never been found."

"I'm so very sorry. It's just so hard to believe."

"I asked you here because there is someone I want you to see." Émile removed a gold watch from his vest pocket and flipped open the cover. "Two-thirty, it's time."

Teresa heard a bell ring. Several minutes later, the front doors of the convent opened. Out came the Sisters and many little girls who skipped and giggled as they ran to play. Teresa smiled as she watched the little ones, then she turned to Émile, "Who is it that you'd like me to see?"

"Look carefully at each little girl."

After focusing on each girl, Teresa jumped from her seat." I can't believe my eyes!" Teresa pointed. "Is that? It cannot be! That little girl looks exactly like our dear Lola!"

Émile stepped beside her. "Ah, so you see what I see. She is Lola's daughter."

"Yes! She has the same black hair and blue eyes. Her face! I would swear that's Lola!"

"The Sisters call her Mimi. Her name will remain Mimi La Fontaine. I've been responsible for expenses since she arrived as an infant. She'll soon be four years old.

"For the first few years, I remained bitter and refused to see Mimi. But after I retired from the government, I grew very lonely. My friends would boast of their grandchildren and I realized that I might have another chance. I want to start over with Mimi. But this time I will never reject her. She'll have everything she wants. I won't make the mistake I made with Lola. I will refuse Mimi nothing.

"I want to bring her home with me today. You've been the nanny and chaperone for my wife, Doña Dolores, and you were the same for Lola. So, I want you to take care of Lola's daughter. My only request is that you never tell her about her mother. When Mimi asks, tell her that her father, a military officer, died in service, and Lola died after giving birth to her. Will you agree?"

Teresa thought a moment. "Monsieur La Fontaine, I am thrilled at the thought of caring for Mimi, but you must realize I'm much older now. I'm not sure I have the energy for a little girl."

"I've been a proud fool for many years, and pride has cost me more than I can bear. There are many others I can ask to take care of Mimi. But there is no one else that I care for and trust, as I do you. Teresa, will you help me?"

She smiled, "How can I resist? Yes, of course, I'll be happy to be Mimi's nanny."

21

Dance with the Devil

Chapter 4

Who is this woman? Michael James O'Reilly wondered as he sat beside her coffin. *I saw her every day of my life, but I never knew her.*

As per custom, Michael had laid his mother's body out for viewing. He could only afford a cheap wooden coffin. He placed it on two chairs in the kitchen of his paltry Arkansas cabin. Well-wishers came to pay their respects, just as they had done one short year ago for his father. He thanked them when they patted him on the shoulder and offered their condolences. Ma had been with him then. He had been brave for her. He has no one to be brave for now.

He sat by her coffin all that day and the entire night. As the day had surrendered to darkness, he had lit oil lamps which gave her pallid complexion a warm, rosy glow. He had never asked her anything about herself and she had never offered.

Michael knew little about her family. Her name was Dierdre. She had accompanied his father as his bride when they came to America from Ireland. They had traveled together on one of the rickety, overcrowded vessels known as 'coffin ships.' Her younger brother had been with them, but he had died on the long, grueling journey. He was one of the many poor souls who had succumbed to malnutrition and disease.

Michael knew more about his father, Terrence. His father often told him how much he missed the green hills of Ireland and of the good times he shared with his family. His father also told Michael of the horrors he had witnessed during the Potato Famine. He spoke of his parent's sacrifice when they insisted he leave for America with Dierdre and her brother, while they were still strong enough to survive the voyage.

His father clenched his fists as he described his anger and humiliation when he and his family, like thousands of others, were evicted from the land they had worked for generations. Michael couldn't bear to look at the tears in his father's eyes as he recounted the day he left Ireland. He heard the heartbreak in his father's voice as he told of his guilt and helplessness knowing his parents would soon die from famine and sickness.

Terrence had brought a deep love of the land with him. A love he had tried to instill in his young son, Michael. As when he scooped up a handful of earth and said, "Michael, smell this, smell the richness of it! Everything comes from the earth. The sun and rain are in the earth. We're alive because of what grows from it, and when we die, we become a part of it."

Before Michael was born, there had been many years when the harvest was good and the crop prices were high. But the Civil War had caused an overwhelming burden on farmers. As a result of the war the Southern economy was devastated, and so was Terrence. The harder he tried, the poorer they got. His pa always dreamed of becoming rich from his land. He loved the land until he hated it. Dejected and defeated, Terrence had worn himself out trying to make a living for his family. Sick with tuberculosis and the stink of poverty, he died.

Michael had continued to work the land after his pa died, but having no more success than his father, he had never developed the love his father felt for the land. To Michael, land meant drudgery and disappointment.

He stared at his mother's serene face and tried to recall everything about her. He believed she had been deeper and more complex than his father, but now he'd never know. To him, she was always just ma. He touched her thick red hair and thought that she must have been beautiful once. Michael tried to imagine her as the pretty, young woman his father married. Her smile must have dazzled him.

In his seventeen years, Michael seldom remembered her having a reason to laugh. When she did, her big green eyes sparkled. However, when he misbehaved, he remembered how he feared the anger in her eyes. They were more terrifying than his father's strap. Mostly he remembered the misery he saw in them. When a crop failed, or they couldn't afford shoes for him, or they had no money for pa's medicine.

Ma's skin was paper-thin and rubbed raw from endless toil. She was strong because she had to be. She had worked in the fields as hard as he and his father. Yet she had also performed her daily labors of cooking and cleaning, washing and mending their clothes. Ma was the first to rise each morning to make breakfast and feed the animals and was the last to go to bed at night. She had never once complained.

He clasped her cold hand. *I wish I got to know you better. I wish we sat and talked about your life and your dreams. I wish I told you that I loved you.* Now he would never know her. At thirty-nine, she was dead. Dead from heart failure. Dead from heart sickness. Dead from nothing to look forward to but more misery. Now she was about to be buried. *Goodbye Ma, it's time for you to rest in peace.*

Michael cried at his mother's funeral. He was sad about his mother's hard life. He didn't know what unkept promises his pa had made to her, but he made a promise to himself. An unbreakable oath. *No matter what, I'll give my wife a good life—a happy life—without worry or pain. I'll have enough money to keep her happy, or I'll never marry.*

Chapter 5

After his mother's funeral, Michael felt hollow, alone and angry. Angry at himself for not appreciating his mother. Angry at his father for not giving his mother a better life. Angry at enduring a life of poverty and despair.

Michael had never been anywhere outside the boring little town of Allenville, Arkansas. With his parents dead, he had no reason to stay. He sold the farm for the little it was worth, packed his meager belongings and mounted his horse.

He headed to Ft. Smith, where he picked up the trail of the old Butterfield Overland Mail route. This route used was by stagecoaches carrying mail and passengers west from Missouri to California. Over time the route had become obsolete.

He wandered from town to town along the mail route taking jobs where he could find them. In Ft. Smith, Arkansas he built wagons. He moved on to Tulsa, Oklahoma where he pumped oil. While in Santa Fe, New Mexico, he laid railroad ties for the Atchison, Topeka, and Santa Fe Railroad.

Easy-going, Michael enjoyed talking with others. He made friends easily. After work, he often joined his pals at the local tavern for laughter and camaraderie. However, if he over-imbibed, the liquor let loose angry demons, and, at times, caused him to end up in a fight and a night in jail.

There was never a reason for Michael to stay in a town longer than a year or two. Most men he met were like himself. They worked hard and drank hard but they seemed as lonely as he was. Most of the young women he met were looking for husbands. He'd never met a woman who interested him. Even if he had found someone, he insisted on keeping the promise he made to himself. He'd not marry until he could afford to take care of his wife and keep her happy. He stayed in each town until he got bored and ready for something new.

Once again, he had the urge to leave. This time he headed to Arizona. He didn't know what he was seeking, he only knew he hadn't found it yet.

He quit his job at the railroad and purchased the goods he needed for his long journey and set out to continue along the mail route. Although he liked spending time hunting, cooking his meals and sleeping under the stars, Michael was grateful for the remaining waystations he came across along the trail. He appreciated a roof over his head, sleeping in a bed, having dinner at a tavern and the opportunity for a hot bath.

Michael traveled many long days over dusty desert terrain, looking for a waystation where he could relax for a while. In the late afternoon, hot and thirsty, He reined in his horse and took a long drink from his canteen. With his bandana, he wiped the sweat from his neck and looked out over the landscape.

Waves of heat shimmered from the hot barren land. Before him, he saw a few tall, multi-armed saguaro cactus and the twisted branches of mesquite trees. The blazing sun melted behind distant hills. Deepening shades of blue began to swallow the pastel sky. Soon it would be night. Relieved to see a town in the distance, Michael nudged his horse to move on.

A small dusty outpost in the Arizona desert, Dragoon Springs Station, had a ramshackle hotel, a livery stable, a saloon, a post office, a general store, a restaurant and a jailhouse.

Michael rode into the outpost. Shouts and laughter rollicked through the doors of the nearby Hellbenders Watering Hole saloon. He left his horse at the livery and headed inside. This place was no different from other saloons he'd seen, with its high ceiling of pressed tin, dirt floor, and a bar of half-hewn lumber and wood slat walls that sported bullet holes. He walked to the bar through the haze of cigar smoke and the bitter smell of beer.

A crowded row of men stood at the bar. Every man wore a hat and spurs, many had hair to their shoulders, and each wore a mustache. Michael squeezed between two men, ordered a whiskey and swigged it. The rough taste of it felt good as it scorched his insides. He continued to enjoy several more until a man pushed beside him. Michael complained, "Hey! You spilled my drink!" A scar from eyebrow to chin on the man's face made him look hard and nasty.

The man turned his back to Michael and ordered a drink.

A voice from the crowd shouted, "Hey Barret, looks like this corncracker's got a beef with you!"

Barret received his drink and replied, "I think you might be right, Joe." Barret faced Michael, and with a twinkle in his eye, he sipped his whiskey.

Michael leveled a cold stare at Barret and demanded, "You spilled my drink, now you owe me one!"

29

"Ain't that a shame," Barret snarled. How 'bout I give you some a' mine?" He threw his drink in Michael's face.

Michael punched him. Blood flowed from Barret's nose. He fell against those near him, spilling their drinks as he hit the floor. After his friends helped Barret rise he swung. But Michael blocked his arm and socked Barret again. A mob surrounded Michael and pummeled him. One man after the other fell from Michael's blows but the crowd persisted. A man joined the melee. Rather than beat Michael, he helped him fight off the assailants.

A gunshot stilled the room. Michael turned to see the sheriff and two deputies standing in the entrance. The sheriff shouted, "Stop fighting or you'll all be spending the night as my guest!" The crowd settled down. "We don't allow no fightin' in Dragoon Springs Station. Aw right, who started this?"

Blood trickled down his nose and bruises began to appear on Barret's face as he shouted, "We was mindin' ar own business when these two loco sons-a-bitches started shoutin' and punchin' for no reason a'tall." He looked at the other patrons and asked. "Ain't that right? None a' us started the fight, right?"

The sheriff walked to Michael and his defender, "Is it true you two started the fight?"

Michael said, "No sheriff, that ain't how it—"

Barret pointed at Michael and demanded, "Ask him, ask him who threw the first punch!"

The sheriff looked at Michael, "Is it true you threw the first punch?"

Michael replied, "I suppose so, but—"

"Never you mind. Looks like you two started this, so you both got a bed on me." The sheriff called to his deputies, "Lock 'em up."

The deputies grabbed the two men and marched them across the street to the jailhouse. Michael and his fellow pugilist shared a prison cell. Michael put out his hand and announced, "My name's Michael O'Reilly. I thank you for backing me up but you don't even know me. Why'd you help me out?"

His jail mate shook Michael's hand and said, "Glad ta know ya. I'm Cyril O'Keefe. I never like it when ten men need ta pile on one. If ya cain't fight one on one, that makes ya a yellow belly. An' I cain't tolerate no yellow belly."

Cuts and bruises covered Cyril's face. His eye, purple and bulbous, looked as if it was about to pop, and made it hard for Michael not to laugh at Cyril's attempt to be earnest.

Michael's face had as many bruises and blood oozed from his split bottom lip. He wiped the blood with his sleeve and said, "Well, I surely do appreciate your help. Do you live hereabouts?"

"No, I jus' got here. I'm only passin' through. I got business in another place. So, where'd you come from pardner?"

Michael shook his head, "Nowhere, uh, everywhere, I guess. And you?"

"O'Reilly, you say? You're Irish ain't ya?"

"Yeah, well my family was."

Cyril looked thoughtful, "My family's Irish too. Though, I'm the only one left. My pa and uncle came from the ol' sod. We worked the coal mines of Pennsylvania till we heard about California gold. We packed our bags and set off to get rich and by golly, we did! We hit a bonanza! As God is my witness, I

31

tell ya we was rich! We got enough a'that blessed shiny stuff ta fill this miserable jail cell!"

Michael took a closer look at Cyril and frowned, "If you're so rich, what're you doing here?"

Cyril shook his head. "Ah, the sad truth of it is, some claim jumpers got the better of us and killed my pa and my uncle. I was jus' a youngun then. I played dead or they wouda' killed me too."

Michael said, "Sorry for your troubles."

Cyril's eyes grew hard, "Thanks, Michael. But I gotta tell ya, God owes me, and I want what's rightfully mine! No damn claim jumper's gonna take my hard-earned stake away from me again!"

"I wish you luck, Cyril."

Cyril stared at Michael as if he was trying to figure something out. "Say, I'm lookin' for a pardner, someone who can work with me and make sure we keep them cutthroats from stealing our claim. I can see you're not afeared of nuthin'. So, Michael, how 'bout takin' a chance with me?"

Michael scratched his head, "What're you talking about?"

Cyril stood against the bars to see if anyone could hear. Then he stepped back and sat on Michael's bunk. Leaning close, Cyril whispered, "I'm on my way to Rimrock Springs, Arizona. There's been a big gold strike and I'm gonna get me some."

"Rimrock Springs, you say?

Cyril looked around then back at Michael, "Hush! Do 'ya want the world to know?"

Michael lowered his voice. "How'd you know about the gold strike?"

"I don't know. Well, what I mean is, I heard talk an' I'm gonna see for myself."

"Nah, sorry Cyril, I'm not interested."

"I know ya think I'm full a horse feathers, but I had the taste of it before and I want it again. Ain't got a reason not to check it out. Why not come with me?"

"I'm not the right man for you. I've done a lotta things, but I never done any mining."

"Don't worry about that. I'm not one for braggin', Michael, but I been hangin' round 49er's since I was a little pup. My pa taught me all about it. If it's there, I'll find it."

"I don't know much about mining, but I know you'll need a grubstake. I'm broke and can't help you there."

"I'm not askin' ya for money. I ain't got much, but I've got enough to get started. I feel in my gut that one day we'll be pulling nuggets out of the ground the size a' my fist!"

Michael laughed hard. "Ow!" He said as the tear in his lip ripped open. He wiped the blood on his sleeve. "Cyril, don't make me laugh. That's a great dream you have. But I don't think I'd be much help to you."

"Lord knows why, but Michael I feel I can trust ya'. I'd like ta pardner up with the likes of your ugly mug. Wouldn't ya like to be rich?"

"Sure, but the chances aren't very good."

"Look, Michael, what've ya ta lose? Let's take a look. It's about a week's ride from here. We'll snoop around, keepin' our eyes and ears open and see if anything looks interestin'. If not, we'll just toast to better times with a handshake and a drink, and I'll have been proud to have known ya. Ya got somethin' better to do?"

Dance with the Devil

Chapter 6

Michael and Cyril headed to Rimrock Springs. For a week, they survived a relentless sun and rain-parched land of scrub, mesquite and prickly pear cactus. They worked well together, calling upon each other's experiences under similar circumstances and enjoyed each other's company. Evenings around a crackling campfire, they joked and talked about their past.

On the last night before they reached Rimrock Springs, their discussion turned to the future.

Cyril asked, "So Michael, what're your plans for all the money you'll be needing to spend when we strike the big one?"

Michael laughed, "Since I never imagined I'd have enough money to do more than make it to the next town, I have no idea what I'd do."

"C'mon Michael, there's more to you than that." Cyril poked the campfire with a twisted stick. "There must be somethin' rattlin' around in that skull of yours. You'll have the whole world at your feet. There must be somethin' you want more than anythin'."

Michael scratched his head and thought. "Well, if I had lots of money, I'd like to spend it on a woman. Not any woman, but a special woman. Someone I'd love with all my heart and who loved me in return. I'd build her a big house and buy her everything. We'd have lots of children and—"

"You're quite the romantic, Michael. Just you be careful now, there's many a young sage hen lookin' to hogtie a man with pockets full a' hard money. They'll do everythin' they can to score off you. Make sure the woman you go sweet on is the real thing and loves you for yourself and not your money."

"Don't you worry about me. When I meet the right woman, I'll know. So, what about you? What'll you do with all your riches?"

"Aaah! When I was with my pa and uncle in California, we saw some of the most amazin' cattle ranches. I'm gonna get me a large piece a land and run some thousand head of cattle on it. That's my dream!"

"Well, whatever happens, Cyril, I sure do hope one day your dream'll come true." Michael yawned, "I guess we be better be getting some sleep. We got lots to dream about and tomorrow we got a busy day."

The next afternoon they arrived at the bustling town of Rimrock Springs. Cyril and Michael agreed that they needed to gather as much prospecting information as possible.

Larger and busier than expected, they were disappointed to see an incessant stream of wagons and men on horseback traveling through Rimrock Springs in every direction. Everyone seemed to be in a hurry. Men shouted, "Out of the way!" as they navigated their wagons through the crowded streets. They heard the whinnies of horses and the rumbling of wagon wheels against the dirt-impacted streets. The town crackled with excitement, as if everyone vied for a front-row seat at a grand celebration.

Cyril shook his head. "I'd bet there ain't a farmer in this territory who's stayed home to bring in the harvest or a cowpoke who ain't pawned his watch to git here and an' start diggin'. Looks like the whole world knows there's gold in these parts."

Michael frowned, "Do you think we're too late? Are we wasting our time?"

"I don' know. But I ain't ready to give up til we start prospectin'. I tell you what, there's a hotel cross the street. Let's get a room, get some grub, a bath, and a little sleep, then we'll check out this town."

Crossing the street, they dodged loaded carts and agitated horses. Checking into the Rimrock Springs Hotel, they discovered exorbitant prices for a night's stay. Michael asked the desk clerk for a cheaper place in town to stay. He told them no other hotel had rooms. Desperate for a hot bath they agreed to pay for one night's stay.

The posh hotel exhibited velvet-covered settees and Persian rugs in the lobby and had a restaurant with cloth-covered tables and a small bar. Their room had two comfortable brass beds, a stand with a water pitcher atop, and lace curtains surrounding a window that overlooked the noisy main street. Michael and Cyril took turns bathing in a large wood-covered tinware plunge bath.

After a few rested hours and a light meal, they were impatient to harvest information. Cyril announced, "The best place to learn where to search is at the local saloons where we kin find loose-tongued braggarts and barmen who soak up gossip like hogs in a trough. So, Michael, if you're up to it, it may be necessary to exhaust every watering hole in town. Whadaya say?"

With a wink and a smile, Michael agreed. "A man's gotta do what a man's gotta do!"

Together they entered the Wet Your Whistle Tavern. Shoulder to shoulder men crowded the busy bar. Most men stood with a foot rested on the brass foot rail running the length of the bar. A line of spittoons sat at even distances along the rail. Every man wore a hat as varied in size and shape as their facial hair. Some wore chaps, vests, or had kerchiefs dangling from their necks.

Behind the long mahogany bar, whiskey bottles rested on shelves attached to a large mirror. Dark brown paneled wood wainscot covered the other walls. Above the wainscot, deer, elk and bull antlers hung against striped red and brown wallpaper.

Cyril and Michael struck up conversations with patrons and bartenders but had little luck gleaning information. They continued to every saloon along Whiskey Row until they came to the last one. Their hopes were low as they entered The Last Chance Saloon. The small, dark room smelled of dust and rotten wood. At the bar, Cyril asked, "Hey, barkeep, my name's Cyril, what's yours?

A cigarette hung from the grubby bartender's lips. He turned his disinterested face to Cyril and said, "You must have tried every saloon in town. Betcha you're trying to find out where the gold is."

"You're right there. They weren't kiddin' when they named this place The Last Chance Saloon. So, kin you help us out? Everyone seems to know where the gold is at but us. If'n you can give us a hint, we'll make it worth your while."

The bartender smirked, set three shot glasses on the bar and filled them with whiskey. "This round is on you, boys."

They each swigged down the shot. The bartender poured himself another and pointed to an old man at the end of the bar. "If anyone knows where's there's gold, it's Sam. He's been prospecting around Rimrock Springs for years. I don't think he's ever found anything, but at least he can tell you where it ain't!"

They looked at the man at the end of the bar. His head rested on folded arms as he leaned against the bar. Michael asked the bartender, "Is he asleep standing up?"

"Sam!" The bartender shouted. With no response, the bartender shouted louder "HEY, SAM!"

Sam lifted his head and looked around the room as if he didn't know where he was.

"Sam, these boys wanna talk to you."

He narrowed his eyes and looked them over. "Wha'd a ya want?" Deep ragged crevices appeared on the areas of Sam's sun-scorched face not covered by greasy hair and an unruly gray beard. He wore a sweat-stained shirt, a dusty vest and a large floppy hat. His bloodshot eyes looked as if he hadn't been sober for a long time.

Cyril said, "We jus' wanna ask ya what ya know about findin' gold in these parts."

Sam's rheumy brown eyes widened. "Ya got whiskey money?"

In a lowered voice, Cyril asked Michael, "Ya think he's got anythin' to tell us?"

"It's only gonna cost us a bottle of whiskey to find out."

Cyril said, "Yeah, we got whiskey money."

Sam smiled, "Well, c'mon over boys, we got plenty to talk about!"

Michael ordered a bottle of whiskey. They watched Sam as he shuffled on his old bowed legs toward a table in the furthest corner from the door. They joined him there.

After Michael filled their glasses, Sam slugged his down and poured himself another.

When Sam reached for the bottle again, Cyril pulled it away and asked, "Whaddaya got to say 'bout the gold aroun' here, ol' timer?"

Sam looked Cyril in the eye. "What's your name boy?"

"I'm Cyril," he tilted his head, "and this here's my pardner Michael."

"Pleased ta meet ya fellas. I been prospectin' in these parts nigh on ten years. Been up and down every stream bed and valley in this territory. The closest I ever come to finding gold is—how 'bout a nuther shot of lighting boys?"

Cyril poured Sam another glassful.

Sam swigged it down and put out his glass for more. Cyril didn't fill it.

"Now boys, ya' gotta unerstan', what I'm 'bout to tell ya is worth way more'n a bottle a rotgut. If ya ain't a little more genrous I maybe might furgit some a da details, catch ma' drift?"

Michael and Cyril looked at each other, then Michael pushed the bottle toward Sam.

Sam filled his glass. "Aw right, listen up fellas. I ain't told nobody what I'm 'bout to tell you. First off, you the only boys who's ever was willin' to buy me a bottle. But the other reason I'm tellin' you is cause it's too late fur me, I gots me the roumatiz. There ain't no way fer me ta mine the stuff myself, not wit' all my aches and pains. 'Sides I'm an ol' man an even if I was t'mine the gold, what would I do with the money? Got nobody I care 'bout to give it to. My times up fellas. Better for you young'ns to enjoy it."

"Thank you kindly, Sam," Michael said.

"Yeah, Sam," Cyril said. "We 'preciate it. So, where's the gold?"

Sam took a swig from the bottle then coughed hard. After a few minutes, he took a breath. "Okay, boys, listen up. When you leave town head straight to the mountains. When you reach the base a' the mountains, turn right 'bout ten mile. Look for a crick in a pass between two mountains. That's the last place I looked 'for I give up prospectin'. I found me some quartz in that crick. It had veins that looked rusty. Do you boys know what that means?"

Michael shook his head but Cyril's eyes gleamed. "Where there's quartz veins with rusty lookin' fractures, that's where you kin find the greatest amounts a gold."

Sam slapped his hand on the table and shouted, "That's right, boy! That's where the gold is!" Sam reached into his pocket and pulled out a piece of quartz. "Here's what I found."

Cyril examined the quartz for a few minutes, then looked at Sam. "This is what you found in the creek?"

"Sure t'is."

"So where 'xactly is this creek?" asked Cyril as he handed the quartz to Michael.

After gulping down another shot of whiskey Sam said, "Well, I tell ya. When I first found it, I thought maybe I'd go back to the crick when I was feelin' better, so I put my mark on the mountain. What I dun was, I dug me a hole on the side of the mountain and put a wood cross wit ma name on it. If it's still there, you'll find it awright."

Michael examined the quartz piece and handed it back to Sam.

41

"Naw, you keep it, boys. I ain't got no use for it no more."

Michael looked at Cyril as if as confirming a tacit agreement. Michael announced, "If we find gold 'cause of what you told us, we'll cut you in for a third of what we find."

Cyrus put the quartz in his shirt pocket and said, "Yeah, that's right. If what you told us gets us to the right place, we'll take care of ya."

"Well fellas, I surely hope you strike it rich an' apriciate you wantin' to give me a piece, but by the time you hit it big, I'll be planted 'neath the daisies. Best a' luck to ya."

Cyril and Michael shook Sam's hand and thanked him.

Michael pulled a ten-dollar bill from his pocket. "Here, Sam, the drinks are on us!"

After they left the saloon they smiled and patted each other on the back. Cyril said, "I gotta good feelin'. I think that ol' man knows what he's talkin' 'bout. Let's go celebrate!"

"I hope you're right 'bout Sam, but I don't think we should spend any more money. We got a lot of supplies to buy."

"C'mon, Michael. We're not comin' back to town for a long spell. Let's give ourselves something to remember while we're here. Don't know 'bout you, but I'm ready for some vittles and that place over yonder looks mighty fine to me. Smell them sizzlin' steaks! C'mon Michael, ain't ya hungry?" Cyril put his arm around Michael's shoulder as they headed for the saloon.

The Golden Slipper Saloon sat apart from Whiskey Row. More than a saloon, it was more of an elegant restaurant and casino. When they stepped inside, a man in a tuxedo greeted them, brought them to a table and handed them a large menu.

"Cyril, look at this place. I never seen anything like it!" The spacious saloon had gilt-edged mirrors, sparkling chandeliers, a long, polished mahogany bar and a big stage with red tapestry drapes. Raucous patrons milled around gambling tables

"I cain't hear ya. It's too damn noisy in here." An orchestra played, but with all the laughing and shouting, they barely heard the music.

"Look at these prices! I thought the hotel had high prices!" Michael said as he pointed to the price of steak listed on the menu. "Is this the price for a piece of steak or the whole cow?"

Cyril nodded, "Ya gotta be rich to live in this town. That's cause there's gold in these parts! Now, let's get a drink. But none a that fancy French bubbly stuff, just a beer."

"I don't know, Cyril, I think we should leave. We need money to get our supplies tomorrow, not waste it on this fancy stuff."

The room darkened. A hush came over the crowd and a man in a tuxedo appeared on the stage. He announced, "Good evening ladies and gentlemen, I'm Frank Walters, and as the owner of The Golden Slipper Saloon, I'm very proud to present Lola's Ladies for your entertainment pleasure."

The orchestra began to play a saucy tune. "Cyril, we gotta get outta here." Michael rose to leave. "We'll be lucky to afford a beer!"

"Hold on Michael, take a gander at them beauties!"

Michael looked at the stage. He saw stunning women wearing large feathered hats, low-cut bodices and ruffled skirts short enough to expose

43

their legs. He sat staring with a mixture of fascination and embarrassment as the ladies lined themselves shoulder to shoulder and simultaneously lifted their right knees high, circling their pointed toes and swirled their skirts with enthusiasm.

Captivated, Michael watched the dancers run around the stage shouting and laughing, taking turns doing cartwheels or standing on the toes of one foot, holding the other foot straight into the air with one hand, and spinning round and round. Not inexperienced with women, Michael had seen more than one naked lady, but he'd never been to a performance where so many women danced with such immodesty.

A waiter arrived. Michael whispered to Cyril, "We should go. I think we'll be spending too much money here and we need to get an early start in the morning."

Cyril didn't take his eyes from the stage. "Hold your horses, Michael. Let's get one beer. If you still want to leave after we've finished our drink, that's what we'll do."

Michael sighed and ordered them each a beer. He returned his gaze to the stage. By the time their drinks arrived, Michael felt more comfortable watching the ladies dance suggestively. The gentleman in him wanted to lower his eyes, but the man in him couldn't stop staring.

Just as they finished their beers, Lola's Ladies left the stage and the host returned. He asked the crowd, "Did you enjoy our wonderful dancers?"

The crowd whistled and cheered. "Well, my fortunate friends, you're about to see a most spectacular performance by the one, the only, Miss Lola Dupin. Formerly a star performer at the famous

Moulin Rouge in Paris, France. I guarantee this will be a performance you'll never forget. Now, please join me in welcoming Miss Lola Dupin!"

Michael demanded, "Okay Cyril, let's go."

The crowd stood and shouted, "Lola! Lola! Lola!"

Cyril asked, "Wait! How can we leave now? Let's just see what she looks like, then I promise we'll leave."

Michael rose and insisted, "No Cyril, it's time to—"

At that moment, Lola appeared on stage. Michael's mouth froze open at the sight of Lola. Sleek and exquisite, the white silk dress hugged the curves of her shapely body. Small red flowers interweaved within her up-pinned shiny black hair and exposed the soft curve of her graceful neck. Lola's sapphire blue eyes were large and set above pronounced cheekbones and her red lips were full and sensual. Entranced, Michael watched as Lola moved like a rolling sea, with swaying hips and shoulders, as she sauntered across the stage.

Michael's gaze swept along Lola's body. His knees caved as he felt heat rise through him. He melted into his chair.

Cyril said, "You're right, Michael, we should go."

"No!" Michael shouted, "No, we can't leave now!"

Cyril laughed and said, "Okay, if you insist!"

Lola's lips curled into a slow, lazy smile. She purred, "Bonsoir, boys. My name is Lola and we're going to have fun tonight. If that's all right with you, say *oui!*"

The audience clapped and shouted, *"Oui! Oui!"* Michael shouted with the others.

Lola turned and made her way towards a swing rigged to the upper rafters. A sprig of white nosegays lay on the swing's seat. Lola held the sprig, sat with her back leaning against the rope swing, and with a sad countenance sniffed the bouquet. The orchestra played, and in French-accented English, Lola sang, "A Bird In A Gilded Cage."

At the sound of her voice, Michael felt his heart pound. He had never heard anything so beautiful.

Lola threw the bouquet into the audience and several men scrambled to catch it. She stood and began a series of dance steps, leaping and twirling across the stage. In between dances she sang bawdy songs including 'A Maiden Did Bathing Go," "A-rovin," and "The Comical Dreamer." The crowd enthusiastically clapped and stomped along with the beat of her songs.

When she finished singing, a stagehand presented her with a crook. She took it and sat on a swing that raised her into the air. She flew through the air a hair's breadth above the crowd. With the crook in hand, she playfully removed men's hats and tapped the heads of men who tried to pull her off. Lola sang to them and eventually threw them souvenirs of her clothing—a glove, a handkerchief and a garter. The spectacular sensation drew grateful gasps from the crowd.

For the finale, Lola's Ladies returned to the stage, each holding a nosegay as they formed a line. Lola spun and gathered a nosegay from each of the ladies. A she twirled passed them each in turn left the stage. Holding the bouquets, she danced like a butterfly, seeming to float as she twirled and leaped in the air. With elegance, grace and romance, Lola performed a variety of dance styles combining ballet and waltz moves.

When she finished dancing, she looked out into the audience. "So, boys, did you have a good time tonight?" Michael joined the crowd as they jumped to their feet, stomping, clapping and shouting, "Lola! Lola! Lola!"

Michael felt a longing he'd never experienced. He realized that if ever there was a woman he'd want to spend his life with, it would be Lola Dupin.

Dance with the Devil

Chapter 7

That night Michael didn't sleep. He could only think about Miss Lola Dupin from Paris, France. He imagined that when he became rich, he would look into her beautiful blue eyes and ask her to marry him. He envisioned she would swoon into his arms and shout in her adorable French accent, *"Oui! Oui! I will marry you!"*

Giving up trying to sleep, he dressed and waited impatiently for Cyril to wake. When he couldn't wait any longer, he shook Cyril's shoulder and shouted, "Get up! We need to get started."

Cyril looked towards the window. "Michael, it's still dark outside. The general store ain't open yet!"

"I don't care, we'll just wait outside till they open. We need to get started right away!"

Cyril raised himself to a sitting position and turned up the oil lamp. He tilted his head, looked at Michael and chuckled. "You weren't in such a gol durn hurry to find gold 'til you saw that French lady. Is she what's gettin' you all fired up?"

Michael tossed Cyril his pants and said, "Never mind! Get dressed. We got a lot of work ahead of us, so get crackin'."

They packed their belongings and headed to the general store. Cyril sat on the store's front step as Michael paced. The desert night chill evaporated with the rise of the morning sun. Shopkeepers and restauranteurs opened their doors for patrons who'd soon arrive.

49

Cyril pointed and said, "Look, that restaurant's open, let's get some chow."

"I'm not hungry. I want to be here when the store opens so we can get our supplies and get moving."

Just then, the shopkeeper appeared and unlocked the door. Cyril sighed, "I guess they'll be no grub this mornin'." He and Michael stepped inside and bought all the supplies they could afford.

They retrieved their horses and purchased two donkeys from the livery. After loading the donkeys with supplies, they left Rimrock Springs. Following Sam's instructions, they headed towards the mountains. After crossing the plains, they traversed dry and barren hills. By dusk of the fifth day, they reached an area that seemed like the place Sam described but decided to wait until morning to search for the cross with Sam's name on it.

To prepare for the night, they pitched their tent close to the mountain and settled in. Over a dinner of beans, bacon, and hardtack, Cyril explained that gold is generally found along the banks of streambeds and ravines where mountains contain quartz. "An tomorra, I'm gonna check them mountains, but from what I seen, I'm thinkin' we're in the right place."

The next morning, they shouldered their picks and shovels and with gold pans in hand, sallied forth to find their fortune. Cyril examined the mountains for quartz and reported to Michael. "Good news, boy, these here mountains got quartz in 'em! Let's go find that damn cross!"

For hours they trudged in the blazing sun. They checked every creek flowing between mountains but found no cross. The quest continued for days and the days became weeks, but they could find no sign of Sam's cross or any gold.

At the end of another fruitless day, Cyril removed his hat and wiped the sweat from his brow with his forearm. "Michael, I'm thinkin' ol' Sam just wanted a bottle of whiskey and sold us a bill a goods. We're runnin' outta supplies. I tell ya what, let's go back to Rimrock Springs and rethink where we should be lookin'."

Michael crossed his arms. "No! I don't wanna leave. I believe that old man. Let's keep looking. I know there's gold here somewhere, and I'm not giving up!"

"Awright." Cyril said. "Fine if you wanna give it some more time. But only a few more days 'cause we'll be runnin' outta grub soon." They packed their tools and headed towards their camp. Suddenly Cyril shouted, "Michael look yonder. There it is! It's the cross!"

Michael shaded his eyes with his hand. "Where? Where is it?"

Cyril pointed, "It's back in that ravine! Let's go!"

Michael followed Cyril as they ran towards the cross. They stopped in front of it to find the name Sam had been carved onto it, then laughed and slapped each other's back. "This is it! We're gonna be rich!"

Water splashed as they sprinted along the creek. Cyril stopped short at an area where water flowed over a cluster of rocks. The rippling water glittered in the sunlight as it cascaded to a level of about six inches. Michael, following close behind, almost bumped into him.

Using his shovel, Cyril pushed the mud and pebbles around the stream. "Michael, I see

51

something!" Water sprayed as Cyril dropped to his knees. He scooped his hand into the pebble-filled mud. He had difficulty catching hold of the mud through fingers blurred by fast-flowing water. When he succeeded, he stared at his hand. A wide grin splayed his stubbled face. He yelled, "C'mere! Hurry, look at what I got!"

Michael dropped his pick and shovel and rushed to Cyril.

"Can you see 'em, Michael? Can you see them gold specks?"

Confused, it took Michael second or two for his brain to register what he saw. He put his nose close to Cyril's hand and carefully moved the mud around with his finger. "Are these little bits what we're lookin' for?"

"Yeah, this is just the start." Cyril rose to his feet. "Here, hold this," he said. He brushed the gold-flecked mud into Michael's hand with care. His eyes combed the area, then he trudged a few feet through the water.

Michael watched Cyril kneel in the stream. Cyril pulled out a handkerchief and swished mud into it, then handed it to Michael. He ordered, "Add this to the other stuff." He took a knife from his belt holster and used the blade to dig around a small section of bedrock. He tossed the knife, removed a cluster of small rocks and pulled something out, rinsed it in the stream, and examined it. After a minute, he let out a whoop so loud he lost his balance and fell backward into the stream.

Michael ran to help him stand, but Cyril yanked Michael's arm and pulled him into the water. Cyril gave out a maniacal laugh as he showed Michael what he held in his hand.

"Is that a lump of gold?" Michael asked.

Cyril nodded and they laughed and shouted as they splashed each other with enthusiasm.

Sitting beside Michael in the ice-cold stream, Cyril said, "I tell you what we gotta do. First thing is to build a fire."

Michael frowned. "Build a fire? What for? Shouldn't we be panning for gold now?"

"No. We gotta make sure it's real gold and the best way to do that is to see if it burns. Real gold don't burn."

"I never heard that."

"C'mon, let's start a fire and check it out. In the meantime, keep your eyes open. It seems like we're alone out here in the middle of nowhere but we gotta protect ourselves."

Michael kept watch while Cyril lit a fire and dropped the gold nugget into the bright flame. They held their breath and waited. After a few minutes, Cyril used a stick to retrieve the nugget. A broad smile crossed his face. "It's real awright!"

Michael said, "Yes siree! Let's get panning!"

"No, not yet. I ain't losin' out again. We gotta stake our claim by setting up a monument. Let's get one of those stakes we bought in town. We gotta make sure it's sticking three inches out of the ground in the northeastern corner of the land."

With the task complete, they began to pan for gold. They piled their findings onto a blanket that lay beside the stream. The gold varied in sizes from flakes to nuggets. As night closed in, they dug a hole deep in the ground, tied the blanket and buried it.

At supper, Cyril announced, "One a us needs ta go to Rimrock Springs to the county office."

"Why now? Shouldn't we keep panning?"

"One of us goes and one of us stays and pans," Cyril explained. "We gotta stake our claim right away."

"I'll go."

Cyril laughed. "You gonna check out that French girl, ain't ya."

Michael didn't respond.

"You kin go, but business is first. You go to the county office and stake our claim and then you can find your fancy girl. But ya gotta bring back enough supplies to last for a long time. Okay?"

"I promise I'll take care of it. I'm not going to see Miss Dupin, but I want to tell Sam he was right. You don't have to worry about me. I want to do the right thing for us. But I don't like leaving you here alone. I'll come back as quick as I can."

Cyril looked him in the eye. "Okay Michael, I trust you. Leave at first light."

At dawn, Michael had packed his horse light so he could travel fast. He made it to Rimrock Springs in three days. Arriving in the late afternoon, he checked into the same hotel as before. It felt good to have a bath and freshen up.

The next morning, at the county assayer's office, he filed the necessary papers. Afterward, he went to the Last Chance Saloon to find Sam.

With only the bartender in the saloon, Michael wondered how it stayed in business. "Where's Sam?"

The bartender looked up from wiping glasses, "Hey ain't you that fella that bought Sam some whiskey a while back?"

"Yeah. I came to buy him another bottle."

"Did he steer you right? Did you find gold?"

Michael hesitated. He wanted to brag about their find but clamped his mouth shut. He hated to lie but knew he had no choice. "Uh, no. I just come back to town for some supplies. And while I'm here I figured I'd stop off to see Sam and ask him for more information."

"Sam can't tell you nothing anymore. He's dead."

"Dead? When'd he die?"

"That's the peculiar thing. After you boys left, he spent the money you gave him on whiskey and drank every drop. All the while laughing and talking to himself. He was saying crazy stuff like 'I finally have a purpose in life and maybe somebody will remember me.' He just sat there laughing until he was dead."

Hel removed his hat and shook his head. "I'm sorry to hear that. Is he buried around here somewhere?"

The bartender pointed over his shoulder. "Yeah, there's a cemetery just behind the church."

Michael thanked the bartender and tipped him. He stopped off at the cemetery, paid his respects to Sam, he bought another donkey, tied it and his horse to the rail outside the general store.

Inside the store, he had a stock boy gather all the goods he needed. When the boy accidentally dropped a hammer near his boot, Michael jumped back and bumped into another patron.

He heard a lady with a French accent say, "Oh, pardon, *monsieur*."

When he turned to apologize, his eyes popped. Michael stood face-to-face with Lola Dupin.

"Forgive my clumsiness," she said.

"Uh…uh…" Michael lost his tongue when Lola looked into his eyes and offered a bright smile. He felt heat throughout his body and his jeans tighten. He removed his hat and covered his loins. When he found his voice, he said, "Oh no, Ma'am, I'm the clumsy one. Please forgive me."

Lola offered her hand and said, "My name is Lola Dupin. It is a pleasure to meet you."

The sound of her voice made his heart pound. "I'm the one who's pleased, Mrs. Dupin."

"It's Miss Dupin, but call me Lola. With a dazzling smile, she asked, "And you are?"

He took her hand and felt his fingers tingle. "My name is Michael. Michael James O'Reilly. But please call me Michael."

"*Enchanté*, Michael. Are you staying in town?"

"Uh, no. I got some business outside of town and I have to leave right away."

"That's too bad. I perform at The Golden Slipper Saloon. I would love for you to come tonight to see the show. Are you sure you must leave today?"

Michael couldn't keep from staring at Lola.

"So, Michael, can you stay?" In a teasing voice, she asked. "Would it make a difference if you stayed one more day? I'll be happy to save a table for you near the stage."

He couldn't believe that she wanted him to stay and to watch her perform. "I, oh, Miss Dupin, I sure do want to but—"

"It's settled then, I will make arrangements for you for this evening."

Chapter 8

Michael finished purchasing his items. Upon leaving, he smiled, tipped his hat to Lola, and said, "It sure is a pleasure to meet you, Miss Lola."

With alluring eyes, Lola said, "Until this evening, Monsieur Michael." She turned to the proprietor to finish purchasing the fabric that had arrived from Paris. Annie Bodine, best friend and one of the "Lola's Ladies" dancers, stood beside her.

Annie whispered to Lola, "I'm surprised! Men are always chasing after you, but you're so choosy, you seldom accept their advances. This is the first time I've seen you so forward with a man. What's going on?"

Offering a sly smile, Lola said, "Have you had a good look at Michael? Did you see that twinkle in his blue-green eyes? I wouldn't mind running my fingers through his thick, wavy hair. He's so big and muscular with those broad shoulders and those strong arms. I could feel very happy in those arms." Lola thought for a moment. "But it's not only that he's handsome and sexy. I think there's something special about him and tonight I plan to find out what makes him so different."

With mischievous eyes, Annie asked, "And how are you planning to do that?" Annie blushed and they both giggled.

When they returned to The Golden Slipper Saloon, Lola handed the fabrics to Annie and said, "Give these to the ladies so they can begin sewing their new costumes. I'm going to my room for a while."

Lola climbed the stairs and entered her suite of rooms. She felt grateful to Frank Walters, the owner of The Golden Slipper Saloon, who had provided the entire second floor to her. Frank no longer lived in the saloon after he married and he had offered her the suite in appreciation for the tremendous success his saloon experienced due to her popularity.

The suite consisted of three rooms, a drawing-room, a bedroom and an office all sparsely decorated with masculine décor. Lola had made only a few changes. She had converted the office into a dressing area with a large wall mirror and vanity. Throughout the suite, she had added a few prints by her favorite artists, new bedding and curtains, and made the atmosphere more feminine with plants and accent pillows.

Lola sat on the sofa in her parlor and stared at her favorite poster, 'La tournée du Chat Noir de Rodolphe Salis.' In the picture was a black cat sat on a fence against a yellow background. Whenever she looked at it, she remembered Rodolphe Salis for his kindness to her when she was penniless in Paris. She remained grateful to Rodolphe for introducing her to the owners of Le Moulin Rouge where she had begun her career as a professional entertainer. He had also introduced her to Charlie Sloan, the only man she had ever cared for.

Lola couldn't believe it had been only three years since she had left Paris and had come to America with Charlie. During those three years, Charlie had been in and out of her life. Each time he had left, he had caused her misery. Despite the problems he had caused, she believed no man could ever compare.

Not only because of his good looks, charm and the sexual excitement she had felt with him but because he made her feel special. He had made her feel like the most important woman in the world. Since she'd been in Rimrock Springs there had been many opportunities for her to be with men, but no man she had been with made her feel as good as Charlie had.

Now, after much hard work, Lola had achieved a successful career in Rimrock Springs. Men here were rich with pockets full of gold. They promised her expensive baubles and to give her a luxurious life if she would marry them. She had no interest in their money. She wanted to meet a man who could release her from her loneliness in the way Charlie had.

Of course, it was too soon to tell, but in a few moments, Michael had made her feel something she hadn't felt in a very long time. Tonight, she must get to know him better. She couldn't help but hope he'd be the man who could make her forget Charlie.

As she dressed and prepared for the evening's performance, her stomach churned with butterflies at the thought of seeing Michael again.

She checked her appearance in the dressing room mirror and thought, *I'm such a fool to feel this way about someone I don't know What if I make another mistake? I can't let myself be disappointed again. Michael's probably not right for me. Already he's telling me he can't stay in Rimrock Springs. But those beautiful eyes, and that handsome face. No! Stop it! He may not even appear. Of course, he will his eyes told me so.*

The time ticked slowly as she waited to make her stage entrance. Lola wanted to peek outside the curtain to see if he sat at the table she had reserved for him, but she kept herself aloof.

After "Lola's Ladies" finished their introductory dance and returned backstage, Lola caught Annie's arm, "Did you see him? Is Michael here?"

Annie shook her head. "I'm sorry, Lola, I was so busy dancing I didn't think to look for him. I'm sure he'll show up. How could he resist you?"

When Lola heard Frank introduce her, she adjusted her dress and readied her mind for her performance. She walked onto the stage in her usual suggestive manner. She tried not to look in the direction of Michael's table, but she did. *He's not here! To hell with him! I'm better off without him!* Lola continued to perform. In mid-swing, she noticed that Michael had arrived. Upon seeing his handsome face, she threw herself into her act with more vigor.

At the end of her performance, she mouthed the words to Michael, "I'll be right back," and hurried backstage to change. Soon she appeared and sat at Michael's table. "I didn't know if you would come."

"To tell you the truth, I didn't know if I should come."

To appear nonchalant, she asked, "Why did you bother to come?"

"Please don't misunderstand." Michael said, "I'm happy to be here, it's just that I promised to leave town as soon as I finished my business. I don't like breaking my promise, yet, I couldn't resist the opportunity to see you."

Lola's expression warmed at his words.

A tall, portly man approached Michael's table. He smelled like cow manure. He put his beefy face close to Lola. "Why don't you come and sit at my table, lovely lady? I got plenty to offer you, you know what I mean?" He jiggled the coins in his pocket and put his hand on her shoulder.

Lola shook off his hand and stood. Facing him, she said brusquely, "Please, leave me alone!"

"That's no way to treat a customer. C'mon now." He clutched her arm to pull her away.

Michael stood, gripped the man's wrist and squeezed it hard. He shouted, "Leave her alone or I'll break your neck!"

The interloper winced and released Lola. His eyes challenged Michael as he pulled his hand back and hollered "Let go a' me!" Perceiving Michael's powerful physique, his expression changed from an angry leer to uncertainty. He pushed Michael out of his way and marched from the saloon.

"Let's go to my place," Lola whispered

Michael asked, "Are you sure that's okay?"

She smiled and took Michael's hand. His hand didn't feel smooth like Charlie's had been. Michael's hand felt calloused and rough. Climbing the stairs, Lola thought, *I wonder what his hands would feel like caressing my bare skin.*

Upon entering, she pointed to the sofa. "Please sit. May I get you something to drink?"

"Whiskey, if you have it."

Lola had been well-practiced dealing with bullies but felt pleased that Michael was the kind of man who'd stand up to a brute unafraid. She rubbed the area of her arm where the man had grabbed her and said, "Thank you for rescuing me." She brought him his drink and sat beside Michael. "Do you often defend ladies in distress?"

Michael smiled with a touch of embarrassment. "No, ma'am. The occasion seldom arises, but I'll do what I have to if there's a need."

She bowed her head with grace. "*Merci beaucoup,* Sir Galahad."

"No need for thanks. I'd do it again in a heartbeat."

Michael's eyes reminded Lola of the warm Mediterranean waters of the Côte-d'Azur where she and her father often spent summer vacations. She cleared her mind and said, "I hope whomever you made the promise to will not be too disappointed that you did not leave Rimrock Springs tonight."

He returned her gaze then looked away as he brought the glass to his mouth. He took a sip. "It's just one more day. I'm sure he'll be fine."

A man! At least he's not breaking a promise to a woman!

Lola studied his lips. His bottom lip was full and the top lip had a slight bow. They looked very kissable. She tried to imagine what his how his lips tasted and wondered if his closely cropped beard would tickle her face. His lips began to move and drew her attention.

Michael asked, "What brings you all the way from Paris to Rimrock Springs?"

Lola brushed her skirt as if to dust off imaginary crumbs. "It's quite a long story, but the simple truth is, when I worked in Paris, I was one of many performers who were much more famous than I." With a radiant glow, she looked at Michael. "But here, I am unique and appreciated for my uniqueness. I feel the admiration of the audience more deeply than I have ever felt it before.

"And you Michael, with your mysterious promise, what brings you here?"

Michael cleared his throat. "It's just business."

"Gold business, I suppose. I hope you find what you're looking for."

Suppressing a smile, he said, "I hope so too."

"Where are you from?"

"A little town in Arkansas, doubt you've ever heard of it."

"Is it far from here?"

"Yes, it's quite a ways from Arizona. I'd say over 1,000 miles."

She smiled, "Ah, a well-traveled man."

Michael finished his drink. His arm brushed her skirt with a light touch when he put his glass on the coffee table. It thrilled her.

He said, "Oh, pardon me."

Different from most men who smelled of tobacco and whiskey—or worse—Michael's masculine scent stimulated Lola. It reminded her of fine leather.

"No need to apologize, I didn't mind at all. Would you care for another?" She laughed, "Whiskey, I mean."

"No thank you. I should be going."

"Going? So soon? But why?" she asked.

"I find you very attractive and I, well I'm tempted to—"

"Tempted? Tempted to…kiss me?" She lifted her face to his and saw the kiss in his eyes.

Lola closed her eyes. Her stomach fluttered when she felt the touch of his lips against hers. The sensation left in an instant. Lola opened her eyes to see him searching her face for approval. She smiled.

Michael's hand reached under her hair below her ear. His thumb caressed her cheek. He kissed her again, this time with passion. She felt his arm curl around her waist and gasped at his strength as he drew her close. Their breaths mingled. Once again, they kissed. Lola could feel his muscles as she caressed his back. She wanted to feel more of him, but he pulled away.

"What's wrong?" she whispered.

"Wrong? Nothing's wrong. I just have to leave." Michael rose from the couch.

"I don't understand."

"Lola, if I stay any longer, I may do something I'll regret. This is hard for me to admit, but even though we don't know each other, I feel I've been waiting for you all my life. There's something about you that I find irresistible. Something more than your beauty and passion. As much as I want to be with you, I'm afraid."

"Afraid? Of what? Of me?"

"I know I'm crazy or just plain stupid to leave you." he said, "but I'm afraid I'll fall in love with you and I can't allow myself to. I have to go, but I'll be back. Maybe you won't want to see me again and I wouldn't blame you. But if there's one promise I'll keep, it's that I'll be back for you and when I come back, if you'll have me, I'll never leave you again."

Chapter 9

The brutal rays of the sun pierced through a cloudless sky and beat down on Michael. Distracted by thoughts of Lola, he didn't notice the heat as he rode back to camp. Just the thought of her aroused him. Her silky skin, her warm, moist lips, the way her body had molded to his when he held her tight and the feel of her fingers as they roamed his back. *Lola is the woman I need. I must have her. No matter what it takes, I have to get rich. 'Cause I can't marry her until I can give her everything!*

Cyril's wave and broad smile welcomed him as he approached the camp. Michael assumed that he either wasn't aware that he took an extra day, or maybe he just didn't care. Michael slid from his horse and stood before him. "How's everything going?"

"Tie up your horse an' follow me!"

Michael pursed his lips. "Is everything okay?"

"Jus' come with me. Hurry!"

Michael followed Cyril into a cave-like opening in a nearby mountain. When he entered, Michael's mouth dropped. Pails of gold flakes and buckets of nuggets sat everywhere.

"I wasn't even gone three weeks!" He exclaimed. "How'd you manage to get all this gold by yourself?"

"This ain't nothin'. There's plenty more where this came from."

Michael picked up a nugget and stared at it for a minute. "You ain't joking? This is all real?"

"It's real, awright! There's enough gold out there to set us up for the rest of our lives!"

Michael needed to digest the fact that he would be a rich man. Thoughts of Lola popped into his mind. He removed his hat and ran his hand through his hair. "We're gonna be rich? You really mean it?"

Cyril's smile stretched across his face.

"How much longer is it gonna take?"

"It depends on how hard you wanna work, pardner."

Michael looked around at all the gold Cyril had accumulated. "What are we waiting for, let's get to it!"

For months, they worked feverishly, stopping only to eat and get a few hours of sleep. On one typical workday afternoon Michael heard a horrifying scream. He looked around to determine where it came from. "Cyril! It's Cyril!"

Michael threw away his shovel and ran towards the sound. "Oh God! What's happened?" He saw Cyril laying in a pool of blood that oozed from a cut on his left arm. Michael ripped off his shirt and tied it around Cyril's arm, just above the elbow. He lifted Cyril, whose lean but muscular build seemed weightless, carried him to their makeshift lean-to and laid him on a cot.

He tried not to panic. He searched for something to clean the wound but found only old rags. Cyril attempted to speak but soon passed out. Michael tore off Cyril's shirt and used it to wipe the bloody arm.

Michael saw a long, shallow cut inside his forearm. Grateful that Cyril had passed out, Michael poured whiskey on the wound and tied it tight with rags. He applied pressure in the hopes that the bleeding would stop, but he knew Cyril needed stitches.

Heartsore after finding nothing he could use to sew the wound, Michael knew he had to cauterize it. Outside the cabin, he built a blazing fire and heated his hunting knife. When it glowed red, he returned to the cabin. Cyril's blood leached from the wound.

Cyril lay unconscious. "I'm sorry, partner," Michael murmured. "This is the only thing I can think of. I sure hope I don't kill you."

Michael wiped the sweat from his face and took a deep breath. He cradled Cyril and held his arm tight. With a shaky hand, he applied the fiery knife in several places along the wounded arm. He used all his might to keep Cyril from fighting him off. Although the putrid smell of burning flesh nauseated him, and Cyril's shrieks made his insides curdle, he continued to cauterize the cut until it stopped bleeding.

Michael watched over Cyril the rest of the day and all that night. He felt frustrated at his inability to do more to save him. In the morning, happy to see Cyril survived the night, Michael wished he could do more to alleviate his pain.

Looking at his bandaged arm Cyril muttered hoarsely, "What happened to me?"

"I don't know," Michael said. "I saw your pickaxe dropped beside you. I think a sharp rock flew up and cut you. Your arm was bleeding bad and you were out cold. I brought you here and tried to stop the bleeding but it wouldn't stop. I had to burn it closed. I'm sorry, but I couldn't figure any other way."

"Gimme some whiskey, Cyril rasped."

Michael brought him a bottle and watched Cyril drink deeply. He continued to drink until the bottle dropped from his hand as he passed out. With a heavy heart, Michael paced as he tried to decide what he should do. Flushed with fever, Cyril was getting worse. His fear for Cyril became unbearable. The next day Michael shook Cyril awake and said, "I'm taking you to a doctor."

Weak but firm, Cyril shouted, "No! We can't leave. I ain't goin' nowhere."

"You have to. I ain't gonna let you die!"

"Forget it! I ain't going. If you wanna go and get me some medicine, fine! But I ain't leavin'!"

"How can I leave you here alone?"

"Just git on your horse and git back soon as you can!"

"I don't wanna leave you. You could die while I'm away."

"Listen to me." Cyril clasped Michael's arm. "I ain't gonna leave an' that's final! I don' want no claim jumpers' takin' our gold." He stopped to take a few raspy breaths. "Leave me with a rifle, some ammunition and some food. Most especially leave me with some whiskey. Get back soon as you can."

"But—"

"Git the hell outta here, ya hear me?"

Michael considered carrying Cyril out and tying him to his horse, but he realized the journey would probably kill Cyril. He supplied him with what he asked for and readied for the trip to town.

"You better not die on me or I'll kill you!" Michael said, as he mounted his horse and left.

Michael rode non-stop, taking less than two days to arrive at the doctor's office, tied his horse and rushed inside to find the office empty. Outside the doctor's office, two men sat on a bench. The older man had a long, brown beard. The younger man, except for a thin black mustache, had a clean-shaven face. Michael shouted at them, "Where is he? Where's the doctor?"

The younger man said, "He's not here."

"I can see that! Where can I find him? It's an emergency!"

"Well, I think he's at the Fredericks' ranch. I hear tell his wife was havin' their ninth child." The man chuckled. "You'd think she'd know by now how to have a baby without help."

The older man said, "Well, the way I heard it, she was bleedin' a lot. I think maybe that poor woman is plum tuckered out from havin' babies."

The younger man smirked. "Now, I don't think—"

"Shut up! Michael yelled. "My friend's dying and I need to find the doctor!"

The older man said, "Well, the doc's out quite a ways. What's wrong with your friend?"

"He got cut bad so I had to burn him. Now he's got a fever. I think he's gonna die!"

"Why don't you go over to the general store? Amos knows lots about medicine. I bet he can make you something."

Michael's heart pounded in his ears. "How far away is the doctor?"

"Well, the Fredericks' ranch is about fifteen miles yonder, but it ain't a straight shot. You got to go around the mountains and such. Might take you at least a day to get there on a fast horse."

"That's too long!" Michael ran to the general store and interrupted a sales clerk, "I need to speak to Amos right away!"

A portly grey-haired woman wearing a silly hat said, "Excuse me, young man. I was here first. You'll just have to wait your turn."

"Sorry, ma'am." Michael turned to the clerk and demanded, "Mister, I need some medicine. My friend is dying and the doc's out of town. Please help me!"

The proprietor stepped up to the counter and announced, "I'm Amos, What's the problem?"

"Well! I never!" The old woman said as she stuck up her nose and marched from the store in a huff.

Michael explained to Amos what happened. "You gotta help me!" He pleaded.

"I see." Amos scratched his chin. "Well, I can make you some medicine, but I can't guarantee he won't die anyway."

"Do whatever you can, but please hurry!"

"It'll take a while, but I'll be as fast as I can. Come back in half an hour."

"I'll wait outside." Michael left and paced in front of the store. After ten minutes, he heard someone call his name. He turned towards the sound and saw Lola.

She walked to him and said, "What a surprise to see you. Have you been in town long?"

"I just arrived." Michael removed his hat and thought about his promise to her. "Lola, um, please understand. I know I made you a promise but I can't stay now. I'm only here because there's been an emergency and I have to leave right away."

Lola's tone of voice changed from pleasant to annoyed. "Oh, I see. Well, Michael, don't let me keep you. I hope everything turns out all right. Good day." She turned to walk away.

"No, Lola, wait!" Michael took her hand and brought her through an alleyway to the back of the store. "Listen, Lola, you must believe me. I care for you...very much. You're all I think about." He moved closer but she looked away. He couldn't see her face. Her perfume flooded his senses. "Please look at me." He put his finger under her chin and guided her face towards him.

She allowed his touch but didn't look into his eyes.

"Lola, please, look at me." Their eyes met and her face softened. "Oh God, Lola, I'm crazy about you." He pulled her close and kissed her.

After the kiss, she asked, "I don't understand. If you are, as you say, crazy about me, why must you leave?"

"My partner had an accident. I came here to get medicine for him, and I have to bring it to him right away. I'm afraid he might die before I get back."

Lola searched his face as if deciding whether to believe him. With sincerity, she uttered, "I'm sorry about your friend." Then folded her arms across her chest and demanded, "Why do you think you can kiss me whenever you want?"

"Lola...I...don't you care for me at all?"

"How can I know if I care for you? I only see you for a few minutes each time we meet."

"You don't seem to mind when I kiss you. You must feel something for me, don't you?"

"Well, if you want me to care for you, you will have to spend more time with me, so I can decide."

"Look, I'm working on something. If everything turns out okay with my partner, I'm hoping that my work will be finished in a few months. I promise I'll be back for you as soon as I can."

She looked askance. "I like you, Michael and I hope your partner recovers quickly. But I don't think—"

He put his body next to hers and leaned her against the building wall. With no space between them, he could feel her heart pounding against his chest. His eyes said, "I love you." They melted together and kissed deeply. He felt as if their souls had touched.

Suddenly he heard loud giggling. "Hey mister, your medicine's ready!" He reluctantly pulled himself away from Lola to see a young freckled-faced boy with a sly smile standing close by.

Frustrated by the interruption, Michael looked back to see Lola laughing. Embarrassed, he said, "I'm so sorry. I have to go."

"No need to apologize," she said. "Go take care of your partner."

After Michael left, Lola headed toward the Golden Slipper Saloon. Michael filled her thoughts. *Why do I care for him so? Yes, his body is powerful and I want to feel his hands touch my skin. The magic of his passionate kisses makes me feel like dancing! Am I a fool to fall for him? What is it about the men I'm attracted to? Why is it that they always run from me?*

Annie spotted Lola as she arrived at the saloon. She walked to her and with a puzzled expression, she asked, "Where've you been? Your face is flushed. Are you feeling all right?"

Lola felt the warmth of her skin. *Mon Dieu! She's right!* I bumped into Michael."

Annie's eyebrows shot upwards. "Michael's here in town and he didn't come to see you? How long's he been here?"

"Come to my room. Let's talk."

They climbed the stairs and sat together on the sofa. Concerned, Annie took Lola's hand and said, "I can see by your face something's going on with you. Tell me all about it."

"Annie, I'm so confused. Michael's left town."

"I don't understand, I thought he cared for you. Why would he come to town and leave without seeing you?"

"He said his partner was injured and might die. He came to get medicine and had to leave right away."

"Do you believe him?"

"I can only assume he's telling the truth. He did seem worried. Oh, Annie, I'm not sure. I care for him, but I don't know why. I don't know him, but every time I see him, I can't resist his kisses."

Annie smirked, "Kisses! So, you've had enough time together to enjoy his kisses?"

"Oh yes! They're delicious! But Charlie had been a good kisser and he caused me nothing but trouble. I don't want to get into a relationship with another undependable man."

"Well, there's no hurry. Give him some time. If he doesn't come back, there are plenty of eligible men around. I'm sure some of them are good kissers too."

Chapter 10

Michael rushed back to camp to find Cyril moaning and talking gibberish as he lay on his sweat-soaked cot. After placing the medicine bottle on the table, Michael ran to get some fresh water from the stream just outside their lean-to. Dipping a rag into the bucket, Michael wiped Cyril's flushed face and chest hoping it would cool him down.

"C'mon, wake up! I got to give you some medicine." Michael patted Cyril's face. "Open your mouth!" Having no response, Michael slapped him hard. Cyril's eyes shot open. Michael pulled his jaw downward and poured some of the medicine into his mouth. Cyril spluttered but swallowed most of it.

Michael carried him to his own cot and laid him there, changed Cyril's clothes and covered him with a blanket. Outside Michael washed Cyril's bloody clothes and put them on a rock to dry and continued to nurse Cyril until he recovered.

After a few days, a grateful Cyril resumed work. They worked relentlessly for several months until they realized their claim had played out. But it didn't matter, they had enough gold to last them for the rest of their lives.

Keeping a wary eye, they spent several weeks breaking down camp, packing their belongings and the accumulated gold. They traveled to Rimrock Springs as fast as their load allowed. After having their gold assayed, they deposited their fortunes in the Bank of Rimrock Springs.

Later, they rented a room at the Rimrock Springs Hotel where they stayed while they finalized their business arrangements. Desperate to see Lola, Michael forced himself to wait until his business had been completed. At last, he was ready to see Lola. He turned to Cyril for advice. "How can I propose to Lola in a way that would convince her that I love her?"

"What makes you think your Paris lady wants to marry you?" Cyril asked.

"Maybe it's what I want to believe. But when we're together she makes me feel like she cares for me."

"Michael, that don't mean she wants to marry you. I think you need to get to know each other better before you go off half-cocked and screw things up."

He paced and ran his fingers through his hair. "I can't wait! All I do is think about her. I'm going crazy! I'm going to ask her to marry me. If she turns me down, I'll keep asking her until she changes her mind."

"Best be careful. Pushing her too hard might chase her away."

"I can't help myself. I love her, but how can I make her believe me?"

Cyril thought a moment. "I'm not romantic guy, but I know ladies like flowers. Why don't you get her some flowers, maybe take her to dinner and see how it goes? If she likes you as much as you say, she might just marry you. But I think you best take a bath first and maybe get some nice clothes."

Michael knew he should court Lola, but he couldn't wait. Over the next few days, he bathed, shaved, bought a suit, a buggy and a diamond ring.

Today, he will ask Lola for her hand in marriage.

As he stood before the mirror in his room, he thought, *what will I do if she turns me down? I can't live without her. I must convince her to marry me.*

He adjusted the angle of his Stetson hat and straightened his black string tie. He thought he looked presentable in his grey frock coat, matching vest and black pants. He hoped Lola would be impressed with the gold studs he purchased for the buttonholes on the front of his white pleated shirt. Staring into the mirror, he said aloud, "Michael, this is your chance to be happy forever. You can't take no for an answer!"

Michael's excitement overwhelmed him as he peeked over the barroom doors of the Golden Slipper Saloon. In the middle of the afternoon, he saw only the orchestra, a bartender and a few patrons. His heart pounded as he watched Lola stand on the stage rehearsing with Lola's Ladies. He took a deep breath and marched in.

Lola, busy directing Lola's Ladies choreography for a new dance routine, had no idea Michael had entered the saloon. Feeling arms encircle her and lift her body from the floor, she screamed. "Let me go!"

Cradled in Michael's arms, he carried her off the stage. Flailing her arms and legs, she yelled, "Are you insane? Let me down!"

The musicians put down their instruments, the patrons set their drinks on the bar and Lola's Ladies stood with their jaws ajar.

Outside the saloon, curious townfolk surrounded a flowered-covered buggy. A shocked silence filled the air when Michael burst through the saloon doors carrying Lola who struggled in his arms. The saloon emptied as everyone followed Michael and Lola into the street.

Lola's mouth dropped at the sight of the beautiful buggy. But she regained her disquiet when he placed her on the carriage bench. Lola felt a storm brew inside her body as she watched Michael climb to sit beside her. She shrieked, "Where do you think you're taking me!"

With a firm voice, Michael said, "I'm taking you to the preacher so we can get married!"

All eyes fixed on Lola as she scolded, "Is this some kind of joke?"

She moved to exit the carriage when Michael grasped her elbow.

"Wait! I need to speak with you. Please sit."

Lola hesitated, then sat beside him.

Michael looked into her eyes. With a tender voice he said, "Lola, I'm not joking. I love you."

Lola could see the look of love in his eyes. Her heart melted. Her voice softened, "But Michael, I can't marry you!"

"Don't you like me?"

"We've only just met, how can I know if I like you? I need to get to know you before I make such a big decision."

"Lola, it's true we haven't had much time together, but I adore you. I wanted to marry you from the minute I laid eyes on you. But I was broke.

There was no way I would allow myself to be with you until I had enough money to treat you the way you deserve. That's why I had to leave. I was gold mining and worked as hard and as fast I could to make my fortune. Now, I have enough money to give you everything. I'm afraid if we don't get married right away, someone will steal you from me. I couldn't bear that. I love you and promise to make you happy no matter what it takes."

"But how can you love me when you know nothing about me? I might be a terrible person. I could be a shrew."

He laughed. "I don't believe that. Lola, you're a beautiful woman, but what's more important to me, is that your beauty comes from within you. I don't understand why I feel this way but I know it's true. I need to spend the rest of my life with you. I promise I'll be good to you, please believe me."

She saw the kiss in his eyes as he leaned towards her. She tried to keep a cool detachment as their lips touched. His embrace made her swirl with emotion.

Why do I trust him? I'm so confused. I want to love him. I was never certain that I loved Charlie, yet I believe I can love Michael. What is this madness I feel for him? Could this be love? How ridiculous! I don't know him. Yet, he's unlocked something deep inside, something I desperately need.

Michael pulled a large diamond ring from his pocket and pleaded, "Please marry me."

Lola wrung her hands. She looked to the surrounding crowd. All eyes were on her. Everyone seemed to be holding his or her breath in anticipation of her answer. "But Michael I—" She closed her eyes and expelled a deep breath. "Yes! I must be crazy, but I will marry you!"

The crowd clapped and cheered.

Michael took her hand, placed the ring on her finger and said, "Thank you. You've made me the happiest man in the world!" He hugged her, then took the reins to set the horses in motion.

Lola grabbed Michael's arm. "Where do you think you are you taking me?"

"You said you'd marry me, so we're going to the preacher."

"Oh, no, we're not getting married today! I want to get to know you better, which we can do while we prepare for our wedding."

"Wedding? Uh, sure. Whatever you want is fine with me."

Lola's inner voice would not be stilled. *Will my life with Michael be beautiful and happy? Or will this be a huge mistake?*

Chapter 11

Although pleased that Lola asked to have her wedding at The Golden Slipper Saloon, Frank wondered if Lola would return to her important role in the show. She and Frank discussed options and decided that Annie would replace her until she returned.

Shapely and beautiful, Annie's blond hair and large chocolate-brown eyes made her very attractive. Although the crowd might be disappointed at first, with her lovely voice, exceptional dancing skills and splendid sense of humor, Lola and Frank believed she would be a well-suited substitute. Annie agreed to take the position. She and Lola spent their remaining time together working out routines with Lola's Ladies.

For the wedding, Lola designed a menu including the finest beef, the best champagne and a variety of hors-d'oeuvres. The guest list comprised of the many people Lola had befriended since she came to Rimrock Springs. Annie would be her maid of honor and Cyril would be Michael's best man.

With all the wedding planning and development of the new show routines, the couple had little time to be together. When they were apart, Lola had doubts about her decision to marry him, but when Michael held her in his arms, her doubts faded and she longed to be his wife.

The day of the wedding arrived. The mossy, sweet aromas emanating from the abundance of flowers filled the air and the lilting music played by the orchestra added to the festivities. Chattering well-wishers drank champagne in the packed saloon. Many attendees slapped Michael on the back and told him how jealous they were and congratulated him for being lucky that Lola chose him.

The preacher stood center stage. Lola's Ladies gathered behind him, each holding a small bouquet of white carnations. They wore off-shoulder, deep purple satin dresses painted with La France roses and drapery of pink under ruffle of plissé mauve mousseline. The Ladies sang several songs including, "Au Clair de la Lune" and "Beautiful Dreamer" as the crowd awaited Lola's appearance.

Michael stood before the preacher. Waiting for Lola to take the stage beside him, his heart thudded and his fingers seem to have a mind of their own as they drummed against his legs. He asked Cyril, "Why's she taking so long? Do you think she's changed her mind? Should I check on her? Maybe she's not feeling well."

"Calm down, boy!" Cyril laughed. "You're as nervous as a cat in a room full of rocking chairs. It'll be all right. She's already agreed to marry you, the hard part's over."

Michael's eyes were on Annie who stood near the preacher. As Lola's best friend she would know if he should be concerned. Her wink and smile relieved his anxiety.

At last, the orchestra played Mendelssohn's "Wedding March." Michael's eyes shot to the top of the stairs. *There she is, the most beautiful woman in the world!*

Lola's Ladies sang the wedding march in soft harmony. Lola descended the stairs to meet Frank and take his elbow.

Michael's heart swelled as he watched the woman he loved approach him. *Am I dreaming? The most stunning woman in the world is about to marry me. Is this really happening?*

Lola wore a wedding gown of her own making. During her early days as a cancan dancer, she learned to sew her costumes. Lola had never imagined she would use her skills to design wedding gown for herself.

Elegant but simple, her design had white hand-appliquéed Battenburg lace flowers and a slim fitted floor-length skirt. She held a large bouquet of white roses. When Lola stood next to Michael and smiled, he almost fainted at the sight of her beauty.

With the nuptials complete, the orchestra played dance music. Annie sang "I'll Take You Home Again Kathleen" and "While Strolling In The Park One Day."

Frank made a speech about his appreciation for Lola. He said, "I'll never forget the day I first laid eyes on Lola. She barged into my saloon and announced, 'My name is Lola Dupin. I am here from Paris, France. I am a singer and dancer extraordinaire.' Then she said, 'You are the most fortunate of men Monsieur Walters because I have decided to entertain in your establishment.' I didn't believe her at first, but I was curious so I gave her a chance, and I'm happy I did. The rest is history. We will miss you, Lola."

He raised his glass as he turned to Lola and Michael, "We congratulate you and wish you the very best. Three cheers for the young couple."

With tears in her eyes, Lola kissed Frank on each cheek. She wrapped her arm around Annie and said, "I know you'll do a good job while I'm away. Maybe everyone will like you so much, they'll forget about me."

Annie laughed, "No one could ever forget you, Lola. Now, have a wonderful time."

Tears flowed as Lola's Ladies smothered her with hugs and well wishes. Afterward, Lola looked for Michael. She saw him talking to Cyril and watched them laugh and hug. When Lola approached, Cyril took her hand and said, "Michael sure is a lucky man! I wish you both happiness." He turned to Michael. "You better take good care of her, ya hear?" He smiled, tipped his hat and left the saloon.

They watched Cyril leave. Michael said, "I'm sure gonna miss him."

Lola asked, "Do you know what Cyril will do now?"

"He put money down on the California ranch he's been dreaming of."

"Do you think we'll see him while we're honeymooning in San Francisco?"

"Not likely. He says he's going to Ireland to buy some special breed of cattle. I don't know how long he'll be there. But one thing I know for sure, when Cyril sets his mind to do something, he'll get it done, and get it done right!"

"I'm happy for him."

"Me too. Hey, we don't want to miss our train. Shouldn't we get going?"

Lola gave Michael a loving look. "Yes, we should." They made their way through the crowd of well-wishers. At the saloon exit, Lola laughed as all the ladies ran for the bouquet she tossed. She blew a kiss and said, "I love you all!"

Some of the wedding party followed the bride and groom outside and watched as they climbed onto the rose-draped buggy. Several youngsters laughed and whistled as they chased after the newlyweds.

It hadn't taken long for them to arrive in San Francisco by rail. When they exited the Great Overland Railway station, Lola gave a surprised grin feeling the lively Pacific trade winds swirl, making it necessary for her to hold on to her oversized hat.

The carriage charged with bringing them to the Palace Hotel awaited them.

Lola felt excited to see her first glimpse of California. En route to the hotel, she saw Spanish ladies wearing scarlet sashes, striped rebozos slung over their shoulders and long, flaring skirts. The carriage passed shops containing Oriental goods and she saw Chinese men in blue blouses wearing soft slippers and long-braided queues swinging behind them. She observed swaggering sailors, and stiff military officers, looking smart in their uniforms as they strode along streets. Among the day-to-day shoppers, she noted those who dressed in their finery. Ladies who wore rich velvet cloaks and the latest in afternoon wear, and men in Prince Albert coats who might have just stepped from the Astor house.

The driver worked his way around traffic busy with streetcars, horse-drawn wagons and pedestrians heading in every direction.

As they approached an imposing white building with a myriad of bay windows, the driver explained that the Palace Hotel occupied the entire block, bounded by New Montgomery, Market, Jessie and Annie streets.

Their carriage entered the Palace Hotel through an immense circular driveway leading to a central court. A marble-tiled promenade adorned with statues representing the four seasons and several artistic fountains surrounded the court.

When the amazed couple dismounted the carriage, they saw above them a crystal-roofed garden and many balconies crowded with elegant urns and vases of rare and beautiful flowers and plants. Delicious fragrances filled the air. To their delight, a band played compositions from a music pavilion.

Michael watched Lola point her finger and count. She said, "There are seven floors."

He scratched his chin. "That's a lot of stairs to climb if you're staying on the top floor."

"No sir," said the driver. "We have elevators that take you to every floor."

"Elevators? What are those?" Michael asked.

"They're sort of moving rooms that carry you to your floor. I think you'll like the ride."

Michael and Lola looked at each other with surprised delight.

"I'm looking forward to it," Lola said.

Arm in arm, the couple entered the lobby. Its cavernous ceiling, magnificent décor and spaciousness impressed Lola. She was surprised to see a hotel in America that could compete with the finest European hotels.

A courteous attaché greeted them and asked if they would like a tour of the hotel. Confused by the expression on Michael's face, she asked, "You're looking a little dazed, are you feeling well *mon amour?*"

Michael looked at the well-dressed hotel guests in the lobby and uttered, "I'm afraid I'll embarrass you."

"Embarrass me? How could you possibly? I don't understand."

"I never imagined that a hotel could be as grand as this. And the people, they're all rich! I feel so out of place. I'm sorry. I don't have any fancy manners. I feel there are rules I should know how to follow. I'm not sure what I'm supposed to do."

Lola caressed his cheek. "Oh, Michael, please don't be concerned, you could never embarrass me. People may believe they're better than everyone else because they're rich. Just because they eat with the correct knife and fork doesn't make them superior. Mostly they're shallow snobs, who follow the rules because they fear they will be detested if they break their code of arrogance. I love who you are, so please just be yourself. Come, let's take the tour and enjoy our honeymoon."

Looking relieved, Michael smiled and said, "Sure, Lola, whatever you want."

The attaché showed them the breakfast room, the grand dining room, the music and ballroom, the women's lower reception room, the reading room, the bar and the billiard rooms.

He brought them to the elevator. When the doors opened, Lola asked, "Is it safe?"

The attaché reassured them, "Oh yes, it's very safe. Just enjoy the ride."

Michael held Lola tight as they were lifted off the ground."

"How does this thing work?" Michael asked.

"It's called hydraulics. Water is transmitted to various hydraulic motors and hydraulic cylinders and becomes pressurized—"

Michael interrupted, "Uh, never mind, so long as it works."

They stepped out of the elevator on to the second floor where the attaché showed them the private dining rooms, the children's dining hall, and the ladies' drawing rooms. At the end of the tour, he showed them to their suite. Lola uttered, "What exquisite furnishings!"

The attaché told them that the banker, William Chapman Ralston, had built this lavish hotel. He had spared no expense in his desire to create the most commodious and elegant hotel in San Francisco. The attaché pointed out that the heavy, beautifully designed carpets were manufactured exclusively for The Palace Hotel. Of original and unique design, the furniture had been made from the finest and most beautiful woods. Their suite had a parlor and a private toilet, an ample clothes closet and a fireplace.

Throughout the suite, wonderful fragrances wafted from flower-filled urns. A bowl of fresh fruit and a chilled bottle of French champagne sat on the parlor table.

"Mister O'Reilly, would you like me to open the champagne?" asked the attaché.

Michael eyed the bottle. "Uh, no, thank you, I'll take care of it."

"Very good sir. Unless you have some questions, I'll take my leave now."

Michael said with enthusiasm, "No questions, you can leave."

The attaché announced, "We at the Palace Hotel wish you and Mrs. O'Reilly a good day and a very pleasant stay." He cleared his throat.

Lola poked Michael with her elbow and looked towards his pocket.

"Oh, uh." Michael reached into his pocket and gave the attaché a tip.

When the attaché left, Lola giggled and put her arms around Michael's neck. "Did you hear what he said? He called me Mrs. O'Reilly. That's the first time I've ever heard anyone say my new name, Mrs. O'Reilly!"

Michael smiled. "Well, Mrs. O'Reilly, would you like some champagne? It's French, you know."

"But of course, Monsieur O'Reilly!"

"I'm very pleased with this hotel and grateful that Frank recommended this special place."

Michael concentrated on the champagne bottle. He twisted and yanked the cork with all his might. The cork exploded out of the bottle and flew into the crystal chandelier causing the crystal pendants to dance and tinkle, followed by a cascade of champagne. He turned to Lola with a sheepish grin, "I guess you made me pop my cork!" They broke into a fit of giggles.

After they toasted and finished the remains of the bottle, Lola asked, "*Mon Cher*, would you be terribly disappointed if I take a bath now?"

Now! I want to make love to her so bad I'm gonna burst! I can't wait another minute and she wants to take a bath! He took a breath. *Calm down. You waited this long...*"Sure, honey. Take your time."

He watched her disappear into the bathroom. It gave him great pleasure to hear her sing as the water flowed from the tap. However, his patience waned when it seemed like hours until he heard her lilting voice call to him, *"Mon amour, entrez, s'il vous plaît."*

He entered the bathroom and gasped. Lola sat up to her neck in bubbles with hair her piled high on her head. Michael's words were almost prayer-like, "My God, you're beautiful!"

Lola said, "So! What are you waiting for? Do you think I wish to make love with a man who is so stinky? Get in the tub!"

She barely finished her sentence when Michael ripped off his clothes and jumped into the tub so fast, he forgot to take off his Stetson. "Oh Michael, you have such quick reflexes." Lola laughed as she used her toes to flick his hat from his head.

They sat across from each other laughing. He felt the cool smoothness of the porcelain tub against his back, the heat of the water against his skin, the bubbles tickling his nose, and the tantalizing silkiness of Lola's long legs against his.

Michael marveled at Lola's perfection. Fascinated by her, he studied her face and her expressive blue eyes that emphasized her every word. He marveled at her perfect white teeth and the sweetness of her smile. *Good God, I'm a happy man!*

Lola surprised him when she reached into the water and grabbed his ankle to study the bottom of his foot. She frowned as if she found something interesting but couldn't figure out its meaning. She looked at him with confidence and said, "Now, Madame Lola will read your fortune." Michael chuckled as Lola continued, "My very first observation is that you have big feet, *oui?*"

Michael nodded and grinned.

Lola pursed her lips. "Let me see, oh yes, I can see that you are in very bad need of a pedicure."

"A what?"

"No, no!" Lola wagged a finger at him, "Do not interrupt Madame Lola. Now, where was I? Oh, *oui.*" She ran her finger along the bottom of his foot. He pulled his foot back a little. "Ahh, Madame Lola can see that Monsieur Michael is very ticklish."

Michael laughed, "You got me there, Madame Lola."

"What does this line say. Hmmm. It says you are married to the most perfect wife in all the world and you will be very good to her. That is so, is it not?"

"Madame Lola, I do declare you are the best fortune teller I have ever come across in a bathtub."

He grabbed her foot and tickled her toes. Laughing hysterically, she splashed him with the sudsy water, then they splashed each other. With little water left in the tub, she stopped and said, "It's time to exit the bath, *mon cher.*"

Michael stepped from the tub. With a mixture of awe and lust, he watched as Lola rose from the tub and looked like a picture of a painting he had once had seen in a book. He recollected the painting had been called Botticelli's "The Birth of Venus."

Small bubbles clung to several tendrils of Lola's perfumed hair. Other bubbles slid down her body, leaving one breast bare, with a perfectly round, engorged pink nipple peeking through. He continued to watch the bubbles as they teasingly revealed her voluptuous curves. When he brought his eyes to hers, he saw her passion for him.

A thunderstorm brewed outside. Heavy raindrops pelted against the bathroom window, but Michael didn't hear them. He needed to touch her, kiss her mouth, her stomach, her breasts. He thought he should be gentle with her. His calloused hands were made for chopping wood and laying railroad ties rather than tenderly touching a woman's delicate skin, but that wouldn't stop him.

Lola handed Michael a towel and turned her back to him. She felt pleased and somewhat surprised by his gentleness as he dried her back. She looked over her shoulder and saw him toss the towel aside.

She lay her back against Michael's chest. His wet skin made her body tingle. When he ran his fingers lightly along her neck, goosebumps spread throughout her body, bringing a spike of pleasure to her center.

The brush of his beard tickled Lola as he kissed her shoulder. His lips followed the sweeping curve of her neck to her ear. He nibbled it lightly. His warm breath on her skin excited her. She pressed her body into him as Michael's fingers explored her breasts, pinching her nipples. Then he slid his hands down her waist toward her lower regions. Lola rocked slowly as Michael's fingers massaged her with delicacy. She wanted more and clasped his hand, pushing it deeper inside. She could feel her body on fire.

Lola felt him swell and throb against her buttocks. She turned to face him. They looked intensely into each other's eyes. He brought his feverish lips to hers. They kissed long and fathomless. Michael swooped Lola into his arms and carried her to the bed where he lay her down. Lola opened herself and welcomed him. He entered her hard and deep. Lola licked her lips. With her voice barely above a whisper, she asked, "Oh, Michael, what kind of spell have you cast upon me?"

She wished she could have taken his entire body inside her as he surged harder and faster. Her pleasure felt almost unbearable as her entire body pulsated to his rhythm.

The storm raged outside as their bodies melted together, captured by their frenzied desire. Lightning lit the night sky. Thunder approached roiling and booming louder and louder, reaching a crescendo as they exploded into a paroxysm of passion.

In ecstasy, Lola thought, *Have I finally found complete happiness?*

Dance with the Devil

Chapter 12

Over the next week, except for the occasional visit to the hotel breakfast restaurant, Lola and Michael ordered room service and luxuriated in bed.

In time they saw the sights of San Francisco. They stopped at famous places like Nob Hill or enjoyed the amazing views of Russian or Telegraph Hills. They often ended their day gorging on delicious Italian food at the restaurants in North Beach.

Other days they visited Woodward Gardens, an amusement park that took up two city blocks, where they delighted in roller-skating, watching zoo animals and admiring paintings in the art gallery. They saw performers and curiosities from all over the world.

In their several visits to Golden Gate Park, they listened to band concerts, rented bicycles or picnicked as they watched ladies and gentlemen parade by on their horses or in their fine carriages.

They dined at many restaurants. Charmed by the Lick House, Lola loved the décor based on one of the rooms at the Palace of Versailles. Diners sat comfortably under a stained-glass domed ceiling forty-eight feet above. Along the walls of the dining room, Lick placed nine by twelve-foot mirrors of French plate glass.

At the Tadich Grill, considered the oldest restaurant in San Francisco, they dined in private booths while waiters in crisp white jackets and black pants served them a delicious meal of Dungeness

Crab Cocktail appetizer, garlic bread and Cioppino made up of clams, prawns, scallops, bay shrimp, crabmeat, mussels and white fish simmered in a tomato-based sauce.

At Aunt Chovie's place, they drank a Moscow Mule with vodka, lime and ginger beer and they couldn't resist trying the Smelly Fish Mint Cooler with bourbon, fresh mint and lime.

Walking along streets like Sutter, Montgomery, and Clay, they visited exclusive shops like Bello Frères, Ville de Paris and Davidson and Lane's. They often stopped at Peter Job's place for ice cream and cake. Lola purchased gifts for her friends in Rimrock Springs and souvenirs for herself. She insisted that Michael purchase clothes to add to his limited wardrobe.

On Sundays, the city had a general air of festivity. Shops were open, and much to Lola's delight, the theaters gave both matinée and evening performances. They often went to Lucky Baldwin's lavish hotel. The hotel occupied an entire city block. The ground floor of the hotel had many large stores and a theatre entitled Baldwin's Academy of Music, featuring touring performers. As the most elegant venue in the city and the only place for high-class productions, seeing David Belasco, James A. Herne, Tom Maguire and James O'Neill perform thrilled Lola.

Before they knew it, several months had passed. Lola contacted Frank who said that the patrons of the Golden Slipper Saloon had accepted Annie. Lola felt relieved knowing that Frank had no problem with her spending so much time away.

However, she began to think about how much she missed performing and, although she loved the wonderful time she had been having in San Francisco with Michael, Lola knew she had to decide what to do about their future. *I love performing, but what if Michael objects? Will I be upset? I'm his wife and should abide by his wishes. But it should be up to me, not him! Do I really want to talk about this now? It might spoil everything. It's best I sleep on it.*

The next morning, Lola awoke with Michael asleep beside her. She stared at his handsome face for a moment, then whispered in his ear, "You taught me what love is. Thank you for giving me this present." When she leaned over to kiss his cheek a wave of nausea overcame her. She ran to the bathroom and retched violently. Afterward, she sat on the floor and leaned her back against the wall. The cold tile felt good against her sweaty body.

What's wrong with me? Could it be last night's dinner that's made me feel so ill? I haven't felt this horrible since I was —

She clutched her stomach and grimaced. An anguished cry escaped her throat. Fat tears cascaded from her eyes.

Michael knocked on the door. "Lola, what's wrong?"

She couldn't answer.

"Lola, I'm coming in."

Hiding her face with her arms she shouted. "No, don't come in. I don't want you to see me like this!"

"Nonsense!" He opened the door and reached down and helped her rise. Grabbing a towel, he wiped the sweat and tears from her face. "You're sick. I'm sure there's a doctor in the hotel. I'll call for

97

one right now!" Michael brought her to the bed and helped her to sit.

"I don't need a doctor."

"Of course, you do!" He raced towards the door.

"No, wait! I don't need a doctor. I know what's wrong with me."

He sat beside her. His frightened eyes searched her face. In a solemn voice, he asked, "Are you dying?"

Chapter 13

Lola caressed his face. "No, *mon amour*, I'm pregnant."

"Pregnant? Are you sure you're not sick?"

"Yes, I'm sure."

"Why are you crying? Are you in pain?"

She looked away from him "Yes, but not in the way you think."

He sat beside her on the bed and with his hand he gently turned her face to his. "Lola, you must tell me why you're so sad. I haven't asked you anything about your life. I figured you'd tell me when you want to share. I don't care about your past so long as we're together. But now, I need to know what's wrong and I won't leave your side until you tell me."

"I'm sorry, Michael. I should have told you before. I hope you won't hate me when I tell you what I've done."

"Hate you? I could never hate you."

"It's a very long story."

"I'm not going anywhere."

Lola sighed. "I was born in Paris to an aristocratic family. I had to adhere to a strict code of conduct. I felt imprisoned by a life I hated, where arrogance and pretentiousness are expected behavior. At sixteen, I disobeyed my father and refused to marry a man I didn't love. When I told my father my wish to be an entertainer, he forbade me. I ran away. He disowned me and left me penniless. Determined to be an entertainer, I worked hard to improve my skills. A friend introduced me to one of the owners of the Moulin Rouge. They hired me and it was there that I met Charlie Sloan."

Lola paused and gave Michael a sheepish look. "Please don't be angry with me. We had an affair."

Michael's eyes were soft as he gently stroked her cheek. "Lola, you're so beautiful. It comes as no surprise that men want to be with you. There's no reason for me to be angry, after all, I'm the one you married. But I still don't understand why you're crying."

Lola sighed. "Although I cared for Charlie, I never loved him the way I love you. Charlie's a gambler and always running to or away from something and one day he disappeared. I waited for him to return but when he didn't, I made a foolish mistake. A German officer came to my dressing room. I'll never forget his name, Baron Freiherr Diedrich von Breckendorf. He convinced me to join him for dinner. He was charming and handsome so I agreed. But that night I drank too much and—"

"It's all right. You don't have to tell me."

Lola exhaled a ragged breath and wiped her tears. Then punched her hand. "I was so angry when I realized he made me pregnant!"

Michael brushed the hair from her damp face. "It hurts to see you so upset. If you want to talk about this another time, I—"

"No, it's better that I tell you everything." Lola felt ill again and ran to the bathroom.

Michael followed her. He wet a towel and wiped her face. "Can I get you something? Some water?"

"No, I'm fine."

Together they sat on a sofa in the parlor. Lola cleared her throat. "I didn't know what to do. At the time, I shared an apartment with my good friend, Sophie Duchard. She wanted Diedrich to take responsibility for the baby but I wouldn't allow her to tell him. I didn't like his brutal, arrogant nature. If I hadn't had too much to drink, I never would've been with him. Besides, he returned to Germany the next day.

"Where's the baby now?"

Lola covered her eyes and mumbled, "She...she died."

Michael took her hand. "I'm so sorry. What happened?"

"I don't know! I felt her strong legs kicking and always moving inside me. But they told me she died because the umbilical cord wrapped around her little neck and strangled her. I didn't believe it until they showed me her lifeless body." Lola's chin trembled as a groan escaped her.

Michael held her close as she cried into his shoulder.

After a few moments, she uttered, "I'm afraid it will happen again. I couldn't bear it. I'm so frightened."

"Don't you worry, we'll get you the best doctor in San Francisco."

"Michael, I want to go home. Would you mind if we left San Francisco and returned to Rimrock Springs?"

"Go back? We can afford to live anywhere in the world, why not San Francisco or Chicago or Paris?"

"Paris! Never! The memories of my life in Paris sadden me. I will never return there. My friends are in Rimrock Springs. It's the only place I've ever been happy. Living there with you will make my life perfect."

101

"What about the baby?"

"I'm confident in Doctor Malone. He's delivered many babies and all the ladies like him so much. When our baby is born I want to be with people who love me. Can we please return to Rimrock Springs?"

"Of course, honey, anything you want. I'll arrange it right away. But what will we do about a place to live?"

Lola's eyes brightened. "That's no problem. I know the perfect place. My friend Betty misses her family and she and her husband Edwin are moving back east. They have a wonderful house on a hill with a view of Rimrock Springs. I helped her decorate her home. It's all ready for us to move in. I love the house. Can we buy it?" She smiled, "Would that be all right with you, *mon amour?*"

He hugged her. "Anything for you, Lola."

They returned to Rimrock Springs and Michael purchased the ten-room stone mansion with its polished oak floors and picture windows overlooking the town. Lola and Betty had decorated the house in the popular Art Nouveau and Craftsman styles.

Frank threw a party at the Golden Slipper Saloon in honor of their return. Frank asked Lola what her plans would be after she had the baby. Michael stood at her side when she replied, "Although I love to perform, I'm a wife and soon to be a mother, I don't know how I'll feel in the future, but for now I have two wonderful people to take care of."

Frank turned to Michael, shook his hand and said, "Michael, you're a lucky man!"

"Thanks, Frank, don't I know it!"

The months flew by quickly and soon the time had come for Lola to give birth. Doctor Malone, Annie and Lola's Ladies rushed to Lola's side when Michael informed them that her water broke. Despite the assurances from her friends, Lola remained frightened for the baby.

Lola insisted, "Dr. Malone under no circumstances will you put me to sleep while I'm giving birth. I want to be awake during the entire procedure. I need to know exactly what's happening."

"You needn't fear, Mrs. O'Reilly. I never administer chloroform during childbirth. Your baby will come into this world as natural as can be."

Michael sat at Lola's side holding her hand, "Please don't worry. I'll be here with you the entire time. Everything will be all right."

"Maybe you shouldn't be here with me. It may be difficult for you to see me in pain."

"You're right. It will be difficult but I want to watch over you. No matter what, I promise I'll stay."

Lola felt the pains begin. Dr. Malone tried to keep her calm, but she asked repeatedly about the baby's welfare. The ladies took turns dabbing the sweat from her face, patting her hand and singing to her.

Michael asked Dr. Malone every few minutes if Lola was all right. The doctor insisted Michael take a walk outside. He refused and continued to ask about Lola's welfare. The doctor and the ladies all shouted at him to leave so they could concentrate on Lola. Michael turned pale when Lola let out a great scream and ran from the house yelling, "Be sure to come and get me when it's over!"

The time had come for Lola to give one final push. She heard a slap and loud cry from her baby and joyful shouts, "Congratulations! It's a girl! A strong, healthy baby girl!"

Lola could barely contain her excitement. She sat up with difficulty and watched as they cleaned the infant. "Doctor bring her to me! I must hold her!" Lola's tears of joy streamed her face as she cradled the baby girl in her arms. She kissed her and said, "Welcome my precious baby. I love you."

When Michael was summoned, he stormed into their bedroom and asked, "How are you? I'm so sorry I left, but you were right, I couldn't stand to hear you in such pain."

Lola held her newborn little girl. "It's all right *mon amour*. I want to introduce you to your baby daughter." Lola held her up and said, "Baby Rita, meet your poppa."

Tears came to his eyes, as Michael looked at his sweet baby girl. "She's beautiful! The most beautiful baby in the world! Now everything will be perfect."

Chapter 14

Lola cherished Rita. She designed her clothes, played with her, sang to her and loved to dance while holding Rita in her arms. Over the months, Lola could see how much Rita resembled Michael, the same thick, gold streaked red-bronze hair and his large blue-green eyes.

Although she missed performing, Lola treasured her role as wife and mother. However, she frequently used her talents to perform for charity events.

One day, while reviewing choreography with Annie and Annie's Ladies for an upcoming charity event, Hattie, Rita's nursemaid, sat with Rita on her lap. Rita insisted on climbing up onto a table and then began to imitate Lola's dance movements.

"Mrs. O'Reilly," Hanna called out. "Take a look at what Rita's doing!"

Lola turned to see Rita performing her little girl version of the cancan, shaking hips in time with the music. Then as Hanna held her hand, Rita lifted her little leg and awkwardly twirled her foot.

Her heart melted as Lola watched her rosy-cheeked baby girl dance. She rushed to Rita, "You're only thirty months old, how do you know to do this?" Lola picked her up and gushed, "Oh, my sweet darling, how much I love you!"

From then on, Lola rehearsed with Rita at home in their dressing room at home. She taught her songs, and although Rita couldn't pronounce all the words, she was more adorable because of it. Lola designed matching costumes for the two of them to wear when they performed charities together.

Once, when Lola entered her bedroom, she discovered Rita wearing one of her father's cowboy boots. With a frustrated face, Rita struggled to put on the other one. Lola laughed. "What are you doing?"

Rita looked at her mother. Her expression showed hope and yearning. "Momma, help me. I want Poppa's shoes."

"Oh no, my darling, they're much too big for you."

"Please Momma! I want to ride the horsey and I need Poppa's shoes."

Lola's heart filled with love as she looked at her little daughter's face. Her large eyes, her little nose and her heart-shaped lips. Lola scooped Rita up and danced with her kissing each cheek, her nose and her sweet little lips.

One day when Michael sat on the living room sofa reading the newspaper, Rita stuck her curly-haired head under the newspaper and peeked at him. Michael laughed at his little girl and pulled her onto his lap.

"Horsey," Rita announced.

"Horsey? Where?"

Rita pointed to a picture of a horse at the back of the newspaper.

"Yes," Michael agreed, "That's a horsey, all right."

"I want horsey!" Rita insisted.

"You're too young little one."

106

"I want horsey."

Michael looked at Lola, "Should I take her for a ride?"

Rita pointed to an ad in the newspaper. "Oh, Michael! Look! She's pointing to an ad for the circus!" Lola picked up the newspaper and read to Michael that the circus would be arriving in Phoenix the following week. "We must take Rita!"

Arriving in Phoenix, they were excited to attend the circus. Rita laughed at the clowns and her mouth dropped at the sight of acrobats flying through the air. She enjoyed all the other performers as well.

The ringmaster entered the center of the ring to announce Helene Bonner, a lady trick rider of great renown and her horse Sir Galahad. Helene galloped into the ring on a shiny black stallion. Rita jumped from her seat, pointed and shouted, "Horsey, Momma, horsey!" Michael had to hold Rita back to keep her from running into the ring towards the horse.

Rita stared in fascination at Helene's thick red hair and the train of her sparkling sequined white gown that wafted behind her.

Helene stood atop the horse. With much poise, she removed her train, twirled it through the air, and let it loose to spin and float to the ground. With her horse in a gallop, Helene pivoted her body until she faced backward sitting on the stallion's neck, then she reversed her trick and returned to the saddle. To follow, she stood atop the horse and with a lasso shaped rope and passed it from hand to hand as it spun.

107

The more tricks the Helene performed, the more excited Rita became.

For days afterward, Rita repeated incessantly, "I want to ride horsey!" Lola knew that the time had come for Rita to have a pony.

Lola and Michael rode to their ranch of their neighbor, Smitty Smithson. They had become friends with Smitty when Michael purchased race horses from him at his Double SS Horse Ranch.

The ranch brought back Lola's memories of how much she loved horseback riding. She would allow herself only a few fond memories of her father, but her heart softened when she thought of their rides together through the Bois de Bologne in Paris.

Smitty had the features of an overweight cherub. Everything about him was round. His face had chubby round cheeks, his round belly protruded over his belt, and when he walked the cheeks of his behind bounced like two dancing balloons. With a quick smile and an easy laugh, she and Michael grew fond of Smitty and often invited him to dinner at their home.

Lola told Smitty of Rita's fascination for the trick-rider at the circus. He approached Rita and knelt with his face close to hers. "So, you want to learn how to be a trick-rider, eh?"

Rita pointed to the horses in the corral. "I want to ride horsey!"

Smitty looked at Michael and Lola, "I know she's young but some of my ranch hands are expert trick-riders. I believe they'd be willing to teach her some tricks."

Michael shook his head. "I don't think that's a good idea. It's too dangerous. Let's just get her a gentle pony."

Over Michael's objection, Rita ran towards the horse pen where several horses were munching hay. "Momma, Momma look! I want to ride horsey!"

Smitty rubbed his stubbled chin and thought for a moment. "Of course, I understand why you just want a pony for her, and I have some gentle ones. But I know my ranch hands and they'd take good care of her. Why not let her take one lesson? You can hang around to keep an eye on her. If you think it's too dangerous, we'll just end the lesson."

Rita pleaded, "Momma, I want to ride. Please!"

Michael and Lola looked at each other. Lola said, "Let's at least let her sit on a pony and see how she reacts."

Smitty called to one of the ranch hands and said, "Go fetch Trevor and tell him to bring Sweet Eyes."

"Okay, boss," the ranch hand said and ran off.

A little while later, a man approached. His eyes and skin were the color of black coffee. He was tall and broad, with powerful, oversized hands and thick fingers.

Lola looked at him with concern. "The man is very big. Do you think he can be gentle with Rita?"

Smitty smiled. "I know he's a big, strong buck but they don't come any gentler than him."

Trevor brought a well-built pony with a big hip, wide chest, plenty of bone, a baby doll head and kind eyes. The mare had a sorrel coat, a color similar to the color of Rita's hair. Lola said, "I know this breed, it's a Percheron." She confirmed with Smitty, "This pony, she is from France, no?"

"You're right, Lola. Imported here from Le Perche, France. If you know this breed, you know she's gentle."

"Ah, *oui*. Yes, of course." Lola stroked the pony's nose and whispered in her ear.

Michael asked, "What did you say to the pony?"

"Since she understands French, I asked her to be very kind and gentle with Rita."

They all laughed.

When Rita saw her mother approach the pony she ran over and pet its nose. "I love you," she said as she looked into the pony's eyes. "Momma please, I want to ride Sweet Eyes!"

Lola looked into her daughter's pleading big, blue-green eyes. "All right. Smitty let's see what happens. But Trevor, please be careful."

Trevor's smile "Yes ma'am, I surely will." Trevor saddled the pony and adjusted the fit for Rita. He placed her in the saddle and handed her the reins. "Hold on tight, little one."

Rita shook the reins and kicked her feet to make the pony go fast, but Trevor held her tight to keep her safe.

Smitty suggested, "If you think Rita will be okay, why don't we go inside and have a cup of coffee while they get to know each other."

Reluctantly, they agreed and followed Smitty inside the ranch house. Lola and Smitty sat drinking coffee and chatting. Michael stood watching Rita from the window. After thirty minutes, Michael said, "I don't believe it!"

Lola ran to the window followed by Smitty. In unison, they shouted, "What's the matter?"

They shook their heads in disbelief. With a beaming smile, Rita sat atop the pony. With Trevor's help, Rita had the pony walking backward, then forward, then backward again.

They all ran outside. Lola applauded Rita. *"Ma cherie,* you're wonderful!"

Trevor removed her from the saddle and said, "This little one's a natural!'

From that day forward, at Rita's insistence, Lola brought her to Smitty's ranch every chance she had.

Dance with the Devil

Chapter 15

Trevor could see, that even at three years old, Rita's riding ability had great promise. When Rita became comfortable riding Sweet Eyes, Trevor allowed her to increase the horse's pace. Rita's enthusiasm for developing her riding skills and love of horses impressed him.

Pleased at her progress, Trevor began to teach her tricks. Easy tricks at first, but as Rita's skills and confidence developed, the tricks became more daring.

Rita had her father's good looks and his brilliant smile. But she had her mother's personality. Vibrant, outgoing and easy to get along with, Rita could be stubborn too, especially at learning tricks.

No matter how much practice it required to learn a trick, she would settle for nothing less than perfection. Rita displayed her temper when she couldn't get a trick right after several tries. Lola and the ranch hands laughed at Rita when she stomped her little feet hollering at herself, "Rita, no good! No good!" Then the determined little girl would get back on her horse and practice until she did the trick correctly.

Lola missed entertaining and believed she would return to the Golden Slipper when the time was right. For now, Lola enjoyed their simple and happy

113

life. Michael spent most of his time in town at business meetings or working alone in his study. Lola busied herself with running the house, charity work, visiting the Double SS Ranch and tutoring Rita.

Although affectionate and indulgent with Rita, Lola insisted her daughter have a good education. In addition to academia, she taught Rita to believe in herself and not live up to anyone's expectations but her own.

Filled with toys, dolls and children's furniture, Rita's bedroom had been designed for a little princess. The bed had a headboard and footboard of brass with soft down pillows covered with pink cases and a down cover with pink and white flowers. On Rita's bed were dolls in a variety of sizes and outfits along with many toy horses. The armoire, end tables, framed mirrors and desk were of French provincial style and painted white with pink undertones. On pegs hung colorful umbrellas, hats and several small purses.

Her many toys included a baby doll carriage, a mechanical merry-go-round and a bone china tea set sitting atop a small table with two chairs. Rita often required her parents to join her in an imaginary cup of tea. Watching her father struggle into the child-size chair always resulted in gales of laughter for the young family.

<hr />

One day, Lola entered Rita's bedroom to see her sitting at her writing desk coloring. "What are you coloring?" Lola asked.

Rita held up her paper and said, "It's the pretty lady standing on her horse. This is how I will look."

"Yes, my dear, but you'll be even more beautiful."

Rita looked at her mother. With a puzzled face, she asked, "Momma, how many names do you have?"

Surprised by the question, Lola queried, "How many names? Why do you ask?"

"My friend Jeannie said her momma has her given name and two surnames."

Lola smiled. "She must mean she has a maiden name and a married name."

"What's that mean?"

"Well, my love, my family name is La Fontaine. When I became a performer, I used the stage name, Dupin. When I married Poppa, I gained the name O'Reilly. So, my full name is Lola La Fontaine Dupin O'Reilly."

"That's a lot of names."

"*Oui, ma cherie,* that is a lot of names."

Rita screwed her face in thought. "Momma, how many names do I have?"

"You have two names, Rita and O'Reilly."

"Why is my name Rita?"

Lola looked kindly at her daughter. "Because one day I was very sad sitting alone in the park and a little girl came to me and cheered me up. When I asked her, she said her name was Rita. I told the little girl that if I had a daughter, I would name her Rita. You remind me of her. She was pretty and had beautiful red hair just like you." Lola tapped the tip of Rita's nose. "So, my sweet girl, are you ready to get dressed and celebrate your birthday? After all, you've reached the ripe old age of five years."

Rita sneezed and looked flushed. Concerned, Lola touched Rita's forehead. "Oh, my little one, you have a fever!"

Hattie sat in a nearby rocking chair. Lola asked her if she knew about the fever "Yes, Mrs. O'Reilly, I was about to tell you she has a little fever. It doesn't seem serious but I think she should stay in bed. I tried to get her to lie down but she'd have none of that!"

"Now, Rita you must listen to Hattie and get right into bed."

Giving her mother a bright dimpled smile, Rita insisted, "Momma, I feel fine. I'm going to town with you." Rita sneezed again and wiped her nose with her hand.

Lola looked at Hattie as she wiped Rita's runny nose and said, "No, my little one. You're sick and you must go to bed." Lola picked her up and sat on her bed with Rita on her lap.

"But Momma, I want to go to town with you."

Lola kissed each dimple. "No, *ma petite chou*, my sweet little cabbage, you cannot."

"But Momma, today's my birthday! You said you would take me to town and buy me presents!"

"I know *ma petite*, but I want you to get well quickly, so you must stay home. However, if you promise to be a good girl and stay in bed, I'll bring you a very special present. Would that be all right?"

Her golden-red curls bounced wildly as Rita bounced up and down, "Yes, Momma, I'll behave."

Lola instructed, "Hattie, make sure she stays in bed. I'll be right back." Lola left to find Michael. She found him at his desk in his study writing a note. Concerned at the sullen look on his face, she asked, "Is everything all right?"

"Uh, yeah, sure. But I'm busy right now. What is it you want?"

"My sweet, I'm off to town to check on the gowns I ordered and to run some errands. I wanted to take Rita and buy her some gifts for her birthday but she's ill. She's so disappointed that I decided to give her our special gift before I left, and I wanted us to give her our present together."

Michael grumbled, "You bought more gowns? Why do you need more clothes? You have enough clothing to outfit a small town! And why does Rita need more toys?"

Lola felt alarmed. "I don't understand. Why are you so upset? In the six years we've been married you've never taken that tone with me. Could it be that you're working too hard? You've been spending many hours away from home and then you spend more time working in your study. Something's not right. Are you not feeling well? Rita is sick, maybe you're sick too?"

He gave Lola a weak smile and in a soft voice, he said, "I'm sorry Lola. It's just that…uh…never mind. I guess I am feeling poorly just now. Can you give Rita the present without me? I don't want her to catch anything I might have. Go get your dresses honey, and as many presents for Rita as you want."

Lola searched Michael's face. *Something troubles him. Should I push him to tell me? No, I'll wait and talk to him when I return.* "All right, it may be best that I give Rita the present myself."

About to leave, she stopped and thought for a moment, then walked to him and sat on his lap. "I think I know what the trouble is." She put her arms around his neck and whispered into his ear, "It's

117

been too long since we've made love. When I come back, we will make glorious love, *oui*?"

With a tight-lipped smile, Michael helped her off his lap, "Go get yourself some real pretty dresses, honey." He picked up the note he'd been writing and tucked it into an envelope. "Since you're going to town, can you stop off and give this note to Mr. Wilson, the manager of the Miners Bank and Trust?"

"*Mais oui, mon amour*, I'll be happy to." She kissed his cheek and left to get Rita's present.

Lola entered Rita's room to see her daughter in bed playing with her toy horse. "I have something special for you. Poppa wanted to be here so we could give this to you together, but he's not feeling well, so he asked me to tell you that he loves you very much and hopes you like our gift."

Rita sat up straight. Her eyes grew wide with anticipation.

"Close your eyes and put out your hands,"

Rita obeyed but quickly opened her eyes. She gasped to see a golden heart-shaped locket with a tiny diamond centered in the face, surrounded by fancy scrollwork. "Oh Momma, this is beautiful!"

"Can you open the locket?

Rita's little fingers fumbled, so Lola helped her. Inside the locket were two pictures, one of her mother and one of her father. Rita kissed each picture.

Then Lola closed the locket and showed her an inscription on the back. "Can you read what this says?"

Rita struggled but then read it aloud, "To our dearest Rita, always in our heart. Love, Momma and Poppa." She threw her arms around her mother's neck. "Momma, I love you so much! This is the best present ever! Help me put it on. I will wear it every day for the rest of my life!"

After putting the locket around Rita's neck, Lola said, "I'm so glad you like it. Now you must rest *ma petite*. She lifted the covers and helped Rita lay back. Lola said, "Dream of me and know that I will always watch over you." She sang her a lullaby and soon Rita fell asleep. Leaving her in the care of her nursemaid, Hattie, Lola said, "I'm so sorry to leave her. Please take care of my little one for me."

Dance with the Devil

Chapter 16

Lola approved the custom gowns she ordered from Paris and purchased the doll Rita had wished for. She also bought a sheer, lacy nightgown, smiling to herself about the special night she would have with Michael. Lola asked to have her purchases delivered to her home. Outside the store, Lola stood by watching the stock boy load her purchases onto a buckboard, when she heard someone call her name.

She turned to see the chiseled features and striking good looks of the man she once thought she loved. "Charlie? Charlie Sloan?" Seeing his face made her body stir. "*Mon Dieu!* What are you doing here in Rimrock Springs?"

"I thought it was you." Charlie smiled with approval and took her hands in his. "You look as beautiful as ever!"

At the touch of his fingers, a tinge of electricity ran through Lola.

"Sweetheart, you look stunning!" Charlie's smile widened to a grin. "Even better than I remember. Let's go someplace and have a chat. We have a lot of catching up to do."

"Yes, we certainly do!" She walked with Charlie to Minerva's Tea Parlor. Lola's emotions were in chaos. Although angry with him, he brought out a yearning in her.

The tea parlor had frilly lace curtains, linen tablecloths, an antique walnut wall clock with a ticking brass pendulum and a delightful chime. Lola smiled to herself as she watched women patrons strain their heads in curiosity when she entered the shop with this handsome stranger. Lola knew she would be today's hot topic of gossip.

They sat at a table near the window. Lola couldn't take her eyes from him. *He hasn't changed at all since I saw him last. He looks so fine in his immaculate white suit, black satin string tie and silk paisley black and silver vest.*

Her thoughts were interrupted when the eyes of a waitress lingered on Charlie as she handed him a menu. In a dismissive tone, Lola ordered them each a cup of Earl Grey tea.

"It's so good to see you, Lola." Charlie said and gave her a warm smile.

The sound of his voice made her heart flutter. *Those lips, so soft and warm. I wonder if they still taste like fine champagne. Never mind! The pain he caused me is unforgivable.*

As the waitress filled her cup, Lola said, "Charlie, you were brave to catch my attention, I should be furious with you."

Annoyed that the waitress stood and listened to their conversation, Lola said, "Just leave the teapot and that will be all."

The waitress left in a huff.

Charlie reached across the table to touch Lola's hand. "I knew it might be a risk. I had no right to expect you would even talk to me. But I couldn't resist."

Lola moved her hand away and in a firm voice she said, "All those years ago, I traveled here to Rimrock Springs. I came because of your letter. You asked me to meet you here. But when I arrived from New Orleans, you had already left along with the money I gave you. Charlie, you abandoned me!"

He lowered his eyes. "I can't blame you for being angry. I treated you badly and I feel terrible."

Lola shouted. "You should feel terrible!" She looked around to see prying eyes staring at her and lowered her voice. "How do you think I feel? I had no money and no idea what to do. Even worse, Monique almost died because of you! Instead of paying The Black Hand gang the money you owed them, you ran away and in revenge they kidnapped Monique!"

Charlie leaned forward and stared into Lola's eyes. She thought he looked sincere as he said, "I am truly sorry. You deserve my deep gratitude for saving Monique's life." With pleading eyes, he asked, "Can you ever forgive me?"

Lola turned her head and stared out of the window in silence.

After a few moments, Charlie said, "I had every intention of waiting in Rimrock Springs for you to arrive. But I entered a large poker tournament here. I'd been very successful at playing poker up to that point. When I wrote the letter asking you to join me, I had been close to winning a huge pot. It would've been more than enough to pay back the money you loaned me and for us to enjoy each other while traveling to wherever you wanted to go. However, I lost everything. To be honest, Lola, I couldn't face you." He cleared his throat and looked sheepish. "So, I left town."

Lola thought, *What would my life be like if Charlie had won the poker game?*

She cleared her throat. "Where did you go after you left me?"

"I hit one town after another, meeting people and gambling. You know I'm a wanderer by nature."

123

"Meeting people? You mean meeting rich women?"

He sighed. "You know me too well, Lola."

"Why are you in Rimrock Springs? Another poker game perhaps?"

"Yes. I suppose you know Rimrock Springs has an annual Championship Poker Tournament."

"Yes, I'm well aware."

"And you? Why are you in Rimrock Springs?"

Lola took a deep breath. "The only reason I'm not killing you now is that, in a way, it was a blessing I arrived here. I've been very happy living in Rimrock Springs."

His eyebrows shot up. "Happy? In Rimrock Springs? I thought you'd become a famous entertainer in San Francisco or New York. What is it about this town that makes you so happy?"

"After you deserted me and left me penniless, I persevered and achieved success as an entertainer. Not only have I enjoyed my life performing here, but I'm also happily married and have a beautiful daughter."

Charlie beamed, "Lola, I'm not surprised at your success. You'd be a success anywhere. But married! And a daughter! Congratulations! Maybe I did the right thing for you after all."

Lola's chest tightened. "No Charlie, what you did was wrong. I'm successful because of my talents and strength of will. The important thing is, now that I am Madame Lola O'Reilly and have my sweet little Rita, I'm happier than I've ever been."

"I hope your husband is smarter than I was, and he will always treat you well."

Lola's eyes brightened, "*Oui!* Michael is the best husband in the world! We're very much in love, and our little Rita, she's just five years old but so smart and talented. You should see her dance. One day she will sing better than I do! Not only is she pretty, smart and talented, despite her young age, she's also very good at trick riding."

"She sounds special. She must take after her mother."

"I'd love for you to meet her. How long will you be staying here?"

"The tournament is over and I'm leaving today. I'm on my way to Canada to meet someone and then invest in an important business deal."

"A business deal or a gambling game?"

He laughed, "A snake can't change its nature, you know."

"Charlie, I don't live far from here. You must come with me to my house. I think it would be marvelous for you to meet my husband Michael and my little Rita."

"Does that mean you forgive me?"

"No, I can never forgive the pain you've caused, but that's in the past. I will not dwell on it. But I'd like you to see how well my life has turned out. You'll be impressed."

"I would love to meet the man that captured the heart of the fabulous Lola, but I must be on my way." Charlie pulled a gold watch from his vest pocket and checked the time, "I'm running late as it is, but I couldn't pass up the chance to spend a few minutes with Lola the fantastic!"

Lola withdrew a picture from her purse. "Well, you must at least see a photograph of Rita. This was taken at a recent charity performance." She pointed at the photograph. "As you can see, that's me and there is my beautiful Rita. She has thick red hair and

125

bright blue-green eyes. She looks like her handsome father. We'd just performed a ballet duet. We are in matching tutu outfits and have garlands in our hair. Oh, how I wish you could meet her."

"What a delightful picture. Rita is adorable! May I keep it?"

Puzzled, Lola frowned. "Why do you want it?

Charlie looked at the picture again and said, "I will place this picture in my wallet next to my heart and look at it often."

Although skeptical, Lola said, "Of course you can have the picture, but I must inscribe the back." Lola wrote:

To my dearest Charlie,
Wishing you good luck always.
Lola and Rita O'Reilly
August 20, 1895

Charlie read the inscription and smiled. "Lola, I wish I'd been man enough to marry you. I'm so sorry for the pain I've caused. I wish you unending happiness. I hate to leave without seeing your family, but maybe we will meet again the next time you're in Paris."

"Paris. No! I never want to see Paris again! Nothing good is waiting for me there."

"Nothing good? What about your daughter?"

"A daughter in Paris?" Lola smiled and shook her head. "No, you are mistaken. Rita is my only daughter."

"Hold on. I've seen newspaper articles about Mimi La Fontaine. She's famous for her outlandish behavior."

"This is not possible. I have no daughter in Paris. I don't understand."

"I don't understand either," he said with a shrug.

"Charlie, are you sure her name is La Fontaine?

"Oh, yes. I'm certain."

Maybe she's the daughter of another La Fontaine family."

Charlie shook his head. "I doubt that. I've seen her pictures in the newspaper. She looks exactly like you."

"Are you sure?"

"Yes. I've seen pictures of her with her grandfather, Émile La Fontaine."

"*Papá?* But...how can this be?" Lola drew a hand to her mouth. "My baby died when she was born." Lola thought for a moment. Her eyes narrowed. "How old is Mimi?"

"I don't know but at the time she must have been about ten or so. Why?"

"She might be the right age. Do you remember that when we came to America, I felt depressed because I lost my baby girl?"

"Yes. Before we left for America, Sophie told me you had a miscarriage and you wanted to commit suicide."

"Commit suicide? I was depressed but...No, this must be some mistake."

"Lola, there's no mistake. That girl must be your child. No one else could look so much like you."

She rubbed her fingers against her forehead. "Sophie told me my baby died. I held the dead little girl in my arms. How...? This is too terrible. Sophie was good to me. She told me having a baby in the hospital was dangerous. That many women die because of puerperal fever. She insisted that she be my midwife. When I refused, she had Madame Rosalie....*Mon Dieu!* Do you think Sophie switched my baby for a dead baby? Is she capable of such treachery?"

"I know Sophie has done some unsavory things, but switching babies? I can't imagine—"

Lola gathered her things. "I'm sorry, Charlie, I must leave. I must go to Paris immediately! Sophie has explaining to do."

"I understand. I wish I could go with you but I'm leaving for Canada immediately. I have obligations I cannot get out of. Lola, I wish you well." Charlie kissed her hand and left.

Lola rushed home. "Michael! Michael, I must talk with you!" She found Michael in the bedroom and closed the door.

"What's the matter, Lola? You're white as a sheet. Are you all right?"

"Michael, I just found out that my baby, the one I thought died in childbirth, is alive and living in Paris. I must leave immediately and find out if this is true."

"Whoa, Lola. Not so fast. How did you hear about this?"

"Charlie just told me."

"Who's Charlie?"

"He's the man I told you about. My first lover. I met him in town."

"You met your lover in town?" Michael's eyes locked on hers. His jaw muscled tightened. "Lola, what's going on?"

"It's a long story. Please, I must leave right away for Paris."

Michael laid his hands on Lola's shoulders. His voice softened, "I need you to explain yourself. This sounds like a fairy tale. You have a daughter right here to take care of."

"Please, Michael, out of my way. I must pack. "She moved away from him.

His eyes flashed in anger. "I said NO! You can't do this."

"I must and I will! Please take care of Rita. I will be back as soon as I can. I'll write to you when I know what's going on."

Lola began to pack.

Michael grabbed her wrist. "LOLA, YOU CAN'T GO. I MEAN IT!"

She removed his hand and continued to pack. "I AM LEAVING AND THAT'S FINAL!"

Lola brushed past Michael and went to Rita's room. "Hattie, how is Rita doing?"

"She's fine. After you left, she fell asleep. When she woke her fever was gone and she's been playing with her toys."

At the sight of her mother, Rita ran to Lola and raised her arms for a hug.

Lola picked her up and brought her to her bed, sitting Rita on her lap.

With happy eyes, Rita asked Lola, "Did you bring my present, Momma?"

"Yes, sweetheart. Poppa will give it to you later. I must tell you something. Something very important."

Rita knitted her eyebrows. "Is this something bad?"

"*Ma cherie*, I must go away for a while. You will stay here with Poppa and Hattie. I'll return as soon as I can."

Rita pushed out her bottom lip. "I want to go with you."

"I'm sorry my little one, it's not possible. But I'll be back soon with a very special present for you. I love you so much."

Rita's eyes filled with tears. "Momma, I don't want you to go."

"I wish I could stay. You'll be a good girl for Poppa, won't you?"

Rita crossed her arms and frowned.

"Now, Rita. Promise me you'll be a good girl."

Dejectedly, she said, "Okay, Momma. But I will miss you."

"*Ma chou*, whenever you get lonely, look at my picture in your locket. When you see my face, you'll know I am thinking of you."

Lola hugged and kissed Rita.

"Hattie, please take good care of Rita. I'll return as soon as possible."

Looking concerned, "I hope everything is all right, Mrs. O'Reilly."

Lola kissed Rita's head and left.

Chapter 17

Pearly gray fog obscured the waning crescent moon. Perfect for skulking among the baggage containers crowding the dock.

Willy Dressler, with his peacoat collar turned up and his stocking cap pulled low, had disguised himself as a stevedore. He passed among the dockworkers unnoticed.

After loading several suitcases onto a wheeled cart, he made his way up the gangplank. Willy's dark eyes checked the surroundings. With no one watching, he fled to the ship's cargo hold. Crouching between the bulk cargo, he prepared himself to wait until the ship left port from the New York harbor on its from the way to Le Havre, France.

Scrunched between containers, he fumed as he thought about Mortimer Wallace. *That bastard! Him and his highfalutin ways. I never should've got involved with him. Swindling me out of my share of the bank heist. We were partners. He made the plans and I blew the safe. I took all the risks and that masher takes off for Paris to screw French tarts with my money. Nobody cheats me and gets away with it! If he doesn't give me my cut, it's lights out for him.*

Willy removed the gun from his coat pocket and checked the chamber for bullets. He returned it to his pocket and patted it like a good friend. His eyelids grew heavy with sleep when a thought shot into his head. He felt his right hand. *I never shoulda got this tattoo, but I couldn't resist. Maybelle was so impressed when I showed her my spider. Jees, I don't want anybody to remember me by my tattoo. Ah, screw it. I'll slip off the ship as sneaky as I got on. Nobody's gonna remember me.* He pulled his stocking cap over his eyes and drifted off.

The commotion of staff and crew hustling to board passengers and settle them woke Willy. He remained still awaiting the hoist of the anchors and the engines to fire up. Stiff from crouching all night, he stood slowly and stretched his back and legs. Willy's stomach growled. *A man's gotta eat.* He headed for the ship's galley.

In the galley, the frenzied staff readied for the first meal of the day. Willy arrived unnoticed and removed one of several aprons from a shelf, grabbed a broom and pretended to sweep the floor until one of the chefs stopped him. "Hey, you! You're in the way. See those dishes over there? Pile them up and put them with the others."

Willy smiled knowing he's getting away with his disguise. "Yes, sir. I'll take care of it right away."

The chef called out, "Wait a minute!"

Willy's heart pounded. "Is there something else?"

"You new here? I don't remember seeing you before."

"Yeah. This is my first time on a cruise ship. Hope I don't get seasick. Ha! Ha!"

"If you do, make sure you don't throw up on the floor or you'll have to clean up your mess. Now get to work." The chef turned and walked away.

"Yes, sir!" Willy whistled while he stacked the dishes.

Lola grabbed her bag, left home and proceeded to the Rimrock Springs train station. During her trip, she tried to remember every detail of her pregnancy and the day Sophie and Madame Rosalie delivered her baby.

With her travel arrangements set, Lola boarded an ocean liner heading to Le Havre, France from the port of New York.

The next day, Lola walked along the deck to get some air. Her mind was aflutter with questions. *Is Sophie so cruel that she would kidnap my baby? Why? I wish I asked Charlie more questions. I must get to the bottom of this!*

Her reverie was interrupted when she passed a cabin with an open porthole and overheard two men arguing inside. One man, with a spider tattoo, shook another man by the lapels and shouted, "Give me my money or you'll be sorry!"

Puzzled, Lola dismissed their argument. She was more interested in her problems. A short while later, a man bumped into her from behind. She turned to see one of the men who had been arguing in the cabin. Tall and well-dressed, he had a pock-marked face and piggy, dark olive-green eyes. His expression, annoyed at first, changed when he looked at her face. He gave her a smarmy smile and tipped his hat. "Pardon my clumsiness, Madame. My name is Mortimer Wallace and you are...?"

She gave him an abrupt smile and strode away. From that moment, Lola felt he watched her. In the corridor or on deck, Mortimer brushed by her often, lingering for a moment too long, and always offering a salacious smile. She tried to avoid him, but he seemed to know her every step. He never spoke to her but she could feel his staring eyes.

Mortimer gave her the shivers. At first, she believed it was a coincidence. But as the journey continued, she knew he followed her. She wanted to confront him, but the voyage would only last a few more days, so she ignored him.

At dinner, two evenings before docking, Mortimer sat at a table across from Lola. With a vulgar stare, he observed her every move, always with a lewd smile plastered across his face. Men like him had accosted her at the Golden Slipper Saloon and she had once been attacked by a man who waited in her dressing room. She would not let that happen again. It was time to put a stop to Mortimer's behavior! Lola walked to his table. "Why are you following me?"

With an innocent expression, he looked at her. "What are you talking about? I'm not following you."

"You know exactly what I'm talking about. I see you every place I go to."

"Madame, we are on a ship with few public places. It's an easy coincidence that we are in the same place."

"STOP FOLLOWING ME!"

Lola felt the eyes of the dining passengers on her.

The man looked around the room as if pleading his case to the diners. Mortimer said with disdain, "Madame, I have no reason to follow you. You may be the victim of hallucinations or woman's hysteria. I believe there is a physician on board who can provide you with medical attention."

Lola's face reddened. "Leave me alone or you'll regret it!" She stormed from the dining room.

In the kitchen, Willy was folding napkins when he saw several busboys crowd the door listening to the dining room commotion. He pushed his way through them to the door in time to see Lola threaten Mortimer. He smiled. *Mortimer didn't believe me when I threatened him. He walks around like a peacock while I'm figuring the best way to get away with bumping him off. How lucky can one man get! This is the perfect setup. This lady's gonna take the fall!*

Unbeknownst to Mortimer, Willy spied on his every move. He knew Mortimer's reputation for taking advantage of women and expected that this woman will have trouble with Mortimer before they disembarked at Le Havre.

Later, Willy peeked out of a companionway door to watch Mortimer's cabin. When he saw Mortimer's cabin door open, Willy pulled back. *I'll give him some space. I don't want him to know I'm right behind him.*

He watched Mortimer check his pocket watch and followed him to Lola's cabin. The cabin stewardess was leaving Lola's room with used linens and about to lock the cabin door. Mortimer said something to her. She looked concerned but when he placed a coin in her hand she smiled and walked away. Will saw Mortimer slip inside the cabin.

Relieved when a day had passed and she hadn't seen Mortimer, Lola thought she scared had him away. After dinner, she approached her stateroom and discovered the door slightly ajar. *How unusual. Had one of the staff left it unlocked after cleaning it?*

Lola stepped inside. From behind, she felt arms pull her back and toss her onto the bed. She saw his face. Mortimer Wallace! She tried to scream, but he covered her mouth with his hand. "You think you can snub me in front of everyone, you teasing slut! I know this is what you want and I going to give it to you!"

Despite his strength, Lola defended herself viciously. They tumbled around the room knocking over objects and furniture. She tried to run, but he caught her and knocked her down. Her head smacked against an end table. She lost consciousness from the blow.

At the explosive blast of a gunshot, her eyes flew open. A man leaned over her. His face was fuzzy but his spider tattoo on his hand was clear. She watched him run for the door and she passed out again.

Shouts and loud voices floated into her cabin. Lola blinked her eyes. The voices got louder. Someone repeated her name. She tried to sit up.

"Madame O'Reilly put down the gun." Pleaded a crewmember.

Lola was in shock. The crewmember's words didn't register.

"Please, Madame. You must put down the gun!"

Lola stared at the gun in her hand. Someone shouted, "Make room for the Chief Mate!"

Through the crowd of passenger onlookers and crew, The Chief Mate worked his way into Lola's room and crouched down. With his handkerchief, he removed the gun from Lola's hand and rose. He made his way to the man on the floor laying in a pool of blood. He put his hand to the man's heart and announced, "He's dead." He turned to Lola, "Why did you kill him?"

Lola shook her head. "Kill him? I...I didn't kill him."

The ship's doctor arrived. He glanced around the room and hurried to the dead man. He felt for a pulse and took a closer look at the wound. He checked his pocket watch and called to his assistant, "Note the time of death at 8:47 pm." He stood and removed his handkerchief to wipe the blood from his hand. He went to Lola and examined her head. "No blood but there will be a sizable lump."

The Chief Mate asked the doctor, "Is she well enough to answer some questions?"

"She appears to be dazed but I see no reason why she can't answer questions."

"Is this your gun?" asked the Chief Mate.

Through woozy eyes, Lola stared at the dead man. "A gun? No. I don't own a gun. How—?"

"Why did you kill him?

"I...I didn't."

"Doctor Miller, is she in condition to be brought to the brig?"

He looked at Lola. "As far as I can tell bringing her to the brig would not be injurious to her health."

"All right. Men take her to the brig."

"No! Wait!" In a cold sweat, Lola insisted, "You cannot take me. I didn't kill him!"

"This will have to be sorted this out in port." The Chief Mate said, "Meanwhile, you must stay where you can be watched."

Dance with the Devil

Chapter 18

Arrested at the Le Havre Port, Lola sat alone in a prison cell of La Sûrité nationale de Paris for endless hours. The sound of a metal key turning the lock perked up her ears.

A guard opened the jail cell door. "All right you, come with me."

She followed the guard to a small poorly lit, windowless room. A man in plainclothes sat behind a table. "I am Inspecteur Ulysse Curieux of La Sûrité nationale de Paris. Have a seat, Madame O'Reilly."

Lola sat. "Why am I in prison?"

The Inspector wore an ill-fitting suit, a thin mustache and smoked a cigarette. He blew a puff of smoke. "Why? Why not? Is the better question. You are a murderess."

Lola insisted, "I didn't murder anyone."

"So you say. You were found in your stateroom with a dead man near you and a gun in your hand. You are a murderess."

"As I've explained many times before. The man attacked me, we fought, then someone shot him. But not me."

"You were seen arguing with this man, ah..." Ulysse opened a folder that lay on his desk. "Monsieur Mortimer Wallace."

"I don't know him."

"You don't know him? Yet, you threatened him. He was with you in your cabin. Now he is dead. And you say you don't know him."

139

Lola slammed her fist on the desktop. "No! I had no gun. He was in my cabin when I entered. He attacked me. Someone else shot him."

The detective laughed. "If not you, then who?"

"The first time I saw Monsieur Wallace, he was arguing with a man who had a spider tattoo on his hand. I saw them through the porthole. He probably killed him."

"Then why was the gun in your hand?"

"He must have shot Monsieur Wallace and put the weapon in my hand."

"So, you're saying someone with a gun just happened to pass by your stateroom, saw the man attacking you, shot him and put the weapon in your hand? Come now, Madame O'Reilly. Surely, you can come up with a better story than this!"

Lola felt anger boil within her. "*Inspecteur*, you are wasting time. Someone killed that man, but not me.

"You say you saw him arguing with someone. Who?"

Lola sighed. "The man with the spider tattoo!"

"What does he look like?"

"I saw him only for a moment. I didn't get a good look at his face. Instead of grilling me, a victim of that man's lascivious behavior, your time will be better spent finding his killer. I told you what happened. It is the truth. Most likely, I am not the only woman that Wallace man accosted. I suggest you investigate other passengers and find out who had a motive to kill him."

"So, now you are telling me how to do my job. I think returning you to your cell will give you time to come up with a better story." He snapped his finger. "*Officier*, take her away."

Ren'e Fedyna

Dance with the Devil

Chapter 19

Michael paced the floor of his living room. His nerves were on edge and he grew tired of answering Rita's questions about her mother. It had been three weeks and he had heard nothing from Lola. Frantic with worry, he was frustrated at not knowing what to do.

When the postman arrived, Michael grabbed the mail and searched through it. Relieved to see a letter from Lola, he tore open the envelope.

Dear Michael,

I'm sorry I could not write sooner but I am in an unbelievable circumstance. I am in Le Conciergerie Prison on Île de la Cité in Paris. I was arrested and charged with the murder of a man I don't know!

Michael fell into the nearest chair, unable to believe the words.

When I was on the ship to Paris a strange man followed me. He later sneaked into my room and accosted me. In my struggle, I was knocked out and someone shot him, either to protect me or for some other reason. While I was unconscious the killer put the weapon in my hand and ran away. The police accuse me of killing this man, Mortimer Wallace. I know I don't have to tell you I am innocent. I need an avocat. Please provide what help you can as quickly as possible.

With deepest love to you and darling Rita.

Lola

His mind spun with disbelief. *How can this be? Am I having a nightmare?*

Michael packed a few things, sped from the house and hopped on to his horse to head for Smitty's horse ranch. There he saw Hattie watching Rita performing tricks with Trevor's help.

Without dismounting he approached Hattie and said, "I need to speak to you!"

Hattie looked at Michael with consternation. "What's wrong? Is it Mrs. O'Reilly?"

"I must leave right away. I'm going to get Lola and bring her home."

"Where is she?"

"I don't have time to explain. Please take care of Rita. I'll be back as fast as I can."

"Let me get Rita's attention so you can let her know."

Michael watched Rita laughing as she raced Sweet Eyes in figure eights around two large barrels. "Leave Rita be. She's having fun and I don't want to make her sad. Tell her I love her and I'm gonna bring Momma back to her. I'll write to you and let you know when we'll be back. Take care of yourself and Rita."

Michael galloped away.

Smitty came out of the horse barn laughing with two of his wranglers. Noticing Hattie's expression, he asked her. "Hattie, what's the matter? You look sick."

She wrung her hands and the lines in her forehead deepened into crevices. "Mr. O'Reilly just left. He said he would get Mrs. O'Reilly and bring her home. He didn't even say goodbye to Rita."

"Jees, do you have any idea what's going on?"

"No. I only know that on Rita's birthday, Mrs. O'Reilly went to town to buy Rita some presents. She was also supposed to deliver a note to the bank manager. A couple of hours later, she runs into the house looking for Mr. O'Reilly. They go into their bedroom, and in all the years I've worked there, I never heard them quarrel. Never even a disagreement, until that day. Mrs. O'Reilly said goodbye to Rita and rushed out the door. I haven't seen her since."

"Do you know where Michael's going?"

"No. All I know is Mr. O'Reilly galloped off to fetch his wife." Hattie put her hand to her face and blubbered, "How can I tell Rita both her parents have gone away and I don't know where or when they'll be back? Oh, dear Lord, what am I going to do?"

Smitty patted Hattie's arm. "Please don't cry. We'll figure something out." He rubbed his beard in thought. "Jees, this is a mystery all right. I tell you what, you can bring Rita here every day. I'll try to keep her busy learning tricks. Hopefully, she won't take it so bad that her parents are away."

Hattie wiped her tears and her face brightened. "Thanks, Mr. Smithson. I appreciate your help. I feel so bad for Rita. I'm sure hope they'll return soon and life will go back to normal."

Dance with the Devil

Chapter 20

With his copper hair blowing in the wind, Michael stood on the bridge of the tramp steamer, the first ship on which he could book passage to France. Crushed that Lola left on a fool's errand and overwhelmed with anxiety as he imagined Lola in prison, his mind swirled with emotions.

How is it possible you're in prison for murder? How could you leave us based on the word of an unreliable man? Why did you meet with your old lover in secret? Is it his fault you're in prison? What's so important that you had to leave? If you only knew how Rita cried when you left. Oh, Lola, why did you do this to us?

That night a furious storm struck. Monstrous waves crashed over the steamer.

Michael fell out of his bunk. Impossible to stand, he held onto anything sturdy. Between intervals of violent motion, he pulled his way towards the cabin door. Jammed shut, he lunged at the door with all his might until it yielded. He fell forward into the passageway and landed on his back into ankle-deep saltwater.

The clang of metal crashing against metal, the foreboding creak of wood, the tumultuous shouts of anxious men, and the roar of an angry sea brought a ferocious fear to Michael's heart.

He hauled himself up the companionway and raised his head above the open hatch where pandemonium ensued. Men held on for dear life as hostile waves slammed against the deck. He ducked his head when a giant wave swept over the ship's bow and showered him with seawater. With great effort, he pulled himself to the top of the companionway. Three containers broke free from their moorings. Horrified, Michael watched as the containers propelled two hapless crew members into the ocean.

Every man and object slid towards the stern as tons of steel rode upon Satan's back forcing the bow to pierce the black angry sky. For a few terrifying moments the ship suspended in the air then dropped into an abyss of the raging ocean. Only to rise and crash down once more.

A seaman wailed when a heavy metal trunk crushed him. Michael worked his way to the man and with the help of a wave, he pushed the trunk free. Just then an upsurge dragged the seaman to the edge of the ship. Michael gripped his hand but he was no match for the unrelenting power of the sea.

Unable to help, Michael's heart broke to see the poor soul swept away into the blackness. Hearing another shout for help, Michael fought the lashing wind and pelting rain to a seaman who clung to the starboard railing, his face twisted in fear. Michael grabbed the man's arms to haul him aboard but he slipped from Michael's grasp when another wave crashed onto the deck and knocked Michael down. Michael lifted his head in time to see the man swallowed by the ocean.

Heavy objects rained on Michael as he grabbed a rail and hauled himself up. He staggered along the lurching deck with frantic hands clutching the railing.

A fierce wave broke over him. His strength gave out and he lost his grip. His screams could not be heard above the ocean's roar as his body plunged into the raging sea. Desperate to remain afloat, Michael flailed his arms. With each surge, he sank below the chaos and with thoughts of Lola and Rita he fought to rise again. When he could rise no more, he held his breath until his chest was about to explode.

A frantic gasp filled his lungs with salty water.

Then all went quiet.

Dance with the Devil

Chapter 21

Titillated by the latest gossip, Sophie Duchard lay on the chaise lounge in her boudoir, reading the morning newspaper as she sipped her coffee. Curious about her many underworld friends, the crime reports were an endless source of information and entertainment.

Mon Dieu! Sophie almost dropped her coffee cup. She picked up the newspaper with both hands and took a closer look at the article.

Alongside the assailant's picture, it told of a woman arrested for murdering Monsieur Mortimer Wallace on board the SS Poisson during its voyage to Le Havre. She read, "The accused killer, Madame Lola O'Reilly resides in Rimrock Springs, Az, États Unis. and is charged with a murder that took place under particularly odious circumstances."

Sophie squinted her eyes at the small photograph. She exclaimed aloud. "Lola O'Reilly!" She took a closer look and thought, *Could she be Lola? Lola La Fontaine? She killed a man? Quel imbécile! This is not good for me. If she contacts her father, they will talk of me and what I did. No! I will not allow this! I must go to the prison and see if this is truly Lola La Fontaine.*

Under her coat, Sophie wore a low-cut dress that seductively exposed her cleavage and clung to her shapely curves. From her fashionable hat, she lowered her veil to disguise her face.

Arriving just west of the Île de la Cité, Sophie exited the fiacre at Conciergerie Prison. She felt a twinge of nerves in her stomach. *This ugly building is a gloomy medieval fortress. I shudder to think of being a prisoner here.*

Sophie approached a large open area leading to the cells where she spoke to a gendarme. "I must speak with Louis Gaspar, perhaps you know him. He is one of the prison guards."

The gendarme asked, "How do you know him?"

She offered the gendarme her gloved hand. In it, she held a silver 5-franc coin. "He is my brother. He has a bad cough and I promised to bring him some medicine."

The gendarme looked in his hand. "*Oui,* of course, Madame. I would not want your brother to be without his medicine. Follow me." They traveled down a short corridor. "Louis, here is your beautiful sister. She's come to save you from your terrible cough."

"Who? My sister? I don't have a—"

Sophie sidled to him and lifted her veil. "Poor Louis, you are so brave to work with your bad cough." She winked and removed a bottle of brandy from her satchel.

Louis coughed. "Oh, thank you. What a thoughtful sister you are."

After the gendarme left, Louis smiled. "So, now you are my sister, eh? I think from now on that's what I will call you. So, my sexy sister, to what at do I owe this delightful visit?"

"I must see one of your prisoners, but I do not want her to see me."

"So much intrigue," he said. "What's in it for me?"

"Louis, you know I always treat you right."

He placed his hand Sophie's shoulder and slowly slid it down her coat to her breast. With a little squeeze, he asked, "And how will you treat me right?"

Sophie sighed, "Here, take this." She took a silver coin from her pocket and offered it to him.

"That's a good little sister. Who is it you wish to see?"

"Lola O'Reilly."

"The murderess?"

"*Oui*, but this is very important. I don't want her to see me."

"Hmmm. All right. I will take you to her cell. Keep your veil lowered. I'm about to bring her supper. When I open her cell door you can peek in but stand back in the shadows."

"Perfect. Let's go."

When Sophie saw Lola's drawn face, she gave a silent gasp. *That is her! I cannot let her contact her father. She's lucky to be in jail. If Apash saw her, he'd kill her.*

Louis exited the cell and locked the door. Sophie rushed him away and whispered, "It is very important she see no visitors and has no contact with the outside world. Can you arrange that?"

He pinched his lips with his fingers and thought for a moment. "No, I don't have control over her communications."

"Who does?"

"Only the judge *instructeur* who is handling her case."

"Who is he?"

"That would be Paul Chatelain."

Sophie's eyes glistened. "*Quelle bonne chance!* I know him...intimately. Can you bring me to him?"

"I don't know, little sister." He rubbed his fingers.

Sophie rolled her eyes and pulled another silver coin from her pocket. "Here. Now take me to see Paul."

They walked together to the nearby Palais de Justice. "Wait here," instructed Louis. He knocked on the door labeled Honorable Judge *Instructeur* Paul Chatelain, and when permitted entry, he closed the door behind him. After a few minutes, he opened the door and said, "Come in."

A portly man with large jowls, oversized blubbery lips, and popping eyes said, "Sophie! What a nice surprise. Louis, you can leave us now."

Louis winked at Sophie and left the room.

"What can I do for you, Sophie?"

Sophie locked the door and sauntered to him. "I haven't seen you for a while." She ran her fingers through the sparse hair on his balding head. "I have been missing you."

With lecherous cravings, Paul's eyes popped further. He watched her fingers play with the top button of her coat opening each button one at a time. When she finished with the bottom button, she stretched her neck, threw her coat back and exposed her shoulders to emphasize her cleavage.

With impatience, he pulled her to him, his mouth opened wide.

Sophie stepped away. "Not so fast. There is something I need to talk to you about."

He grabbed her. "We can talk later."

"Behave yourself. Think where you are."

Paul looked at the door. He released her. "All right. What do you want?"

"You have a prisoner here, Lola O'Reilly."

"Yes. So what?"

"I need you to prevent her from seeing any visitors or communicating with anyone."

"Why?"

"The reason is not important. You will do this for me, *oui?*"

"This is an unusual request."

Sophie threw off her coat and stood with her hips against his. She put her arms around his neck and gave him a slow, sensual smile promising wildly, wicked things and whispered, "I like doing unusual things. Don't you?"

Dance with the Devil

Chapter 22

Hattie was leaning against the corral fence watching Rita perform a new trick when her eye caught the Sheriff riding onto Smitty's Ranch. He rode to Hattie and dismounted, tipped his hat and said, "How do, Hattie?"

She smiled. "Good morning, Sheriff. What brings you here?"

Tying his horse to the fence he said, "I need to see you and Smitty. Is he around?"

Hattie's eyebrows rose. "Me and Smitty? What's this about?"

"I'll tell you when we're together. Is he in his office?"

"I believe so. I think he's meeting with Benjamin Moss, the ranch manager."

"Would you mind walking over with me?"

"All right, Sheriff." She called to get Trevor's attention. "I'll be gone for a bit, keep a watch on Rita."

Trevor smiled. "It'll be my pleasure, ma'am."

Smitty and Benjamin sat at his large, round conference table having a discussion. Surprised to see the Sheriff and Hattie together, Smitty smiled. "Hi, Sheriff, have a seat and a cup of coffee. You too, Hattie." Smitty poured them each a cup from a nearby coffee pot. "So, what brings you here?"

The Sheriff eyed Benjamin. "Smitty, I have something important to discuss."

"It's okay, Sheriff," Smitty said. "Benjamin is like family. I'd like him to stay if that's all right with you."

"I'm sorry to say I got some bad news for Rita."

Hattie brought her hand to her lips. "More bad news. Oh, poor Rita," she muttered.

The Sheriff continued, "Mr. Havermeyer, the President of Miners Bank and Trust came to my office this morning. He told me the bank is gonna repossess Michael O'Reilly's house and properties."

"What!" Smitty looked at the Sheriff like he was crazy. "Why?"

"I hate to say this but Michael's broke."

They all shouted at once. "BROKE!"

"Yeah, I'm sad to say Michael did a foolish thing. About eight months ago, Michael came to see Mr. Havermeyer and asked for a loan against his house. He said he made some bad investments and lost everything. He made Mr. Havermeyer promise not to tell Lola. Michael's bank account is empty and with him and Lola being gone, the bank has no choice but to repossess the house and all the property."

Smitty lowered his eyebrows. "Have you had any word about Lola or Michael's whereabouts?"

"No. It's like they disappeared off the face of the earth."

Hattie pulled her handkerchief from her sleeve and sniffled. "Poor Rita. How could they do this to her?"

Smitty asked, "What will happen to Rita?"

"Well, as far as I know, she's got no relatives. Unless you know of any, she's gonna have to go to an orphanage."

Smitty raised his voice. "OVER MY DEAD BODY! I'll take care of her. She can stay here on my ranch."

"Well, it's not that easy," the Sheriff said. "You ain't got no kids and you ain't married. What do you know about taking care of a little girl?"

Smitty took a deep breath and scratched his unshaven chin. He turned to Hattie, "Will you come to work for me and take care of Rita? I'll pay you the same wages you earned with them. This is a big place. Rita can have her own room and you can live here too. Without her parents around, she needs someone she's close to. What do you say?"

Hattie wiped her eyes. "Yes, of course, I'll stay. But, who's going to tell Rita?"

Dance with the Devil

Chapter 23

When Rita finished her practice, accompanied by Smitty, Hattie took her home. Rita ran through the door and sat on the parlor sofa and began to play with the doll she had left there.

With eyes on Rita, Hattie whispered to Smitty, "Oh Lord, how can we tell her?"

Smitty shook his head. "We have no choice."

Hattie took a seat beside Rita.

Smitty pulled up a side chair and said, "Rita, "We have something to tell you."

Rita knitted her eyebrows. "Is this going to be a bad talk?"

Hattie went pale and her hands fidgeted. About to rise, she said, "Rita, I'm going to get you a glass of milk."

She stopped short when Rita shouted "I don't want any milk! Tell me, is this about Momma and Poppa? Did something bad happen to them?"

Tears swelled in Hattie's eyes. She sat beside Rita, put her arm around her shoulder and said, "Rita, you know I love you, don't you?"

Rita pouted. Her chest heaved. Her lashes became heavy with tears. "They're never coming home! They're dead, aren't they?"

Hattie held her close. "No! No, Rita baby. We don't know where they are, but I'm sure they're alive."

Rita pouted and punched her thigh. "Tell me the truth! What's happening? Where is Momma? Where is Poppa?"

Hattie looked at Smitty for help.

Smitty took Rita's hand. "I'm gonna need for you to stay at my ranch for a while and Hattie will stay with you. You and Trevor can ride Sweet Eyes every day. Isn't that great!"

Rita pulled back her hand and wiped her snotty nose. She gave Smitty a suspicious look. "Why can't I stay here? What changed?"

Hattie and Smitty looked at each other.

Smitty took a breath and said, "Since your Momma and Poppa haven't been here for a while there's no one to pay the bills. So, until they return, the bank is going to hold on to the house and everything. When your parents come home, everything will be straightened out. In the meantime, you and Hattie will live on my ranch. Is that okay?"

With her voice high pitched and thin she asked, "I don't understand! Where's Poppa? Where's Momma? Why aren't they here? Don't they love me anymore?" Rita jumped from the couch and ran into her room. She flopped belly down on the bed and sobbed into her crossed elbows.

Hattie hurried to Rita's room. Hearing Rita's racking sobs shredded her heart. When she tried to hold her, Rita pushed her away. Hattie tried again. Rita accepted her hug.

After a long while, Rita's crying slowed. Silent tears rolled down her cheeks as she looked at Hattie with red eyes and a runny nose. With a face that reflected abject misery, Rita asked, "Why don't

Momma and Poppa love me anymore? Did I do something wrong?"

"No, my darling. They will always love you. They went away because they had no choice. They would be here with you if they could. Smitty and I will take care of you until they return. Remember what your Momma said before she left?"

Rita wiped her nose on her sleeve. She sniffled and took the locket from inside her shirt and opened it. "Momma said, whenever I get lonely, I should look at her picture and when I see her face, I'll know she's thinking of me." Rita kissed her picture.

Smitty knocked on Rita's open bedroom door. "Rita, we're gonna take everything you want to bring over to the ranch. Will you help Hattie put everything together? I'll have the ranch hands come by and bring it all to your room at the ranch. Is that okay?"

Rita sniffled, "I guess so."

Dance with the Devil

Chapter 24

Lola paced in her cold dungeon-like cell. *What is happening to me? Why haven't I heard from Michael? I should have taken the time to explain everything to him. Is he so angry with me that he refuses to help me? And what of my poor little Rita? What have I done to my family?*

Rubbing her arms for warmth, she sat on the wooden bench sealed into the wall and looked to the skylight high above her head. *Should I write papá? What good will that do? He hates me. I have no one to turn to. I am doomed.*

The guard opened the door to her cell. "Come with me, the judge *instructeur* wishes to see you.

Lola followed the guard into the judge's office and sat in the chair he indicated. On the other side of the desk sat an overweight man with big blubbery lips and popping eyes. The expression on his face made her heart lurch knowing this man held her fate in his hands and it wouldn't be a good one.

He leaned his back into the chair. "As judge *instructeur*, it is my job to determine whether to bring your case to trial. Now, I must tell you it is very difficult for me to believe you are innocent of this vicious crime. Our detectives viewed the crime scene and the district police commissioner questioned the ship's crew and passengers. No one remembers a man with a tattoo on his hand.

"In addition, your fingerprints are on the gun. While it is the belief of our justice system that you are innocent until proven guilty, our investigations have given us no reason to believe you have not committed this crime. Can you tell me why we should believe in your innocence?"

For a moment, Lola held her face in her hands. Then she straightened and held head high. "Your honor *judge instructeur*, you are accusing an innocent woman. As I said before, I did not shoot this man. I own no gun. I fought with him, yes, but only in self-defense. My fingerprints are on the gun because the killer placed the gun in my hand. To accuse me of a crime I did not commit is to allow the real killer to go free. To serve justice, you must investigate further and find the real killer."

While Lola pleaded her case the judge *instructeur* looked at his nails with a bored expression.

Lola screamed, "Why are you not looking at me when I speak! I am innocent! Do you hear? I AM INNOCENT!"

"Enough!" He shouted. As if he took notice of her for the first time, he gave her a lascivious look and said, "You are a desirable woman. During your trial, you will be before three judges and six male jurors. My advice to you is to present your...well-endowed assets to these men and if they enjoy what they see, rather than the guillotine, your sentence may only be twenty years."

Lola burned with anger. She sneered. "You swine!"

The judge shouted, "Guard, take her to her cell!"

The guard grabbed her arm and led her to the open cell door. Lola pulled her arm from him. "I must write a letter. I demand a pen and paper immediately!"

The guard pushed Lola into her cell. "You can send no letters and you can see no visitors!" He slammed the cell door.

Lola yelled through the bars, "WAIT! YOU MUST ALLOW ME TO WRITE A LETTER!"

The guard turned his back and walked away.

Dance with the Devil

Chapter 25

On the enchanting left bank of Paris stood the residence of Émile La Fontaine. His granddaughter, fifteen-year-old Mimi La Fontaine sat atop her bed in the same lovely bedroom in which her mother Lola had once slept.

Mimi's young lady friends joined her. Each the progeny of the nobility with a title such as Baroness, duchess or marchioness.

Browsing through the latest Bon Marché catalog, Eugénie and Louise sat with Mimi on her elegant Louis XV Mahogany four-poster bed. The bed had fluted and leaf-carved front columns, an ebony pediment with gilt metal figure mounts, and tied-back raspberry silk drapes with a sunburst sewn into the canopy.

Next to her bed sat a tortoiseshell table encrusted with ebony and ivory. Atop the table sat Mimi's silver and *plique-a-jour* enamel cigarette case.

Adélaïde stretched out on the raspberry velvet banquette near the open French doors. She enjoyed the sunlight and the soft, warm breeze carrying a floral scent from the garden.

Margot sat at the Queen Anne dressing table primping herself in the mirror.

"What will you wear to the masquerade ball, Mimi?" asked Eugénie. "You always surprise us with your wicked sense of humor."

Mimi took a drag of her cigarette and blew the smoke into the air. "Well, my sweet, if I tell you, you won't be surprised, will you?"

Eugénie pleaded, "Oh please, give us some idea. Your costumes are always magnificent. You've been a gypsy and a pirate and your best, and most appropriate for you, an evil witch!" The group chuckled. Eugénie continued, "Come now, Mimi, we must know! After all, you wouldn't want us to come with the same costume."

Adélaïde chimed in, "I doubt any of us have as much imagination as Mimi. Say, I have an idea. Mimi, why don't you come as yourself?"

"Myself? And what would be the point of that?"

With excited eyes, Adélaïde suggested, "Everyone says you look exactly like your mother, Lola. If you come as yourself, you could pretend to be her and shock everyone."

"No! Absolutely not! I'm sick of hearing how much I resemble my mother and how sweet she was. I'm not my mother and I refuse to be compared to her!"

Margot's green eyes flashed as she turned from the mirror to face Mimi. She broke into a mischievous smile and said, "I've heard rumors that your mother was not so sweet as people claim. I've been told that she ran off to be a cancan dancer. Maybe you can dress in the costume of a *demimondaine* and show off your *derrière!*"

Louise beamed, "Yes, I've heard that too. My *grand-père* swears he saw your mother perform at the Moulin Rouge. He said her dancing was quite risqué."

"That old man is always seeing things." Margot laughed. "The way your grand-père guzzles his liquor, I'm sure he sees pink elephants and snakes in his shoes too!"

"Humph!" Louise crossed her arms against her chest. "Margot, you always have something wicked to say about everyone!" The others giggled at her reaction.

Mimi looked nonchalant. "I don't care who my mother was. My *grand-père* told me she died when I was born. I suspect that's not true. He never speaks of her and there are no pictures of her or my father, whoever he is. Supposedly, he was a German officer killed in some war. I don't even know my father's name. My *grand-père* took me from the Augustine Convent Grandchamp when I was four years old, so I may be a bastard child. What does it matter? If my parents don't care about me, why should I care about them?" Mimi rang for a servant who promptly arrived.

He stepped into the room and asked, "*Oui*, Mademoiselle, Mimi, what may I do for you?"

"Get me *grand-père's* Courvoisier L'Esprit de Cognac and glasses for everyone!"

"*Mademoiselle*, are you sure that's what you desire? It's your *grand-père's* favorite and—"

Mimi screeched, "Do you hear me? Must I repeat myself?"

The servant bowed. "I will bring it to you at once, *Mademoiselle*."

Eugénie asked, "Won't your *grand-père* be angry with you?"

Mimi drew on her cigarette. "*Grand-père* allows me to do anything I want."

"But still—"

"Still nothing! I could run naked through the streets of Paris and he wouldn't stop me."

171

Louise interjected, "So does that mean you'll dress...or undress as Lady Godiva?"

The room filled with laughter.

"I'll not give the partygoers such a treat. Let's see, I will come as..." Mimi put her finger to her lips. "As Queen Tamar, the daughter of the Georgian King Giorgi III. She founded a magnificent empire and was known as "King of Kings and Queen of Queens" by her people."

Margot arched an eyebrow, "Rather a lofty ambition. Are you planning on ruling an empire?"

"Is there a reason I shouldn't?"

Chapter 26

It hadn't been easy for Rita to adjust to her new life at the Double SS Horse Ranch. Smitty and Hattie treated her well but she yearned for her parents. Even though six years had passed, she still believed she must have done something wrong to make them leave. The pain in her heart never left her.

Rita had loved the scholastic lessons her mother had taught her. She had a way of making learning fun. Public-school bored her. Worst of all, the students made fun of her for always wearing britches instead of pretty dresses. All Rita cared about was riding horses. She saw no value in wearing dresses and worried that her underwear might show when she performs a trick.

Her one close friend was Annabelle. Both eleven years old, Rita and Annabelle believed they'd be friends forever. Even though they were different as day and night, they were very close.

Annabelle considered herself a young lady, but Rita loved being a tomboy. She was always ready to climb the highest tree, leap over a dead animal, or sock any boy who pushed her too far. But Rita would rather ride a horse than do anything else.

Today, as with most days, they walked to Jerome Peak, their favorite place. The outcropping rocks of Jerome Peak provided an excellent aerial view of the outskirts of Rimrock Springs. Annabelle lay on her belly with elbows and knees bent and rested her head in her hands as she swayed her feet in the air.

Rita mimicked her as they looked into the distance. In the vast area below, they saw many types of flora near the streambeds, including cactus-like Beavertail Prickly Pear, Blue Myrtle, and Buckhorn Cholla.

Annabelle asked, "Will you ever leave this town?"

Rita cocked her head, "I know that look. What're you thinking about?"

Annabelle's lower lip pushed forward. "Well, I'd like to leave someday. I want to see the world. There must be more than boring old Rimrock Springs. What do you think is out there, beyond all those ugly red rocks?"

"When I was really young," Rita said, "my parents took me on some faraway trips, but I don't remember any of it. The one thing I do remember is going to the circus." With dreamy eyes Rita continued, "It was the most exciting day in my whole life. I saw elephants and monkeys and clowns and people performing all sorts of amazing tricks."

Her face glowed. "But what impressed me most was a beautiful lady in a flowing white gown covered in sparkly sequins riding a shiny black stallion. She had long red hair like mine. She was so beautiful! And the tricks she did were wonderful. When I grow up, I want to join the circus and be just like her."

Annabelle gushed. "I'd love to see the circus! It's never been to Rimrock Springs. Maybe one day it'll come here, but even if it doesn't, I'll see it. Someday, I'll be in a big city and see the circus and go shopping and meet lots of boys."

Rita screwed up her face, "Boys? Boys stink! They're always ready to start trouble. I don't want anything to do with them. Ever!"

Annabelle laughed, "Oh, I bet one day you'll be plenty interested in boys. You're too immature now."

"Immature! Who're you calling immature?" Rita gave one of Annabelle's braids a playful tug. Then Annabelle began to tickle Rita. They shared little girl giggles.

Rita sat up, crossed her legs, flipped back her reddish-gold pigtails and said, "There's one special thing we've got in Rimrock Springs and that's horses, beautiful horses. There's nothing more beautiful than a horse. They're strong and brave and fast and nothing can outrace a horse."

Annabelle's held her nose. "Oh, you and your horses! They're just big old smelly things."

Rita laughed, "Annabelle you're so silly. Speaking of horses, I got to get going."

"Time for you to go riding, I suppose?"

"You betcha," Rita grinned, stood and skipped on her way.

Rita had developed into a skilled equestrian. In their spare time, the ranch hands taught her rodeo tricks like calf roping and bareback riding. She even learned how to shoot guns and rifles. They told Rita she was a natural. She learned quickly and was always eager to try new things no matter how dangerous. The more dangerous, the more she enjoyed performing them, even if it meant getting hurt. She had already dislocated her shoulder and broken her wrist. She was fortunate that the wranglers, who had been injured many times

175

themselves, knew as much as any doctor about fixing broken bodies.

The ranch hands came in all shapes, sizes and colors. About half of them were white men but the rest were Mexicans, Blacks and Indians, all excellent equestrians and they treated Rita with respect. She loved the attention the ranch hands gave her when they praised her accomplishments.

Her favorite wrangler, Trevor Corwin, had taught her tricks beginning when she was three years old. He took good care of her. He gave her ointment for a cut when she fell hard after doing a trick or delicately massaged her sore shoulder with Sloan's Horse Liniment. He spoke softly and always encouraged her. But he was tough on her when she tried to blame the horse instead of herself. Trevor was the kindest, wisest man she knew.

Returning through the Double SS gate, Rita spotted Chance, another of the ranch hands she liked. Chance had taught her how to shoot rifles and six-shooters. Tall and gangly, Chance was so bowlegged you could pass a barrel through his legs and he'd never feel it.

Chance offered his standard greeting to Rita. He waved and called out, "Hey Rita, how's tricks?"

His clothes smelled of horses and leather as she approached him. "Hi Chance," Rita smiled and asked, "Can I ride Blaze today?" Of all the horses she'd trained on, Blaze responded best to Rita.

"Not now, better git to Smitty's office, he sez he wants to talk to ya."

"Do you know what he wants?"

"Dunno, he jus sez he wants to see ya pronto!"

Rita couldn't imagine what Smitty had to say and hurried to his office. She hoped this wouldn't be bad news. She entered his office and gave him a big round wave. "Hi, Smitty, how're you doing?"

"Hello Rita, have a seat."

Rita hoped he'd have news about her parents but feared disappointment. Warily, she asked. "What's up?"

"You know the rodeo is coming here in a few weeks. I think it's time you did some of your fancy trick riding."

Rita's eyebrows shot up, "Are you joshing me?"

Smitty smiled. "No indeed, young lady. I'm not kidding. You've been working hard all these years and it's about time to show Rimrock Springs what you've got. Are you up to it?"

"Up to it! You just let me at 'em! Can I ride Blaze?"

Smitty grinned, "Sure thing, I wouldn't have it any other way."

"Oh, Smitty, I love you!" Rita ran over and gave him a smooch on his chubby cheek. "I guess I better get some practice in. Can I ride Blaze today?"

"Sure, tell Trevor, I said it's okay. Have fun!"

Rita had outgrown the pony Sweet Eyes and now loved riding Blaze, a black quarter horse, perfect for trick riding. Among the many tricks she had perfected were the Two Hand Horn Spin, the One Foot Layover, the Lazy Back, the very dangerous Death Drag and her favorite, the Hippodrome Stand. The feel of the wind in her hair thrilled her as she stood on the back of the galloping horse.

Rita thought, *Finally, I have a chance to show the world what I'm capable of!*

Dance with the Devil

Chapter 27

For several days the Double SS Horse Ranch and the Arizona Round-Up cowboys had been preparing for the rodeo event. Rita could barely control her excitement. She'd practiced hard and knew she'd be ready for tomorrow's rodeo. *This is what I've been waiting for. Nothing that can stop me!*

The morning of the big event the atmosphere at the ranch buzzed with enthusiasm. Rita sat on the corral fence feeling restless butterflies in her belly as she watched the ranch hands hustle in preparation for the show.

Suddenly, she heard frantic shouting. Everyone stopped their chores. The ebullient atmosphere changed to an air of apprehension. Ranch hands stopped what they were doing and ran towards the shouts.

Rita followed to see a large crowd gathered. She pushed her way inside. All she could see was someone laying on the ground.

Someone shouted, "Make way for the boss!"

Rita looked for Smitty to come through the crowd but instead, Benjamin appeared. His face was rigid as he kneeled next to the injured man. He put his hand on the man's chest and his ear to the man's mouth, then leaned back on his heels and shook his head.

Rita gasped. It was Smitty who lay on the ground! She dropped down heavily next to him and shouted, "Quick! Someone call a doctor!" Feeling helpless to see Smitty lay pale and motionless, she cried out, "Wake up, Smitty. Please wake up!" Rita lifted her head to the crowd and shouted again, "THE DOCTOR! WHERE IS THE DOCTOR!" She felt chills seeing his eyes open but not awake. Rita thought, his eyes look empty, like a...like a dead man's eyes.

The crowd separated for Dr. Malone. He kneeled by Smitty and felt for a pulse. He opened Smitty's shirt to listen with his stethoscope.

"Looks like Smitty's had a heart attack," he said solemnly. He closed Smitty's eyes and stood. Dr. Malone shook his head and said, "I'm sorry, Smitty has passed away."

Rita hugged Smitty's lifeless body. His cold and clammy skin made her feel as if she were falling through a bottomless hole.

"Smitty, please don't be dead. I love you. Please don't leave me alone."

Chapter 28

Rita sat on the corral fence petting Blaze's nose as she stood beside her. Rita's sadness had no depth. For years, she had no word of her parents and assumed they were dead. Now that Smitty had died, Rita felt her world had collapsed. Even Hattie wasn't here to console her.

Hearing men's voices, Rita turned her eyes from Blaze to see the Sheriff and Mr. Havermeyer talking as they entered the steps to Smitty's office. Rita felt anxious. She was sure this was going to be more sadness for her. After a few minutes, she creeped up the steps, held her ear to the closed door and listened.

"I am sorry to say that I have difficult news to report," announced Mr. Havermeyer. "I've received a letter from the attorney of Mr. Oliver Smithson, Smitty's brother. He makes it very clear that as the sole and rightful heir to Smitty's property, Mr. Smithson has sold the Double SS Ranch and all Smitty's holdings to the Arizona Mining Company. The mining company intends to excavate the entire property for copper. Effective immediately, all residents and employees have thirty days to evacuate."

Startled by the bang of a fist against the table, Rita jumped back from the door. Benjamin shouted, "That son of a bitch! How could he do this to us? Doesn't he realize there are at least fifty men he's putting out of work?"

Mr. Havermeyer spoke softly. Rita had difficulty hearing and leaned her ear closer to the door. She could only make out the words, "They'll have to leave."

"Damn that bastard," Benjamin roared, "what are we supposed to do about Rita? She's got no family to speak of and since Hattie left to help her sick sister, she's got no one to take care of her."

The Sheriff spoke up. "Looks like there's no other option. It's sad but she'll have to go to an orphanage."

Rita froze. She felt like shattered glass. Acid burned her belly and rose to her throat. *Why does no one want me?* She was about to cry until anger set it. She pursed her lips and thought, *An orphanage! I'm not going to any orphanage. I gotta figure something out.* She ran to her bedroom and closed the door.

She sat on her bed and removed the locket from inside her shirt. Looking at her mother's picture, Rita thought, *Momma, what am I supposed to do? I have no one to turn to. You know I can't go to an orphanage. I have no choice. I gotta run away.*

Rita looked around her room deciding what bring with her. Her piggy bank sat on the dresser. She cracked it open and filled her pockets with coins. Pulling her rucksack from the closet, she stuffed it with her essential belongings. Then Rita ducked into the kitchen, packed some victuals, and filled several canteens with water. She also grabbed a knife for protection.

That night, she sneaked into the horse barn and saddled Blaze. *I hate to leave without saying goodbye, but I'm afraid I'll get caught. No one's gonna put me in an orphanage!*

She whispered into Blaze's ear. "I know I shouldn't be stealing you, but that rotten Oliver man sold you and I don't know what they're planning on doing to you. I'd rather steal you than have them turn you into glue. Let's get out of here before someone finds us."

It was too dark to travel so she rode to the edge of the ranch and hid in the bushes. While grazing on grass, Rita petted Blaze's head and spoke to her. "What am I gonna do now? I have no one but you, Blaze. Don't get me wrong, I love you but I gotta protect us. I guess we'll have to find a rodeo or maybe a circus that'll take us on. We're good enough to trick ride anywhere, right Blaze?"

Blaze snorted and nodded her head.

"Hey, I got an idea! Let's head to Phoenix. That's a real big place. I bet we can find work there."

At daybreak, Rita awoke to the sound of footsteps. She pulled out her knife. Feeling someone grab her arm from behind, she struggled and screamed, "Let me go!"

"Goddammit, Rita. Stop fussing. It's me, Trevor."

Catching her breath, she said, "Oh, Trevor, I'm sorry. How'd you know where to find me?"

Trevor leaned against a boulder and faced Rita. "Everybody's looking for you. I noticed Blaze was missin', so I figured you musta took Blaze. Why you tryin' to leave?"

"I have to."

"What do you mean, you have to?"

"Smitty's brother Oliver is kicking everybody off the ranch because he sold it to a mining company. I don't have any place to live so they're gonna put me in an orphanage." Her lips turned down. "I'll never be able to ride Blaze again."

"Yeah, I heard the bad news. But, I'm sorry girl, you ain't got no choice."

"I do have a choice and that choice is to get away!"

With soft eyes, Trevor said, "Rita, an orphanage is the only safe place for you."

She insisted, "I'm not going to an orphanage. There are other places to go."

"Other places? Like where?"

Rita lifted her chin and said proudly, "I'm gonna find a circus somewhere."

"A circus! That's little girl talk."

"It's not little girl talk! Rita protested, "You said yourself, I'm as good as any trick rider you know."

"Yeah, that's true enough but you can't jus' get on Blaze and ride off. It's dangerous."

"I have no choice."

He leaned forward and looked intensely into Rita's eyes. "You're gonna get yourself killed for sure!"

Rita crossed her arms against her chest. "No, I won't, I can take care of myself!"

"You been living on the ranch with Smitty, in a town where everybody knows you. You been safe here but it ain't safe for a young girl to go out on her own."

"You make it sound like I'm a little girl. Well, I'm not! I'm twelve years old. You told me you were only nine when you were on your own." She grumbled.

"Don't go comparing yourself to me, and don't change the subject. You have no idea what it's like to be alone and unprotected. You gotta understand that there's lots of evil people who'll want to take advantage of you and hurt you in ways you can't even imagine."

"It won't do you any good to try to scare me." With her countenance firm, Rita persisted, "My mind's made up! Trevor, you know when I set my mind to do something, I do it! No one can stop me. If you take me to the Sheriff, I'll run away from him. If he finds me and brings me to the orphanage, I'll run away from them. I'm leaving and there's nothing you or anyone can do about it!"

He shook his head. "Rita when you get like this there's no way of changing your mind. You're stubborn as all get out."

"Say, Trevor, I got an idea. You're gonna have to leave the ranch too. Why not come with me? We can join a rodeo together and then you won't have to worry about me. Wouldn't that be great?"

"Yeah, it sure would, but it ain't possible."

Rita tilted her head. "Why not? Don't you want to?"

Trevor smiled sadly. "I can't. If folks see a big, black buck like me with a young white girl, they'll string me up on the nearest tree and you'd end up in an orphanage for sure."

"Why would they do that?"

"See, this is what I mean when I say you're too young and innocent to go out on your own."

"Trevor, I appreciate your concern. I really do. But I'm going and that's all there is to it. I don't have time to talk about this anymore, I gotta go."

"There must be something I can do to convince you that you're making a mistake. You think you're tough enough to handle yourself but suppose some man, big and strong like me, grabs you and tries to hurt you. What'll you do then?"

Rita showed him her knife. "See Trevor, I'm prepared."

Trevor laughed. "Do you know how easy it is for me to take that from you?"

"You can try to scare me all you want but you can't change my mind. I'm leaving and that's it!"

Trevor hesitated. He had the look of surrender in his eyes. Reaching into his pocket, he said, "I tell ya what, here's some money. I ain't got much but—"

"No thanks, Trevor, I have money," Rita smiled triumphantly and pulled some silver from her pocket.

"Girl, where'd you git that?"

"It's from my piggy bank. From time to time, Smitty would drop some coins in it for me."

"Well, you better hold on to it real tight and don't let no one know you got any money. They'll steal it from you before you can blink an eye."

"I'm not stupid. I'll hold on to it so tight it'll squeal, ha! ha!"

"Rita, please take care of yourself. If anything happens to you, I'll never forgive myself."

She hugged Trevor and kissed his cheek. "Thank you with all my heart for everything. I love you and I'll miss you so much."

With a tear in his eye, he watched Rita gallop off. He laughed when she looked back, waved her hat in the air and yelled, "Yee Ha!"

Chapter 29

To avoid detection, Rita took seldom-used trails towards Phoenix. She galloped for a long time, often looking over her shoulder to be sure no one followed her.

Rita noticed the changes in the terrain as she descended from the high elevation of Rimrock Springs. The rugged canyons and moss-covered rocks became sparse as the scrubby vegetation of the lowland desert stretched out before her. The closer to the desert floor she came the higher the temperature rose.

Although this was Rita's first time traveling outside of Rimrock Springs alone, she felt unafraid. So long as she had food, water and Blaze, she believed she'd be fine.

Overtaken by weariness and a grumbling stomach, Rita searched for a place to camp. Surrounded by cactus, sagebrush, rock and dirt, she saw no water or shelter anywhere.

Rita settled at the mouth of the canyon pass she had just come through. An amazing desert panorama fanned out before her. Purple mountains shimmered in the distance along with cactus of all sizes and shapes. Aside from the shrubbery, the mesa was brown, bare, dry, hot and lifeless. Occasional sandy whirlwinds provided the only movement.

"Well, Blaze, looks like another night of sleeping under the stars." She patted Blaze's neck. In an attempt to remain cheerful, she said. "I bet camping outdoors in wide-open spaces will be fun." Rita dismounted and prepared camp.

She turned her hat upside down, poured water from one of her canteens into it, and offered Blaze a drink, then pulled a stack of hay from her saddlebag for Blaze to munch on.

Proud of herself for remembering matches, Rita started a fire using the ribs of a dead saguaro cactus and creosote branches. She set the coffeepot to boil, heated beans, munched on slices of smoked ham and two biscuits.

She talked to Blaze while she ate, telling her horse about the beautiful lady in the circus and how one day she'd be just like her.

The setting sun painted the sky with broad brushstrokes of yellow, pink and purple. Rita asked, "Isn't that just beautiful, Blaze?"

Darkness soon arrived and her fire dwindled. Rita yawned and stretched. "Well, I guess we better get to sleep, eh, girl? Got a lot of traveling to do tomorrow."

She laid out her blanket and used her saddle as a pillow. The ugly, oil tar smell of creosote bushes filled her nostrils and she heard the yipping of coyotes in the distance. Rita felt small and defenseless in the desert's vastness. She hugged Blaze around the neck and said, "Don't be scared girl, I'll protect you."

Rita checked her sleeping area to be sure nothing unwelcome crawled around, then lay down and pulled the blanket around her. She closed her eyes but couldn't sleep. She realized she was alone. Alone in her mind, body, soul, and most of all, her heart.

Pulling her blanket closer, she tried not to fear her loneliness. Not only alone in the desert but alone in the world. She had no one to care whether she lived or died. *Momma and Poppa, where are you? Why did you leave me?* She felt like a deep, dark hole had swallowed her. Tears filled her eyes. *I have no family, it's as if I have no past, it's like I don't even exist.*

She heard Blaze snort. Rita leaned on her elbow, regarded her horse and smiled. *I'm not alone. Blaze loves me.* Rita lay back and relaxed. She gazed at the stars. They looked like diamonds in the vast black sky.

They reminded her of a dress her mother used to wear, black velvet with sequins that shined like diamonds in the light. She clutched her locket and remembered being cradled in her mother's loving arms. She imagined the smell of her mother's perfume and her sweet voice as she sang French lullabies. Her memories made Rita feel safe, loved and protected. She drifted into a deep sleep.

Rita didn't feel the strong, hot winds that came sweeping across the arroyo, churning dust into thick clouds that blotted out the black velvet sky. Nor was she aware of the thunderheads rolling down the mountains bringing streaks of white lightning and earthshaking thunder. Not even the first fat drops of rain disturbed her heavy slumber. It wasn't until she heard the boom of a fiery shaft of lightning strike a cactus, turning it into a flaming torch just a few feet from her head, did Rita jump in fear.

The clouds ripped open followed by a deluge. The force of the rain felt like metal pellets buffeting Rita's skin. At the bottom of a narrow gorge, slick rock walls towered above her. Rita could see nothing in the total darkness. But she could hear the wild, churning fury of the river's force and the crunch of boulders smashing along the stone walls.

Panic captured her when the brilliant flash of lighting exposed great torrents of water roaring towards her like a runaway train. She had to save herself and Blaze. She grabbed her horse's reins and tried to run but floodwaters overtook her.

Tossed like a ragdoll in the churning water, she struggled to avoid the dangerous obstacles in her path and to keep her head above water. The absolute blackness of the sky, interrupted by sheets of pure white lightning, set the sky ablaze, turning night into day,

Choking and desperate, Rita grabbed onto the limb of a floating tree branch. It kept her afloat but debris smacked into her, impeding her efforts to hold on. When a branch smashed her head, she passed out.

No longer hemmed in by sheer walls, the deluge inundated the flatlands and spent its force. Only the rapid diminishing of floodwater saved Rita from drowning. She lay semi-conscious and exhausted in the muddy streambed. She coughed to expel water from her lungs.

Rita looked to the sky. The lightning had stopped and the thunder sounded a hundred miles away. Clear, black velvet starlit skies returned as if nothing had happened. Too tired and too bruised to move, Rita passed out again.

She awoke to a dazzling blue sky. Rita sat in the muck and rubbed the painful knot on her head. Her lungs burned and every part of her body hurt. Frantic, her fingers searched her neck, she was relieved to feel her locket. Her panic returned when she looked around to see Blaze had disappeared. Rita had no food, no water, and worst of all, no Blaze!

Rita had lost one of her boots and the other boot had no sole. *How am I going to get anywhere this way?* Desolate and devastated, Rita sat in the muck and tried to recover her wits to determine her next move.

She noticed a lone desert primrose poking out of the mud. Despite its mangled and muddied leaves, the flower must have bloomed overnight. The cheerful yellow bloom seemed to be looking at Rita as if to say, "Don't give up, just like me, you can survive if you want to."

Encouraged, Rita took in her surroundings. Surprised how the lifeless desert had changed from brown and dry to a desert awash with color, she felt as if she floated into a land of enchantment.

The landscape glistened and sparkled in the bright sunshine. Everywhere the parched earth bloomed with flowers. Golden poppies, blue lupine, pink owl clover and bright yellow clumps of brittlebush blanketed the horizon. Small green leaves covered every branch of the creosote bushes, ocotillo and mesquite trees. Even the cacti were tipped with delicate blossoms of pink, peach, white and yellow.

It was as if Mother Nature threw a party and invited every living thing. Hummingbirds fluttered their iridescent royal blue and purple plumage as they raced with honeybees to gather rich floral nectar. Rock Wrens and quails sang, ground squirrels and cottontails scurried, insects buzzed and lizards sprinted. Rita saw two red-tailed hawks soaring overhead as if performing for the audience below.

Rita tossed off the useless boot, picked herself up and wiped the muck from her clothes. She tried to get her bearings but had no idea where she was. She assumed with the morning sun on her right side, she should continue following her original northwest direction. It would not be easy without shoes or drinking water, but she expected there should be waterholes along the way due to the heavy rain.

With little strength and a great deal of pain, Rita made her way, scrounging for water and food. She came upon a small hill and reaching the top, she saw a patch of giant cactus. She watched as a woodpecker flew toward one, then disappeared.

Hoping the bird might have been heading towards water, she walked to a large cactus and peered inside an opening. "Holy Cripes!"

Rita jumped back when she saw two big eyes staring out at her from within the cactus. She realized it was an owl nesting inside the trunk and smiled when she heard the chirping of baby birds.

"Can I crawl into your cozy little nest with you and your little ones, Mrs. Owl? I guess not. Wise Mrs. Owl, can you tell me where the nearest waterhole is?"

While keeping an eye out for Blaze, Rita continued to search for water the entire day. She found some here and there but not enough to quench her thirst. The temperature rose and scorched the beautiful plant life. She was hot, thirsty and miserable. The hard desert floor felt like hot coals under her torn and blistered feet. Only the incessant biting of insects took her mind off her painful feet.

Drained and exhausted, Rita stopped to rest. She found a bit of shade under an outcropping ledge.

Dropping down hard, she closed her eyes. *Oh Blaze, where are you? Are you safe? I miss you so.*

Rita fell asleep. She awoke to a sound that made her blood run cold. *Oh no! A rattler!* She froze. With half-closed eyes, she peeked towards the terrifying sound. From its ugly head appeared a flicking tongue and two beady eyes that stared straight at her. *I'm done for!*

A roadrunner scampered towards her. Using his tail as a brake, he stopped short in front of the rattler and chased it from the shade into the hot sun. It didn't take long for the searing sunlight to kill the cold-blooded rattler. The roadrunner picked it up in its beak and began to beat the snake against a rock. She watched slack-jawed as the bird swallowed the whole snake headfirst, saving the rattles for dessert. Relieved, she stayed for the night hoping her roadrunner friend would keep unwanted guests away.

Unable to sleep, Rita shivered from the desert's night chill. At daybreak, she resumed her vigil. Once again, she found some water and some berries, but just enough to keep her alive. The air soon warmed and the sun beat down on her unprotected head. Her skull felt as thin as an eggshell and it didn't take long for pain in her feet to intensify.

By late afternoon, she was crazy with thirst. She wondered why, despite the blistering heat, she wasn't sweating. Her skin felt as dry as parchment. The hot desert air sucked every ounce of liquid from her body. She had heard that putting some pebbles in her mouth would get her juices flowing, but they just rattled around her mouth like a pair of dice, so she spit them out.

Rita's lips were open sores. Her tongue swelled and felt too big to keep in her mouth. She felt like throwing up but all she did was dry heave. Her mind began to wander. Imagining she was inside a hot oven, she tore off some of her clothes. The sound of flowing water was driving her insane. *Why am I hearing water when there isn't a drop anywhere?*

Then she saw it! The most beautiful sight in the world. Water! A tremendous pool of sparkling blue water appeared just a few yards ahead. Ignoring her pain, Rita ran towards it. The closer she came the farther away it seemed. She ran and ran and ran. Until she had to face what she didn't want to believe. There was no water, only rocks and sand.

Rita hated everything. She hated the sky and the sand. She hated the rocks and the cactus and, most of all, she hated that goddamned sun!

Plopping down in the meager shade of a yucca, she cried. Stinging hot tears rolled down her blistered, sunburnt cheeks. She couldn't believe that tears could come from her dried-out body. She cupped her hands to catch her tears and licked the tiny salt droplets. Rita tried to force tears, but no more liquid came. Disheartened, she looked at her raw and bloody feet. They reminded her of two skinned rabbits as she removed cactus thorns from various places on her body.

She used her hand to block the sun as she looked into the distance. Rita could see only veils of heat shimmering above scorched earth. Everything was lifeless except for insects and dust devils.

Why go on? What's the use?" Yet, something inside of her wouldn't accept defeat. She pulled herself up, shook her fists at the desert, and shouted, "First you try to drown me, then you try to fry me! Goddamn you! I won't give up. I will keep going so long as I have breath in my body and to hell with you!"

Rita forced herself to hobble onward. She approached an area of steep rocky ridges and had no choice but to climb. *I have no strength left and no hope that I'll make it to the top. But what else can I do? I can lie down and die here, or I can die trying.*

Rita clawed her way upwards, clinging to the rocks with her raw, bloody fingers, pulling her pain-racked body up with nothing but the sheer force of will.

Near the top, she sniffed the air. *I swear I can smell food cooking. Food cooking? In the middle of nowhere? Girl, you are going crazy. Hot dang, the smell is getting stronger. Please, oh please, don't let this be another mirage.* Rita climbed as fast as her worn-out body would allow. She reached the top and peered over the edge.

Rita screamed as she fell. She smacked her head on the hard ground and lost consciousness.

Dance with the Devil

Chapter 30

Below the ornate ceilings of the magnificent Pavillon Ledoyen, one of the oldest restaurants in Paris, Mimi sat having lunch with her friend Adélaïde. Mimi ran her finger around the rim of her wine glass and looked at the elaborately terraced gardens through one of the huge picture windows. "I'm so bored!" she carped.

Before them lay their exquisite lunch. Adélaïde feasted on the roasted blue lobster with peppered olive oil and stewed green cabbage accompanied by tangy turnip jelly.

Mimi ignored the duo of tender poached breast of Bresse capon, bathed in a creamy, caviar-spiked sauce. She complained to her friend, "I'm seventeen years old. I've done everything, seen everything, tasted everything and have been with every man in whom I've had the vaguest interest. What will I do with the rest of my life?"

Partaking her sumptuous delights as she read the notes on the back of the menu, Adélaïde barely listened. "Did you know that this restaurant was the haunt of Robespierre? He dined here two days before they executed him!"

She moved her greasy finger along the words as she read.

"Also, this restaurant was the breakfast place of duelists, who, after shooting at each other in the Bois de Boulogne, reconciled over breakfast. Oh! Even better! Napoleon and Joséphine met at this

197

restaurant!" Adélaïde quickly turned her head and scanned the room.

Annoyed, Mimi asked, "Who are you looking for?"

"It says that the artists Degas, Monet and other famous people frequent this restaurant. Do you think they are having lunch now? Wouldn't it be exciting to meet them?"

"You're such an imbecile!" In a vociferous voice, Mimi said, " You're just like the rest of my friends. I don't know why I bother wasting my time with you!"

Adélaïde placed the menu flat on the table and regarded her friend. "Mimi, why are you so upset?"

"I told you, I'm bored. I need some excitement, something to make my heart pound."

"Oh, that's easy, have an affair. Have you seen Duke d'Amboise?" Adélaïde's eyes went dreamy as she hugged herself. "Mmmm, he's so handsome and so rich. I'll wager he'd make your heart pound!"

"So, what if he's handsome and rich? It means nothing to me. I'm beautiful and rich. Bedding him would be to his benefit, not mine! I'm tired of these tedious affairs. These fools profess love for me or they're only invested for a minute's gratification. Either way, there's no challenge."

"What kind of challenge do you have in mind?"

Mimi's eyes shimmered with naughty delight. "Something dangerous."

"Well, why don't you roam the streets of Montmartre? You can meander among the pimps and gangsters. Most likely, you'll be robbed, or better yet, murdered! Surely, some excitement would await you there."

Mimi's face brightened. "Yes, what a grand idea! I'll do that tonight!"

"Very funny." Adélaïde's eyes brightened. "Let's go to Le Bon Marché and buy everything in the entire store. Wouldn't that be fun?"

"What a simpleton you are! I'm going to Montmartre. Now that will be delicious fun." With a twinkle in her eye, Mimi smiled. "Would you care to join me?"

"Me? No! Are you insane? Of course not! I was only kidding. You can't go!"

"I can, and I will!"

That evening, Mimi had a carriage brought around to the front door of her home. She ordered her driver to take her to Montmartre. With each bounce and shake of the carriage as it rose to the top along narrow, twisting, cobblestone streets, Mimi's enthusiasm for a great adventure grew stronger.

Into the warm night air moistened by a drizzle, Mimi alighted the carriage. The hazy moonlight offered a pallid glow. She took no particular route. She eyed men who passed her, some took no notice of her in the poorly lit street, while others ogled her with lewd intentions but she found them to be uninteresting. Mimi turned a corner and saw light through a tavern window, she heard shouts from within.

Mimi entered and ordered a glass of wine at the bar. A young man standing atop a wooden table giving an impassioned speech attracted her attention.

His large feverish eyes were like bright moons protruding from his gaunt face. Sweaty droplets bounced from his long, curly brown hair as his head jerked in time with the pound of his fist. His frame was excruciatingly thin, but his zeal made him seem large and powerful.

She scanned the room to see all eyes riveted on this man as they cheered and encouraged him to continue. Mimi assessed him from head to toe. She had never seen this kind of passion. She worked her way to the table where he stood. His words meant nothing to her, but she found his ardor irresistible. She wondered if he was this passionate in all things. Her loins were on fire at the thought.

When his voice became dry and raspy, Mimi reached up and offered him her glass of wine. He paid her no attention and continued. Unaccustomed to being ignored, her desire for him increased. Soon his hoarse voice all but disappeared and another speaker took his place. When he descended from his perch, Mimi, once again offered him her glass of wine. He grasped the glass with two shaky hands.

Mimi put her hands over his to stop the glass from quivering. He noticed her for the first time. She gave him an alluring smile. They exchanged no words. He took her arm and led her up creaky wooden stairs to a tiny garret above the bar.

The unlit room was hot. It smelled of stale cigarettes and musty books. She heard the scrape of a match against a rough surface. He lit a candle. The candlelight threw shadows against the wall. She thought she saw a mouse scurry from the light.

It wasn't much more than a hovel. The roof pitched low at the farthest end. A dresser topped with books bore cigarette burns, deep scratches and a broken drawer. Coffee-stained newspapers lay on a small table, along with an empty coffee cup and a chipped plate with crumbs from a half-eaten slice of bread. Each leg of a wooden stool was of a different length. Bedclothes on a narrow cot were in disarray.

Mimi had never seen a place like this before. This was the living space of a poor man. The impoverished surroundings enflamed her passion.

She felt his eyes on her and turned to see his face. The candle's flame reflected in his dark eyes, making him appear as if he was on fire from within. She ripped open his shirt. He screamed as her nails scraped his chest and raised bloody welts. She kissed him hard. He slammed her against the wall and leaned into her. She slapped his face. He slapped her back.

Mimi's eyes dazzled with lust as she watched him pull off his jacket and shirt, exposing his skinny frame.

He pushed her onto the bed. The grip of his bony fingers pained her as he clamped her wrists and forced her arms above her head. He sat with his knees astride her. When he leaned forward to kiss her his sweat dripped onto her face. She took delight in his scream as her teeth clamped onto his shoulder. His vice-like pinch caused her to release him.

His scuffled beard scratched her face when he covered her mouth with his, forcing his reptilian tongue into her mouth. Their tongues danced and darted, rotating their heads as their lips crushed together. She bit his lip and drew blood. He slapped her, then grabbed her dress and ripped it apart, exposing her naked breasts.

When he bit her nipple she shouted, "Harder! Bite me harder!"

201

He clenched his teeth.

She let out a blood-curdling scream. He lifted his head with a shadow of concern on his face. Mimi laughed. She demanded, "Take me!"

Gyrating against her, he refused. "You're not ready yet." He looked down at her with a malicious smile.

"Take me, I said!" She dug her nails into his back, "You're driving me mad! Give it to me or I'll kill you!"

"Ow!" He screamed as her claws pierced his skin. He jammed himself inside her. Again, and again, pumping harder and faster, until he was spent.

With nonchalance, she asked, "Is this your best? You disappoint me."

He accepted the challenge and they continued with tempestuous ferocity, until, in the early hours of dawn, they fell asleep.

Mimi woke lying upon the tiny cot covered by a cheap, scratchy blanket. The foul smell of dirty wool, wet with the odors of sweat and sex, filled her nostrils. She lay thinking she was right about his passion. Never had she experienced sex as intense as she had with this young man.

They stayed in that claustrophobic room for several days, only exiting to get a bite to eat and a drink of wine. One day, he conveyed his fanatical convictions to her.

Mimi lay naked on the cot with her only adornment, a red ribbon, tied at her neck. She focused her attention on the apple she was eating.

Her lover, Edouard Furieux, told her of his life and his politics. He explained that his parents worked themselves to death and after their deaths, his uncle, an honest, hardworking member of the

Bourgeoisie, had taken him in. His uncle treated him well and sent him to *école normal* where his friends taught him about the glories of rebellion and revolution.

Pacing back and forth, the naked Edouard jabbed his finger in the air or slammed his fist onto his fragile table for emphasis. He reminded Mimi of Rodin's sculpture of the naked St. John the Baptist, preaching to the uninitiated.

In his strident voice, he sermoned, "God intended that no man should own property. Property leads to corrupt institutions. If no one owned property, no man could live off another man's labor. Government and law must be eliminated! These institutions are designed to help the powerful at the expense of the powerless.

"Only after the old system is pummeled beyond repair can a new social order be born with complete equality and no authority for anyone. Only then, will there be enough of everything for everyone. No more tears from babies with empty bellies. No more slaves to work seventeen hours a day, seven days a week, for thirteen centimes an hour. Once the oppressed classes become convinced of their right to happiness, they will joyfully unite and put asunder the entire malignant system.

"It's only with death and destruction that freedom will come. Yes! Only with bombs and assassinations that our point is made. The revolution is coming and I will strike a blow for justice!"

Mimi stopped eating and looked at him as if he were a stupid fool, "Do you think blowing up a building will put food in a baby's belly? Do you believe that killing someone will change the way the world has been since time began?"

He sat on the bed and looked deep into her eyes. His face aglow with sweat and passion, he replied, "Yes, I believe it and I'm not the only one. Do you know that leaders of six different countries have already been assassinated?"

Mimi stared at him in disbelief.

He smiled, "Yes, already they have assassinated five heads of state." Edouard counted them on his fingers. "You know of President Carnot of France, then Premier Canovas of Spain, followed by Empress Elizabeth of Austria and just recently, King Humbert of Italy. True believers assassinated each of these leaders dying glorious deaths for the coming revolution. So, you see it's not only I who believes the world must change." Then he looked around the small room and whispered conspiratorially, "And tonight...tonight I will blow up Le Bon Marché!"

"The department store?" Mimi raised an eyebrow, "Are you serious?"

Bubbling with excitement he said, "Yes, isn't it perfect? What better place to destroy than that mercenary temple of greed flaunting itself like a cheap *mondaine* in front of the poor. It's the sweaty labor of the poor, who make the goods, which they can never afford to buy. Can you imagine what a statement that will make?"

Mimi was beginning to believe he would do it. She imagined Le Bon Marche blowing up with corsets and chamber pots flying in the air. "Yes, that would make quite a statement," she laughed.

Exhilarated, Edouard beamed, "I'm so happy you understand." He drew close to her ear and whispered, "Come with me tonight. Help me blow up this unholy shrine of decadence."

Mimi was about to refuse, but then she thought how exciting it would be to blow up a building. "Yes, Edouard. I will help you."

The moonless night made it impossible to see anything in the alley, but it also made it impossible to be seen. Edouard told Mimi that he had waited in this alley often, timing the patrol of the gendarmes, so he knew when to proceed.

They'd been waiting there more than an hour and Mimi's anticipation was building. She couldn't remember ever feeling nervous excitement like this.

It was time. Edouard peered out of the alley to be sure no one was about. Holding her hand, he circumvented the street light as he led her to the back of the department store. He took a rock from his satchel and broke a window large enough for them to climb through.

Once inside, Edouard brought out a lamp, its weak, amber light made everything within its beam appear jaundiced. The atmosphere was as eerie as a morgue.

Following behind, Mimi's pulse pounded. She felt warmth in her loins. Her breath caught in her throat. She saw someone. "Edouard," she whispered, as she tugged at his jacket, "Look!"

Edouard paused for a moment. His eyes searched the darkness. He put his mouth close to Mimi's ear. "It's all right. It is only a mannequin that will die tonight."

They arrived at the center of the store. Edouard reached into his satchel and brought out a bundle of dynamite with a lengthy fuse and laid it on the floor with great care. He whispered, "Now we will strike a blow for all mankind." He bent to light the fuse. Mimi grabbed his shoulder.

"No…don't." Mimi's voice was low but firm.

"What's the matter?"

She bent down next to him, "I want to do it. I want to light the fuse."

He smiled and handed her the match.

After lighting the fuse, they ran from the store and hid in an alleyway several blocks away. Exhilarated, they waited and held their breath. Mimi's stomach fluttered. The delay was more than she could bear.

The explosion boomed louder than Mimi expected. It fascinated her to see hundreds of pieces of concrete, glass and debris project into the air and fall in every direction. When the fires began, Mimi lost self-control. She pushed Edouard against the wall of the alley and grappled with his trousers. They copulated to the sound of the fire engine's blaring wails.

Back in the garret, they slept late. Moved by hunger, they went downstairs to the tavern. Edouard purchased all the newspapers he could find. Over cappuccino and croissants, they read the accounts of the bombing.

Delighted at the extent of the destruction, Edouard proudly read to Mimi the details and the angry reaction of the police, government officials and the public. "Oh, Mimi isn't this wonderful?"

"Yes, that was fun last night, but I must be going."

"Going? What are you talking about? We have—"

Edouard looked around the empty tavern. He whispered, "We have only just begun to make an important statement for humanity. How can you leave now?"

"It's time for me to leave. It's been too long since I've had a bath. I stink enough to kill a rat. And my hair! I would break the mirror that would see how I look."

He scoffed, "I can't believe you could care about such insignificant things."

Mimi's chair scraped the floor as she rose.

When she began to walk away, he grabbed her wrist. "You must stay," he commanded.

Mimi gave him a scorching stare. She growled, "Must?" Her voice dripped with acid. "Who are you to command me!"

Edouard released his grip. He said, "You're right. I misspoke myself. I can't believe I've done to you what I have been fighting to eliminate. A man should never order another human being to do anything. Can you forgive me, Mimi?" Then with urgency, he continued, "Please come back to the room with me. There is something important I must tell you."

Accepting his contrition, her anger changed to petty annoyance. "No, I don't think so. It's time for me to leave."

Edouard took her hand and with imploring eyes he asked, "Please come with me for just ten minutes. I have something very important to tell you. I assure you it will be worth just ten minutes of your time."

"All right, but it had better be worth it!"

Before entering his room, Edouard peered down the stairway and scanned the hall. Followed by Mimi, he stepped into the room and locked the door.

Mimi sat on the cot and asked dully, "What's so important that it's worth taking my time?"

Edouard put his finger to his lips. He went to the dresser, opened a drawer and removed what looked like a bundle of rags. He held the bundle with both hands as if he was holding the most important possession anyone could have and placed it before Mimi. With eyes aglow, he said, "Unwrap it."

Puzzled, Mimi looked at him.

"It's okay, open it."

Mimi shrugged and opened the bundle. "So, you have a gun, I'm happy for you," Mimi said dully as she tossed it on the cot and started to leave.

With a furrowed brow, he beseeched her, "Wait! It's not just the gun. It's what I will do with it that matters."

Mimi sat again and pulled Edouard down next to her. Her eyes narrowed, "And just what are you planning to do with this gun?"

Edouard licked his dry lips and breathed in her ear, "Tonight, I will assassinate the Minister of Justice, Monsieur Jules Boudreau." He looked at Mimi as if he just received his favorite toy for Christmas.

In a loud voice, Mimi asked, "Are you insane? Do you actually think you will kill Monsieur Boudreau?"

Once again, he put his finger to his lips. "Sssh!" His pupils dilated with rapture, he whispered, "Yes! Can you imagine the chaos that will cause?"

Mimi asked, "How do you plan to do this? Have you thought this through?"

His face flushed with pride. "Oh, yes, I've watched him for months. He goes to the Salles des Cuisines every night at 8 pm, always sitting in the same booth. At 8:15 tonight I will rush past the *maitre'd*, barge up to him and fire between his eyes before he has a chance to react."

Mimi sneered and said, "That's not much of a plan. It won't work. One look at your filthy clothes and you'll be caught and thrown out before you can get near him." As Edouard started to protest. Mimi held up her hand and said, "Wait, let me think a minute."

She leaned back on her elbows and thought for a few moments. She sat up and said, "I have a much better idea. You should assassinate the ex-Minister of Finance!"

Edouard raised his eyebrows, "Monsieur La Fontaine? But why? Who cares about an ex-Minister?"

"First, he will be much easier to assassinate because he is no longer protected. Second, the Minister of Finance is responsible for the wages of the proletariat. Who better to blame for the misery of poor people?"

Edouard brushed his fingers against his mustache as he thought for a moment. "Yes, that would be even better. But how can we find him?"

Mimi put her face close his. "I know the people who work for him at his house. They will let us in. While he's sleeping, you can shoot him and no one will be there to stop you."

Edouard could barely contain his exhilaration, "But how can you be sure they will not tell Monsieur Le Fontaine?"

"I know these people well. You can believe me when I say they will do me this favor. Leave this to me. I'll make the arrangements. Meet me on the corner of Boulevard des Invalides and Rue de Grenelle at midnight the day after tomorrow. Bring your gun and your lamp. Everything will be ready."

They met as agreed and entered the grounds of Émile La Fontaine's townhouse. Mimi took Edouard's hand and led him through the French doors of her bedroom, the same French doors that her mother sneaked through so many years before.

They tiptoed through the bedroom, out into the hallway and up the stairs. Just outside Émile's bedroom, Mimi pushed Edouard against the wall, "This is for the pleasure you've given me."

After she kissed him with passion, she whispered, "Are you ready?" When he nodded eagerly, she took his hand and opened Émile's bedroom door. She peeked in. All was black and quiet. They entered and she flashed the pallid lamplight at the humped bedcovers. Edouard pulled the gun from his waistband and fired three times.

"Get him!" Yelled the Prefect of Police.

On went the room lamps, the light blinding Edouard. Before he could react, the gendarmes rushed him. They grabbed him and knocked the gun from his hand.

Émile came into the room and kissed Mimi on the cheek. Smiling with pride and satisfaction, he placed his arm around her shoulders.

Edouard screamed, "What's happening?" He stared at Mimi, his face a mixture of rage and confusion.

With cold eyes, Mimi sneered at Edouard. "You donkey's ass! You drivel-headed imbecile! Your stupidity knows no end! I'm one of the richest women in Paris, and you talk to me of eliminating wealth and destroying powerful people!

"Émile La Fontaine, the man you tried to destroy tonight, is my grand-père. Do you think I would let a worthless piece of dirt like you waltz in here and assassinate him? Your neck will feel the blade of the guillotine as it removes your stupid head! Take him away. I never want to see his face again!"

The police dragged Edouard from the room as he screamed. "But Mimi, you said you believed in the cause—" He continued to scream, "MIMI!" as he struggled to escape while they dragged him from the house.

Émile beamed at his granddaughter. "How did you find out about this anarchist?"

Mimi went to the mirror to fix her hair. "Oh grand-père, you should know by now that I have my ways. However, I think you should have the chambermaid change your bedclothes before you retire." Mimi laughed. "I don't think pillows with bullet holes will be very comfortable to sleep on."

Dance with the Devil

Chapter 31

Ahanu, a curious three-year-old, was tending a flock of sheep with his older brother Keme. It had been a long time since their first meal of the day, so Keme built a campfire to heat the stew their mother had prepared for them.

While he waited for his lunch, Ahanu peeked over the edge of outcropping rocks. He never expected to see a wild, red-haired monster with cracked lips and bloodshot eyes peeking back at him. Terrified, Ahanu screamed. He watched with fascination as the redheaded monster fell from the edge of the cliff.

Blistered, bloody and bruised, Rita lay semi-conscious on the hard earth. Unable to move in mind or body, she felt too tired to think, too tired for regrets, and too tired to pray.

Rita didn't hear the light tread of moccasins approaching, but she felt a respite from the brutal sun when a shadow fell across her face. She forced her eyes open. The shadow appeared to be a black figure in the shape of a man. The sun's rays projected from behind his head like a halo.

Is he a mirage? Is this what it's like to be dead? Has Jesus Christ come to take me to heaven?

"Stupid girl."

Did I hear this…ghost call me stupid? Oh, no! If Jesus is calling me stupid, I can't be in heaven. I hope I'm not dead. But if it's not Jesus… what if he's…the devil?

The voice grew louder, "Wake up, stupid girl."

She felt a rough hand smack her face, then strong hands lift her and flop her belly down onto a horse's back. Breath whooshed from her body just before she passed out.

Rita woke choking. *Is that water? Yes! Precious, wonderful water!* She opened her eyes to darkness. She could sense water dripping into her mouth. Swallowing was impossible. Her throat muscles refused to cooperate and she coughed hard.

She heard a woman's voice, "If you can't swallow, rinse water in your mouth then spit out." Rita tried to see the face of the person speaking but her vision wouldn't focus. She thought she must be dreaming but did as instructed. After several attempts, she could swallow a little water.

Rita tried to grab the source of the water to drink it in larger gulps, but she couldn't move. Again, she heard the woman's voice, gruffly this time, "Stay still! Don't be greedy. Stupid Girl, you must drink slow."

Cool water on her blistered face helped her eyes to focus. Wrapped in a wet blanket, she lay in the arms of a woman, who dripped water into her mouth. Rita looked at her with grateful eyes. She tried to speak, but she had no voice. The woman seemed annoyed and told her to be quiet.

The woman stayed with Rita for a long time. When the woman left, she took the water with her. Rita croaked, "No…please…I'm so thirsty…please give me more water." The woman ignored her and left. Rita felt a little less miserable in the wet blanket and fell into a deep sleep.

When she woke, Rita had no idea where she could be. She lay on her back and blinked the sleep from her eyes. Through a hole in the roof, she saw a bright, cloudless blue sky. Rita wondered why the roof had a hole in it. Her pounding head and itchy skin from beneath the dry blanket overtook her curiosity. She attempted to stand but weakness prevented her.

Although sore, Rita realized that her bandaged feet felt better. She threw off the blanket and curled up on the sheepskin rug she found next to her. Rita lay in the room's coolness and hoped the Indian woman would soon return with water. She fell asleep remembering the water's sweet taste.

The sound of laughter awakened Rita. She raised her head to see a little boy with black button eyes. He sucked his forefinger and slobber hung about his chin. He pointed his wet finger at her and called out, "Stupid Girl."

Rita looked past the boy to see a group of Indian women sitting cross-legged on sheepskins with their eyes on her. The woman who'd given her water sat in front of the others. She had thick, black hair, a strong face with prominent cheekbones, weathered, coppery skin and two straight brown lines for lips. She wore a velveteen blouse with silver and turquoise necklaces and a cotton skirt.

"My name is Pahana," she said. The other women, of varying ages, were dressed in a similar fashion.

Rita laughed at the boy's description of her. In a voice that sounded like the crunch of gravel, she said, "I guess you're right, I was stupid to be out alone in the desert." She looked at the woman who gave her water and croaked, "Thank you, Pahana, for saving my life. I'm grateful to you. But please, can you tell me where I am?"

Pahana handed Rita a jug of water. "This is the Nedero Reservation and we are of the Dry Lake Clan. Keme, son of Mahela, bring you here. You almost dead. Why you in desert alone? Where are your people?"

Rita didn't know how to respond. Afraid to tell the truth, she took a deep sip of water, thinking up a plausible story. Then she blurted out, "I...uh...I was on my way to San Francisco to visit my aunt. I had lots of provisions, but there was a cloudburst and I got washed off the trail and nearly drowned. I lost my horse and everything I had. I couldn't find my way back to the trail and had no idea which way to go."

Pahana looked at her with suspicion but said nothing.

"I can't tell you how much I appreciate your saving my life. But can you see your way to a little food, and maybe I can buy a horse from you?" Rita reached into her pocket of her tattered jeans for money but found only a handful of sand. "Uh oh, I seem to have lost my money in the wash too."

Pahana said something in Nedero to another woman. The woman left and returned a few minutes later with a bowl of corn mush.

Handing the bowl to Rita, Pahana advised, "Take this food, but you must eat slow or you will be sick."

Rita eyed the bowl hungrily and ignored the woman's advice.

They watched as Rita grabbed the bowl and shoved the mush into her mouth repeatedly with her fingers. Rita's eyes grew wide. She scanned the hut and then ran outside and threw up.

Rita returned to the hut to see Pahana shaking her head. "Stupid Girl, I told you to eat slow."

The little boy laughed at her. Pahana said something to a woman, who then handed Rita a bowl of foul-smelling grease. Pahana told her to rub it all over her body and they all left the hut.

After rubbing the grease on her body, exhausted, Rita fell back to sleep. The next morning, she awoke and felt better. Her injured feet still hurt, but she could hobble and her cracked and dried skin felt less painful. But she was starving!

She searched the hut for food. The dome-shaped hut had a hole in the roof for smoke, an earthen floor with a fire pit in the center and walls made of timber that were covered with bark and dirt. The hut contained a clutter of hides, old tools, bundled pelts, saddles, ropes and miscellaneous possessions that hung from pegs, but no food.

Rita was about to leave when Pahana entered with a group of women. They brought her more mush. This time she ate slower. Pahana spoke, "You say you have no money and no horse."

Feeling stranded, Rita panicked. She put down her bowl and took a deep breath. "You've been kind to me and I have no way to repay you. I don't want to be a burden to you, but I have no provisions and no money. If I could stay here for a while, I'll work to repay you. When I've saved a little money, I'll leave."

Rita held her breath. If Pahana didn't accept her offer, she'd be cast into the desert with nothing. She'd be worse off than when she left Rimrock Springs.

"You must return to your family. You have no horse so we will take you back."

Rita's heart pounded. She hung her head, "I'm ashamed. You saved my life and instead of telling you the truth, I lied. I have no aunt. I have no family." Rita's voice pinched as she forced back her tears. She was about to put into words the frightful reality of her life. "I don't know where my parents are. I have no one."

Rita paused with her lips clenched. She tried not to cry but the tears came. She wiped them away. Clearing her throat, she continued in a quivering voice, "There's no one in the world who cares if I live or die."

Pahana nodded. "This does not surprise me. A girl alone in the desert. Not hard to think you run from something. But you cannot stay here. We will bring you to sheriff tomorrow."

"No, please, Pahana, don't make me go. They'll send me to an orphanage. That would be worse than prison. I'll do anything. Please don't bring me to the sheriff." Rita gulped back her tears. Pahana stared at her without a word. Rita lifted her tear-stained face and looked at Pahana with pleading eyes, "Please, please let me stay."

After what seemed like forever, Pahana said, "I believe that this orphan place must be a bad place. A place that make you so afraid you risk your life to run from it. Many Indians know the misery of being forced to live in a bad place, so I will let you stay. If you stay here, you must work hard. You must do everything we ask with no question, no complaint. Many Nedero people do not like white people. They will mock you and make you want to leave. You must obey our laws and honor our people. You agree?"

Rita clasped her hands as if in prayer and said, "Yes! Oh, yes! Thank you. I'll do whatever you say."

Pahana called out, "Mahela!" A pregnant woman with a hair lip waddled forward. The annoyed expression on her face gave Rita the impression that Mahela's underwear must have been chafing her. "Mahela will help you learn our ways. You must follow her in all things. You will stay in her hogan. Stupid Girl, you are welcome here if you do as she say. But Mahela does not speak your language so her daughter Dakoda will be her voice."

A girl, a little younger than Rita, came forward. Plump, with a pleasant round face, broad flat cheekbones and long, shiny black hair. Her dark almond-shaped eyes twinkled at Rita and she offered her a wide smile.

Rita stood and took Mahela's hand to shake it. She said, "Pleased to meet you, my name is Rita O'Reill—." Mahela gave her a dirty look, so Rita dropped her hand as if she was a snapping dog. Rita figured she must have done something wrong and looked at Dakoda, who grabbed Rita's hand instead. In a firm voice Dakoda said, "Pleased to meet you, Stupid Girl."

Rita started to object but thought better of it. She smiled. "Well, I guess I better get used to being called Stupid Girl."

Pahana gave a command and left. The other women remained. Rita started to ask Dakoda a question when the group of women rushed at her. "Whoa! What's happening?" They grabbed Rita and dragged her out of the hogan. They were giggling and chattering, as they towed Rita along.

219

Alarmed, she shouted, "Let me go! Leave me alone!" Rita tried to wiggle loose. The more she yelled, the more they laughed at her. *Are they going to kill me?*

They brought her to a lake and pushed her in. Rita screamed as they all jumped in with her. They ripped off her clothes and pushed her head under water.

They're going to drown me! Rita managed to stand. She choked, then drew a deep breath. They pushed her under again. She continued to struggle until she realized they were trying to bathe her.

They gave her a good scrubbing. Soon she relaxed and began splashing water and playing with them. When they finished, the girls pulled her out of the lake and dried her naked body with blankets. They rubbed her with salve and re-bandaged her feet. One girl placed moccasins on her feet and gave her an outfit like theirs, but with no jewelry and they all walked back to camp, still chattering and giggling.

As the group returned, Rita observed the camp. It was comprised a complex of scattered structures, each separate but all close together. There were dugouts for storage and a sheep corral. Beyond were garden plots that looked as if they contained corn, wheat, tobacco and maybe squash, melons, and beans.

The huts, or *hogans* as Pahana called them, were like the one Rita had been in, but smaller. The one Rita slept in had a large fire pit next to it. Near the pit were some trees with small objects tucked inside. It looked like they used the trees as cupboards. Other trees had ropes joining them where clothing, blankets and sheepskins hung.

Under a tree, a man tanned a hide. A woman sat in front of a crude rug loom, weaving a blanket. Several small children scurried around playing with a dog, and in the distance, an older boy herded sheep. Ignoring several lambs bleating near him, a man sat making a piece of jewelry. He was using a small hammer and a metal die to tap a design into a piece of silver. Rita could see a corral with many horses and wondered if Blaze might be in there. She'd check as soon as she had the chance.

Rita felt better. She was still sore and walking was painful, but she was clean and surrounded by women who were laughing and happy. She felt relaxed and part of the group.

Until, the next day, Mahela, who hadn't joined in Rita's bath, ran towards her with a butcher knife. Rita stopped in her tracks. She was about to run for her life when Mahela shoved the knife into her hand and shouted at her in Nedero.

Rita stood stiff and blinked in confusion. Mahela pointed to the sheepherder and continued shouting. Rita thought the crazy pregnant woman with a harelip wanted her to kill the sheepherder. Dakoda worked her way out of a crowd of women and explained, "My mother says you must butcher a sheep."

Relieved to learn the only death involved a sheep, Rita looked at the butcher knife and groaned, "But Dakoda, I never butchered a sheep in my life. I don't know where to start."

Dakoda furrowed her brows, "Stupid Girl, I will help you but if you refuse to do this you will be banished."

Rita looked at the knife and sighed. "I hate to kill an animal but if it's him or me, I guess it'll have to be him. Let's go!"

Dakoda smiled with relief. Although Rita did all the work, Dakoda explained how to catch the sheep, butcher it, remove the internal organs and prepare it for use. After completing her task, Rita ground meal on a metate, a flat stone with a depression for holding maize. Dakoda showed Rita how to grind the maize with a mano, a stone-like rolling pin. Many of the women sat together. They reminded Rita of a quilting bee as they talked and laughed while grinding the corn.

Rita saw Pahana with several women at the large open fire pit. She watched one of the young girls assemble pots and pans around the glowing coals of a cedar fire. Pahana sang as she added corn to a large pot of lamb stew.

The young girl mixed a large pan full of dough that she kneaded from flour and baking powder. She smiled as she sang with Pahana. The girl shaped a tortilla, throwing small portions of the stiff dough from one hand to the other. At her side, a frying pan rested on hot coals. She shaped one tortilla and watched as another tortilla fried in the pan. She flipped it with skill and continued cooking them until the pile of tortillas was high. Then she measured coffee from a paper sack and poured it into the coffeepots.

Cooking aromas drove Rita crazy. The women who'd been grinding corn rested and fanned themselves with flour sacks when a group of men arrived with loads of firewood.

The young tortilla chef laid several sheepskins wool side down on the ground and set down large bowls of stewed meat and corn-flavored broth. She brought a pile of tin cups, huge stacks of tortillas, pots full of coffee and a jar of sugar and placed them in the center of the skins.

Everyone sat around in a circle on the sheepskins and the meal began. Rita threw herself into her meal with gusto. She enjoyed every ounce of the tender meat, savory broth and tasty tortillas. She washed it down with several cups of rich, sweet coffee.

There was plenty of friendly conversation during the meal. One wiry, wrinkled old man must have been the comedian of the group. He seemed to be telling stories that broke everyone into fits of laughter. Rita wished she could understand what he was saying.

At the end of the meal, Pahana brought out a huge watermelon and threw it on the ground, splitting it. The children shouted with glee. Everyone picked up a piece of the sweet treat and had a great time.

After dinner, Rita watched the men began to chant. The chant was high-pitched and hypnotic. The consistent rhythm was like a drumbeat and the melody would rise, fall and rise again.

Dakoda sat next to Rita and whispered to her that the ceremony was to honor the Earth Mother and thank her for the meal. Everyone looked peaceful as the chant continued. Rita asked Dakoda if she could join in. It pleased her to see Dakoda's nod. She closed her eyes and, losing herself in the chants, Rita enjoyed a new sense of tranquility.

223

At twilight, everyone sat around a blazing fire, while one of the old men told stories to the children. Rita couldn't understand what he was saying, but she was certain that they were scary stories, because the moon-eyed children were frightened. This went on for some time and until all the children ran screaming into their hogans. The adults laughed and followed them in, but they showed signs of fright as well.

Rita asked Dakoda why everyone seemed so frightened. Dakoda explained that adults tell scary stories to children about the coyote's mischief. The coyote is a messenger, but his news is usually bad. They tell the children scary stories of the coyote to make the children brave and strong. Parents want their children to know that the coyote is always lurking and is always hungry and always dangerous. But they're assured their family will protect them.

A group of men extinguished the fire, and everyone went their separate ways. Dakoda directed Rita to her hogan. As they entered, Rita saw Dakoda's large family already undressed, laid out on the floor atop sheepskins and ready for sleep. Arranged like spokes of a wheel, their feet pointed towards the fire pit in the center of the room. This hogan was smaller and more crowded than the one Rita had slept in.

Dakoda whispered to Rita, "Be sure not to step on anyone, it would be a very unlucky thing to do."

Rita was very careful as she found herself a spot and fell sound asleep. It seemed like she just drifted off when she felt the nudging of an impatient foot. Lifting her head, she saw the hogan was empty except for Mahela, who nudged her. Rita groaned under her breath.

Rita forced her sore body to rise. Mahela held a sheepskin and growled something at her. She pushed Rita from the hogan and Mahela shook it roughly then put it into Rita's hands. She made Rita shake it. She pushed Rita back into the hogan and showed her how to roll it up.

Then she directed Rita to pick up another one and go outside to shake it. Rita understood and took all the sheepskins outside, shook them and rolled them up, placing them along the walls.

When Rita saw Dakoda approaching, she smiled and said, "Sure glad to see you. But I have to ask you something. Why's your mother so mad at me?"

Dakoda looked sad and said softly, "It's not you she is angry with, it's all white people. Indians have suffered so long at the hands of white people that many of us think all white people are bad."

"Do you think all white people are bad?"

Dakoda paused, "All my life I have heard the tales of terrible white men. But I have also heard the tales of some bad Apaches and Utes and other Indians. I know that there are even some bad Nedero. But most Nedero are good and caring people. I think there must be good and caring white people too. I hope you are one of them."

Rita grinned and said, "I think you are a very smart Nedero."

Dakoda smiled and took Rita's hand, leading her towards a woodpile. "Today you must chop wood."

Rita groaned. She spent the day chopping wood, eating breakfast, helping to gather crops, eating lunch and learning how to make tortillas for dinner. The day ended just as the previous evening had.

225

The days became months. Rita learned more about the Nedero People's ways and their language. She learned that Pahana's name meant "filled with wisdom" and that she was a respected advice-giver.

Rita learned that the Dry Lake Clan was highly admired for their skills at weaving blankets and that Pahana was the best weaver. She admired the intricacy of Pahana's rug designs. Loving the vivid colors and Pahana's ability to create a six-foot rug in just a week amazed her.

Performing the same duties as the other women, Rita fell into the routine of the village. Except for Mahela, everyone seemed friendly towards her. Feeling like an integral part of the group thrilled her.

One night while the family slept in their Hogan, Mahela started to moan. Men ran from the hut and chanted prayers.

Crowding into the hogan, a group of women arrived with two long, heavy, carved poles and many blankets. Three women staked the poles into the ground and tied the top portion of the poles to pegs hanging from the ceiling. Mahela stood gripping a pole in each hand.

Dakoda explained that this was the Nedero way of giving birth. She grabbed Rita's hand and joined the women who formed a circle around Mahela. They danced and chanted in the Nedero Circle Of Life Ceremony.

They sang and danced for hours until, with the help of gravity, Mahela gave birth to her fourth little girl, Pipaluk, meaning Sweet Little Thing.

Much rejoicing greeted Pipaluk's arrival. The woman Elu was the first to grasp the emerging baby, so she had the privilege of being the first to bathe and anoint her with corn pollen. Tibone, Mahela's husband, chanted while he made a cradleboard for his new little daughter. The men slapped Tibone on the back congratulating him on another healthy child, his seventh.

Rita thought Mahela was the one who should be congratulated.

Dance with the Devil

Chapter 32

When Rita wasn't busy doing chores, she and Dakoda would take walks by the lake or sit in the shade of a tree where they discussed the traditions and the daily life of the Nedero people.

In their discussions, Rita learned that Earth Mother built the first hogan out of turquoise and shell and gave the Nedero people the gift of corn. Rita learned how their ceremonies blessed or healed, to appreciate food and nature, and about the rites of passage for young men. Most important, Earth Mother taught mortals to live in harmony with nature.

On one blustery day when they sat alone inside Mahela's hogan, Dakoda explained about the Holy People. She said, "The Holy People are strange and powerful spirit beings who travel on the wind and on sunbeams, on rainbows and on thunderbolts."

"However," she explained, "these spirits are not always good. We must appease them with offerings, ritual chanting and cleansing ceremonies to keep them from using their power to harm."

Rita asked, "Is that why children are so frightened of the night?"

"Yes, but not only children. What we all fear most is *chinde*, the dead who are the ghosts of the Earth Surface. These spirits are evil and cannot be appeased."

Thunder clapped nearby and both Dakoda and Rita lurched at the loud boom. Dakoda peeked outside the hogan.

"Wow! That was close! Rita jumped up and stood next to Dakoda. "Is everything all right?"

Dakoda looked worried. "Maybe we should talk about this another time."

"Please, Dakoda, I want to learn more, if that's all right with you."

Dakoda took a deep breath and returned to her seat. "I'll tell you more, but I hope I'm not making the ghosts angry."

"I don't want to get you in trouble, so if you don't want to tell me, it's okay."

"No, I think it's important that you learn about this. The Nedero believe the evil part of a dead person returns to the place of its dying to torment the living for some oversight or insult. Even the ghost of a loved one, one who had been a good person when alive, is feared. We so fear the places of death that, when a person dies inside a hogan, they burn it down rather than remain living there. You were very lucky my brother Keme found you. If another Nedero found you, they might have left you to die."

"Jeez, that's a scary thought. How come Keme saved me?"

"Keme is not afraid because he, like many young boys, was forced to go to the white man's school to learn English and the white man's ways. These white men made our young boys cut their hair and wear the white man's clothes. They were taught to be ashamed that they were Indian and made to forget the Nedero language and the Nedero ways. They were told to teach our clan to be like white people. That's why me and Pahana speak English, but my

230

mother and other Nedero refused to learn. They wish to keep the old ways.

Rita shook her head, "That's awful. I don't know why folks can't let people be."

"We are sad because Keme and the others have a sickness in their hearts. They feel they're not Nedero and they're not white. Pahana says that the world belongs to the white people now and soon we must learn how to adjust to their ways or one day all the Nedero will be gone."

"That's terrible! I hate to say it, but I'm ashamed that white people are so mean. That they force gentle people like you Nederos, who live in harmony with nature, to become mean like them. Maybe they should be chased by…what'd you call it…*chinde?* "

Another boom of thunder sounded in the distance and rain pounded the earth outside.

Dakoda looked frightened. "I don't think we should say that name anymore."

"Maybe you're right." Rita agreed. "Say, have you ever seen a ghost?"

"No. But I've heard stories from many Nedero's who have. They tell of the ghosts they've seen at night in the shape of a wolf."

"A wolf! What happens when they see these wolf ghosts?"

Dakoda's eyes grew large. "Ghosts have mutilated livestock and leap upon the living to claw at their clothing or inflict the dreaded Death Sickness."

Rita's mouth dropped open. "Death Sickness? What's that?"

"I hope you never find out."

A few days later, Rita was herding sheep, when Dakoda came running to her. "Rita! My baby sister, Pipaluk, laughed for the first time!"

"Did she? That must have been fun to see."

"Yes. It was. You must come to our celebration. All the Clans are here."

"What kind of celebration?" Rita asked.

"A baby's first laugh is very important," Dakoda said. "All the Nedero clan join in the celebration. Come, come! The celebration is about to begin. Hurry!"

By the time they returned to the village, the largest hogan had been filled with people.

Propped up on pillows, Pipaluk was the center of attention. A woven basket filled with cakes, tortillas and blue ears of Indian corn lay in front of the baby.

Dakoda pointed to a woven basket. "That basket was used as part of my mother's marriage ceremony. Our people accept gifts from the basket. The basket is a symbol of the gift that this child is bringing to the world. Hoping her life and all who take a gift, will always be blessed with laughter."

At the end of the ceremony, Rita left the hogan and noticed a group from another clan mounting their horses. Recognizing Blaze her heart raced and her skin tingled. She yelled, "Blaze! Blaze, it's you!" Rita ran towards Blaze and hugged her neck.

An Indian boy who sat atop Blaze screamed something. Rita focused on Blaze and ignored the shouts. The boy dismounted. He shouted at Rita and pushed her. Rita held on to Blaze and disregarded him. A powerful blow on the side of her face knocked her to the ground. Rita surged forward and punched the boy. They tussled on the ground, punching and biting each other. Two men pulled them apart and held them back. Blood ran from the boy's nose as they leered at each other.

Pahana yelled, "What are you doing, Stupid Girl?"

Consumed with anger and breathing heavily, Rita pointed at the boy and shouted, "He stole my horse!"

Pahana glared at Rita, "That cannot be your horse, Stupid Girl, you had no horse when you came here."

Rita caught her breath. With a caustic stare at the boy, "Blaze is my horse," she declared. "The storm frightened her and we got separated. She's *my* horse and I want her back! I'm sorry if I got rough with him, but he slugged me first!"

Pahana turned to the boy. Rita didn't understand what she said to him, but there were heated words between them. A man with a nasty sneer and haughty attitude stepped forward and shouted at Pahana.

Kishel, Pahana's husband, came forward and words got louder still. The boy hopped onto Blaze. The nasty-faced man mounted his horse and his entire clan rode off. Rita tried to run after them but she was restrained. Pahana ordered Rita into an empty hogan and told her to stay there until Dakoda came for her.

Rita obeyed. She stayed in the hogan and paced the floor. *I miss Blaze so much. I have to see her again. I know I'm gonna be kicked out of camp now. What am I going to do? All I know is, whatever it takes, I will get Blaze back!*

The next morning Dakoda entered the hogan and said, "You must come with me." Seeing the sad expression on her face, Rita knew she was in serious trouble. On the way to Pahana's hogan, Dakoda explained that the boy was a member of the Lizard Clan. "They are not good people," Dakoda said. "We believe them to be witches and to cast spells, causing much trouble for the Dry Lake Clan."

Pahana sat cross-legged on a sheepskin, her face more stern than usual. Her husband and several other serious-looking men sat by her side. In a grave voice, Pahana ordered, "Sit down, Stupid Girl."

Rita was contrite. "Pahana I'm so sorry for any trouble I caused and I—"

"Do not talk, Stupid Girl. Esadowa found the horse you claim to be yours roaming freely, and as is his right, he gave her to his son Chunta. You have insulted Esadowa and Chunta. You have taken honor from the Dry Lake Clan. The only way to redeem yourself is to work for them until you repay your debt of insult. I have agreed to this arrangement."

Rita didn't like the way this was going. Especially since Dakoda said that clan was full of witches. "How long do I have to stay with the Lizard Clan?"

"That is their decision. You will stay until it satisfies them."

Rita felt panic grip her chest. She looked into Pahana's eyes and asked, "Isn't there any other way?"

"You brought shame on the Dry Lake Clan, something I told you never to do. You may leave the reservation if you wish. But if you do not repay your debt, Dakoda will go in your place."

Rita looked at Dakoda and saw terror on her face. Rita took a deep breath. "I will go."

Dakoda returned with Rita to her hogan. As they walked back, Dakoda's voice was anxious. "You must be careful of the Lizard Clan." She said. "They are very dangerous. For years, they have been envious of the Dry Lake Clan. In the night, they have stolen our cattle and our sheep. They have put spells on many of our people and some have died because of these spells."

Rita knew the Nedero were superstitious people. She didn't believe in these things, but hearing about this witch stuff made her nervous. She asked Dakoda, "How do they become witches?"

Dakoda's eyes grew large. She whispered, "It's not hard to become a witch. Anyone who has hatred or desire for vengeance or wealth can be a witch. But they must do unspeakable acts. They must commit incest or eat the flesh of humans or live animals. Or, worst of all, rob a grave. Any human can be a witch and you won't know it. During the daytime, they look like any other Nedero. But at night they turn into 'skinwalkers', wolves who turn back again the next day."

Rita felt chills down her spine. "Are you trying to scare me? 'Cause you're doing a good job."

"I'm sorry, Rita, but this is the truth," Dakoda said. You embarrassed Chunta and his father when you fought back and bloodied his nose. They may want to punish you for this insult. Dakoda handed Rita a pouch.

Rita opened it, sniffed it and grew faint from the smell. She pinched her nose as she said, "Whew! What is this stuff?"

"It's a preparation made from the gall bladders of mountain lions, bears, eagles and skunks," Dakoda said. All Nedero carry it. It will protect you from the

235

Death Sickness. If a witch wants to make you sick, he can prepare a potion of the dried flesh and the brittle bones of corpses and mixes it with poison. He makes a powder and blows it in your face. The only way to save yourself is to swallow this."

Damn! Swallowing this foul-smelling stuff will probably kill me faster than any powder blown in my face. "Thank you for your kindness Dakoda. I appreciate your concern and your help."

That night, Rita couldn't sleep. She would have to leave camp in the morning and tried to figure a way out of this mess. Potions or witches didn't scare her but she feared getting a knife in her back. She needed a weapon and tiptoed to the cooking area. She didn't like to steal, but she believed she had no choice. She grabbed a knife, hid it in her clothes and sneaked back into the hogan.

The next morning, Dakoda accompanied Rita to the Lizard Clan's village. Along the way, Rita asked Dakoda, "If the Lizard Clan has caused so much trouble for the Dry Lake Clan why don't your people do something about it?"

Dakoda explained, "In the past, they had many wars with each other and many Nedero died. When the white man began killing Nedero, the Lizard Clan and the Dry Lake Clan had a peace ceremony and agreed never to fight each other again. The Lizard Clan has broken the peace many times. They sneak in the night and are never caught, so we have no proof."

"Why don't your men stand guard and catch them in the act?" Rita asked.

"The night is full of danger. The ghosts of the dead walk in the night and if they catch you, they will kill you." Dakoda shivered. "Even the braves do not go out alone at night. They will only go out in groups, and only if necessary. Since we don't know where or when they will raid us, the men refuse to stand watch."

"What would happen if they knew when they would be raided?"

"I don't know. Pahana would decide that."

Rita shook her head, "I thought Pahana was beginning to like me. Why do you think she would make me go to be with the Lizard Clan if they're so evil?"

"Pahana is angry with you for betraying her trust and dishonoring the Clan. She will always put the best interests of our Clan first, and there is no choice between you and the Clan. "

They reached the outskirts of the village and Dakoda said, "I must leave you now."'

Rita took Dakoda's hand. "You and Pahana have been very good to me. Even your mother who hates me has allowed me to live in your hogan. I'm grateful to all of you, and I feel bad that I have brought shame to you. As much as I love Blaze, I'd give her up, rather than cause any harm to your Clan. If there's any way that I can make up for this, I will do it gladly. Please tell Pahana how I feel." They hugged. "Thank you, Dakoda. You've been a tremendous help to me and no matter what happens, I'll always remember your kindness."

Rita saw tears in Dakoda's eyes as she left.

Dance with the Devil

Chapter 33

Rita considered her options. *Nothing good will happen to me in the Lizard Clan village. They'll punish me and maybe kill me. I should run away. Maybe, I can steal some provisions and somehow find Blaze. I learned a lot from my Indian friends about how to survive in the desert. But if I run away, I'd bring more trouble for the Dry Lake people and especially for Dakoda. I can't do that. I gave my word. No matter what happens, I'll just have to face the consequences.*

Entering the village, the putrid smell of garbage overwhelmed Rita. She wrinkled her nose and thought, *This must be the wrong place!*

The vast difference between the two villages made her cringe. Dry Lake village was clean and organized. Both men and women used their skills and everyone took pride in their appearance.

In the crowded Lizard Clan village, she saw men laying about smoking and talking, while children ran around naked, either playing with filthy dogs or fighting amongst themselves. Only the women worked, hauling pails of water, chopping firewood or tending gardens.

Rita felt sick at the sight of this village. Children had long, stringy hair with grimy hands and faces. Rita heard two women screaming as they fought over an article of clothing. Mangy dogs prowled, growling and snapping at each other, protecting their meager finds from the piles of refuse strewn everywhere. *Oh my god, I've entered hell! I can't stay here! There must be another way!* She scrunched her eyes and pressed her lips together. *I have no choice. I can't let Dakoda be punished in my place.*

With a heavy sigh, she approached a scraggly, loose-skinned, toothless old woman cooking a foul-smelling concoction in a kettle. Using her meager knowledge of the Nedero language, Rita bid her greeting and asked where she might find Esadowa.

With a hostile frown and narrowed eyes, the woman looked at Rita through the curling steam rising from the kettle. She turned to a little boy and shouted something. The little boy looked at Rita and ran off.

Rita's eyes scoured the camp looking for Blaze but the horse was nowhere in sight. The boy returned, grasped Rita's skirt with a dirty hand and tugged it. She had to run to keep up with him. She felt the old lady's eyes burning into her back as she left.

The boy brought Rita a short distance and together they entered a hogan that smelled of rancid sheepskins, stale food, urine and sweaty bodies. There were various animal skulls, and what may have been human skulls, scattered around the hogan.

The way Esadowa looked at Rita made her skin crawl. She had never felt so trapped and helpless.

With a devious smile, Chunta swaggered to Rita. Being shorter than she, he stood up as straight as possible. Rita remained motionless as Chunta sauntered around her, assessing her as if measuring for her coffin. He sneered with ugly, twisted lips, and his eyes riveted on hers with menace. He removed a large hunting knife from his waistband and brought the very sharp point to Rita's chin. Her heart thumped wildly. The knife pricked her and she felt a trickle of blood.

I'd love to stab him with his knife! But even if I could, the others will kill me.

Rita glowered at him. Hoping they would respect bravery, she spit in his face. Surprised, Chunta jumped back and wiped the spit. The others laughed at him.

Flushed with anger, Chunta raised his arm to thrust his knife into her heart. Esadowa yelled. At the sound of his voice, Chunta stopped short of plunging it into Rita's flesh. His face contorted into a sanguine mask. He raised his arm again, about to finish her when Esadowa grabbed his wrist and screamed at him. Before Chunta resumed his place with the others, she thought she heard a low growl come from his throat.

Esadowa shouted again. A young woman entered the hogan. She appeared to be several years older than Rita. She might have been pretty, Rita thought, but she was as unkempt as the others. With shoulders bent forward and downcast eyes, she carried herself with a woeful air.

The young woman's eyes remained downcast as Esadowa barked more instructions. She tugged at Rita's sleeve and led her to a wretched garden where they picked something resembling weeds.

Rita attempted to exchange names and speak the few Nedero words she knew, but the young woman didn't speak or look at her. After several backbreaking hours, they carried their baskets of weeds and returned to the young woman's hogan.

When Rita saw that the scraggly, loose-skinned, toothless old woman lived in the same hogan, she feared she would have to eat the foul-smelling thing the old woman had been cooking.

Rita cringed as she watched the young woman spoon a ladle of greasy soup and a few scrawny vegetables into bowl. She handed the bowl to Rita. Raising her bowl, Rita paused then swigged a hungry gulp. Her tongue caught fire and tears flooded her reddened face. She spluttered and coughed and couldn't catch her breath.

The old woman laughed at Rita, a loud, toothless old-woman cackle. She poked the young woman in the ribs with her elbow as if to say, white girl can't take a little heat.

Rita continued to cough and gasp for breath. The young woman grabbed a jug and handed it to Rita, who drank the foul-tasting concoction until the fire abated. Rita realized the soup was loaded with hot chilies and chewed on a tortilla, but it was dry and tasteless and she lost her appetite.

I don't have to worry about being murdered here, this food will kill me!

That evening a group of women carrying an odd-looking piece of clothing entered the hogan. They spoke to the old woman, who eyed Rita and nodded.

Rita got the impression they would make her change her clothes. She worried they'd find her knife and take her locket. Turning from them, she removed the knife from her pocket and the locket from her neck. She let them slip from her hand and she kicked them under a sheepskin.

The women replaced Rita's clothes with a dress made of sheepskin. It stank of body odor and dead animals. She wondered who might've been in this outfit before her and if she was still alive.

Rita understood resisting these women would be useless. She let them bring her outside the hogan where they tied her to a pole near a smoky fire and dispersed.

Her eyes wide with terror, Rita watched as men with hideous monsters painted on their bare chests, wearing black masks with bulging yellow eyes, surrounded her.

Passing a bucket, they drank deeply and howled to the night sky. They whooped and danced with wild, menacing motions and in her face they shook rattles made of skulls. Rita's stomach lurched with fear.

When the dancing and shouting stopped, an ominous silence filled the air.

Rita sensed something approach. She thought she heard hissing. The hissing grew louder and now she heard dragging and slithering. She tried to see what was creating the sounds but the flames and smoke blocked her view.

The men began a low, rhythmic chant in time with their skull rattles. Rita felt something at her feet. She screamed and struggled to kick it away, but her feet were bound to the pole. Her eyes popped as she looked down. A giant lizard nipped her bare toes. Fear paralyzed her as the lizard clawed its way up her body, its tongue flickering as it climbed. Its claws pressed into her flesh.

When it reached her neck, she could feel its hot breath. Fearing it would bite her face, she turned her head away. The creature breathed indistinguishable words into her ear. She twisted her head to see the face of Esadowa. He was covered in a lizard skin costume. His claws pressed deeply into her skin as he laughed a crazy, evil laugh. Quaking with horror, Rita screamed and fell into blackness.

Rita's eyes fluttered. She was relieved to be alive after the horrendous ritual. She tried to open her eyes but the glare of intense afternoon sun was too strong. Still tied the post, her muscles ached from being bound all night. Her scorched skin was blistered and she suffered from claw scratches.

Rita struggled to release herself from the ropes, but they were too tight. She assumed they her left to die in the scalding sun.

Several hours passed. Rita, half-conscious, was grateful to see the young woman arrive to free her and help her back to their hogan. She gave her water, after which, Rita passed out.

That night, Rita regained consciousness to see everyone asleep. She wondered if they had given her the Death Sickness. The slightest movement caused her excruciating pain, but at least she was alive.

I know I'll never be able to survive another night like that. I must get away. But how?

Despite the pain, she stepped with care over the bodies sleeping in her hogan and peeked out. Seeing no one, she headed to the corral to find Blaze. When she heard growling noises, Rita stopped and hid behind a bush.

She was shocked to see a dozen men dressed in wolf skins who barked, howled, snarled or chanted. Their eyes radiated blood-red in the light of the dying campfire. She witnessed them mount their horses and ride away, baying wildly. Rita mounted one of the remaining horses and followed them to Dry Lake Village.

In the full light of the moon, she watched with disgust as they ripped open the necks of sheep with their bare teeth. She found the gut-wrenching bleats unbearable as they tore into the flesh and lapped up the blood. In a foul, depraved sacrifice, they gorged themselves on the entrails of the mangled animals. Sheep's blood covered their wolf-like faces. Seeing them rub their chests with the sheep's blood, Rita felt her intestines twist and she vomited.

The 'wolves' mounted their horses and rounded up some of the Dry Lake sheep, cattle and horses. Rita wanted to wake Pahana to let her know what was happening, but being quite a distance from her hogan and she realized by the time she got there the thieves would be gone. Rita galloped back to the corral, tied the horse and sneaked into her hogan.

Lonely and desperate, Rita wished to confide in someone, but trusting anyone was out of the question. Besides, the women of the camp either ignored Rita or were hostile towards her. Her only hope was the young woman.

Dance with the Devil

Chapter 34

That night, while everyone slept, Rita fled to the horse corral. Thrilled to see Blaze, she hugged her neck, kissed and petted her. Rita wanted to escape, but she feared for Dakoda, so she knew she must develop a plan.

Rita waited to see if a raid was scheduled but nothing happened that night. She continued to sneak off every night to be with Blaze and keep watch, but she didn't see raiders again.

Several nights later, while petting Blaze, Rita heard the raiders approach the corral. Hiding, she watched their transformation ritual with disgust. This time they rode in a different direction.

Working her way back to her hogan, from behind she felt a heavy hand on her shoulder. In the moonlight, she turned to see an evil grin on Chunta's face. Rita gave him a defiant look and clutched her knife. But Chunta made no threatening moves. He stood looking at her. She refused to be the first to leave for fear he'd throw a knife in her back. She heard a low growl as he brushed past her.

The next day, Rita's nerves were on edge. She expected Esadowa to punish her, but this day passed like any other.

That night, as she prepared for sleep, a group of men barged into Rita's hogan. She assumed they were coming for her, instead, they ignored her and dragged the old and young women and all four children from the hogan. Rita saw the misery on their faces. Furious that she couldn't help them, she watched them force the family into Esadowa's Hogan. The screams and cries she heard coming from the hogan broke Rita's heart.

Rita waited hours for their return but sometime during the night, she fell asleep. The hogan was empty when she awoke. She found the young woman working in the garden. The cuts and bruises on the young woman's face and the faces of the children working with her brought Rita to tears.

Rita asked in Nedero, "Was this because of me? Did they beat you because I left the hogan?"

The young woman said nothing, but Rita could see in her eyes it was because of her that they suffered.

Seething with guilt and frustration, Rita knew she had to find a solution. She had to prove to Pahana that the Lizard Clan stole from them. Maybe then, Pahana would let her return. If Rita knew when they were planning their raid, she could warn them. But she had no idea when the next raid would be. Rita would find a way.

That night, six men in ugly masks barged into Rita's hogan. The young woman looked defiant but the old woman grabbed her arm as she rushed the family outside of the hogan. Rita panicked. She tried to resist, but the men overpowered her, dragged her outside the hogan and tied her to a stone bench. The six men danced in their ugly masks while two others forced Rita to drink a horrendous liquid. Gripped with terror, she remained conscious but paralyzed.

Yellow-gray tongues of fire rose through thick smoke. Rita heard yips followed by an anguished howl. As if appearing from the fire, someone jumped forward. Rita recognized Chunta dressed in wolf

248

skins. He crept around her on all fours, sniffing her and emitting threatening growls. He smelled like a wet dog and brandished two large, sharp knives. He drew his lips into an evil smile. Rita's body trembled.

Chunta growled. His spittle landed on her face as he danced and waved his knives. He slashed her with little cuts, danced away, then scurried back. He thrust his knives toward her chest, but danced away, only to return and slit her skin again. Rita tried to struggle, but couldn't move.

Esadowa appeared in wolf skins. His ghastly red eyes stared at her with malevolence. He spread his arms and looked up at the sky, howling wickedly at the moon. He spit powder in Rita's face. She knew it was poison. Now blind and paralyzed, she could hear the ritual as they continued to howl and bark and laugh like lunatics. She lay fighting to remain conscious, fearing if she passed out, she'd never wake, but the potion was too strong.

Dance with the Devil

Chapter 35

Rita opened her eyes. She had difficulty seeing, but she was alive and unbound. With no one to help, she crawled to her empty hogan, grabbed the pouch Dakoda gave her and gulped the horrid stuff.

Nauseous and dizzy, Rita sweat profusely and felt as if poison bubbled beneath her skin. Sharp pains cramped her stomach. Unable to tell whether alive or imagined, she screamed when she saw a ghost slither from a grave and stare at her with heavy-lidded eyes. She scrambled away when from its slack mouth, a reptilian tongue reached for her face. Her heart beat so fast she was sure it would burst.

Hearing someone approach, she tried to gather her senses. She lifted her head and saw a shadowy figure enter. *Was she hallucinating?* Her throat too paralyzed to scream, Rita froze when the person kneeled beside her and tried to make her drink.

Rita had no strength to push the jug away.

"You must drink!"

Her eyes focused to see the young woman's face. She drank the water. It tasted sweet and cool.

The young woman went to the entrance of the hogan and peeked outside. She returned to Rita and whispered, "They have given you the Death Sickness."

Her throat was raw, she could only whisper, "You speak English?"

"Yes."

"What's your name?"

"My name is Catori."

"Am I dying?"

"Yes. You have been sick for many days. Throughout the camp, your screams were heard. This is the way of the death trance. You will die in a few days."

"Is there an antidote?"

The young woman's expression was sad as she shook her head. "No, only a shaman can help, but it is too late."

"I took a potion. The person who gave it to me said it would protect me from death."

"I know of no such potion."

"What will happen if I don't die?"

"All who get the Death Sickness die."

Over the next four days, Rita slipped in and out of consciousness.

On the fifth day, Catori entered the hogan and said, "You look much improved."

"Yes, thanks to you, I'm feeling better," Rita said.

"No matter, you must continue to moan and scream and act sick. That will keep everyone from the hogan."

"Will it keep Esadowa from the hogan?"

"Yes. The Nedero's fear death most of all and will not go near a dying person for fear they will die in their presence and the evil spirits will enter them."

"Catori, if all the Nedero fear death, why aren't you afraid?"

Catori's face was bleak. "Death could not be worse than the life I am living. I would welcome it. I hate Esadowa. I wish to have evil spirits enter my body so I can kill him!"

"Why is this camp so different from the Dry Lake Clan?" Rita asked.

"It wasn't always this way. When my father was chief it was like the Dry Lake Clan."

Rita's eyebrows shot up. "Your father was chief?" She saw the pain in Catori's face and asked softly, "What happened?"

"My father no longer walks this earth. His son, my brother, Esadowa, killed him."

"Esadowa?" Rita was aghast. "Your brother...killed his father!"

"Yes. My father was Chief, so Esadowa killed him and became chief of the Lizard Clan. Esadowa has an evil sickness in his head and he likes to see people in fear and pain."

"Why don't the people overtake him and get rid of him?"

"He forces them drink chakumwa. It makes them crazy. They are addicted so it is easy for Esadowa to control them."

"Isn't anyone brave enough to challenge him?" Rita asked.

"All the men fear Esadowa, so they do nothing. He takes all women in the clan and many of the children in the camp are from him, yet the men follow him like sheep and will not disobey him."

Rita croaked, "It makes me so angry that Esadowa can get away with this."

"I am angry too." Catori glared into the distance, her face went rigid and her fingers curled into tight fists. "If I were a man, I would kill him. I hate him, but I fear him. Esadowa beats me and our children."

"You said *our* children."

"All the children in this hogan are from me and Esadowa."

"You and him? You mean your brother—"

Catori dropped her head and nodded. "I must go now," she said and left the hogan.

Rita couldn't stop thinking about what she heard. She knew Esadowa was evil but to kill his father and make his sister have his children was horrible. Her thoughts went to what Dakoda said about incest. *I must find a way out of this.*

The next day when Catori returned to the hogan, Rita asked her if she knew when the next raid would be.

"It will be the next new moon," Catori answered.

Her voice still hoarse from screaming, Rita said, "Perfect, total darkness!" She thought a moment and asked, "Catori, what would happen to my body if I died?"

"The hogan would be burned with your body inside and then a cleansing ceremony is performed."

"I've been thinking of a plan," Rita said. "On the day of the new moon, I'll slip out of the camp. You tell Esadowa that I died so they'll burn down the hogan. In the meantime, I'll sneak over to Dry Lake camp and tell Pahana that Esadowa will raid their camp that night. They will lay in wait for Esadowa. Then I'll dress like a ghost and scare Esadowa because he will think I'm dead. Do you think this will work?"

Catori shook her head. "I do not know. I hope it will work. If they catch you, your death will be a thousand times worse than the Death Sickness."

254

Chapter 36

The day to put the plan into action arrived. Rita sneaked from the hogan and took off for Dry Lake camp. In the meantime, Catori reported to Esadowa that Rita died. They torched the hogan and performed the cleansing ceremony.

At the Dry Lake Village, Rita rushed to Pahana's hogan and found her weaving. Pahana's back was to her as she said, "I'm so happy to see you, Pahana."

Pahana made no attempt to look at Rita or respond. Rita moved to face her. "Please listen to me. I have important news for you. The Lizard Clan will raid your sheep and your horses tonight."

She ignored Rita and continued to weave. Rita kneeled beside her and pleaded, "Please hear what I have to say. I have a way to stop the raiding. But more important, the people of the Lizard Clan are suffering. With your help, I can change that."

Pahana turned to Rita with narrowed eyes. "Why should I listen to Stupid Girl who does not keep her word?"

"You are a wise woman with a good heart," Rita said. "I know the Dry Lake Clan is the most important thing to you. I believe that when the Nedero suffer, you suffer too. Esadowa is evil. He is cruel to the Nedero people. He must be stopped! Please help me rid the Lizard clan of his poison."

Pahana looked into Rita's eyes as if to search her soul. After a long minute, she asked, "What is your plan?"

That night the Lizard Clan raided the Dry Lake Clan's village. Esadowa and Chunta, along with the other men from the Lizard Clan, feasted on the sheep and rounded them up along with much of the cattle and horses and were readying to leave when men of the Dry Lake Clan pounded their drums in the darkness and brought the confused raiders to a halt.

Dressed in black with her face painted white to emphasize her black-painted eyes, Rita stood on the back of a black horse and cantered out from her hiding place. In the darkness of this moonless night, she held a lighted twig below her face giving the eerie impression that her head was disembodied.

She moaned and shrieked and called to Esadowa and Chunta the words Catori taught her in the Nedero language. "You killed me," she shouted. "My spirit will torment you all the days of your life. My hatred will invade you and I will torture your bodies forever. YOUR SOUL IS MINE!"

Standing atop the horse and screeching, she charged at full gallop towards Esadowa. The terror in Esadowa's eyes exhilarated Rita. She hoped he was feeling the fear and anguish he had forced upon his people.

Esadowa neck-reined his horse to escape in the opposite direction.

Rita screamed, "Get him! Get him now!"

From the darkness, men of the Dry Lake Clan attacked Esadowa and the Lizard Clan with clubs and knives. A terrible fight ensued. In the end, Esadowa, Chunta and many of the Lizard Clan lay dead.

The following day, the Dry Lake Clan met with the survivors at the Lizard Clan Village. These discussions lasted for several days. Rita remained at Dakoda's hogan nursing the wounded leg she had encountered during the melee.

When Pahana and her husband returned along with the rest of the Lizard Clan, she told Rita. "The Lizard Clan is no more. Those who survived and wished to join the Dry Lake Clan have been welcome."

Pahana helped Rita outside the hogan where she saw Catori waiting. Catori's clothes were clean and she was well-groomed. Rita hobbled to her and hugged her. "Catori, you're beautiful! Thank you so much, I owe you my life!"

"You owe me nothing." Rita saw a spark of life in Catori's eyes. "Thanks to you our days will no longer be filled with terror and our hearts can be free. Now the Nedero can live as one again. It is I who will be forever grateful to you."

Rita felt a nudge from behind. She turned to see Dakoda holding Blaze's reins. Tears fell as she hugged her horse. "This is one of the happiest days of my life!"

Pahana said, "Rita, you are a young woman of good heart and much wisdom. From now on you will you be known to the Nedero people as Cloud Dancer, a name that is much respected by our tribe."

"Thank you, Pahana, I am honored. I will wear the name with pride."

Pahana added that there would be a celebration in her honor and that she would be welcome to live with the Dry Lake Clan as long as she wished.

Rita couldn't wait until she healed enough to practice performing tricks with Blaze. Although she was happy living with the Nedero people, she knew her life would not be with them. One day soon, she'd head for a circus.

Chapter 37

Ignoring the party guests, Mimi sat on a banquette sipping her third Sazerac in her friend Margot's elaborate chateaux. Margot plopped down beside her.

"Why so glum, Mimi? You're usually the life of the party."

"*Grand Dieu!* After the excitement I enjoyed with that ridiculous anarchist, Edouard Furieux, I'm more bored than ever. I can't continue to blow up buildings to keep from dying of tedium. There *must* be something else I can do."

Margot pouted, "Poor Mimi, what a dilemma, death by ennui."

"Very funny. Are you going to help me or not?"

"Hmmm, let me see." Margot took the drink from Mimi's hand and gulped it down. "Yes! I have an idea. Why not get married? You're getting long in the tooth you know. Maybe it's time."

"Married!" Mimi's sapphire-blue eyes widened in disbelief. "Are you insane? What makes you think a man could make my life more interesting?"

They each grabbed a drink from a passing waiter.

Turning back to Mimi, "Well," Margot advised, "If you married a prince or someone with political clout, you could rule behind the scenes. You always said you'd like to rule the world."

Mimi's voice took on a haughty tone. "It's true. I'd like to rule the world but not as the woman behind the man. If there is a man involved, he'd stand behind me!"

With a mocking smile, Margot said, "I can't imagine it being any other way."

Taking a sip of Sazerac, Mimi gave Margot a sideways glance. "Do you know of a man who might satisfy my requirements?"

"That depends. What are your requirements?"

"Let me see." Mimi tilted her head and looked thoughtful. "He must have enormous wealth and influence, but he must be malleable. Of course, he will acquiesce to my every wish. He mustn't be old or ugly and I won't tolerate a *roué*. I demand that he is devoted to me alone."

Margot laughed, "Is that all?"

Mimi looked confused. "What else would there be?"

"I suppose love is out of the question?"

"Love? Oh yes, it would be best if he loved me with every fiber of his being." Mimi noticed that Margot's gaze turned towards someone. "Who are you staring at?"

"Someone you should meet." Margot rose from the banquette. "Come with me," Margot insisted.

Mimi followed. As they walked together, Margot explained, "I will introduce you to my cousin, Nicholas Willensschwach Von Reichen. His father owns the Tintenfisch Iron and Steel Company, headquartered in Germany. I think he'll be perfect for you."

Intrigued, Mimi asked, "Why is that?"

"Because, my demanding friend, his father has holdings in many countries of the world and he knows most of the world leaders by their first name. Is that good enough?" Margot grabbed Mimi's elbow and led her to Nicholas, who had been conversing with his colleague, Aubert Bruneau.

Drawing their attention, Margot interrupted, *"Excusez-moi Messieurs."* Margot looked at Nicholas and said, "There is someone you *must* meet." She brought Mimi forward to introduce her. "Mimi La Fontaine this is my cousin Nicholas Willensschwach Von Reichen."

She looked at Mimi with a sly smile. "Try to be gentle with him," and strutted away.

His eyes grew wide when Nicholas turned to greet Mimi. He smiled in astonished delight, then uttered, *"Enchanté, Mademoiselle* La Fontaine."

Mimi assessed Nicholas like a piece of meat. He appeared more like a poet than a businessman. He stood tall and slim with wavy blond hair that reached over his collar. Sideburns to his jawline framed a hairless face. Long, blond eyelashes protected large, sad, dove gray eyes. A straight, rather long, thin nose kept him just short of handsome.

After judging him, Mimi offered Nicholas her hand. With the alluring look she used to melt the heart and resolve of every man who had interested her, she said, *"Bon Soir*, Nicky."

Mimi could tell by his reaction that Nicholas was hers to possess and she knew how to make that happen. She removed her hand before Nicholas had a chance to kiss it. She turned her back to Nicholas and said to Aubert, "I've never seen you before." She wrapped her arm in Aubert's. "Let's take a walk in the garden so you can tell me all about yourself." As they strolled away, she looked back and winked at Nicholas.

Dance with the Devil

Chapter 38

Rita loved living with the Nederos and was tempted to stay forever. But practicing her equestrian skills had reintroduced her to the thrill of performing. She realized that life with the Nederos could never fulfill her.

During her time with the Nederos, she acquired many skills, including the ability to weave blankets and make jewelry. Pahana understood that Rita wouldn't remain in the camp so she encouraged Rita to sell her wares and allowed her to keep her earnings.

The day came for Rita to leave the Nedero people. Pahana outfitted Rita with provisions for her trip, which included a new pair of blue jeans. Rita thanked Pahana profusely for her thoughtfulness.

Many of the villagers gave Rita gifts of remembrance. She was pleasantly surprised when Mahela, who she believed never liked her, presented her with a beautiful saddle blanket.

Sadness filled Rita's heart. Pahana, Catori, Dakoda, Keme and Ahana had each taken part in saving her life. Her eyes filled with tears as she hugged the kindest, most loving people she had known. They were her only family and she wondered if leaving was the right thing to do.

Just as she was about to change her mind, Blaze's whinny caught her attention. Looking past Blaze to the road ahead, the lure of destiny pulled at her soul. She mounted Blaze and galloped off.

Many of the villagers accompanied her to the road that led to Flagstaff.

It felt good to be riding Blaze again. She planned to head for San Francisco where she felt confident that she would find a circus or rodeo to join.

For several days Rita traveled without incident. From time to time, she would entertain herself by performing with Blaze. One afternoon, while in the middle of a handstand on Blaze's back, she heard applause and the words, "Brava! Brava!"

She was upside down when she saw a man standing on the seat of his wagon. She righted herself and halted Blaze. A man dressed in a swallowtail coat and top hat applauded her.

"Young Missy," he bellowed. "You are an equestrian extraordinaire. Your prodigious talents are exemplary. Your feats are even more amazing as you are at a tender young age more suited to playing with dolls than taming wild beasts."

Until now, the trail had been uninhabited. Being alone, Rita was wary and ready to put Blaze into a full gallop at the first hint of danger.

The man who spoke to her climbed down from his peculiar-looking wagon, the first of a three-wagon caravan. The first two wagons were embellished in an elaborate script: Doctor Van Sandt's Emporium of Exotic Delights. Painted on their side panels were landscapes of faraway lands. A third wagon, painted in bright reds, greens, and yellows, was intricately carved and highlighted with gold leaf.

The man approached Rita with a broad, beguiling smile. He thrust his hand to Rita for a friendly handshake. Rita's eyes narrowed with suspicion.

In a strong, showman's voice he announced, "My name, dear child, is Doctor Jules Alouiscious Sylvester Van Sandt, the third. And to whom may I have the pleasure of addressing?"

Rita looked him over. She noted a clean-shaven chin, long bushy sideburns that joined his equally bushy mustache and unruly tufts of white hair curling out from under his shiny, silk hat. His ruddy cheeks were chubby and a potbelly strained his brocade silk vest. When he smiled, his lively, affable blue eyes crinkled in the corners.

She liked him but wasn't sure she should trust him. Rita had never heard anyone speak like this strange man and that got her hackles up. "If you're asking for my name, it's Rita. Rita O'Reilly. You sure talk pretty, mister. Is that English you're speaking?"

Doctor Van Sandt leaned his head back and guffawed as he patted his belly "What a delightful waif—talented and with a sense of humor as well." The doctor raised his hat with a flourish and offered a flamboyant bow. "Well, Miss Rita O'Reilly, I am delighted to make your acquaintance."

Confused by the doctor's behavior, Rita thought she might be hallucinating from the hot sun. She asked, "Exactly who are you and what're you doing in the middle of nowhere, Mr…uh, what'd you say your name is?"

"My name is Doctor Jules Alouiscious Sylvester Van Sandt, the third, but you may address me as Doc Van Sandt, or Doc if you prefer. I am on a pilgrimage to deliver a precious cargo of various wares. Wares that are guaranteed to heal both mind and body to all the lovely and deserving people who live in the small hamlets and villages across America."

Rita frowned with consternation, "Heal the mind and body of the people of America?" She wondered if anything terrible happened while she was with the Nedero people. "Is everybody sick?"

"Are the people sick?" He chuckled. "What an adorable little ragamuffin. Yes, yes they're ill." Van Sandt's eyes sparkled with ardor and his arms waved with dramatic flair as if he laid all of America before her. "Their souls are like empty vessels starving for entertainment, and their bodies are weary from relentless toil and lack of proper nourishment. I offer them relief with exotic herbs and potions for their body and visual pleasures to delight their minds. The specialties I offer come from the far-off world of the mysterious Orient where, for time immemorial, they have understood Yin and Yang. How the body and mind must work together in balance."

Rita was awestruck. She scratched her head and asked, "Are you sure you're speaking English?"

"Yes, my dear child, I'm most definitely speaking English. Where may I ask is your abode?"

"My what?"

"Your place of residence?"

"Oh, I'm originally from Rimrock Springs."

"Rimrock Springs? How did such a lovely young maiden as yourself wind up in this vast wilderness void of adult supervision?"

"Huh?" Puzzled by his question, Rita looked blank.

Seeing the confusion on her face he tried again, "Why are you out here all by yourself, little Missy?"

Rita's face relaxed, "Now that's a question I understand. I guess you do speak English after all.

Well, it's a long story, but Blaze and me are on our way to San Francisco to join the circus."

Van Sandt's eyes flashed under a broad smile. "Circus? Did you say you'd like to work in a circus? What a happy coincidence! I was just thinking to myself that I need another bally act. I'm looking for a young person, such as yourself, to join my little troupe. The way you perform with...Blaze, did you say? What a delightful name for such a talented filly. Tell me, are you in possession of talents other than the equestrian ones you've exhibited?"

Rita dismounted. "If you're asking whether there's anything else I can do, well, yes. There's lots of tricks I can do with Blaze and I can shoot a pistol pretty good, twirl a rope, do some bronco busting and...well, I can sing and dance a little too."

"All that talent in one young maiden? I must say I'm impressed. You and Blaze would be a perfect match with my other accomplished performers." Van Sandt swept his arm broadly to show several unusual looking people standing in front of their wagons with their eyes on this young girl and her horse.

Curiosity overcame her reticence and Rita walked with Van Sandt as he introduced her to each performer. "Please allow me to introduce you to my show family. Meet the ever-delightful May and Ling Sisters, dancing Siamese Twins joined at their lower spine and hips. Although they share blood circulation, they share no major organs."

Two pretty Chinese ladies of about twenty years old were giggling behind their hands. They curtsied simultaneously and said, "Nǐ hǎo, Hello." They wore exquisite bright yellow Chinese satin brocaded garments topped with mandarin collars and a white

267

and gold dragon design down the fronts, specially altered to accommodate their joined hip area. Rita's eyes almost came out of her head as she uttered with concern, "Jees, I never saw anyone stuck together like that. Does it hurt?"

Van Sandt continued, "Don't fear for them, young Missy. Wait until you see them do their great Fan Dance. But I'm afraid their conversational skills are limited as they have not taken to the English language." He stepped away from them.

"Now, let me introduce you to Mr. Frump, our India Rubber man, who can tie himself into a variety of knots and manage to undo himself with ease."

Mr. Frump, a tall, thin man showed a pleasant smile and with long, cool, bony fingers, he gently shook Rita's hand. "Very pleased to me you, Miss O'Reilly."

Van Sandt turned to a woman standing beside him. "This lovely lady is Mrs. Frump. As you can see, there is no need to explain the obvious. However, she has many other invaluable talents as well." Short and rotund, Mrs. Frump welcomed Rita with a broad smile and a wink of her laughing blue eyes. The words "Pleased ta meet ya, dahling," worked their way through a thick, strawberry blond beard flowing to her ample waist and tied in increments with blue satin ribbons.

"This young man is our all-around helper, Mullo." A dark-skinned, short, slim young man, Mullo sported a budding black mustache. Dressed in Gypsy fashion, he wore corduroy double-fronted fly pants with stitching around the flap, a bright red shirt, a yellow silk scarf and a large belt. His embroidered vest had gold coins sewn onto it and a broad-brimmed hat sat jauntily on his head.

"This, my young friend, is Diabolicus the Great, our magician and clairvoyant." Diabolicus was dressed in a similar Gypsy fashion. Average looking, he had a dour expression and no distinguishing features except for his mesmerizing eyes. Diabolicus uttered no greeting. Instead he gave Rita a penetrating stare through his two black, mirror-like holes. Through those menacing eyes, Rita felt as if Diabolicus could see straight into her soul. The man gave her the shivers.

"And here is the dear mother of Diabolicus and Mullo, Madam Atokay Boszorkány, or better known as Madame Zorba, our Gypsy fortune-teller. She's a lovely lady but be careful! She loves to put curses on anyone who makes her cross, and it doesn't take much," Doc chuckled.

Rita thought *I won't bother her, I've been cursed enough to last me a lifetime.*

Madame Zorba, a short, white-haired old woman, had a large red pentagram-shaped birthmark centered on her forehead. Her face had the same dour expression as Diabolicus. Madame Zorba wore a Gypsy outfit with a long, brightly patterned voluminous skirt and an elaborately embroidered apron. Her blouse had puffy sleeves and a shawl covered her shoulders. On her head sat a silk turban-style scarf. Necklaces of amber and gold hung from her neck, large gold hooped earrings dangled from her ears and on her fingers were several gold rings

Madame Zorba looked at Rita as if assessing her. She surprised Rita when she grabbed her hand and looked closely at her palm. Madame Zorba frowned and uttered, "Hmmph, pech görl, bad luck showgirl."

Rita asked, "S'cuse me, ma'am?"

269

Doc said, "Don't mind her." With his face full of enthusiasm, he asked, "So, little lady, would you like to join our family?"

Thrilled, Rita asked, "You really want me to work in your show?"

"Most definitely, little Missy, I propose employment to you at the substantial wage of $2.00 per week. I will supply you and your filly with room and board. All I ask is that you entertain where and when I say. The entertainment will consist of those tricks at which you are so adept and whatever other accomplished feats you possess. What do you say, little Missy?"

"Did you say $2.00 a week! $2.00 a week for just doing tricks with Blaze?"

"Yes indeed, little Missy, shall we shake on it?"

"Well, I'll be. You bet I'll shake on it!" Rita spit in her palm and grasped Doc's hand with both of her own. She yanked it up and down as if she was milking an ornery cow.

"Whoa there, little Missy, I appreciate your enthusiasm, but I'll be needing this appendage for the show."

Per Doc's instructions, she tied Blaze to the back of his wagon and climbed inside. Rita couldn't believe her luck. Paid to perform on Blaze! It wasn't until she settled herself inside the wagon that she realized she would be traveling with the strangest people she ever had seen.

Chapter 39

That night, they camped under the stars near a small creek. Everyone performed their assigned chores, including Rita. She fed, watered and groomed the horses, settling them for the night.

Rita's mouth watered as the fragrant dinner aromas wafted through the air. She watched Mrs. Frump, who sat on a stool by the crackling campfire, mothering her cooking preparations. Rita's stomach growled when Mrs. Frump lifted the lid of a well-aged Dutch oven to check on a batch of browning cornbread and in large pot suspended from an iron bar, she stirred a bubbling stew.

"Mrs. Frump, can I help you with anything?" Rita asked.

"Please, call me Ida," Mrs. Frump replied. "No *maidelah*, everything is almost ready."

Rita shook her head in confusion, "Gee, don't you speak English either?"

Ida laughed, "Dahling, I come from a little Jewish town outside of Chicago and believe you me, this is as good as the English gets there."

"You're Jewish? Wow, I never met a Jewish person before." Rita approached Ida and stared at her head.

Ida asked, "What are you looking at?"

Rita shook her head and said, "I knew they were lying. When I was a little kid, some friends of mine said Jewish people had horns like the devil. I didn't believe it. Now I wish I could prove to them they were wrong."

Ida sighed. "*Ech, mishegoss!* Does crazies with their stupid ideas. If we ever go to that Rimrock Springs, I'll personally stick my head in their face and I will tell them *kuch in toches arein*…they can kiss my…"She waved a dismissive hand, "Ach, never mind."

Rita laughed at first, then frowned. "Gee, I'm sorry if I said something wrong."

Ida smiled, "*Nisht* gefilte fish, don't let it bother you dahling. I'm not surprised. That's probably not the worst lie you'll hear about Jewish people. *Gay maidelah.* Call everybody, the food is ready."

Rita gathered everyone. She helped Ida dish the food and she poured steaming cups of coffee. Everyone but the Gypsies, who took their food and disappeared, sat around the fire and ate their meal.

Ida said to Rita, "Don't mind them, they always sneak off together." Ida cupped her hand by her mouth and whispered, "There's something not kosher about those Gypsies. I don't trust them. They always seem like they're up to something. I think maybe—"

Ida was about to elaborate when Rita noticed Mr. Frump shaking his head as if to say don't start rumors. Ida conceded to her husband and smiled at Rita. "*Ess gezunterhait,* dahling. Eat in good health."

Rita took her plate and sat cross-legged on the ground near Ida. She dug into her meal with a hearty appetite. "Wow, this tastes great! Is it lamb?"

Ida replied, "It's one of my specialties." Her eyes twinkled, "It's called 'Bubble and Squeak'."

Looking up from her plate in horror, Rita screeched, "Squeak? What is this? Some kind of mouse stew?"

Ida laughed with vigor. Her beard shook along with her bobbing head and shoulders. Her entire body jiggled as she snorted and squealed. She pointed at Rita, "You should see your face!" Ida removed a handkerchief from her sleeve and wiped tears from her eyes and sweat from her brow. "Trust me, I wouldn't cook mice. They're not kosher, but maybe prairie dog—"

Rita's jaw dropped and Ida began to laugh again. After she caught her breath, she said, "I'm sorry, dahling. I shouldn't have teased you. I got the recipe from Mr. Frump. He says it's an old Irish recipe. A stew of potatoes with cabbage. When we're really lucky, like tonight, we got some lamb. How it got the name, 'Bubble and Squeak', I couldn't tell you, but I get such a kick from the name."

After dinner, Doc and Ida asked Rita questions about her background. She told them how she had learned to trick ride and how the Indians had saved her from certain death.

Intrigued, Doc Van Sandt said, "So that's why you look so much like an Indian. I must admit I was quite perplexed when I first observed your appearance. A young copper-haired, tawny-skinned maiden in trousers. My first impression was that you were a young Indian lad of mixed parentage. But a helpless young white girl, brave enough to escape from ruthless savages! Well, little Missy, that's outstanding!"

Rita bristled, "But Doc, I didn't escape. They let me go, and they're not savages!"

Unruffled by Rita's outburst, he said, "Now, now, my dear, don't despair. We must think of the show. I have my first assignment for you. Wait here."

Van Sandt scurried to his wagon and climbed in. Rita heard the clattering of metal and tossing of boxes and then a loud singsong shout, "Eureka! I found it!"

He exited the wagon holding a red headband with a lone feather attached and a fringed buckskin dress. He made his way to Rita and held the dress before him as if dancing with it.

"We used to have a bona fide Indian Princess in the show until the misguided young lass ran off with Ivan, the strong man.

"Stand up, Rita my girl. Now let's see. Yes, yes, this is good. Very good indeed." The doctor measured the dress against Rita's frame, "Hmmm, looks a little big for you, though. Dearest Mrs. Frump, would you be so kind as to use your formidable sewing skills to adjust the dress for our little Indian Maiden?"

"Indian maiden?" Rita didn't like where this was going. "Why do you want me to wear this thing? It's much easier to do my horse tricks in trousers."

"Ah, well, that may be so, little Missy, but you will need this outfit when you tell the story of how you were kidnapped by Indians and of your successful death-defying escape."

"Whoa! Hold your horses, Doc. That's not true. The Indians saved my life and I left of my own free will. I'm beholding to them."

Van Sandt sighed and put his arm around Rita's shoulders in a fatherly fashion, "I see it's time to give you your first lesson in show business." With an outstretched arm sweeping across the horizon, he continued, "You see little Missy, there are thousands of people throughout this marvelous land of ours whose lives are filled with drudgery. From the crude mining camps and rough frontier towns to sleepy villages and isolated farming communities, there are many poor people. People who sweat and toil week in and week out, with nothing to look forward to but more of the same. Their lives are barren and without joy."

Rita frowned and scratched her head.

He continued, "That all changes when Doc Van Sandt's Emporium of Exotic Delights comes to their little community. We provide them with healthcare for their bodies. Just as importantly, we bring sunshine into their shadowy lives with our uplifting songs, enchanting dances and spellbinding feats of magic."

She wasn't sure what he was talking about, but the pictures he made in her mind enchanted her.

"My dear Rita, can you imagine the elation our little troupe provides? We may offer the only entertainment they will ever have the opportunity to witness in their entire mundane lives. We put on a show for them that they will never forget. We're entertainers of the highest sort, and, as entertainers, we are like players on a stage acting out roles."

Rita's eyes widened. "You mean like real actors? I saw a play once when I was little. I liked it."

"Ah, so you'll understand that when I ask you to tell the story of how you were kidnapped by Indians and of your successful death-defying escape, I'm asking you to act role that will fire the imagination and bring a wealth of everlasting happiness to these poor souls. Don't you think this is a just cause? An invaluable service that far outweighs any little white

275

lies we may tell in the process of providing entertainment?"

Rita rubbed her chin. "Let me think this over. If I get you right, you're saying it's okay to lie to people because that'll make them happy?"

"Well, I wouldn't put it quite that way." Doc placed his hand on Rita's shoulder. "It's not really a lie if it's make- believe, and what we do is make-believe. Some people are worldly enough to know that it's not real and go along with it for the enjoyment. Others are more fortunate because they're transported to an imaginary place. A place much better than where they currently reside. So, will you help me make these people happy?"

Rita sighed, "I guess if it'll make people happy, I s'pose it's okay. But if it's entertainment you're after, then maybe I should tell you what happened when I was forced to live with the Lizard Clan, and how they turned into wolves and poisoned me with death powder."

Van Sandt burst with delight, "Egads! This is fantastic! What a find you are, a true diamond in the rough. Come, child, and let us sit by the fire. Please enlighten us with your exciting tales of danger and adventure."

Rita told them of her life-threatening adventures with the Lizard Clan, enjoying their delighted applause at her story's end.

Van Sandt rubbed his hands together. With a broad smile, he said, "Even I couldn't have invented a better tale than that one. This is most assuredly a crowd-pleasing saga."

Rita frowned. With irritation, she asked, "It sounds like you don't believe me."

Van Sandt said, "Missy, I'm convinced that you are an exceptional young lady and quite capable of most anything. Your veracity is of no consequence. It's only important that you convey your experiences with an enthusiasm that'll fire the imagination of the gills...er...the customers. Now I will turn you over to Mrs. Frump's very capable hands."

As she accompanied Ida to her wagon, Rita turned to see Doc Van Sandt kick up his heels and shout, "Hooray!" as he pranced away.

In the wagon's hanging lamplight, Ida hummed a Yiddish ditty as she altered Rita's costume. Rita enjoyed Ida's sweet and melodious voice and noticed how pretty Ida was. She thought it was a shame the beard hid most of her face. "Ida, can I ask you something?"

Ida was cutting the thread with her teeth, then said, "Certainly *bubbala*. What would you like to know?"

"Um, if I ask you a question about your beard would that upset you?"

With a dismissive wave of her hand, Ida said dully, "Ach, what does it matter? I answer questions about my beard all the time. Just don't yank too hard because it's real."

"Yank? Oh no, I wasn't going to yank it. It's just that it's so different looking from men's scraggly beards. I just wanted to know how you got it to be so soft and shiny." Rita rubbed her hand about her chin. "I was just thinking that if I ever had to have a beard, I'd want one just like yours."

Ida's eyes bulged, "*Oy gottenyu!*" She made spitting noises and said, "God forbid your pretty face should have such a *brokayh*." Ida's face softened, "Such *a sheyne meydl*. That's one of the nicest things

277

anyone ever said to me! A thousand blessings on your sweet head. But dahling, don't you worry. It'll never happen to you."

"Does it bother you much? To have a beard?"

"Sure, it used to. I was a bitter woman for a very long time. I have eight brothers and sisters. All such beautiful children you wouldn't believe. God only knows why I'm the only one with a beard. I had more hair on my face even than my *tatah*, my dear father. I'd pray every night to wake up and be just like my beautiful sisters. But it seemed the more I prayed, the more hair I grew. I thought I must be a bad person and God was punishing me. I was very angry and couldn't stand to be with my family. I felt that I shamed them. My family had been very kind to me, but the more they loved me, the more I hated myself. So, I ran away."

"Really?" Rita felt an unexpected kinship. "Where did you go?"

"Here, there and everywhere, until finally, I met my sweetheart. My dear husband loves me and my beard. If it wasn't for him, I would probably continue to be a bitter woman."

Mr. Frump sat on his bed where he read the newspaper. He took his eyes from the paper and looked to Ida. They smiled at each other with adoration.

Ida turned back to Rita and said, "He's such a *mensch*. He's such a special man who truly makes me feel beautiful. He says he would love me if I had two heads and two beards! So, dahling Rita, to answer your question, no it doesn't bother me to have a beard. *Nah maidelah*, your Indian dress is ready. Wear it in *gezunterhait*, in good health. Now it's time for sleep."

Rita watched Mr. Frump help Ida rise from her stool with the look of love in his eyes.

I hope someday someone will look into my eyes like that, she thought.

Dance with the Devil

Chapter 40

The next day, Van Sandt sent Diabolicus and Mullo to locate an appropriate space for their show, to give out handbills, to put up advertising posters and to achieve several other tasks.

A bright sun shone in a cloudless sky as the parade passed through the town of Jonesville, Missouri. Mullo led the caravan wearing a costume akin to Aladdin. His gold turban had a peacock feather attached, a multi-patterned vest covered a gold satin shirt that was tucked into red harem pants and pointy gold slippers completed the outfit. He pounded a bass drum with a magic lamp fastened to the top.

Doc's wagon followed. He stood and waved, shouting, "Sunset, my friends! Come sunset to see the fantastic, the delightful, and the most amazing adventure of a lifetime!"

A crowd gathered along the route. Men waved their hats, women waved their handkerchiefs and children shouted with joy. Wearing her Indian garb, Rita smiled and waved as she sat next to Doc. She heard steam-whistled tunes blaring from the back of their wagon where Diabolicus played the calliope.

The Siamese twins drove the next wagon. May faced the crowd to the left and Ling faced to the right, waving, smiling and shouting, "Nǐ Hǎo!" Behind their wagon, Mr. Frump performed handstands and various calisthenics.

Driving the last wagon, Madam Zorba held the reins in one hand and shook a tambourine with the other.

At the end of town, the caravan came to a halt. The rest of the day they prepared for the show. As if by magic, the wagons transformed into a stage with a canvas curtain depicting scenes of the mysterious Orient and a runway leading to the audience.

At dusk, they lit the stage with kerosene pan torches. The curtain remained drawn. Diabolicus stood at the gate, keeping a lookout for trespassers, as he collected twenty-five cents a head and provided each customer with a numbered ticket stub.

Mullo set incense to burn in various places. The sweet and pungent aromas added to the Oriental atmosphere. Mullo climbed onto the stage where he paraded and banged a hand-held gong to get the attention of the audience and signal Doc the crowd was large and ready.

Doc leaped through the curtains with arms wide. In a barker's voice, he shouted, "Alagazam! Alagazam! Welcome to all you fine folks. Welcome to Doc Jules Alouiscious Sylvester Van Sandt the third's Emporium of Exotic Delights." He waved his arms and continued, "Gather 'round fine people, closer. Yes! Come closer still. Don't be afraid. You have much to see and hear and I don't want you to miss one itty, bitty little thing."

The crowd listened intently to Van Sandt as they stepped forward.

"Welcome to The Emporium of Exotic Delights, where wondrous pleasures are yours to behold. I have spices to titillate your appetites and potions to heal you. Yes, folks, I will heal your ills. Those of you who are in constant pain and those of you who are dying, I have the cure. Do you have a toothache? A headache? Gout or female troubles? I will cure you. I've traveled the world and bring to you ancient potions known only in the exotic Far East. I learned the forbidden secrets of these potions from Huang Me Chong, a Chinese wizard. Yes, my friends, from a Chinese wizard!"

Mullo struck an oversized gong hanging from a full-height frame with a wooden mallet. The clash of wood against metal reverberated throughout the audience.

Van Sandt scoured his audience with wide eyes. "As a lad seeking adventure, I stowed away aboard a seafaring vessel that shipwrecked just off the coast of China near Tsingtao, on the Yellow Sea. I was the only survivor. Captured by Wizard Chong, I was forced to become his slave and assist him. I saw him cure consumption and neuralgia, diarrhea and diphtheria. I even saw him make blind people see and cripples walk! I watched and learned and practiced in secret. When I knew all I needed to know, I escaped! But he put a curse on me. If ever I am to reveal the secret ingredients of these potions, I will die a most excruciating death!"

The audience gasped and jabbered amongst themselves.

"Yes, my good people. It is my desire…nay…my sacred duty to offer you the benefits of these wonderful remedies. As a man of medicine, I have given my oath to restore your health and zest for life. In addition, I will present to you entertainment as you have never before experienced. Your eyes will be amazed and your ears will be astounded. You will tell your children and your children's children of the happy experiences you've witnessed today.

"And, if that's not enough, I have a wonderful surprise for you. Yes, my dear friends. Look in your hand to see the ticket you were given upon entry. This ticket is an opportunity for you. Yes, the opportunity of a lifetime for one very lucky person. A lucky person who will win...THIS!" With an extended arm, Doc turned toward the curtain.

Mullo came from behind the curtain carrying a large green velvet bag and a small folding table. He placed the table in front of Doc, put the bag on the table and retreated.

Doc beamed, "By staying until the end of the show, ladies and gentlemen, not only will you delight in the pleasures of skilled entertainers, not only will you benefit from my life-giving potions, but one very fortunate individual will win this bag of—" Doc opened the bag and fished his fingers around inside.

The crowd gasped to see him pull a fist full of shiny silver dollars from the bag. He let them slip through his fingers and spill onto the table and to the floor.

"Yes, my friends! One hundred silver dollars will be awarded to some lucky individual whose number is randomly selected at the end of the show. Be sure to hold fast to your ticket stubs, as they will be worth one hundred silver dollars to one of you." Doc looked out to the eager faces in the crowd and pointed to several individuals. "It could be you...or you...or maybe you, my friend."

The crowd buzzed with excitement.

Mullo appeared and gathered the coins, leaving a few on the table, and putting the rest in the bag. He moved the table to a spot where the bag would remain in the view of the audience.

Van Sandt shouted, "Ladies and gentlemen, please may I have your attention! I have one more surprise for you before I present the entertainment portion of the show."

The crowd hushed.

Doc pointed to Madame Zorba's wagon. "Direct your attention to the wagon on your left. This is the wagon of Madame Zorba. Madame Zorba is a gypsy woman, but not just any gypsy woman. She is known as a shuvihani. She is rare indeed. Madame Zorba was born with a unique symbol on her forehead, a symbol of a pentagram. Only the most blessed are born with such a special sign. This symbol means, ladies and gentlemen—"

Van Sandt's face became serious as he panned the crowd and spoke as if he were exposing a great secret, "She has the gift of second sight. Yes, my friends, second sight! Madame Zorba can see into your past and tell you your future. She can answer your questions. Will you be rich? To whom will you marry? Do you want to know what your enemy is up to?

"Her wisdom will give you the answers. For the tiny sum of one dollar—just ten small dimes—you will learn from Madame Zorba the answers to your most burning questions.

"Please, my friends, do not deny yourself the answers that may improve your life. Quickly now, form a line in front of Madame Zorba's wagon."

A group of patrons formed a line and eagerly handed their Morgan dollars to Mullo as they entered the wagon.

"And now, with no further delay," Doc announced, "it's time for the entertainment portion of the show. Ladies and gentlemen, I have the pleasure of introducing to you, The Female Bearded Wonder Extraordinaire." Doc started the applause and stepped behind the curtain.

Ida twirled her way through the curtain. She wore a frilly pink tutu and, despite her bulk, she pranced like a light-footed ballerina onto the stage. The crowd gaped at her luxuriant beard, plaited and entwined with fancy pink and yellow ribbons. She ignored the cruel laughter and standard insults shouted by the onlookers.

"I'd sooner kiss ma dog's butt than kiss that hairy freak."

"I don't think there's a razor sharp enough in this whole territory to scrape off that ugly mess a hair."

"How'd you get that thing? Was yo mama a buffalo?"

Ida broke into song. Her lovely voice hushed the crowd. After several songs, Ida curtsied and left the stage to fervid applause.

Doc appeared and said, "Now that's only the beginning folks. We have much more to show you so stay right where you are. Now get a gander of The Elastic Man of Rubber, our own 'Fillet Phil, the Boneless Wonder.'"

Mr. Frump wore a body stocking the color of his skin. He looked naked except for his black shorts. Mullo provided a drum roll for each stunt Mr. Frump performed, and a bang of cymbals as each stunt ended.

Bending his long, lean body backward, Mr. Frump grabbed his ankles and proceeded to roll around like a human hoop. He tied himself into a knot by crossing his ankles behind his head and holding his torso by his stringy, cordlike arms, turning himself into a human swing and continued to contort in various ways. He received boisterous applause and with one arm in front and one behind, he bowed his head to the floor.

Van Sandt returned to the stage and announced, "Stay right here folks. There's plenty more entertainment. Don't forget, I'm going to cure your ills and provide the lucky winner with a sack full of money at the end of the show.

"With no further ado, I have the pleasure of presenting to you Little Miss Rita O'Reilly. Miss O'Reilly, a young orphaned girl on her way to San Francisco to be with her elderly grandmother."

Doc removed his hat, placed it over his heart, and looked down as if in prayer, "Who since passed. God rest her soul." He replaced his hat and continued, "Our little heroine sat on the railway unchaperoned when ruthless bandits attacked the train. These fiendish assassins robbed and killed all those unfortunates aboard and shamelessly kidnapped this sweet innocent child.

"However, the fast-thinking, Miss O'Reilly managed to escape their vile clutches only to be lost in the merciless desert and then—.

"Well, better to have our heroine tell you the story of her frightful adventures with the terrifying Lizard Clan and how she saved herself and many others from certain death. Miss O'Reilly if you please..."

Doc made a sweeping gesture toward the curtain.

Rita watched the show from behind the curtain and applauded each act as enthusiastically as the audience had. When the Frumps weren't performing, changing outfits or otherwise occupied, they stood with her as she watched. But now that Doc announced Rita's act, she had a terrible case of butterflies. Rita had been through many things in her young life, but she felt making a speech in front of a crowd would be almost as harrowing as her other horrendous experiences.

Ida saw Rita's nervousness and whispered in her ear. Rita giggled. She cleared her throat, wiped her sweaty hands on her buckskin dress, straightened her Indian headband, and walked through the curtain onto the stage ready for battle. Once she saw all those eyes staring at her, waiting to hear what she had to say, she felt a lump in her throat the size of an orange. Rita faltered over her words and wanted to run from the stage.

At the sound of whispering behind the curtain, Rita turned to see Mr. and Mrs. Frump in the wings giving her a thumb's up sign. Ida's advice came back to her: 'Imagine all the people in the audience naked, I betcha they sure are funny looking without their clothes.'

Rita's confidence blossomed.

She orated her story with great relish. The amazed audience cheered her exploits. Flushed with excitement, Rita hurried off the stage to loud applause and ran to Mr. and Mrs. Frump. "Wow, I can't believe they actually liked what I had to say!"

Once again, on stage, Doc announced, "Now my brothers and sisters, from the wondrous land of Siam, where rubber trees are yanked from their roots by unrelenting monsoon winds, and where huge wild elephants and man-eating tigers roam free. From this exotic place come two very special young ladies, May and Ling.

"These young ladies are Siamese Twins, the 25th and 26th daughters of the King of Siam who, because of their disfigurement, were abandoned at birth. When I discovered them in my travels, they were malnourished and so sick as to be near death. My heart went out to these poor wretches so I nursed them back to health with my potions.

"Now, ladies and gentlemen, see for yourselves. The very healthy and talented May and Ling, Royal Siamese Twins are here to delight and entertain you with their amazing Fan Dance."

Doc turned his head from side to side as if about to whisper a secret. "But first, I must caution you, dear people. I hope you understand that they are from a foreign country where the customs and attire are completely different from our modest conventions. If you do not wish to see them in their scanty outfits, please, I implore you to cover your eyes.

"Alternatively, you may attend Madame Zorba's wagon, so as not to be offended as they perform for you, an ancient dance that is the quintessence of femininity and grace entitled 'The Heavenly Dance of the Divine Nymphs."

Doc extended his arm as he introduced the two young women, "Ladies, if you please."

May and Ling appeared on stage. Doc watched the crowd's reaction. He feared being run out of town for promoting lewd behavior. The crowd gawked as if scandalized at the outfits they saw. One woman screamed and swooned, caught, presumably by her husband, who fanned her face with his hand. Another man, most likely the town minister, left in a huff.

Doc smiled as he observed that most of the men in the audience grinned with delight.

Piled high upon their heads, the twins displayed various jewels and combs adorning their shiny black hair. Tassels hung from their short sleeves and colorful vests. Bare midriffs exposed a matching jewel implanted within their navel. Fans were tucked into the tasseled belt of their sheer gauzy harem pants and rings bedecked their naked toes.

Imitating Eastern music, Mr. Frump tapped a drum and Ida played the flute as May and Ling danced. They removed the brightly-colored fans with oriental lettering and simultaneously fanned themselves then tossed the fans high into the air, each caught the other's fan. After returning the fans to their belt they put their palms together over their heads with fingers pointing upwards.

May and Ling thrust their heads forward and moved them side to side in a motion that made their heads look as if they were separated from their bodies. Their hips gyrated in unison, and with their hands clasped, they followed with leaping and spinning. It was like seeing double. At the finish, they bowed their heads to the audience and skipped behind the curtain.

When the applause slowed, Doc stepped from behind the curtains. "Rita O'Reilly will once again appear before you, but this time she will perform equestrian feats of such great skill you will find it hard to believe your eyes. Once more, Little Miss Rita O'Reilly."

Eager to perform and relieved to be wearing her blue jeans, Rita made her way into the center of a prepared ring. While seated atop Blaze, Rita warmed the crowd with two songs. Following, she had Blaze stand on her hind legs and kick her forelegs in the air while shuffling left and right then turn in a circle.

While riding, Rita performed handstands and back-over flips, she jumped off and on Blaze's back and she dropped a handkerchief on the floor, then swooped down to pick it up with her teeth. With each trick, the crowd's applause amplified. They loved Rita, and she loved the applause.

Once again, Doc stepped out onto the stage and waited for the applause to fade before he announced, "And now for the final act of the evening, a magician all the way from Hindustan in the mystifying Far East. So, without further ado...please welcome...the one...the only...'Diabolicus The Magnificent!'

Rita didn't recognize Diabolicus now that he was dressed as a magician. He wore a tuxedo with a high-collared black cape and a false goatee. His turban had a huge fake diamond in its center and his eyes seemed even more black and mysterious.

Doc explained, "Diabolicus is in possession of rare powers granted to only an infinitesimal number of persons in a generation. He has the power of a clairvoyant who can probe the thoughts of others. To prove it, I will go among you, the spectators, and receive several of your articles. While blindfolded, Diabolicus will describe these articles in detail."

After confirming Diabolicus could not see through his blindfold, Doc went to the back of the audience and asked an average looking man to provide him with an article. Doc called out, "Diabolicus, can you tell me if I am standing before a man or a woman?

Diabolicus replied, "A man."

"What color is his hat? Speak out."

"Gray,"

"Can you tell the style of the hat?"

"A fedora."

"What am I holding in my hand? Hurry now." Doc held up his hand to show the audience an article and put a finger to his lips to keep it secret.

"A pocket watch."

"Do you know which metal? Speak loudly?"

"Silver."

"Of what maker is this?"

Diabolicus said in a thunderous voice, "American Watch Company"

Doc continued to make his way through the audience holding up various volunteered objects, asking questions and receiving accurate responses from Diabolicus. The audience murmured with amazement. At the end of the performance, the audience clapped and cheered Diabolicus.

After the act, Doc worked his way back to the stage and announced, "Ladies and gentlemen, now is the time you've all been waiting for. Tell me, my brothers and sisters, do you have arthritis or warts? Do you suffer from liver disease or tapeworms? Are you troubled by gout or halitosis? Do you seek relief from back pain or coughs and colds?" Doc paused for dramatic effect.

"Whatever your trouble, I am here to help you. To offer you the elixir of life that will save you from your pain and help you enjoy life again. Now, at long last, my dear friends, you will be cured!"

Doc clapped his hands, and the curtains opened. The crowd's eyes popped collectively to see an oversized chart of the human anatomy next to a skeleton hanging from a pole, jars of large, ugly tapeworms and other frightful, misshapen creatures. Doc used a pointer to lecture the crowd about the evils that Mother Nature can do to the human body, and how his elixirs can cure those evils. The crowd fixated on his every word.

"Now my good people, I will put my money where my mouth is. I will demonstrate to you the power of Doctor Van Sandt's Chinese Wonder Cure-All Tonic."

Doc picked up a clear glass of water from the table. "With this simple glass of water, I will prove to you that many, if not most of you, are needlessly suffering from catarrh, yes, catarrh. A disease that causes buzzing in the ears and affects your eyesight.

"Catarrh is caused by a hideous germ that enters into an unsuspecting victim and goes through his entire body, planting its evil seed. That evil seed, I'm sorry to say, brings forth to its host. the most dreaded disease, consumption!

"Yes, my friends, consumption, killer of man, woman and child alike. Many of you may have consumption growing within you now, right at this very moment!

"But there is good news, my friends! You no longer need to fear consumption because you will see before your very eyes that Doctor Van Sandt's Chinese Wonder Cure-All will instantly cure you of catarrh and, therefore, eliminate the possibility of consumption!"

Among other items sitting next to the jars on the table was a pitcher of water and several glasses. "Now, who will be the first to help me demonstrate that the poison lies within them? Come on now, don't be shy. I may save your life and all I ask is that you simply blow into this little glass tube."

He scanned the audience and pointed to a man in the front row. "You there, young man, you look the

293

picture of good health. I would appreciate your help with this quick and painless demonstration."

The reluctant young man pushed forward by his friends, made his way onto the stage. "You're a brave young man and I thank you for your aid. You appear to be a strappingly healthy young man. Do you feel healthy?"

"Uh, sure." The young man murmured. "I feel fine."

"Excellent. May I look into your eyes, sir?

"Sure."

Doc stared into the young man's eyes. "Hmmm. Now please sir, if you will stick out your tongue." The young man appeared embarrassed but obliged. Doc shook his head as he said, "Oh, too bad. Young man, how would you feel if I told you that you have most certainly fallen victim to catarrh?"

"Uh, I don't think so. I'm feeling pretty good."

"Of course, you may think so. Catarrh is insidious. You feel perfectly healthy until one day when it's done its work, you suddenly get a buzzing in your ear. Subtle at first, then the ringing starts. The constant, annoying, relentless ringing and before you know it you are dying from consumption!"

The young man looked doubtful.

"I can see by the expression on your face, you doubt my veracity." Doc declared. "No matter, proof is what you require. All you need do is blow into this straw. If the water remains clear, you are indeed the picture of youthful good health. However, if the water should turn cloudy, then my young friend, you are a victim of the insidious catarrh that will surely cut short your life. First, I will demonstrate that it is only water you will be drinking."

Doc poured water from the pitcher into two glasses. He drank from one glass and gave the other to the volunteer. Please take a sip and let me know if this is water, plain and simple water.

The young man took a sip. "Uh, yeah. I guess it's plain water."

Doc put a straw into the glass. "Now, will you do me the kind service of exhaling into this straw?"

"Uh…sure." The young man looked to his friends in the audience with a silly grin. He blew into the tube that rested inside the glass. The water turned milky. The audience gasped.

"Hmmm, just as I suspected. Well then, let's see what we can do about this." Doc took a bottle of his remedy and poured a few drops into the milky liquid. It turned clear. The audience gasped again.

"You see my friends, even those of you who are young and strong can benefit from Doctor Van Sandt's Chinese Wonder Cure-All Tonic.

"My young friend, I need not be a seer into the future to know what your sorry fate will be. I strongly recommend you purchase a bottle, or I cannot be responsible for the dire consequences most certainly headed your way."

The young man stood with his mouth hung open. "But, I uh…sure… uh…how do I get some?"

"Please see Mullo over there. He will sell you all you need."

Doc repeated the experiment again and again with other audience members, all with the same result.

He approached the foot of the stage and shouted, "Come, my friends and be cured. What other brave soul wants to live a painless and happy existence? Who of you is in pain? Who wants to be cured?"

No one stirred until one man at the back of the crowd shouted, "Me! I'm in pain Doctor Van Sandt and I need your help!" The man was of middle age, yet his body stooped forward. His movements were slow and looked painful, as he leaned heavily on his cane. The sympathetic crowd parted and let him make his way to the stage.

Doc helped him onto the stage and looked him over. He felt the curvature of the man's spine. "My poor man, have you had this ailment since you were a child?" The man nodded. "Did it get worse as you grew to be a man, and worse still as the years crept upon you?" Again, the man nodded. "My poor man, I can see you have a condition called Idiopathic Scoliosis.

"My friend, today is your lucky day! Doctor Van Sandt's Chinese Wonder Ointment will cure you!"

Doc grabbed a tube of ointment from the table and raised it in the air with a flourish. "My friend, let me loosen your shirt."

Doc pulled the man's shirt out of his trousers and rubbed some ointment on his bent over back. "Do you feel the power of the ointment as it warms your back? Do you feel it working its magic wonder?"

The man said nothing. In a few minutes, he smiled. "The pain, it's gone! I can't believe it, no more pain! Wait! I think, yes. Yes!"

The man straightened, slowly at first and soon he stood straight. He tossed his cane aside and took a few cautious steps. He marched back and forth on the stage, his back straight as a soldier. He grabbed Doc's hand and pumped it with glee, "Thank you, doctor, you saved my life! I can stand like a man. I can't thank you enough. Please, I want to buy some of your ointment. I got kids at home and I can see

296

their backs starting to bend too. Please, doctor, you gotta sell me some of that wonderful stuff!"

"Certainly, my good man. See Mullo over there, and he will sell you all you need."

The man ran over to Mullo and shouted, "I'll take ten dollars' worth." He jumped off the stage yelling to the audience, "I'm a new man, folks!"

Doc proceeded to work his magic with others in the audience, easing coughs, clearing up deafness and other various complaints until the crowd was chomping at the bit to buy every ounce of his Cure-All potions.

"Thank you all. I am pleased to have provided you with potions to improve your health and quality of life. Now, my good friends, this is the moment you've been waiting for." Doc clapped his hands, and the curtain closed.

Mullo jumped on to the stage. He walked to the little table and carried it and the bag of silver to where Doc stood.

"Containing one hundred silver coins, this bag will be presented to one very lucky individual. To keep the selection honest, I will have one of you, all strangers to me, pick the winning number. Which of you would like to help me pick the winner? How about you, young lady?" A handsome young woman smiled demurely and was helped to the stage by Diabolicus.

Mullo handed Doc a bag. Doc showed the audience that the bag contained pieces of paper with numbers on it. "Young lady, have I ever had the pleasure of meeting you?" The wide-eyed woman shook her head. "Well then, if you will be so kind as to close your eyes and select a number at random."

297

The lady tittered. She reached in, picked a number and handed it to Van Sandt. He showed it to the young woman and then to the audience. "The winning number is—." Mullo played a drum roll. "The winning number is…TWENTY-FIVE! Will the lucky person with number twenty-five on their ticket stub please come forward and claim your one hundred silver dollars?"

A man in the crowd jumped up and shouted, "It's me! I got it! I got the winning number! Hallelujah!" He climbed on to the stage, grabbed the bag of coins and shook the Doc's hands. The man turned to the audience, held the bag high, and shouted, "Bless you, Doc, I cain't begin to tell ya how much this will help me an' my wife an' my twelve children!"

Beaming, Doc replied, "It was truly a pleasure, sir." He turned to the audience and said, "And that, my friends, brings us to the conclusion of the show. We appreciate your patronage and wish you all good night and good health."

Diabolicus and Mullo ushered the crowd away and prepared for a quick getaway. The packed caravan was on the road within an hour.

Chapter 41

With several lit lanterns attached to each side of the wagons, the caravan made its way out of town, hurrying to cover as much distance as possible and to find an appropriate campsite in the dark of night.

Rita sat with the Frumps as Mr. Frump drove their wagon. Still pumping with adrenalin, Rita recalled her excitement during the show. Her bright blue-green eyes flashed in the feeble lamplight as the words flew from her mouth. "Gee, that was a wonderful show. I can't tell you how happy I am to be part of it and how much I enjoyed performing. I mean, at first, I didn't think I could make a speech. I'd rather have faced a raging bull head-on. But once you and Mr. Frump got me started it was, well, I couldn't stop talking! On top of that, I got to perform with Blaze! I'm so happy!"

Mrs. Frump said, "Enough already with the Mrs. Frump this and Mr. Frump that. My name is Ida and this mensch over here," Ida pinched her husband's cheek, "is Phil."

"Mrs., uh, Ida, I think you and Phil are great. In fact, everyone was great. But Doc, he's amazing. The way he cured those people, jumpin' Jehosaphat! I never saw anything like it! I guess he was right when he said he was going to cure the people of America. I had no idea so many people were sick."

Ida's chuckle became laughter and turned into guffaws.

Rita bristled. "Did I say something funny?"

Ida's body jiggled with raucous laughter until tears came. Rita frowned and felt foolish. Phil leaned past Ida to say, "Rita, don't mind her, she's just delighted by your innocence."

"Innocence? What do you mean?" Rita felt indignant.

Ida wiped her tears and put her hand to her bosom as she took a few deep breaths. She recovered enough to speak. "I'm so sorry *shaineh maidel*. Please, I wasn't laughing at you. It's just that you're such a rare thing, so innocent. Listen *bubee*, the Doc, he's a *schmeikel*, a con man. He's a fast talker who takes advantage of the *shmos* with his tricks."

"Tricks? What kind of tricks? I saw him heal those people with my own eyes!"

"*Oy*, my young doll." Ida waved a dismissive hand. "Ech! I hate to wake you up to the truth, but I think it's best you know what you got yourself into. Nothing you saw was real. It was all tricks."

Rita's eyes widened with wonder. "Tricks? But how?" Rita waved a dismissive hand. "Nah, you're joshing me." The Frumps looked at Rita and shook their heads. "But what about that man with that scoli…whatchamacallit, the bent back?"

Phil said, "That man was a shill. He got paid to pretend to be sick, just like the others who were miraculously cured."

Rita's face dropped. "A shill? So, this is all a racket? Like when crooks salt the mines they're trying to unload on to…*shmos*?"

Ida smiled sadly, "I'm afraid so, sweetie."

"So, Doc's just an old swindler. I guess he must be pretty good to fool all those people. How does he do it?"

Ida saw the disappointment in Rita's face. "*Ach*, I'm sorry I told you. I didn't want to hurt you." With an impish smile, she said, "But if you really want to know."

"I sure do. Tell me everything."

"All right, if you insist. Do you remember when Mullo and Diabolicus went ahead to set things up?" Rita nodded. "Well, in addition to finding a place for the show, they were also finding advance men. They pay the shills, and if necessary, provide payoffs to local officials for any required permits."

Rita asked, "Were all the cured people shills?"

Phil answered, "No, not all. Some of the audience wanted to believe so badly that they let themselves be convinced by his spiel."

"But what about the catarrh? I saw the water turn cloudy."

Phil said, "That's a gimmick. Unbeknownst to the crowd, the clear water was limewater. Carbon dioxide turns limewater milky, so when the gills exhaled into the straw, their breath caused the milky effect. Put some acid in vinegar, one of the "cure-all" tonic ingredients, and the limewater turns clear again."

"But Doc gave away the hundred silver dollars, didn't he?" The Frumps shook their heads. Rita's eyebrows shot up, "You mean the money was fake!" They nodded. "But what about the man who...oh, I guess he was a shill too." They nodded again. "But doesn't this make him a crook? How come he doesn't get caught?"

"He has to be careful," Phil said. "Did you notice how fast we got out of town? That's because he doesn't want to give anyone time to catch on, and by the way, you'll never see the same town twice. He doesn't want anyone to remember us."

"But what about you? Don't you think he's cheating people? If he gets caught won't you be in trouble?"

Phil started to respond, but Ida gently put her hand on his knee. "Dahling, you're right," she said. God forbid, if Doc gets caught, we could get in trouble. But it's a chance we take. After all, look at us, Phil and me, a fat lady with a beard, and my Phil, so tall and skinny and good at tying himself into knots. All we got is to be entertainers. What else can we do?"

"I don't know, Ida. I'm so confused."

Ida saw the discomfort on Rita's face and continued, "It's true we're working with *gonifs*, thieves. And although that stuff he sells might be strong enough to take the paint off a barn, it doesn't really hurt anybody. Who knows, maybe it even does some good. For me and Phil, it's *bashert*, predestined. Anywhere we work would be the same thing."

Ida paused and smiled sadly. "But you, Rita. You're pretty and smart and talented, and *oy*, so brave for such a young meydl. You don't have to stay around with this *shmegegi*. You can have a happy life. You can do whatever you want. *Ir farshteyt?* You understand?"

Unsure of her feelings, Rita took time to think this new found knowledge through. After a few minutes, she said, "I would like to join a circus with Blaze but right now the only thing I know is that I really did enjoy myself today. I like you both very much and even though Doc's just a fast-talking crook, I kinda like him too. So, I guess I'll just tag along for a while."

Ida smiled. She put her arm around Rita and kissed her head.

Although often difficult, Rita enjoyed the range of experiences they encountered along the way.

The Emporium of Exotic Delights bumped along the unpaved roads of the country from one small town to the next and, just as Phil said, they never stayed longer than one night.

They traversed through a variety of terrain, much of it beautiful but often hazardous. They forded swift rivers and sludged through the morass of marshy swampland. They made their way up perilous rocky peaks and around treacherous mountain ridges. They continued onward regardless of the difficulty.

Varied weather brought challenges as well. The withering heat of a tireless sun was only relieved by torrential rainstorms that created floods and mud so thick it halted transport. They contended with dense fog, hurricane winds and the occasional twister. But there were rainbows too, and magnificent sunsets and azure skies. They enjoyed the sweet aromas of floral bouquets and the trills and warbles of happy songbirds.

All of America was their backyard. Most nights hillocks or glens were their sleeping quarters, with stars for their blankets. Creeks were their laundry and their bathtub. Dinner was fish if there was any to be caught, or game to be had for the price of a well-aimed bullet. There were sweet berries, apples or peaches for the taking. A poke of greens gathered from the creek bed made a tasty side dish, especially

303

when prepared by Ida's skilled hands. Rita often said, "Ida could make an old shoe taste good."

Despite the hardships, Rita loved the camaraderie. Except for the Gypsies, who kept to themselves, everyone got along well and enjoyed each other's company. Ida taught Rita to sew, and when the ingredients were available, she taught her some Jewish cooking. Rita taught Ida Nedero cooking and taught Mae and Ling some English. The twins taught Rita the dances they knew. In addition to instructing Rita about potions, Doc took an interest in Rita's education. Math, chemistry, biology and history were among her studies. But what she enjoyed most of all, were the wonderful books he supplied, delighting her imagination.

Doc kept the caravan on the move. He always seemed to know the best places to perform, and they never had trouble. On occasion, when they weren't performing, they would spend a day in some town buying clothes, eating in a restaurant and even sleeping at an inn.

The days and months passed quickly. Rita loved performing and her skills continued to improve. The only thing troubling her was not having a chance to meet any friends her age, particularly boys. Everywhere they went, Rita saw young men, she even managed to speak with a few, but she could never get to know them. For now, the care and companionship she received meant more to her than anything, but Rita knew eventually things would have to change.

Chapter 42

As the caravan traveled from town to town, each stop was much the same as the other. Life continued to be uneventful but this day would be different. The show ended, and the crowd was disbursing when someone shouted, "My wallet, where's my wallet?" Then another man shouted, "My wallet! My wallet's gone too!" Several others echoed the same complaint.

Confusion mounted. People pointed at Doc and ran towards him shouting, "Get him, he's the ringleader!"

"Get that varmint and hang him from the nearest tree."

"Yeah, let's grab em. They're all crooks!"

An angry mob headed their way. The blood drained from Rita's face. Her head whipped in several directions looking for Doc. When she saw him, her heart leaped into her throat.

The mob dragged Doc, Mullo and Diabolicus toward a grove of trees. Over thick branches, they threw ropes. Rita's stomach dropped. The Frumps were fighting off some angry customers and the twins were hiding under the stage. Madame Zorba stood on the steps of her wagon flinging objects and spitting curses at the crowd.

All Rita could think of was to create a diversion. Looking around, she saw a barn in the distance. She hopped onto Blaze and raced towards it. Inside the barn Rita found lanterns. She turned up their flames and tossed them into the hay to start a fire. After the fire got going, Rita mounted Blaze and raced back to where the townspeople were ready to string up Doc and Diabolicus. Rita screamed, "LOOK OVER THERE! FIRE! HELP! FIRE! THE BARN'S ON FIRE!" She kept yelling until she heard other people start to yell fire, too.

The mob let loose of Doc, Mullo and Diabolicus and ran towards the barn. "Quick, let's git," Rita ordered.

The frightened troupe ran for the wagons and drove out of town as fast and as far as their cumbersome wagons could take them.

Late that night, with the horses exhausted and feeling relatively safe, they looked for a place to hide the wagons and rested. Doc told Mullo to take the first watch. Diabolicus was to relieve him in a few hours.

Inside his wagon, with their voices barely above a whisper, Rita asked Doc what happened. "Well, my young one, I couldn't say. Maybe they were disappointed with the show and wanted their money back."

Rita replied, "Have you ever been to that town before? Do you think this was about the phony silver dollars?"

In a melancholy voice, Doc asked, "How long have you known?"

"Since the first show."

"Really?" I'm surprised that you had never said anything."

Rita sighed. "I realized my staying or leaving wouldn't change anything and I love being with the show. So, what was there to say?"

"You're quite something, young Missy."

"What do you think happened?"

"Don't worry your pretty head about it. We have a long day tomorrow, just get some sleep."

"But—"

Doc said firmly, "Go to sleep now."

Rita tossed and turned most of the night attempting to sleep but could only think about what transpired. She gave up and through the rear window she watched the dark curtain of night lift to a drizzly gray dawn.

At the sound of pounding hooves and shouting, Rita peeked out of the wagon window and saw that a posse surrounded them. She watched in terror as they burst into the wagon, seized Doc and dragged him outside.

"Unhand me, you rapscallions!" Doc bellowed, "Let go of me, barbarians!"

Rita scrambled outside with a rifle in her hand. Fear and anger colored her words. "Leave him alone, you sons a' bitches!" She raised the rifle barrel to the sky and fired over their heads. Someone grabbed her from behind and twisted the rifle away.

"You bastard!" Rita kicked and punched the man who held her.

"Hey, give me some help here!" He yowled. "This little bitch bit me! Stay still, you she-devil!"

Rita fought so viciously it took three men to subdue her and tie her up. They tossed her into the wagon with the others.

The troupe had been taken to the town of Fredericksburg, South Dakota and put behind bars. The women were placed in one cell and Doc and Phil were placed in the cell next to them. The sharp clang of the metal door striking shut against metal made Rita cringe.

Phil seemed unruffled as he lay on his bunk puffing a cigarette. Ida comforted the twins who were in hysterics.

When Rita realized the Gypsies weren't in jail with them, she asked, "Where the hell are the Gypsies?"

Ida said, They musta snuck off in the night."

Rita scrunched her face in anger. "Those sneaking backstabbers."

Ida shook her head, "I told you I didn't trust them."

Through the bars, Rita looked at Doc. "What's going on? Why'd they put us in jail? Those town folk were awful angry at us. What'd we do?"

Doc said nothing.

Rita turned to Ida, "Somebody tell me what's going on?"

Ida said, "*Sha dahling*, wait, we'll find out soon enough." Rita wanted to ask her again but instead, she plopped down on the cot, folded her arms and pouted.

Several hours later, the sheriff appeared outside their cells. His wrinkled, sunburned face, looked annoyed as he announced, "I'm gonna question each of you one at a time, and if you know what's good for ya, you'll tell me the truth, ya understand?" He pointed to Rita. "You first." The keys jangled as he unlocked the cell door. "C'mon you, hurry up, I ain't got all day." Upon exiting the cell, she looked back. Her heart sank to see her friends behind bars.

He brought her to his office and told her to sit. Rita put on a tough face in an attempt to hide her fear that they'd send her to an orphanage.

"Okay, you, what's your name."

"Rita."

"Rita what?"

She crossed her arms and insisted, "Just Rita, that's all."

"What's your Christian name?" the sheriff demanded.

"What's your name Sheriff?"

"Don't get smart with me or I'll lock you up for good." He demanded, Now, what's your name?"

Rita puffed out air. "Rita Cloud Dancer."

"Cloud Dancer? What kinda name's that? Look you, I got no time for games. Either you tell me your name or so help me the whole lot of ya will be sent off to the county prison." He shouted out the door, "Hey, Slim, get the wagons ready. The prisoners are uncooperative so take them all to the county jail."

Desperate to save her friends, she blurted, "All right! My name's Rita O'Reilly."

"How old are you, Rita O'Reilly?

"I'm eighteen," She announced.

"Yeah right, you're no more than..." He scanned her face and body. "Nah, you're just a little girl, 'bout eleven, I'd say."

Rita boasted, "No, I'm not! I'm fifteen years old! Next month, I'll be sixteen."

"Yeah, that's what I thought," the sheriff said with a twinkle in his eye.

"You knew I wasn't eleven. You tricked me!"

He leaned back in his chair. "That's right. How'd you like it? Not fun, is it? That's how folks feel when they been robbed."

"Robbed? I didn't rob anybody!"

"No? The people in this town say different. How long you and that crook been stealin' from honest, hardworking townfolk?"

Rita lowered her brows in confusion. "I don't know what you're talking about. We're just entertainers."

"Don't act so innocent, kid. How long you been with him?"

"Gee, Marshal I don't rightly know. It must be almost two years now."

The marshal scoffed, "Hogwash, you been with that crook two years an' you don't know he's been pickin' every damn pocket he can git his hands on?"

"What do you mean picking pockets? Doctor Van Sandt's Chinese Wonder Cure-All Tonic is legitimate medicine. You should try some. I bet it'll improve your disposition."

"Very funny, kid." He smirked. "I'm not talkin' bout the rotgut he sells. Heaven knows that's bad enough. I'm talkin' about pickin' pockets. You're all in big trouble so you better fess up."

Rita couldn't believe what the sheriff was saying. "Honest, Sheriff, I don't know what you're talking about. I told you, I've been working with Doc for going on two years and I never heard anyone complain about their pockets being picked."

Taken aback by the Sheriff's accusations, Rita thought for a moment, trying to remember anything suspicious. Then she got angry. "Wait a minute. You're calling Doc a thief. He never picked a pocket in his life. He's no thief! He's a showman, a great showman, and he doesn't need to steal. Why're you trying to railroad him?" Rita's voice rose higher and became more forceful, "Why're you doing this to us? WE DIDN'T DO ANYTHING!"

"Awright, calm down. Slim, take this one back to the cell and bring me the ring leader."

The deputy took Rita's arm in a tight grip and escorted her back to the women's cell. As he dragged her off she shouted, "DON'T YOU GO CALLING DOC A THIEF. YOU'RE A DAMN LIAR! YOU GOT NO CALL TO—"

"Oh, shut up kid," said the deputy as slammed the cell door closed and locked it.

Feeling helpless, Rita stood against the cell bars and watched teary-eyed as the deputy removed Doc from his cell. She cried out, "Doc, don't let'm scare you into lying about yourself."

With Doc out of sight, Rita turned to Ida, "What's goin' on? Why'd they call Doc a thief? They said he's been picking the pockets of all the people in the towns we've been in! Why'd they say that?"

Ida puffed her chubby cheeks and let her breath out slowly. "*Oy gevalt!* Phil, did you hear this?"

Phil rose from the cot and stepped over to their adjoining bars. "Picking pockets? That's a new one. We've been with him for years and he's never been accused of that, unless—." Ida and Phil looked at each other as if they shared the same thought.

Rita felt clueless, "What? What're you thinking?"

Simultaneously, they exclaimed, "Diabolicus!"

Phil said, "Sure, before the Gypsies came, we often stayed longer than one night, especially in the plum towns. But let's not jump to conclusions. We don't know if there's any truth to what the Sheriff said."

Ida's beard swung as her head became animated with emotion, "If that Diabolicus—who I never

311

trusted from the day I met him with those weird eyes—if he has caused us *tsores*, a plague should befall him. His teeth should fall out. A thousand bedbugs should suck his blood from him. He should—"

"Ida honey," Phil cautioned, "Let's wait and see what happens before you use up all your curses, okay?"

Chapter 43

The Sherriff released everyone but Doc, who remained in jail awaiting trial. Rita and the others found a place in town to stay and visited him daily.

The circuit judge arrived, and the trial took place at the local saloon. Most of the witnesses, the jury, and his appointed defense attorney had had their pockets picked at the show, so the trial took less than an hour. The judge sentenced Doc to three years in the county jail and said, "Consider yourself lucky you weren't strung up by your scrawny neck!"

With tears in her eyes, Rita ran to Doc's side. She hugged him and said, "I'm so sorry, Doc"

"Hush, little Missy," Doc patted her back and said, "I'll be all right. Come visit me later. I need to talk to you."

Rita knew Doc was a scallywag but despite it, she loved the old windbag. As soon they would allow it, she went to the jail to see him.

"Doc, did you really pick pockets like they said or are those kangaroos railroading you?" She said with a vengeance, "Because if they are, I'll find a way to bust you out of here, I swear I will!"

He looked at Rita with affection. "Well, little Missy, although I appreciate your unwarranted support and unwavering enthusiasm, I'm a cad and have been one most of my life. I relished the remuneration provided as a flimflam man. However, more importantly, taking advantage of the unobservant and the gullible captivates me. I'm a showman after all, and what higher compliment to one's abilities than to enthrall your audience to such a degree that they are so totally engrossed in distractions that they relinquish their collective conscience and their dollars to me."

Rita felt perplexed by his words. "Doc, let me get this straight. You're telling me that you've been lying, cheating and stealing everywhere we've been? Don't answer me with your fancy words! I want the truth and I mean it!"

Doc sighed, "I'm afraid it's all true."

Rita didn't want to believe him, "Did those Gypsies put you up to it?"

"While I admit I hadn't considered it before Diabolicus joined our little family, I was quite enthusiastic about his idea. After all, he and Mullo did all the work as they distributed the elixir, and I got a share of the bounty."

Crestfallen, Rita asked, "Why'd you do it, Doc? Did you need the money?"

"Ah, Rita, I'm an incorrigible cheapjack." He replied with an element of pride. "I'm a man afflicted, unable to control my wanton need to be an inveigler and a crook."

Rita frowned with concern "Does that mean you're sick? Do you have some kind of inveigle disease? Do you need a doctor?"

He chuckled, "No, Rita my dear, there's no cure for my malady. Unfortunately, this is an illness that provides me with gratification and I have no desire for a cure."

Rita felt increasingly confused. "I don't understand. You're sick, and this sickness makes you do bad things?"

"Yes, Rita, this illness allows me to enjoy doing bad things. I've even taken advantage of you and the rest of the troupe, for which I have great remorse. Although, I'm quite sure I'd do it again under the same circumstances."

"Taking advantage of us? How?"

"Well, let's just say your talents are undervalued."

"Undervalued? In other words, you cheated us by not paying us enough?"

Doc hung his head like a bad puppy.

Rita scowled. "Doc, I don't know whether to feel sorry for you or to be mad at you. You've been taking advantage of us and for that I'm angry. On top of that, to do something so stupid like stealing. I can't tell you how upset I am! You could've gotten us all into serious trouble and you almost got yourself hanged! Now, you're going to jail for three years. Aren't you afraid?"

Doc replied in a soft voice. "You ask me if I'm afraid. Where there is no fear of retribution there is no pleasure in committing transgressions. My nefarious acts give me untold pleasure, but all of life's pleasures come at a price. Now it's time for me to pay the piper. It will certainly be a most disagreeable travail, but as the judge so succinctly stated, this is a temporary inconvenience compared to the everlasting fate I surely would've suffered in other lawless mobocracies."

"Do you think there's any way out of this mess? You're such a smart man…" Rita thought for a moment." Maybe if you tell them you're sick?"

Doc smiled sadly, "No, Rita, my dear sweet child, I don't think there are any options for me, but please don't fret. I'll land on my feet. Besides, it's the adventure in life that I'm after, and surely incarceration is an adventure of sorts."

"I don't think you're going to have much fun in jail."

"I'm quite sure there's no fun to be had. However, Rita dear, it's you I want to talk about. It's time for me to recompense for my felonious behavior. There's someone I want you to meet. His name is Devon Vascom. He owns a wonderful circus and I know he'd want you to be a part of it. I've penned a letter of introduction for you."

Van Sandt removed an envelope from his vest pocket and slipped it through the bars to Rita.

"Mr. Vascom is appearing in San Francisco presently and should be easy to locate. The name of his circus is Vascom's Big Top. I've known him for many years and I think this will be a great opportunity for you, little Missy."

Although she felt bad for Doc, Rita was thrilled by his words. "San Francisco! I always wanted to go to San Francisco. And to join a circus would be perfect! But what about the rest of the troupe? Surely, we could all go together. That is except for that varmint Diabolicus and his family."

"Rita, forget about Diabolicus, Doc said. "If I know him, he and his little group have disappeared and they won't be found. Please don't blame them for this predicament. Just as I follow my nature, they follow theirs. We cannot judge lest we have walked a day in their shoes."

Concerned, Rita asked, "But what about the rest of the troupe?"

"As for the Frumps and the twins, bring them with you to see Mr. Vascom, I hope he'll accept all of you, but most importantly, I hope he will accept you."

Doc fished inside his shirt. He removed a neck chain with a key attached. "Take this. It's the key to my strongbox. The strongbox is under the floorboards of my wagon. I want you to take all the money within it. Please share it with the troupe. Take the wagons as well, to sell or use as transportation. It will no longer be amusing to withhold your earnings since I won't be around to perpetuate my misdeeds."

"But Doc, won't you be needing money, in case you need a doctor or something?"

"Don't you worry about me, Missy." He said with a mock laugh. "I'm off on my next adventure. Fare thee well. May your journey through life be safe, and may your life bring you pleasure. But beware that the cost of your pleasure is not higher than the price you are able to pay."

With tears in her eyes, Rita leaned through the bars to kiss Doc on the cheek. "Goodbye, Doc. Take care of yourself. I'll miss you."

Dance with the Devil

Chapter 44

Rita banded everyone together and informed them that the plan was to go to San Francisco to meet Mr. Vascom and present him with Doc's letter of recommendation. She pulled out the key Doc had given her and brought them to the strongbox. Their mouths dropped when they saw the money inside the box.

Phil let out a long whistle and the twins gasped. Rita shouted, "Jumping Jehoshaphat!"

They laughed when Ida squawked, "Such a *gonif!* When a *gonif* kisses you, you better count your teeth!"

With the money divided equally, they began their journey, singing as the wagons rolled.

Rita felt as if hummingbirds' wings tickled her belly. *I can't believe we're going to San Francisco, where Momma and Poppa honeymooned! And now my wish to be a circus performer will come true!*

Mae and Ling were excited because they wanted to see their uncle who lived in San Francisco's Chinatown. Now that they had plenty of money, they hoped he would accept them as part of his family. Rita and Ida promised they would help them find their relatives as soon as they had seen San Francisco's sights.

Entering the city, the troupe found a livery stable where they had rented space for the horses and wagons. Rita gave Blaze a loving hug and whispered into her ear, "You get a well-deserved rest now, I'll be back for you in a few days." Blaze nodded and pawed the ground as if she understood.

Phil and Ida asked the livery's proprietor where they should begin sightseeing, and if he had heard of Vascom's Circus.

The proprietor's face was barely visible through his scraggly beard and overabundant eyebrows and a wooly head of gray curly hair. He had small round eyes that he kept shut as he spoke as if trying to hinder them from sprouting hair as well. His long arrow-shaped nose poked through his gray, furry overgrowth as his words came through slowly.

He wrapped his fingers around his suspenders and replied, "Guess it's plain as day, youze circus folk. Hmmm, well, lemme see…the circus…." When he scratched his chin, his fingers looked like little snagged animals trying to escape a wooly web. "Yessiree, the circus was heeya, bouts a month ago las' Sundee. Had a big parade with el-e-phants an' ever' thing. Ain't the first circus I'd seen ya know, but this one sure was a purdee fancy one. Anyways, they's gone now. Lef' a few days ago, I'd say. Don' know where, though. As for seein' San Francisco, Market Street's as gooda place as any ta start." Using his nose as a pointer he said, "Jus' hop on that there cable car, an' it'll take yer right there."

Phil announced, "Well then, to Market Street it is."

They thanked the proprietor, the ladies hooked elbows and the troupe went on their way. Chattering and giggling, they ran to the waiting cable car and hopped on. With a clang of the bell, they were off, craning their necks to see the passing sights.

They alighted at Kearny and Market Street and stood with wonder to watch the city pulse with life.

The abundance of shops, restaurants and steel buildings towering into the sky overwhelmed them. They heard street vendors cry 'Pea-nuts, fresh roasted pea-nuts, five cents a bag', mixed with the clang of streetcars and the clomp of hooves against the cobblestones as horse-drawn carriages navigated the busy streets. Everywhere, brilliant colors and sweet fragrances emanated from flower vendor's stalls.

Delighted to be in a shopper's paradise, the ladies hugged each other and jumped with joy. Before them were stores offering a tremendous variety of wares including jewelry, art, corsets, perfumes, hairpieces and even glass eyes. Rita stopped to stare at the toyshop window and said, "Oooh, let's go in here."

Phil spotted a bookshop and announced, "I want to go in there."

Ida pointed to a milliner's shop. "I would love a hat. I'm dying for a new hat."

Rita agreed, "Me too, let's go!"

The women hurried into the milliner's shop to see a saleswoman busy arranging a hat display. When she turned to greet her customers, it was obvious she had never expected to see a bearded lady, Siamese twins, and a cowgirl enter her shop. Her mouth twisted into a sneer. Sniffing with obvious disdain, she approached them. "What do you want?"

The ladies shouted with glee, "We want new hats!"

The saleswoman stared in horror at Ida, Mae and Ling. "You must be joking!"

The ladies looked at each other in confusion. Ida said, "She must think we're poor *schleps*. Girls, let's show her the *gelt*."

The saleswoman peeked into their money-filled purses. Her attitude changed to efficient and polite.

They rummaged through the shop trying on every hat they could get their hands on. Rita and Ida were in hysterics when they saw Mae and Ling trying to go in different directions at the same time to grab for hats.

Proud of their fashionable new bonnets, they continued from shop to shop, browsing everywhere and buying to their hearts' delight. After a while, they realized how hungry they felt and had to decide where to eat. Restaurants were everywhere. A French restaurant just above Kearny named Ma Tanta attracted Rita.

"*Bienvenue, mes amis,*" Ma Tanta said, in greeting to her patrons.

At the sound of her voice, Rita felt a sudden sorrow. This was the first time she heard French spoken since her mother had disappeared. Her heart ached as memories of her mother's love overwhelmed her. Rita couldn't keep from hugging a very surprised Ma Tanta.

Rita apologized. "I'm sorry. You remind me of my mother, who I miss very much."

Ma Tanta patted her back, "There's no need for apologies *mademoiselle.* I'm pleased to remind you of someone you love so much."

The hug helped Rita endure the pain of her loss and they all enjoyed a merry time. After the delicious meal of soup, fish, bread, coffee and dessert, they spent the rest of the day shopping, sightseeing and enjoying the cinema. After dark, revelry from saloons and music from the concert cellars danced in the air as they passed along the brightly lit shops on Kearny Street.

Exhausted after an exhilarating day, Ida announced, "*Oy* my feet are killing me! I'm ready to *plotz*. Let's find a hotel."

Phil agreed, "That's a good idea." He pointed, "Look, there's the famous Palace Hotel. What do you say we stay there?"

Rita exclaimed, "My parents stayed here on their honeymoon. Let's go!"

They proceeded into the Great Court entrance of the Palace Hotel. Their mouths fell open in amazement as they craned their necks upward. Seven stories of lighted balconies overlooked the carriage courtyard lined with palm trees and crowned with a frosted glass ceiling. Ida tugged on Phil's jacket and whispered, "I think this place is too fancy-*shmancy* for us."

Rita saw Ida's hesitation and insisted, "We've got money, I'm sure we can afford to stay here one night. Let's go in and take a look."

They were awestruck by the hotel's grandeur. Phil walked up to the desk clerk and said, "Excuse me, sir, we'd like three rooms."

The desk clerk looked up from his work. With a bilious expression, he said, "We have no available rooms, please leave."

They looked at each other and looked back at the clerk.

Rita didn't like the desk clerk's tone and barked, "If it's money you're worried about, we have plenty." Rita pulled some gold coins from her purse, "See?"

"Your money is no good here. Your kind is not welcome. Leave immediately or I shall call the police!"

Rita's body tensed with rage, "Mister, you don't have any manners. I think you need a lesson on how to get some." She started towards the desk with fury in her eyes. Ida grabbed her arm and whispered, "Rita he's a *shmendrick* and not worth the *tsores*. We're not here to end up in jail. There's plenty of other places. Let's try another hotel."

She fumed then calmed down. "I guess you're right, but I'd still like to knock his block off."

They were about to leave when Ida waved her beard at the clerk. She said with feigned sweetness, "Oh mista, *Ikh hob dir in drerd!*" Then she moved her ample bulk out of the hotel as fast as her feet could take her. Rita asked what she said to the desk clerk. Ida translated: "I told him to go to hell!"

At every hotel they tried, the same situation occurred. Rita blurted, "I don't understand. This is supposed to be a wide-open town, yet all these hotels are so snooty."

Phil asserted, "It doesn't matter what town you're in, it's just a fact of life that people are uncomfortable around you if you're different.

"We've been going about this the hard way. We'll just have to be smarter than they are." Looking at Ida he suggested, "That hat you bought has a veil, doesn't it? Just tuck your beard inside your coat and put the veil over your face."

The next hotel they entered Mae and Ling sat on the lobby sofa hidden by their bundles as Ida stood with her back to the front desk. Rita and Phil obtained three suites with no trouble. After they settled, they all went to Rita's room and ordered a bottle of champagne. They talked and laughed late into the night.

The next day, after a hearty breakfast, they ambled to the cable cars to spend the day sightseeing. It had been a wonderful but exhausting day. On their way to the hotel, Mae and Ling saw a Chinese vegetable vendor in a blue cotton blouse and trousers, with padded slippers and a broad hat shaped like a large inverted bamboo cone. Over his shoulder, he carried a flexible pole. Slung on either end hung two huge baskets overflowing with greens and fruits. The baskets bobbed rhythmically to his swinging gait as he hurried on his way.

From the expressions on their faces, Rita and Ida realized how homesick the twins were.

Rita said, "I promise, no matter what, tomorrow we will find your uncle." The twins broke into big smiles and thanked Rita, Ida and Phil for everything.

Dance with the Devil

Chapter 45

Early the next morning, desiring more sleep, Rita ignored the knocking at her door. The knock got louder.

"Rita. Rita, dahling, open up!"

Yawning, Rita mumbled, "All right, keep your knickers on, I'm coming." She opened the door to see Ida pale and anxious. Concern supplanted Rita's drowsiness. "Ida! Please come inside. What's the matter?"

Ida stepped into Rita's room. With a theatric hand to her head, she said, "*Oy*, don't ask. My poor Phil, he's got such a toothache, you wouldn't believe. He was up all night in pain and where's that *gonif* Doc when you need him? In the clink! But there's a nice man in the room next door to us. He said he's familiar with San Francisco. He says he knows a good dentist, a doctor...uh...McTeague. The man says he's good. We passed his office yesterday, over on Post Street. It's the office with that great big gold tooth hanging out front."

"Give me a few minutes to get dressed. I'll be right with you."

"You're such a sweety. A thousand blessings on your head. But no, dahling, there's no need to spoil your good time. Take Mae and Ling and go shopping today or to a moving picture show. Enjoy yourselves. Tomorrow we'll all go together and take the twins to their uncle."

"Are you sure you don't need me?"

"Yes, dahling, please enjoy yourself."

"I think I'll take Mae and Ling to find their uncle today. I gave them my promise and they're so eager to find him."

"Rita, bubby, listen to me. Chinatown is a dangerous place for young girls to be wandering around. It's full of *meshugana* Tongs and God knows what. They could kidnap you and sell you into white slavery. God forbid! Please, Rita dahling, don't go. Do me a favor and wait for me and Phil. We'll all go tomorrow."

"Ida, please don't worry." Rita insisted. "You know I can take care of myself."

"Rita, telling a Jew not to worry is like telling the sky not to rain. I would feel much better if you waited."

"If it makes you feel better, I'll take my gun along. How's that?"

"I would only feel better if you didn't go. Please, *bubbalah*, my stomach will bubble all day."

Rita smiled, "I'll see you tonight. Tell Phil I hope he feels better soon."

Ida looked up at the ceiling and said, "From your sweet mouth to God's ears." She kissed Rita on the cheek. "I know how you are when you make up your mind. I wish you wouldn't go, but since you're gonna go anyway, please promise me you'll be careful. I'm not going to breathe until I see you back safe and sound."

Rita looked forward to helping Mae and Ling find their uncle. She understood their desire to be with family. The mystique of Chinatown also fascinated her. Rita thought of the search as an exotic adventure and she couldn't wait to get started.

She threw on her jeans, boots, a fringed vest over her shirt, and a wide-brimmed hat. After a light breakfast, they were on their way to Chinatown. Having been advised that Chinatown was a small area, only ten or twelve square blocks, they assumed finding their uncle would be easy. But when they walked through the Chinatown Gate, the immensity of their task dawned on them.

Before them they saw a maze of buildings and wooden structures, streets and narrow alleyways, teeming with Chinese men—hundreds—perhaps thousands of them. Rita and the twins realized they had a slow, laborious task, but they were determined to succeed.

As they perused the crowded streets, Rita felt as if she was a foreign country. Buildings with balconies painted in greens and yellows and bedecked with potted plants abounded. Metal and canvas canopies jutted from storefronts displaying Chinese signs of gold, red and black. Atop most roofs, drying laundry hung from clotheslines. Notices and flyers in Chinese lettering plastered the walls. Lanterns of various shapes and sizes dangled from store canopies. Many restaurants and residences were in basements. The streets were vibrant with the rich rhythms of a lively, thriving people.

Some of the men paraded like peacocks in expensive clothing. They wore skullcaps of finely woven black silk with tunics brocaded in rich greens, reds and purples. From their necks dangled gleaming gold chains set with precious stones. However, most men dressed in plain dark cotton tunics, white socks, cloth shoes, pants and conical bamboo or felt Homburg-style hats. Long hanging queues were ever-present, regardless of dress or age.

The overcrowded streets bustled with a kaleidoscope of activity, overloading the young ladies' senses with colors, sounds and aromas. Along the cobblestones, they heard the bumpety-bump of rolling dollies and clomps of horse-drawn wagons loaded with a variety of goods.

Tourists bustled in and out of curio-shops displaying wares with prices ranging from pennies for cheap novelties to jade and gold works of art costing thousands of dollars. Outside the shops, every conceivable type of merchandise was displayed on shelves and in baskets.

Storefront factory workers hunched over their benches making shoes or cigars, sewing garments, or assembling brooms. Laborers made their way to the various markets carrying heavy wicker baskets hoisted onto their shoulders.

Rita and the twins went from shop to shop asking everyone about their uncle and spoke with the street peddlers, who seemed to be everywhere, but with no success.

Hours passed and lanterns glowed as daylight faded into evening shadows. Their quest seemed futile until they came across a man who was sitting on the steps of a building smoking a pipe. He was cadaverously thin. His face looked like wrinkled parchment, but he had a merry twinkle in his eye and a toothless grin.

Rita asked if he knew of their uncle.

He spoke to Rita in Pidgeon English and then to the twins in Chinese. He said he knew of a man who talked of his nieces, twin girls who were stuck together just like Mae and Ling. The man worked in a laundry near the outskirts of Chinatown. For a dollar, his great-nephew would lead them to their uncle.

Rita could see the excitement in the twins' eyes as they jumped with joy, but she was skeptical and wondered if the old man was taking advantage of them. Rita clung to her gun-filled purse.

The twins gladly paid the old man. He called a fine-featured young man of about sixteen and introduced him as Gim Chang. Walking toward the end of Chinatown, Gim Chang patiently answered Rita's many questions.

When they came to a street populated by dozens of barbershops Rita asked, "Gim, how come the men here wear braids, and why do they need so many barbershops?"

"This street is known as 'Fifteen Cent Street.' Chinese men regularly go to these barbers to have their hair cleaned, braided and oiled and their foreheads shaved an inch above the hairline. During the rule of the Manchu Qing Dynasty braids or queues, were imposed upon Chinese men. Should a man ever return to China not wearing a queue, it would be a sign of defiance, and he would be punished with severe penalties."

Finding it necessary to weave through the jam-packed streets, Rita wondered, "Is Chinatown always this crowded?"

"I'm afraid so. The Chinese population increased with the gold rush, then exploded with the building of the Central Pacific intercontinental railroad. We Chinese were welcome at first, but as jobs became scarce, white workers saw us as competition. Chinatown is the only area where we are safe. They have beaten several of my friends outside of Chinatown's borders."

"Gee, that's awful. Chinatown is the only place you can work?"

"That's right. I work as a guide for my great uncle." He smiled as he said. "My great uncle is a shady entrepreneur who promotes the reputation that the Chinese are evil, vice-ridden, wicked and dangerous to stimulate tourism in Chinatown." He laughed as he told them about how foolish tourists pay him and other guides to take them on adventurous visits to underground dens of iniquity, complete with the smell of opium, "false walls" and evil-looking, sword-bearing "bandits" lurking in the shadows.

"They tell tourists bogus tales of a mysterious labyrinth of secret passages reaching ten stories into the earth."

They stopped for a moment to watch Pekin Two Knife Man, who performed a sword dance, and they tossed him some nickels in appreciation.

Continuing through Ross Alley, Gim Chang pointed out that the street is known for its gamblers and pawnshops. Many cellars are serving as secret halls of vice. A visitor could lose his shirt gambling at games like pi gow, fantan or chuck-a-luck, or lose his mind smoking opium.

Gim Chang expounded that despite street names like Consort of Heaven and Virtue and Harmony, most Chinese were living in filthy, rat-ridden, tightly packed rooms with mocking names like the Palace Hotel.

They passed along Sullivan's Alley where Rita noticed scantily dressed women standing in provocative poses.

"Say, Gim, are those ladies' prostitutes?"

"Sadly, yes. Prostitutes are smuggled in from China, sometimes in padded crates labeled 'freight' and kept as slaves in cells called 'cribs.'

Rita frowned. "That's terrible! Isn't that illegal?"

"Not here in Chinatown. Although it is terrible what happens to these women, it's a necessary evil. After working 18 hours a day, six days a week, the workers eagerly flock to find solace, escape and relaxation. Deprived of traditional outlets and comforts, many of these men gamble heavily, visit their favorite singsong girl, catch part of the latest Chinese opera or smoke opium."

Darkness overtook them as they approached the edge of town. Gim Chang brought them to an old run-down laundry shack. He called out and a man appeared in the open doorway.

The man wiped his sweaty brow with his worn sleeve. His queue was wrapped around his head as he puffed on a tobacco pipe made from a tree branch. When saw Mae and Ling, the man shouted at them and waved his hand, chasing them away.

The twins cried and pleaded with him.

Rita whispered to Gim, "Why is their uncle so upset? Doesn't he recognize his nieces?"

He whispered back, "Their uncle says he doesn't want any more mouths to feed. He calls them worthless women and told them to go back to China."

Rita felt sorry for Mae and Ling as their uncle shouted and waved his arms with more vigor.

His attitude changed when the twins ran up the steps and opened their purses showing him the money they had received from Doc.

Gim Chang offered his goodbyes and left.

The twins told Rita that their uncle was so happy he wanted to treat them to a celebration dinner. He brought them a short distance to a restaurant where they ate, not in the basement with the other poor workers, but on the main floor where businessmen ate.

As they sat, it surprised them to see their uncle rush into the kitchen. He returned with a young man in a white apron, who introduced himself as Tommy Chin. In English, Tommy told Rita that he and the twins were cousins and their uncle was his father. His father was grateful to Rita for bringing his rich nieces. Now he would no longer have to wash dishes or do laundry. He smiled with pride at the announcement that they would use the money to open their restaurant.

Rita looked at the twins and wondered if they were happy that their earnings would not be theirs to keep. But they seemed thrilled to be part of their uncle's family. Rita hoped their newly found family would treat them well.

Tommy also announced that in Rita's honor, he asked the chef to prepare a special banquet. The chef prepared a feast beyond anything Rita could ever have imagined. As dish after dish was set before them in the center of the table, Tommy described each exotic platter. The prodigious colors and heavenly aromas of ginger, garlic, sautéed vegetables, sizzling meats and fish tantalized Rita.

During the meal, Tommy spoke of San Francisco and the plans for the new restaurant. They laughed at Rita's attempt to use chopsticks, and Rita laughed at her clumsiness.

The delightful banquet went on late into the night. Happy for the twins, Rita believed they would be safe and cared for, but it was late and she was getting sleepy.

Tommy frowned. "Rita, the trolley cars have stopped running. It is too dangerous for you to walk alone so late at night. My family will welcome you to stay with us."

"Thanks, Tommy. I appreciate your concern, but I'll be fine."

"Rita, I strongly advise you to stay with us. I fear for your safety."

She thought for a moment. *I have my gun and know how to use it and Ida will be worried sick about me. No, I must get back to the hotel.* "There's no need to worry, Tommy. I've been through many dangerous situations. I can handle myself."

The twins begged her to stay, but Rita insisted on leaving. She hugged the twins, who thanked her a hundred times. Then, upon receiving directions, she headed back for the hotel.

Rita was unaware of how treacherous San Francisco could be, especially in the dark anonymity of night.

Dance with the Devil

Chapter 46

Bordering Chinatown was a God-forsaken section of San Francisco known as The Barbary Coast, where gambling dens, lewd dance halls and saloons such as The Morgue and Devil's Kitchen thrived.

The Barbary Coast provided a sanctuary for murderers, thieves, gamblers, pimps, and degenerates engaged in every form of loathsome behavior. On streets with names like Murder Point and Dead Man's Alley, vice and crime were on constant display. Where debauchery, brutality, disease, insanity, misery, poverty and death were the norm.

It was here that Sluggo Enoch Muldoon made his living engaging in theft, mayhem and murder. Among his nefarious exploits, he was a *crimp*. Shipmasters paid him to shanghai sailors.

Sluggo used two methods of high jacking sailors. He either plied gullible sailors with free drinks laced with knockout drops or used his preferred method, for which he was proudly known, clubbing them over the head. Regardless of the method, the sailors ended up with a headache and empty pockets in the cramped, dank, dirty forecastle of a ship bound for ports unknown.

This night, Sluggo was in a surly mood. What should have been a profitable venture had turned disastrous. He had been arrested when he made the mistake of shanghaiing two undercover police officers. It was only his knowledge of the slimy back

337

alleys, with their vermin-ridden cellars where men, women and booty were smuggled, that enabled Sluggo to escape his pursuers.

To make matters worse, he lost his last cent at Fantan and he knew his bitch of a wife would box his ears when he returned home broke. Sluggo's rage boiled within. He needed to do something mean and ugly. When he saw a girl walking alone in the dead of night, he knew his luck had changed.

Rita clutched the collar of her coat tightly against the misty dampness that chilled her bones. At this late hour, the shops were boarded and the empty streets were dark with only hazy light from sporadic lampposts.

Except for the sounds of her boots clicking against the sidewalk, all was dead quiet. Feeling nervous, Rita tried to distract herself with pleasant thoughts of performing at Vascom's Circus.

When she heard footsteps from behind, Rita hoped it was just late-night stroller, but sped up her pace. When the footsteps behind her sped up as well, she knew someone followed her and was glad she had brought her gun. Rita glanced over her shoulder but could only see a sinister outline in the impotent lamplight. She ran. So did her pursuer.

Rita kept ahead of her stalker, but she couldn't lose him. Her lungs burned as she tried to put distance between them, but the stomp of his heavy footfalls closed in on her. Rita dodged into a garbage-filled alley and crouched behind a foul-smelling garbage can.

She yanked the gun from her purse and assumed she'd have the drop on her pursuer when he followed her inside. If he tried anything, she would shoot him.

With difficulty, she tried to control her heavy breathing for fear he might hear her. Terrified with anticipation, Rita shivered in a cold sweat. In the pitch-blackness of the alley, her ears were alert for the sounds of his footsteps.

In anemic lamplight, she saw a shadow of a man run past the alley. *Thank God!* she thought as she let out a silent breath.

Rita waited for what seemed like forever. She tightened her grip on the gun and rose from her hiding place. She stuck her head out from the alley to see if the coast was clear.

A painful blow to her head knocked her unconscious.

Sluggo smirked at the girl's inept attempt to deceive him. He was a pro and pretended to run past her knowing she would feel safe and peek out. So, he waited with his Billy club at the ready. Now he had his prey and could do anything he wished to her.

He hoisted Rita's limp body over his shoulder. With a wicked grin, he pictured in his mind the gruesome acts he was about to perform on this juicy piece of meat.

He carried her to one of his hideouts, a sleazy rat hole on the fifth floor of an ask-no-questions fleabag hotel. He kicked open the door, dropped Rita on the bed and lit the lamp.

"All the better to see you, my dear," he cackled. He threw off his jacket, poured himself three fingers of cheap hooch and brought the lamp closer to Rita's face. *Pretty girl*, he thought and imagined what she would look like after he carved the word 'bitch' into her face. Or maybe he should carve his name instead. This way, if he let her live, she would always remember him. *Ain't dat romantic!*

Sluggo sat beside her, sipped his drink and enjoyed a smoke. He stared at her helpless body and, as if reading a delicious menu, contemplated his choices. The more he thought about it, the more excited he became.

When he reached the point where his imagination wasn't enough, he climbed on top of Rita and began to rip off her clothes. His spit rolled down his whiskered chin as it drooled onto Rita's face.

Rita moaned. A sharp smack against her face brought her awake. She cried out in pain as the power of the blow jarred her teeth and caused a ringing pain in her ear. His hand had felt as rough as the bark of an old fir tree.

She couldn't focus her eyes. It appeared as if two drooling, unshaven, foul-smelling wretches sat atop her, tearing at her clothes. Her face flooded hot with anger, charging her body with adrenaline. Despite seeing double, she balled her fist and punched one of them hard in the jaw.

Off-balance when her fist connected to his face, Sluggo fell off the bed with a thud.

Rita jumped from the bed. She tried to run but she was too dizzy. She lost her footing and fell to the floor.

Her assailant sprung up and leaned over her. With a smug expression he grabbed her arm, yanked her up and tossed onto the bed. His fiendish eyes glowered as he hastened to her and hissed, "You're awake, eh? So much the better. You demon harlot, you're going feel every ounce of pain I give you. Doesn't that excite you? It excites me."

Rita swung her leg to kick his head but he grabbed her leg in mid-swing and tossed her across the room. Spasms of pain shot through her skull as it bounced against the wall. Rita shook her head to clear the cobwebs.

Her breath came in short, shallow gasps. He stomped towards her. His ugly face twisted with an evil grin and his eyes were glassy with anticipation, like a spider about to devour its dinner.

When Sluggo got close, Rita propelled her leg and kicked his groin with all her might. He screamed. His face contorted in pain and he doubled over, grabbing his crotch.

Rita bolted for the door, but Sluggo caught her by her hair and wrapped a powerful arm around her throat from behind. His hold was so tight she couldn't breathe. Her heart jackhammered when she saw his knife, the treacherous blade glinting in the lamplight.

"Know what I'm gonna do with this knife?" She smelled his reeking breath and felt his slobbery lips press against her ear. He rasped, "I know a thousand ways to give you pain, an' I'm gonna do every single one of them to you."

Close to passing out, Rita willed herself to remain conscious. Fear gave her power. She whipped her foot back and kicked him with her boot, using all the force she could muster.

He howled and loosened his grip to bend forward and rub his shin.

Rita turned and punched him using every ounce of her strength. He fell back against the wall and dropped the knife.

"You goddam hellcat!" He screamed, "I'm gonna kill you!"

Rita gasped for air and fled for the door. He grabbed her arm. She sunk her teeth into his filthy hand. The taste of his blood nauseated her. The blinding pain of his fist smashing her cheek forced Rita to release her grip and she fell backward.

Sluggo searched for the knife. When he bent down to grab it, Rita picked up a chair and walloped him. The force of the blow drove him against the front wall of the building.

About to escape, Rita froze when a deep, horrendous rumble caused a vibration to course through her body. The room shook violently throwing her onto the bed.

In an instant, the floor pitched and rolled and timber groaned. Sounding like nails being ripped from a wooden crate, she felt the building lift from its foundation.

Rita watched in horror as the brick and plaster of the entire front wall disintegrated. She saw her attacker's look of disbelief as he fell with it.

Rita stood in shock, not comprehending what happened.

The front wall of the building was gone. She saw huge spaces of lath work where the plaster had broken away. The loud vibrating rumble and shaking did not stop. Rita fell to the floor. The bed danced and objects bounced about in complete disorder. The gas lamp crashed and flames set the wooden floor afire. Staggering like a drunken sailor, she grabbed Sluggo's coat and tossed it onto the fire, putting it out. Alone in the darkness, the world crumbled around her.

When the rumbling and shaking stopped, she crawled to the edge of the building and looked out into the hazy blue dawn. Sluggo was dead. He had fallen onto a spike-like object that had pierced his neck. He looked like a speared fish with bulging eyes. Startled people ran from their homes to help him until they realized it was too late.

As Rita surveyed the destruction, the horrible noise and shaking began again. The entire city rocked and rolled. Chimneys crashed through ceilings, roofs caved in, brick walls collapsed onto the ground, wood-frame buildings became huge splinters and tall buildings swayed. Plumes of plaster dust clouded the air and jangling church bells played as if announcing a death knell for the city.

When the shaking stopped once more, she ran down the precarious stairway and out of the building.

Dance with the Devil

Chapter 47

Rita stared down at Sluggo. She should feel relieved he was dead, maybe even glad. She should feel grateful to be alive. But she could only feel numb as if she wasn't really there.

She turned to the building. The entire façade had fallen away, leaving her a view of the rooms within. It looked like a huge dollhouse decorated by a drunk. Broken furniture in disarray hung precariously close to the breach.

Rita viewed her surroundings. Downed light poles and church towers had crashed onto the streets. Broken glass, bricks and piles of mortar were everywhere. Stone steps had fallen away from their front doors, streets were cracked and elevated at odd angles, fires had erupted and broken water mains had begun to cause flooding.

Rita couldn't absorb the horror. *This can't be real. This must be a nightmare.*

Frightened survivors scattered through the streets, running in every direction. Their stunned faces reflected shock and betrayal. Their anger and grief seemed to be suspended as if they waited for the right time to scream and cry.

Despite the misery surrounding her, Rita looked at her torn, disheveled clothes and laughed. Her subconscious knew that something terrible had happened to her, something more than the earthquake. The pitch of her laughter rose higher and louder, uncontrolled. She felt herself unravel.

345

Again, the earth shook. She grabbed onto a pole to keep from falling. When the shaking stopped, Rita thought, *Whoa, there girl, you almost lost it. Get yourself together. You have to find Ida and Phil.*

Undecided about which way to go, Rita asked a man for directions. He wore only underwear and a homburg hat. As if he wore a his business suit, and she wore her finest Sunday dress, he smiled, tipped his hat and calmly gave her directions.

Dodging fleeing refugees, police, firefighters, barking dogs and frightened cats, Rita hobbled through the debris. Her thoughts were for Ida and Phil. *Please be where I can find you. Please be all right.*

With great difficulty, she made her way to their hotel. Finding the hotel in shambles, she feared the worst. Rita discovered Phil sitting amongst the ruins. "Oh Lord, no," she whispered. Phil held Ida in his arms. He swayed, weeping and moaning, petting her hair. Her bearded cheeks were wet from his fallen tears. Rita shouted his name and ran to him.

When he looked at Rita, his anguished face broke her heart. His voice cracked. He cried, "She's dead! My dear, dear wife is dead."

"Oh no, please no!" Rita's eyes filled with tears. She knelt and took Ida in her arms, "I'm so sorry, so very sorry." Ida lay ashen and lifeless. Blood oozed from a gash on her head. Rita thought she saw Ida's chest rise and lower and said. "Wait a minute!" She placed her hand on Ida's heart. "I can feel her heartbeat. She's not dead. SHE'S NOT DEAD!" Rita shouted with joy. Rita shook Ida. "Wake up, Ida. Wake up!"

Ida's eyelids fluttered. "*Oy,* stop with the shaking already. Are you trying to kill me?" Ida smiled at

Phil. He leaned over and planted a kiss on Ida, burying his face in her beard.

"Ow!" Ida touched her head, ""*Oy gevalt!*" I got a hole in my head the size of Chicago. Phil, dahling, be sure to catch my brains if they should fall out."

Phil helped Ida into a sitting position. "Don't move, Ida. We've got to get you bandaged up," Rita ripped a piece of her shirt and gave it to Phil to make a bandage.

"I always knew you were hard-headed," Phil grinned with relief.

While Phil bandaged the gash on Ida's head, she looked at Rita. "Rita, sweetheart, we were *meshugeh* worrying about you. Thanks to God you're all—wait a minute! Lemme get a good look at you. *Oy, Gottenyu!* Look at your face!" Ida gently pushed Phil's arm away. "That's enough already with the bandaging."

Ida turned to Phil, "Look at Rita. Her beautiful face!" Swollen, greenish-purple bruises had formed among the cuts and scrapes on Rita's face. "Your head!" Ida shouted. "Look at that bump! Did someone kanock you on the head?"

Phil asked, "Rita, are you feeling all right?"

Just above a whisper, Rita said, "I...I'm okay."

"Rita, sweetie, what happened?"

Rita said, "Never mind about me. We need to take care of you."

"Rita, please stop *machen a tsimmis* over me. Are you all right?" Ida frowned with concern as she cradled Rita's chin and examined her face.

Rita pulled her head back from Ida's hand. "Ida, please don't worry about me. I'm fine. Just shaken up, is all."

Ida shook her head. "I can tell you had some *tsores*. Is that why you didn't come back last night? You had some trouble in that *farcockteh* Chinatown? And where are the twins? Are they okay? Please, Rita dahling, what happened?"

"I'm fine. We found their uncle and he was so happy to see them he gave us all a banquet. The banquet was over very late and...I...uh...I got lost coming home. Something must have hit me on the head, but I'm all right."

With soft and damp eyes, Ida said, "*Shaineh meydl*, look at me, I know something is wrong."

"There's nothing to talk about. We need to get out of here. The fires are spreading."

"*Ach*, all right, already. I'll stop being such a *nudnick*. When you're ready to talk, I'll be all ears."

"Ladies, if you're sure you're all right, we better get moving. Ida, can you stand?"

"Where's my hat?" She turned to Rita, "We couldn't grab much but, for sure, I saved my hat."

Phil handed Ida her hat and said, "That's how she got in trouble. She ran back for her damn hat!"

Rita and Phil helped Ida up, but her twisted leg made it too painful to stand. Phil held onto Ida. Looking around, everyone appeared to be moving westward. Phil called to a man who rolled a desk on casters. He asked where everyone was going. The man told him they were heading to Golden Gate Park. He said, "There were no buildings there to fall on them and no fires."

Phil suggested to Ida and Rita, "I guess that's where we should head."

Ida was too heavy for Phil to carry, so he put her arm around his neck. They started to walk, but Ida was in too much pain.

Rita's eyes swept the area. "If we can only get some kind of...wait, there's a wheelbarrow!" Rita ran to the wheelbarrow. Disappointed, she said, "No help here. It's broken and the front wheel is missing."

Let me take a closer look, Phil said, "Maybe I can fix it. Do you see the missing wheel anywhere?"

Rummaging through the debris, Rita picked up a wheel and shouted, "Hey, maybe this is it but I don't think we can use it."

She handed it to Phil. "It's bent pretty bad but it'll have to do." Rita held Ida as he attached the missing wheel. He managed to jerry-rig some handles to replace the broken ones. "Let's give it a try." Phil wheeled it, but the front wheel made him go in a serpentine direction. "It won't be easy but we'll have to try." He brought the wheelbarrow to Ida. "We're going to put you into the wheelbarrow. Sweetheart, we'll need as much help as you can give us."

Phil backed the wheelbarrow to Ida. She sat as if sitting onto a chair. The handle side of the wagon shot out of Rita's hands and Ida landed on the floor.

"Ow! *Oy gevalt!* I'm such a *klutz!*" Phil and Rita ran to help Ida. Her hefty bulk and painful leg made it a struggle. It became even more difficult when Ida started giggling. The more they struggled to pick her up the harder she laughed. She began her standard body-jiggling laugh. Phil and Rita couldn't help but join in. The three of them, amid fire and destruction, laughing as if someone told them a good joke. They laughed until they cried.

After much travail, they managed to get Ida and their few belongings back into the wheelbarrow and went on their way.

Under less tragic circumstances, a bearded lady with a bandaged head in a Sunday hat, wheeled in a cart that could only go left or right would have been a comical sight. But as they left Union Square and marched up Market Street, they were just one strange sight among many.

They joined a macabre procession of dazed men, women and children from all social classes, carrying whatever bits and pieces of their lives they could save. Most staggered along looking like glassy-eyed, blank-faced mannequins making their way through a blizzard of cinders as voracious fires gobbled up their lives.

Phil and Rita pushed Ida's wagon as they plodded around piles of rubble. Through the billowing smoke, they coughed and strained their muscles hauling Ida over broken sidewalks and up steep hills.

The terrifying smell of escaping gas permeated the air. Fire consumed building after building. It seemed the devil escaped from hell to punish San Francisco. He blew his scorching breath over the hapless city. His fiery tongue lapped up clapboard shanty and stone palace alike.

Chapter 48

Golden Gate Park, a huge expanse of several hundred lush green acres, stretched west to the Pacific Ocean. It had once been an exquisitely landscaped Garden of Eden where happy children rode on a merry-go-round, lovers paddled canoes on Stow Lake, and genteel ladies sipped tea in the Japanese Tea Garden. It had been a place of serenity, where birds sang and bison grazed.

There was no serenity on this day. Thousands of desperate people arrived to find blankets spread out in every direction as if families were on an eerie doomsday picnic. Many people wandered, shouting names as they searched for missing loved ones, while others were on their knees praying. Mourners laments and the cries of the wounded resounded from every direction.

Rita and the Frumps made their way through this sea of misery in search of a clearing where they could rest. A woman waved and shouted at them, "Here! Bring your wheelbarrow over here. We'll make room." Phil waved and directed the wheelbarrow in her direction.

"Thank you so much," Phil said as he and Rita helped Ida roll out of the wheelbarrow. "My name is Phil. This is my wife, Ida, and our dear friend, Rita.

Speaking all at once, they thanked the woman and said how grateful they were for the invitation.

"You're welcome, I'm sure. My name is Greta Minnow. I used to work with circus folk, and I traveled with the Ringling Brothers Circus. I was a seamstress. My husband Herman was a rowdy. That's how we met. But that was a thousand years ago. Gee, it's great to meet some show folk. Too bad it had to be this way." Greta stood and waved her hand as she called out, "Herman, c'mere. Herman, look, circus folk!"

Herman, had been chatting with a fellow refugee when he heard his wife call, excused himself and made his way to them. He shook their hands and offered a big smile. "Pleased ta meet ya, I'm sure."

Greta introduced their family, "This is my son, Andronicus, Andy for short...he's ten. I named him after a lion tamer I used to date who saved my life once. This is my daughter, Annabelle. She's six. No circus relationship, we just like the name. You look like you have some sick people here. Boneless, mind if I call you Boneless? Reminds me of my circus days. Take some blankets. Andy, give the nice people some blankets."

Phil started to protest but Herman held up his hand and said, "We was lucky. We got outta our house in time and managed ta grab plenty a' stuff. My family's all here safe wit me an' Greta. A lot of folks ain't so lucky. In times like these, we gotta stick together and help each other. Ya know what I mean? You need blankets and we got 'em, so don't be proud. I'm sure you'd do the same for us."

Ida gushed, "A thousand blessings on you and your beautiful family. You're good souls. *Zei gezunt*, live and be well and, God willing, this craziness will end soon." Ida rummaged through her purse where she always kept goodies stashed. "Here, *kinderlech*...take some candy." The kids looked at Greta with pleading eyes. She nodded and they gratefully grabbed the candy, thanking Ida. "Such nice *kinder* you got."

Greta smiled at Ida, "Thank you. We sure appreciate all your good words and I hope you feel better soon. Is it serious?"

With a dismissive hand, Ida said, "Ech, don't ask. This is nothing, just a little booboo. A twisted ankle and a hole in my head. But ya know…life is such a strange thing. If I felt like this two days ago I'd be *makhen* such a *gevalt*, such a big deal." Ida put her hand to her face as she weaved her body for emphasis. "But when I look at all these poor hurt people…*ech*, so terrible."

With a pitiful glance at some of their injured neighbors, Greta nodded. "I can't believe this myself. I mean we bin living in San Francisco for ten years and had some earthquakes before and some pretty bad fires an' all, but this! This is the worst thing I ever seen in my life! I had a feeling somethin' was wrong when I heard dogs barkin' like mad last night. I said to Herman, Herman, I sez, I think somethin' bad's gonna happin'. Right, Herman?"

Herman nodded his head, "That's right, that's just what Greta said, sumpthin' bad's gonna happen…an sure enough, she was right!"

Greta nodded. "Say, you people must be hungry. Here, I got some bread. Take some."

Phil shook his head. "Thank you, but no. You have children to feed. We'll be fine, right ladies?" Ida looked longingly at the bread but agreed with Phil.

Greta continued, "I don't know when they'll be feedin' us so if you get hungry just say the word, 'cause I got plenty. Boy, this sure is somethin', ain't it? I gotta tell ya we was all scared to death, right, Annabelle?"

353

Annabelle finished the candy and sucked hard on her thumb. When she nodded her head, small bits of ash floated from her tousled blond locks onto her soot-covered dress. Greta continued, "Mark my words, the worst is yet to come. It's the fires. This whole city's a tinderbox. Right, Herman?" Herman nodded. "My Herman, he works for the city water department now and he sez there's no water. He sez the city's pipe system ain't adakit...ain't good enough to meet how much the fire department needs to fight a big fire, right Herman?"

Herman nodded and said, "It's true."

Phil agreed, "I think you must be right about the water. On our way here we saw huge fires and firemen looking frustrated when several hydrants had no water."

In the distance, they heard a slap and the wail of a newborn baby. Everyone turned toward the sound as if it was the most wonderful sound in the world. Greta smiled sadly. She petted Annabelle's head and said, "That's the fifth baby I heard bein' born since we bin here. No matter how bad things get, like Herman always sez, 'where there's life, there's hope,' ain't that right, Herman?'"

Ida said, "Your Herman is a smart man. With God's help, let's hope he's right." Everyone nodded in agreement.

Herman smiled with pride.

Greta and Herman asked the Frumps dozens of questions about their past and what they were doing in San Francisco. The Frumps were happy to have something to talk about besides the misery surrounding them.

Rita didn't take part in the conversation. She felt overwhelmed with remorse and frightened that Mae and Ling were injured, or worse. *I should've listened to Ida and waited. Maybe we would all be together now.*

Thinking caused her too much grief so she concentrated on the fire. Rita stood amongst a crowd of onlookers and stared in disbelief as a series blazes ravaged the city. She watched in horror as waves of intense heat whipped frenzied flames into scorching upward drafts that caused the fires to leap from one building to another. She hoped with all her might that the twins and Blaze were safe.

As the day wore on, a non-stop procession of refugees provided bits of gloomy news. No one knew what was rumor and what was true.

The earth shook and people screamed, but it was not an aftershock. It was the powerful force of explosives. The army was blowing up buildings to stop the fires. Rita felt each terrible blast of dynamite reverberate in her chest.

The bombardment made everyone even more nervous. Greta continued to ramble. She said her nerves made her talkative. Everyone was glad of it because it kept them from thinking about how frightened they were.

When Phil asked Greta if she knew what happened to Vascom's Big Top, she said, "Oh, they were lucky, they just missed the earthquake. They already headed north. They'll probably play in Oakland and Sacramento, then most likely on up to Portland."

At night, gyrating masses of smoke rose into the glowing red sky. Billions of sparks made the sky look like the Fourth of July celebrations gone mad. They lay on their blankets in fear as incessant concussions of dynamite shook the ground and showers of ash and hot cinders rained down on them.

The constant wail of ambulances and the clang of fire department bells as their horse-drawn steam-pumping engines raced onward, made sleep impossible. Startled by the sound of gunshots, everyone worried looters were on the loose.

Through the night, exiles shuffled their feet, half-choked by the hot cinder-filled air, dragging their few possessions as they continued to enter the camp. The news they brought kept getting worse.

Resolute firemen, police and soldiers fought the conflagration block-by-block and street-by-street with little success. With no water to put out the fires, their valiant efforts were futile. The earthquake had shattered the city's water mains, leaving them little choice but to stand and watch the destruction or make troublesome decisions about how to block its path.

Scores of buildings had been blown and others set on fire to check the flames. The city's magnificent library, holding over one million books from all over the world had been destroyed. Priceless art treasures had gone up in flames.

San Francisco had become a giant kiln in which lead bubbled, wood exploded and glass melted. All along the streets, they placarded dead bodies 'shot for stealing.' A critical water shortage ensued and the stench of death was everywhere.

As morning approached, everyone's eyes stung from the acrid smell of burnt wood and soot-heavy air. Hot, thick waves of heat accompanied the ever-approaching fires. The booming of dynamite increased in intensity. However, a semblance of order began to take shape.

Although there was barely enough water to sterilize instruments, an emergency hospital had been up at the park's main entrance. They also distributed tents and clothes. Squads of soldiers spent the night preparing breakfast for the multitude camped around them. Latrines were prepared and soldiers supervised a bread line. People of all ages, nationalities, and economic groups lined up. Even though the lines were very long, everyone waited their turn.

Ida felt well enough to line up with the rest of them. Everyone was grateful for the food and Rita was happy to trade her torn clothes for a decent, if ill-fitting dress. Rita stayed to help distribute food, while Ida and Phil returned to be with the Minnows.

The fire in the city continued to burn for two nights and three days before it hissed its last steaming breath. Buglers on horseback galloped through the streets announcing the fire was out. It seemed the entire city wept with relief.

It was as if the devil exhausted himself and breathed his last gasp, but he had one final joke.

Now that the flames were out, the sky exploded with rain. Rain, that had it come one day earlier, would have helped save the city. Now, It came in torrents, soaking the refugees as they clung together in leaky tents or under trees. The camp became a swamp, but it couldn't dampen the joy of the people. The devil had returned to hell and now they could try to piece their shredded lives back together.

Rita returned to the Frumps and the Minnows. They were jumping for joy and dancing in the rain, ecstatic now that they could leave. Rita said, "We can head north. I heard the Southern Pacific Railroad is running."

They asked the Minnows if they were leaving too. But Greta said no, they had made several friends in the park and since none of them had anywhere to go they would stay together for now and figure something out. They hugged and said their farewells.

Despite the destruction of their buildings, newspapers published and distributed abbreviated versions of the news.

Someone thrust a publication at them. Phil read it aloud. The headline announced, "IT'S OVER!" He read and that 3,000 people dead, 225,000 left homeless, 28,000 buildings were destroyed and the estimated property damage was more than $400 million. One-fourth of the city, the oldest and most densely populated part had burned to the ground. Throughout the rest of the city, thousands of structures were unsafe to use because of the earthquake damage. But the city had already begun to rebuild.

It was one thing to hear about the tragedy in the newspaper, but it was much worse for Rita to see the devastation with her own eyes. Eerie and heartbreaking emotions overwhelmed her as they trudged through the muck and smoldering ruins. How could this be the same San Francisco she entered a few days ago?

Her thoughts went to Mae and Ling as they entered what was once Chinatown. Aside from looters, there was no one to ask about the twins. With heavy hearts they left, hoping the twins had made it to a safe refuge.

As they made their way to the livery stable, Rita had a bad feeling about Blaze. She clutched her locket for comfort and tried to reassure herself that Blaze had a natural instinct for survival.

The small group gasped in unison to discover the livery stable had been crushed. A building had collapsed on top of it and demolished everything inside.

They approached to see the hairy old proprietor picking through the rubble. His appearance shocked them. Where once there had been a fleecy mane, now only a shiny, hairless egg-shaped dome remained. Scorched stubble appeared where his beard and eyebrows had been. Except for a singed nose and ears, he looked otherwise unharmed.

When he saw them approach he shook his head and said, "I'm awful sorry folks, the horses, they's dead. All of 'em. I was here when that there building fell. I ain't never seen nothin' like it. It happened quick. One minute, ever'things okay, then the next minute the building's on top of us. I went ta git some water for the horses or I'd be under that pile too. I came runnin' back but it was too late."

Rita caught her breath and clutched her chest when she heard him say, "I shot them jus' in case but I don' think they felt a thing. Then the fire started, I tried to save your stuff but I got burned real good and had to git out. Your wagons been destroyed too, but you're welcome to go through an' collect anything you think is you'rn. Like I said, I'm real sorry."

Ashen-faced, Rita stood rigid. She had registered nothing after hearing the horses were dead.

Ida put her arms around Rita. "My poor Rita. How can I tell you how sorry I am? Blaze is in heaven

359

now. Maybe your *Mamala* is riding on her right now."

Phil gave the proprietor some money, shook his hand and thanked him. He put his long arms around the ladies and hugged them. After a few minutes, he said, "It's time we left this town."

Their heads hung as they tread in silence towards the train station. They hardly noticed the tremendous crowds eager to get out of San Francisco. Rita had no idea how long they waited. Eventually, they were able to purchase tickets and board a train headed for Portland and Vascom's Big Top.

Sitting together, Rita rested her head on Ida's shoulder. Ida sang Yiddish lullabies and brushed Rita's hair with her hand. Rita began to weep, quietly at first, trying to hold back. Ida told her she must cry and keep crying until there were no tears left. "Rita, honey, there's nothing better than a good cry. Try it, you'll see. I think if everyone had a good cry on a regular basis, there'd be no wars. Come, *Mamalah*, give me your best cry."

Tears poured from Rita like a burst dam. She sobbed loud and hard. After a while, Ida said, "Now you need to get it all off your chest. Tell me what happened to you the night of the earthquake."

Between gulps and tears, Rita told Ida everything. She told her she had been attacked, how scared she was, and that she thought she would die. Rita told Ida about how guilty she felt for not listening to her. She said it was her fault the twins were not with them now. Rita continued to blubber for a long time until the tears stopped flowing and she became calm.

"Good *shaineh meydl*, good. Get the past out of your system so you can look towards the future."

Rita dropped off to sleep in the comfort of Ida's arms. When she awoke, Rita thanked Ida and said she felt better.

"Good. Now let's talk of the circus. We will need to make you a nice costume. I been thinking, how about an angel in a white dress, with a diamond tiara? I'll even make you wings. Whadaya think?"

Rita smiled, "It sounds wonderful, Ida." She hugged Ida and all three soon drifted off to sleep.

Dance with the Devil

Chapter 49

Excited to arrive in Portland, the troupe scanned local newspapers and learned of the circus location. Fearing the circus would leave before they arrived, they chose not to take time to freshen up.

The trio hugged and jumped for joy at the sight of the pennants waving above the circus tents.

They hastened to a red wagon with a painted Ticket Window sign. Rita's heart skipped a beat when she asked the man inside, "Where can we find Mr. Vascom?"

A portly, balding man with a red-veined nose and a bloated face gave them a quick once over. Not bothering to remove the cigar from his fish-like lips, he waved a pudgy dismissive hand. "G'wan. Git movin'. Got no time for tramps!"

Rita boiled with anger. Her eyes flashed like lightning in a fierce storm. "We're not tramps, we're performers and we're here to see Mr. Vascom."

Busy counting money, the man didn't bother to look at them. "G'wan, I say or I'll sig the boys on ya."

Phil stepped in front of the ladies. In a stern voice, he said, "There's no need for threats, sir. We have business with Mr. Vascom."

The man's blubbery lips twisted into a sneer. He judged them with cold, hard eyes. "For the last time, I'm tellin' ya get lost or you'll wish ya neva bin born." He reached down, pulled out a tent stake and pounded it against his meaty palm.

Rita's throbbing face turned scarlet and shouted, "Listen, you. You don't scare us. We're here to see Mr. Vascom and we won't leave without seeing him!"

Ida bellowed, "That's right! We're not leaving until we see him!"

A woman stepped outside a nearby wagon and asked, "What's all the commotion, Rosy?"

She appeared to be well over six feet tall with broad shoulders, narrow hips and a made-up face as long as a size twelve shoe. She wore a beautifully tailored red suit and a double-breasted jacket with a black velvet collar. On her head sat a large, broad-rimmed black hat adorned with fancy bows, velvet muslin roses and ostrich feathers. Finely stitched kid gloves covered her huge hands.

The voice of this elegantly dressed woman was thunderously deep, yet rich and lilting. Daintily, she brought her hand to her mouth. "Oh," she uttered.

"Dolly, what's the scoop? What goes on out there?" Out from the same wagon popped a short, thin man about five feet tall with a generous handlebar mustache whose ends twirled to thin points. He wore a smart one-button cutaway frock of silk and cashmere. His long, snout-like nose gave him the appearance of a well-dressed fox.

Rita asked, "Are you Mr. Vascom?"

Rosy growled, "Scoot, I says. Stop botherin' everyone."

The tall woman asked, "What do you want with Mr. Vascom?"

Ida spoke calmly. "Please, listen a minute. I know we look like *bumicas*, but we really are performers. We look like this because we just came from the earthquake in San Francisco." Ida grabbed her beard and waved it. "See, I'm a bearded lady." And my Phil here, he's Phillay Phil Da Amazing Boneless Wonder. Wait till you see him. He can tie himself into knots and roll around like you wouldn't believe."

Ida put her arm around Rita, "And this...this beautiful young lady is Rita. You should see her when she's cleaned up."

Ida withdrew a soiled hanky from her sleeve and licked it. She was about to wipe some smudges from Rita's face until she saw a don't-do-that look in Rita's eyes. Ida smiled and continued, "This Rita...she's beautiful and she does tricks on a horse that'll make your hair stand up with how she flips and jumps and whatnot. You should see how the crowd goes crazy for her."

Once again, Dolly put a hand to her astonished mouth, "Oh, my goodness, you poor people, the earthquake! Duncan, these poor people have suffered so. We must help them."

"Jees," said Duncan, "The earthquake, eh. That must have been sumpthin'. Yeah, okay, sure. We'll give a hand."

Rita spoke up, "It's not a handout we're looking for. We really are good at what we do. In fact, we have a letter of recommendation from Doctor A. Van Sandt, lll. Uh...at least we did, but it got destroyed with the rest of our stuff."

Vascom's eyebrows shot up with pleasant surprise. "Doc! Jee's, you know Doc? How is that old scoundrel? I haven't seen that son of a gun for...jees...it must be ten years, easy."

Rita bowed her head, "I'm sorry to say he's in jail. He got three years for theft. But he's all right. He was happy to get off so light. He said they could've strung him up."

Vascom looked at the troupe as if he was seeing them for the first time. "So, how'd you meet Doc?"

Phil said, "We did mud shows with his Emporium of Exotic Delights through all the backwater towns."

Vascom scratched his ear and smiled. "Emporium of Exotic Delights, eh? So, Doc's still a grinder pitchin' the chopped grass and flea powder? Jees, I never thought the fuzz would catch him though. He musta slipped up on the fix. Well, that could happen to anyone, even the best of 'em."

Rita asked, "It sounds like you know him pretty well. How'd you meet him?"

Vascom said with pride, "We met in jail when we was just kids. We used to grift together as young men. Sleight of hand and the short con was my game." He laughed. "Jee's, I was just fourteen when we got together. Doc stood on a corner selling Miracle Soap out of a suitcase, see. When a crowd gathered, Doc would pitch his spiel, telling the suckers his soap cured corns and all kindsa skin diseases. While Doc was selling soap, I was picking pockets."

The trio gave each other a knowing look. Ida said, "So, Doc's been a *gonif* since he was a kid. No wonder he's so good at it!"

Rita said, "Doc said you'd let us stay with the circus."

Dolly replied, "Oh, yes. We must let them stay."

"Okay, Dolly." Vascom looked at the trio and said, "I tell you what. Get yourselves fixed up and we'll have a look at ya. If ya pass muster we'll sign you up." Vascom turned to Rosy and ordered, "They can stay for now. Get 'em fixed up and give 'em whatever they need."

"Um, Mr. Vascom," Rita asked, "I'm afraid I lost Blaze, my trick horse, in the earthquake. Is there any way I can borrow a pony?"

Dolly answered, "Sure, honey. Rosy will take you to Mr. Merryweather, the ringmaster. Just tell him Dolly said to give you a good rosinback from ringstock. Now you go get yourselves cleaned up and fed in the cook tent and go enjoy the show tonight."

Turning to Rosy, Dolly said, "Make sure they get the bible seats."

As they walked away, Ida whispered to Phil, "That Dolly. She's such a nice lady. But ya know...I think she's a *faigelah*."

Rosy had one of the roustabouts show them their sleeping quarters. Ida and Phil were in the married people's car, filled with thirty-two other people. They were happy to be sleeping in a real bed of sorts. But they were disappointed at being separated into upper and lower single berths.

Rita fared only a little better. She would sleep in the single women's car where the berths were stacked three high on two sides and being a 'First-of May' newcomer, she got the top bunk.

A roustabout said he would bring them some water to wash with and meet them at the dressing tents. News spread on the back yard that the First-of-Mays had experienced the San Francisco earthquake and fire. It was big news.

As Ida, Phil and Rita waited for the water, show folk came by and offered them clothes and whatever help they needed. They asked questions about the earthquake and the fate of San Francisco.

Astonished by the sudden attention and the variety of people, Rita was too overwhelmed to speak. Before them were midgets and giants, people with various oddities and many beautiful ladies.

One man, handsome and well proportioned, came forward leaning on a cane. He shouted, "Leave them be! Give them a chance to catch their breath." The crowd scattered. "I apologize for their rude behavior. It's not our way to ask questions."

Rita smiled. "No need to apologize. They were just being friendly."

The man stared salaciously into Rita's eyes and announced, "My name is Rudolfo Tonelli, of the Magnificent Tonelli's. I am an aerialist extraordinaire. But as you can see, I am grounded like an eagle with a broken wing."

"Pleased to meet you. I'm Rita O'Reilly and this is Ida and Phil Frump. Did you have an accident?"

Rudolpho ignored the Frumps. He stared at Rita. "Oh, yes. I'm one of the few flyers who can do the extremely difficult triple somersault. Alas, my clumsy catcher missed his timing, and while he's healthy, I can only sit like a townie and watch the show."

"Is it serious?" she asked.

Rudolpho stared more deeply into Rita's eyes and said, "I fell from the heavens, but now that I've met you, I'm beginning to feel much better." He kissed the back of Rita's hand.

Rita blushed and fumbled for something to say. "Uhh. I'm a... I'm quite a sight, I should get cleaned up."

"If you look this beautiful now, I can't wait to see you after you have freshened up," Rudolpho said. "If you are going to the show this evening, I would very much like to accompany you."

Pleased to be treated like a grown woman for the first time in her life, Rita's body tingled at his words. "Yes, I would be very happy if you would accompany us to the show tonight."

Once again, Rudolpho kissed her hand, "Until tonight."

Rita and Ida went into the ladies' dressing tent and giggled about Rudolpho's flirtations. Two women entered and offered some clothing. They were identical twins, both tall, shapely and beautiful. Not only did they look exactly alike, but they also spoke at the same time, almost like hearing in stereoscope. "We're the Melon Sisters, I'm Jean and she's Irene, we're chorus girls. We thought you could use some clothes."

Rita said gratefully, "Thanks, we appreciate this. Our clothes are only rags. We'll return these to you soon as we get ourselves settled. I sure can't wait until the water comes. I feel like I've been rolled in mud and set to dry."

In unison, they said, "Don't expect much water, everybody gets two buckets a day. That's for bathing, washing your hair and your clothes."

Ida exclaimed, "Just two buckets, *oy gevalt!* I don't think that's enough even to wash mine *toches!"* Everyone laughed when Ida slapped her oversized rear end.

They spoke quickly, barely taking a breath. "It's the same for everyone, even the stars unless it's really, really hot. Then we get two more after the matinee. There are lots of rules we got to follow too. Like everybody only gets two trunks for their stuff, one for your costumes and one for personal stuff. Oh, and payday is Thursday. Say, you're going to need a grouch bag, a place to hold your money. That's what everyone uses. We keep ours around our neck. That way you'll never worry about losing it."

Ida said, "Such a good idea!"

The twins pointed to each other. "Oh, the cook tent!" They spoke faster. "Everyone sits in their place. The first table near the door is for Mr. and Mrs. Vascom. Next to them, sit Rosy, Mr. Bradington, the equestrian director, and Mr. Merryweather, the ringmaster, and the other managers. Then come the performers. The equestrians always get the best seating 'cause that's the tradition, then the aerialists. In the back of the tent are the roustabouts. When you hear someone say, 'The flag is up' it's time to eat. But don't delay because everything here is on time. Breakfast at a half-hour after we arrive, lunch eleven to noon and dinner from four-thirty to six. At six they pull the cook tent down and it moves out with the first departing train."

"*Oy!*" Complained, Ida. "My head is spinning. Please, can you talk a little slower?"

They looked at Ida and said, "Oh, the prodigies can eat at any time since they're always showing and they can eat in their costumes too, but everyone else has to dress properly."

Rita and Ida both questioned, "Prodigies?"

"Oh, the grinders used to call them freaks, but Mrs. Vascom won't let anyone use that word. Mrs. Vascom used to be in the sideshow and hated when someone called her a freak."

Ida lifted her eyebrows and shook her head, with mock self-importance she said, "So how do you like that? I got a fancy name now, I'm a prodigy."

"Well, we gotta get going. Just let us know if you need anything else."

Ida and Rita thanked the twins, proceeded with their bathing and retired to their bunks to nap before dinner. After a tasty meal of fried chicken, mashed potatoes, green beans and apple pie for dessert, they were off to see the show.

Dance with the Devil

Chapter 50

Ida, Phil and Rita joined the crowd traversing the midway. They bubbled with excitement relishing the sounds, smells and colorful banners. The concession stands filled the air with aromatic clouds of popped corn and sweet candy. Shouts from candy butchers rang out, "Git your pink lemonade and fairy floss right chere! C'mon kiddies, git your hot dogs while they last. Popcorn for you and peanuts for the elephants. Soda water...all flavors. How 'bout a big red candy-coated apple!"

Stepping into a world of wonder, Rita chatted and laughed as they passed the bugmen hawking chameleons and shouts of "Souvenirs! Get your circus souvenirs right here. Lookie! Lookie! Lookie! Bring home a circus souvenir."

Hurrying along the midway towards a row of booths, they saw canvas banners each portraying exaggerations of the attractions within. Ida pointed at the banners. "Look Phil...you and me...we're gonna be up in lights just like them!"

The spiel of the ticket seller enticed them as he emphasized every syllable. "Step right up, la-deez and gen-tul-men, step right up. For one thin dime, yesss, just one tennth of a dol-la you will ex-per-iennce the thrills of a lifetime. Just beneath yon canvas, we have cure-i-a-si-ties and mon-ster-a-si-ties that will dazzle and de-light you. Hur-ray, hur-ray hur-ray...step right up...you don't wanta miss a thing"

With expectations of delight, they entered the sideshow tent. Among the sights was a three-legged man, the fat lady, a fire-eater a sword swallower, a snake charmer and, Rita's favorite, the eight-foot giant surrounded by singing midgets.

On their way to the big top, the trio passed the menagerie where they saw scores of exotic creatures on display including camels, an anteater, zebras, a kangaroo, baboons, a python, cheetahs, a black rhino, a giraffe, leopards, chimpanzees, a gorilla and several elephants.

After marveling at the variety of animals, they made their way to the main entrance of the big top. Just inside the front entrance, Rudolfo waited for Rita. He kissed her hand as he greeted her, *"Buona sera,* Miss O'Reilly. You look lovely." Rita suppressed a giggle as she thanked him for his compliment. "Follow me," he said. "I will show you to your seats of honor."

They sat several rows back but centered from where they had an excellent view. Thrills shivered through Rita. She became the little girl who, so many years before, accompanied her parents to the circus.

The lights dimmed. In a spotlight stood the equestrian director, distinctive in his black silk top hat, bright red jacket, white riding breeches and shiny patent-leather boots. His voice boomed, "Ladies and gentlemen and children of all ages, welcome to Vascom's Big Top. And now on with the show!"

Music blared and the spectacle began. A lavish parade, including all the extravagantly dressed performers and animals circled the hippodrome track. Rita couldn't wait to be part of the parade. With difficulty, she controlled the urge to jump up

374

and yell, "Hey everybody, look at me, I'll be parading with you soon!"

The amazing circus production ended all too soon. The trio talked excitedly of the various performances as they made their way back to the train. Rudolpho accompanied them, interjecting his critiques of the performers and their skills.

After about a quarter of a mile, they reached their individual sleeping cars, Rudolpho said, "Rita, my dear, I cannot tell you how much I'm looking forward to spending time with you. Please call upon me if there is any way I can be of service. Have a good night, lovely Rita, and pleasant dreams. I will count the hours until the sun rises and I see your beautiful face once more."

It was difficult for Rita to keep from laughing at Rudolpho's silly words. But she managed to say, "Thank you for a pleasant evening Rudolpho, but I'll be busy preparing my act and doubt I'll have much time to socialize. Good night."

Rudolpho sensed the rejection but smiled as he bid her good night. Rita waited until he was out of earshot, then she rolled her eyes at Ida and Phil as if to say, "Thank God, he's gone."

Rita smiled as she lay in her bunk. *My dream is about to come true. I made it to the circus! I'm sorry Blaze can't be here with me and I wish Momma and Poppa could be here to see me perform. One thing is for sure, I will be a famous circus performer and nothing can stop me!*

Dance with the Devil

Chapter 51

Over the next few weeks, Rita joined with Ida and the circus seamstress as they worked together to design her equestrian costume.

The ringmaster took a liking to Rita and saw that her athletic skills could be honed into a first-rate routine. He told her of famous female equestrians like the graceful Ella Bradna, who included a variety of horses, dogs, birds and even a singing Hungarian midget in her act.

There was Mae Wirth who could perform amazing feats like a double backward somersault from one horse to another while blindfolded.

Rita strived to become as accomplished as these and many other female equestrians. She worked hard to make her act special and today she was to perform in full dress accompanied by the circus band for Vascom and Dolly's approval.

Phil and Ida peeked from behind the bleacher seats watching Rita's performance with nervous anticipation. Phil whispered to Ida, "Good heavens! She's all grown up and has become a beautiful young woman."

Ida got weepy and wiped her nose with the hanky she removed from her sleeve. She sighed, "Oy, such a beauty." She sniffled, "Look at her, like a ballerina on a horse, and such a fast horse yet."

Phil whispered, "I knew she was capable of many tricks but I've never seen her perform like this before. She's so professional and so graceful. I have to say that as a fairy princess, she's so beautiful and so believable that anyone who doubts that there are fairies in the world will be immediately converted!"

They looked at each other and smiled lovingly.

The Vascom's were impressed with Rita's routine but wanted to see the audience's reaction. That night Rita gave her first performance. She entered the ring to the romantic waltz from Tchaikovsky's "Swan Lake." She sat atop a sturdy white rosinback Lipizzaner steed made up to be a unicorn with a horn that sparkled like white diamonds, his tail enmeshed with white ribbons, flowers and strands of pearls.

Rita's gown of white satin brocade covered in white pearls and a slit skirt, made her appear as a vision of loveliness. Her long. shapely legs, so like her mother's, were crossed at the knee as she rode sidesaddle. A sash of white roses and pearls crossed her left shoulder and passed over her bosom attaching to her tiny waist. Rita's thick red hair, lacquered into big curls, bounced below a pearl tiara. Attached to her back she wore silver-sequined wings and atop her shoulders sat two trained white doves that she petted and kissed.

After prancing around the ring several times, the tempo of the music changed to the exhilarating "Danse Russe" from *Tchaikovsky's Nutcracker Suite*. Releasing the doves into the air, Rita jumped to the ground and began to turn cartwheels and somersaults alongside the horse as it cantered. Then with her body poised to meet the horse's motion, she vaulted from the ground to the back of the horse.

As the horse loped beneath her, she stood erect, with hands out at shoulder height. Rita balanced on one leg and leaned forward, like a vision of Mercury in flight. She brought her arms forward rested them on the saddle and turned her supple body into a handstand. Rita followed with a series of backward and twisting somersaults sailing high into the air with the grace and charm of a butterfly and landing firmly onto the broad back of the proud steed.

The crowd went wild with applause.

The Vascom's were so thrilled with the audience's reaction to Rita's routine that they told her she would appear as the third act after one of the main attractions and signed her to a season contract for $150.00 per week. They said if she continued to be such a big hit with the audience, next season they'd give her a big signing bonus.

Rita couldn't believe that she could make so much money doing something she loved. She laughed to remember how thrilled she had been to receive $2.00 a week from Doc, the old scoundrel.

I'm so happy, but there is one more thing I need to make my life complete...

Dance with the Devil

Chapter 52

The bright morning sun filtered through the lace window curtains as Émile sat in his exquisite dining room about to enjoy his *petit déjunener*.

Fresh cut daffodils and roses wafted their fragrances from the vases placed throughout the room, blending with the tantalizing aroma of warm, baked goods.

Covered with the fine linens, the grand table was laden with croissants, brioche, pain au chocolat, pain aux raisins and chausson aux pommes. Toppings included chocolate, butter, honey and a variety of marmalades.

Sterling silver pots of coffee and *chocolatine*, a cut glass pitcher of fresh-squeezed orange juice and mini-pots of espresso were available to be poured by the attentive serving staff.

Off in the distance, Émile heard church bells chime the ten o'clock hour.

Émile was surprised to see his granddaughter, Mimi, enter the room. He could only think how closely she resembled his beautiful daughter, Lola, with her lustrous black hair, large sapphire blue eyes set above pronounced cheekbones and full red lips. Believing Lola's suicide had been his fault, guilt and regrets boiled within him. Regardless of the humiliation Mimi often caused him, indulging his granddaughter excessively was his way of atoning for his tragic mistake.

She waited while a servant pulled a chair for her to sit across the table from Émile. *"Bonjour Grand-père,"* Mimi said smiling.

With his reverie interrupted, Émile returned a pleasant smile and said, "You're awake quite early this morning. How unusual for you."

A smartly dressed servant placed a napkin on her lap with flair as she responded, "I woke early this morning especially for you. I wanted to catch you before you left for your morning stroll. I have something to tell you."

"It must be important for you to rise before late noon."

"Yes, it is." Mimi announced, "You'll be happy to know that I've decided to marry."

With the look of astonishment, Émile leaned back in his chair. "Marry? Are you serious?"

Mimi laughed, "I know it's hard to believe." The servant held a silver platter before her. She selected a single chocolate croissant for her plate.

"You told me that no man could ever be acceptable to you as a husband. This man must be very special indeed to have captured your heart. Who is he?"

"It's not that he's captured my heart nor is he special." Mimi took a sip of coffee.

Puzzled, Émile asked, "Then why do you wish to marry him?"

"I've grown bored with Paris. It's time for me to spread my wings."

"I don't understand."

"He has worldwide connections and I'm intrigued by him."

"Mimi," Émile cocked his head, "You are marrying this man not for love, but for his connections?"

With nonchalance, she said, "Yes. He's far from handsome and he's rather dull. But he comes from a family of enormous wealth and power and he's devoted to me. His family has holdings in many parts of the world including Germany, France, Russia, Mexico and South America."

With a bemused smile, Émile said, "It seems as if you're making a business arrangement rather than a love match."

"You surprise me, *Grand-père.* Aren't most arranged marriages business transactions? Think of it this way. I've saved you from the impossible task of finding me a suitable match."

Émile's expression turned wistful as he remembered Lola's wrathful reaction to the matrimonial match he made for her. "Yes, it is best that you've made your own decision about whom you chose to marry. Who is this fortunate man?"

"He is a cousin of my friend Margot. His name is Nicholas Willensschwach Von Reichen. Although born and raised in France, he's of German heritage. His father owns the Tintenfisch Iron and Steel Company, headquartered in Germany."

Émile's face flushed. He threw his napkin onto the table. "German! You know I despise—"

"Yes, I know," Mimi said flatly. "In 1870, Old Prince Otto, The Iron Chancellor, provoked poor France into the Franco-Prussian war and we lost miserably. They made France pay five billion francs in reparations and give them the territories of Alsace and Lorraine. And I know how you cried when you saw the German army parade victoriously through Arc de Triomphe de l'Étoile."

Émile set his mouth in a hard line and clenched his jaw. His voice was firm as he said, "I'm dismayed that you plan on joining our family with...Germans! Of all the men for you to choose from, why did you have to choose a German?"

"I'm sorry, *Grand-père*, but I've made my decision. Nicky's father is aging and in ill health, so he gave his only son full authority to oversee their holdings in Russia, Mexico and South America, to prepare Nicky to be at the helm of his worldwide operation. I find that incredibly beguiling."

Mimi finished her breakfast as Émile stomped from the room. She then returned to her boudoir to contemplate her marriage details. A wicked smile crossed Mimi's face as she thought how easy it had been to snare Nicky. Her crusade to find the right husband had worked perfectly. It surprised Mimi that, despite his wealth and worldliness, at twenty-five, Nicky could be so unsophisticated with women.

She, a guileful spider, had left a trail of temptation for him to follow. He, enticed by the promise of her incredible delights, had eagerly entered her intricately woven web and once entrapped, had become a willing prisoner. Snaring him into her web had been almost too easy.

"I hope you know what you're doing!" As they sat together outside the civil ceremony office awaiting Mimi's arrival, Nicky's best friend, Max admonished him. "There are so many reasons you shouldn't marry Mimi." He pointed to his fingers and counted the reasons. "Your parents hate her. She has slept with half the men in Paris. She's selfish, opinionated, unpredictable and annoying. She'll take advantage of you and she's just not right for you."

Nicky's wavy blond hair brushed his collar as he shook his head and laughed. "Have you finished? Or will you remove your boots and count on your toes?"

"This is not funny!" Max insisted. "Why must you marry Mimi? Why not have an affair with her? You'll soon tire of her and then she'll be out of your system for good."

"My dear Max, I appreciate your concern, and you are correct. She is those things you say. However, none of that matters. I can sum up all of the reasons I wish to marry her with one finger." Nicholas pointed to his heart and said. "I love her!"

To Émile's disappointment, rather than a grand affair at the magnificent Church Madeleine, Mimi chose to marry in a private civil ceremony. Instead, she threw all her energy into a grandiose and scandalous wedding party.

Nicholas went along with Mimi's ostentatious scheme, but it outraged his parents that their only child had chosen to marry a French woman, especially one of her notoriety. They hadn't met her, but they despised Mimi for her reputation as 'verdorbene frucht,' spoiled fruit, and refused to attend the marriage ceremony.

Mimi convinced Paul Poiret, a famous French master couturier, to host her party. Poiret was known as a designer who, by dismissing the use of corsets and eliminating layered petticoats, had radically changed the feminine form with his new fashion designs. He had also gained fame for hosting the most prestigious and extravagant parties in Paris.

She informed the invited party guests they must wear Persian-styled costumes. Most of them hired Poiret to create their costumes, as did Mimi and Nicky.

Mimi had her exotic costume designed in vibrant glowing colors and beaded embellishments. She wore a Lampshade style tunic with a knee-length triangular shift wired at the hem and edged with fringe. Blousy Harem pantaloons and jeweled slippers completed her outfit. Nicky wore a fur-bordered caftan and a jeweled turban.

Guarded by half-naked blackamoors, the venue had been transformed into an Arabian palace. Brightly lit trees with live parrots and monkeys sitting on branches enhanced the exotic atmosphere.

An orchestra led by French musician, Alfred Lemair, played traditional Persian music using indigenous shawms, horns, trumpets, and percussion. Spicy fragrances of curries and every kind of exotic delicacy filled the air. Clear long-necked carafes and crystal ewers contained a palate of fluorescent colored liqueurs including Creme de Violette, garnet bitters, yellow-green chartreuse and ruby grenadine, expertly mixed to create mysterious and sinful drinks.

Their wedding party made bold headlines in the society pages and announced their honeymoon plans to visit the heads of state of Russia, Argentina and Mexico. Upon their return to Europe, the couple would reside in Germany.

On their honeymoon, Mimi planned to meet some of the most powerful men on earth. Although Nicky had met with these men several times in the past, it had always been as his father's son. Now that his father's illness had grown worse, the senior Von Reichen had insisted that, for the sake of maintaining a strong relationship, Nicky meet them as the head of the company.

Nicky resisted at first, but Mimi maintained this would be a perfect honeymoon, and besides, he could introduce them to his dazzling wife. Nicky acquiesced.

Mimi thought: *How clever I am to find a man willing to open the doors for me to meet and mix with powerful heads of state. I feel a glow all over just thinking about the power they possess!*

Their first stop on the multi-nation journey was Russia where they met with Czar Nicholas II and his wife, Czarina Alexandra, aboard The Imperial Romanov Yacht Standart. The flag, with its regal double-headed eagle, fluttered in a stiff breeze as the couple approached. They boarded and were greeted with an offering of bread and salt, the traditional Russian symbol of hospitality.

Fitted with ornate fixtures, mahogany paneling, crystal chandeliers and other luxurious amenities, The Standart presented a floating palace for the Russian Imperial Family.

The Czar, dressed as a British yachtsman, had a carefully tended brown beard and mustache. His captivating eyes, creasing around the edges when he laughed, were his most distinguishing feature. Charismatic and cheerful, the Czar and his wife had

387

opposite personalities. Despite her attractive features, she appeared shy and stiff. She spoke little with a face both rigid and unsmiling.

Nicholas tried to hide his consternation, when over lunch prepared by a French chef, Mimi asked the Czar, "Your Imperial Majesty, I wonder, what does it feel like to be the Emperor of All Russia? To rule as an autocratic monarch requiring over 130 million people to obey your supreme authority?"

The Czar answered her questions politely but quickly changed the subject to business.

After several days of sightseeing, Mimi and Nicky were off to Argentina where they met the Chief Executive, Julio Argentino Roca. Mimi asked Roca what it was like to rule his country. Roca began a long dissertation about his glorious career. His announcement that under his leadership, Argentina had become richer than France, Germany and Italy surprised Mimi.

With the morning Argentine government conferences completed, Nicholas and Mimi tried their luck at the Palermo Hippodrome Horse Racing Track. At the racing enclosure and the grandstand, they encountered the well-heeled gentry in all their finery, showing off their wealth and extravagance.

Afterward, they enjoyed Giuseppe Verdi's Aïda at The Colón Theater, one of the world's top opera venues.

Late that evening, guides transported Mimi and Nicky around the city, ending at the main thoroughfare, Calle Florida, a commercial street located downtown.

As if in a magnificent ballroom, sparkling lights festooned the streets. The couple watched as a varied procession of spectators passed them, including powdery old ladies in the shelter of their broughams, google-eyed tourists, and sailors who swaggered along the sidewalks. Out from the music halls strolled chanteuses, lavishing seductive smiles as they passed young men who playfully twirled their black mustaches.

Although charmed by the district, Mimi soon became bored and decided it was time to leave. When the sudden sight of tango street dancers displaying their talents caught her attention, she shouted, "Stop the carriage!" At its sudden halt, she jumped from the brougham and stood to watch their performance in awe.

Nicky and their guide alighted the carriage to stand with her. She demanded of the guide, "What is this dance?"

"It is called Tango and it is very popular here."

"I must learn how to dance this Tango. Teach me!"

"Oh, Señora Von Reichen," the guide said with a hint of embarrassment, "I'm sorry, I cannot dance the Tango."

"Then take me someplace where we can learn!"

"We?" Taken aback at the thought, Nicholas balked. "I can't learn this dance!"

With a sharp look, Mimi insisted, "You can, and you will!"

"With your permission, Señor Von Reichen, I will take you to a Milonga where you may learn." Nicholas sighed and shrugged his shoulders and they piled back into the carriage.

They practiced the dance every night until it was time to leave for their next meeting.

Their next stop was to meet Porfirio Díaz, President of Mexico. When Mimi asked him about ruling Mexico, he ignored her.

She interrupted Diaz and repeated her question. He smiled and said, "Señora Von Reichen, I hope your husband won't mind when I say you are a beautiful woman. But I do not wish to muddle your brain with serious political issues."

Mimi was about to explode when Nicky intervened, "President Diaz, you displeasure me when you speak to my wife in such a condescending manner."

"There's no need to defend me, Nicky," Mimi looked at the President with disdain. "Obviously, the troubles with his political opponent, Madero, weigh heavily on the mind of Señor Diaz. Perhaps Mexico is not a secure country in which the Tintenfisch Iron and Steel Company should continue to invest."

Diaz glared at Mimi, then immediately changed his expression to a forced smile. He said, "My apologies to you, Señora." He turned to Nicky, "and to you as well. I misspoke. I beg you to forgive my rudeness. I will be happy to answer all questions you—"

"What is that?" Mimi had heard noises from the street. She strode to the window to observe a procession of people carrying cardboard puppets, ceramic sculptures, posters and papier-mâché skulls and skeletons.

Nicky and the President joined Mimi at the window.

Diaz replied, "Today is the Mexican holiday, Día de Los Muertos, The Day of the Dead. Every year it takes place over the first two days of November. The holiday is of Aztec origins and, in the 1500s Spanish missionaries introduced All Saints' Day and All Souls' Day, mixing Native American traditions with Catholic holidays."

"Worship of the dead?" Mimi raised an eyebrow, "It sounds irreligious to me."

"Here, death is not seen as the end of one's life, but as a natural part of the life cycle. The observances include spending time at cemeteries, making shrines to the dead and displaying artistic representations of calacas, or skulls and skeletons."

Mimi's eyes flashed, "It sounds marvelously gruesome."

Actually," he said, "it is a festive occasion, rather than a morbid one. Some families go to the graveyard to celebrate through the night. They clean and decorate the graves, sometimes they set up offerings on the gravestones, as bells are rung.

"Nicky, let's see the parade and follow them to the cemetery." Mimi gave Diaz a challenging stare. "I would prefer to spend time with the dead!"

Dance with the Devil

Chapter 53

With business completed in Latin America, the couple returned to Germany. On their arrival in Berlin, Heinrich Schnauzer, a corporate assistant employed at Nicky's, Tintenfisch Iron and Steel Company, received Mimi and Nicky ebulliently.

Schnauzer, a tall, gaunt, nervous man, sported a long, pointy nose that protruded from his jaundice-colored face. Thinning blond hair exposed Schnauzer's pink scalp. His small dark brown eyes were in constant motion, like two flies searching for a place to land.

He welcomed Nicky with the traditional deference to his authority and followed by lavishing the couple with sugarcoated praises. Schnauzer reached for Mimi's hand and greeted her in French. Mimi snubbed him. Irritated by his fawning behavior, she snapped, "My German is a little rusty, but your French sounds like a pig squealing in pain. Speak to me in English if you can, or don't speak to me at all!"

Red-faced, he bowed and apologized, "You are correct, Frau Von Reichen. Please forgive me, my French is abominable. Most Germans of importance speak English in Berlin, even our beloved Emperor, so you will have no trouble with the translations."

A chauffeur-driven company's limousine awaited to take them to Nicky's ancestral family home, Schloss Von Reichen. During the ride Schnauzer chattered incessantly. He sniffed as he spoke, exposing very long front teeth. With his eyes constantly in flight. Mimi thought he resembled a demented bunny rabbit. She and Nicky gazed out of the automobile windows, ignoring his sycophantic babble.

They rode through the long Seigesallee, the Victory Boulevard in the Tiergarten where thirty-two marble statues lined the wide, tree-lined boulevard. Mimi asked Schnauzer about the statues.

Schnauzer sniffed with a wrinkled nose. He turned to Mimi with a proud smile. "Ah, so you take an interest in our proud Germanic heritage, ya? These are statues of former Prussian royal figures. Exquisite are they not? They were sculpted by—"

Mimi sneered, "I've never seen anything so ugly!"

Snauzer's fly eyes spun wildly. He sniffed a few times, brought his finger to his shirt collar and pulled at it. He cleared his throat and changed the subject. Brimming with German pride, he announced, "So! Frau Von Reichen, it is my understanding that you have never been to Berlin before. So, I am pleased to have the honor of informing you of the proper Berlin etiquette for women." With a pompous air, he removed several papers from his satchel as if they were the Ten Commandments handed to him by God.

Mimi turned to Nicky with a surprised smile. She couldn't believe Schnauzer was serious. "I never realized you Germans had a sense of humor!"

Nicky groaned under his breath and slumped into his seat.

Schnauzer cleared his throat. With a loud, firm, voice he read:

"Number one: no lady may walk in the streets of Berlin wearing anything but the color black.

Number two: never allow a man into your home when you are alone.

Number three: never speak to a man when you are alone.

Number four: always step off the sidewalk to let an officer pass.

Number five: never tap on the privacy glass of a taxi with a stick or umbrella

Number six---"

Mimi tapped the privacy window with her umbrella to get the chauffer's attention.

"No, no, Frau Von Reichen, you must have misunderstood. This is not permitted!"

Mimi ignored him. When she had the driver's attention, Mimi ordered him to stop the car. The driver pulled over. Mimi reached across Schnauzer's lap and opened the car door.

"No, no, Frau Von Reichen, das ist nicht zulässig!"

She pushed Schnauzer out of the car.

"No, no Frau Von...das ist nicht......achhh!"

Mimi motioned for the driver to continue, leaving Schnauzer laying on the sidewalk with his fly eyes searching for a place to land.

On their way to the Schloss, they rode over gentle forest-covered hills with idyllic rivers, storybook castles and palaces perched atop cliffs. Mimi took a minimal interest in the scenery and was relieved, at long last, to arrive at the family's ancient home. Nicky advised Mimi that his parents preferred to remain at one of their many other residences. She was pleased they weren't there to greet her.

Mimi found the castle to be ugly and uncomfortable. The big hall had little furniture and what there was of it was large, heavy, over-gilded and at least 150 years out of date. Dozens of family portraits hung along the depressing chocolate-brown colored walls. Mimi could feel the sneer of her mother-in-law's eyes when Nicky pointed to her portrait. "That's the first thing to be removed from this dreary place!" Mimi insisted. She was sure her mother-in-law had furnished the castle. It was just like her: large, heavy, over-gilded and at least 150 years out of date!

Lined along a huge winding staircase, the entire household staff assembled in their best liveries. The men wore blue coats with white gaiters and gloves. The maidservants wore short crimson dresses, white aprons and stockings with white cambric caps and plaited hair hanging down their back. Mimi laughed at the ridiculous outfits and quantity of staff it seemed necessary to take care of two people.

The organization of the household followed strict military lines, requiring every servant to perform a daily drill. The staff had rules for everything. When Mimi wished to exit one room for another, one servant rang a bell and another servant opened the door. A footman walked in front of her wherever she wished to go. Amused at first, Mimi quickly lost patience with German etiquette. The servants scattered like frightened children when they heard the blasphemies Mimi shouted, demanding that they stay out of her way.

At a dinner party, Mimi conversed with Rudolph, a friend of Nicky's. When he asked her impression of Berlin, he was astonished by Mimi's reply.

"Despite Berlin's overbearing pomp and obsession with German militarism," Mimi said, "I find it to be a city pulsating with growth.

"Of course, Berlin will never match Paris, Vienna or London for style or class. However, I'm impressed by the peoples' arrogant pride and determination to become the wealthiest capital of the most powerful nation on the European continent.

"I see Berlin as a city of the future. I think of it as the powerful throbbing of a young man's first erection—strong, hard and ready to explode!"

Dance with the Devil

Chapter 54

Mimi looked forward to the schedule of parties and dinners. Their first would be tonight's party at the home of Herr Große Böcke, a rich industrialist.

The home's massive stone exterior belied the Beaux-Arts interior style. Designed to impress, Mimi took notice but had little interest in the extravagant ornamentation of the statuary, arches, balconies or the triangular pediments with classical relief sculptures that greeted her.

The guests indulged in appetizers and cocktails as they mingled about in the opulent ballroom. Nicky introduced Mimi to many of the guests. Mimi enjoyed the attention of the men who ogled her and found the pretentious smiles of jealous women amusing when they glared at her beauty.

Mimi soon became bored and scanned the room. It didn't take long for her eyes to home in on one man. Mimi grabbed Nicky's arm and pointed to a handsome young military officer. She whispered into Nicky's ear, "Quick, come and introduce me."

When Nicky saw who she pointed to, he scowled. "Why do you want to meet him? There are many people of importance here. He's just a soldier."

With a coy expression, she said, "Nicky, are you jealous?"

He looked at her with his sad, dove gray eyes, "Yes, I am."

"Well, Nicky, you'd better get used to being jealous. This is just the beginning!"

He reddened from his neck to his scalp. "Never forget, you're married to me!"

"Never forget, I will always do as I please!"

Introducing her with a tinge of bitterness, Nicky's eyes bored into Friedrich Joséf Von Brandt. "This is my wife, Frau Mimi Von Reichen, whom I dearly love."

In a blasé tone, Mimi said, "Nicky, be a dear and get me another glass of champagne."

Nicky opened his mouth to speak but pursed his lips and gave Mimi a brooding look. He turned to Fritz, and, with a taut voice, he excused himself and marched away.

Crowned by sun-bleached golden hair, Friedrich's tanned face emphasized steely blue-gray eyes.

Like a hungry tigress about to devour her catch, Mimi's eyes flashed as she admired Friedrich's Adonis-like features.

"*Enchanté*, Frau Von Reichen." He smiled at Mimi through flashing white teeth, dramatically clicked his heels and bowed to kiss her hand.

Mimi gave him her most delicious smile, "Oh no, Frau sounds so old and stuffy. Call me Mimi, everyone does."

"Ah, then you must call me Fritz. Everyone does."

Mimi teased, "Everyone? Aren't you a general of some kind? Don't you lead tin soldiers around in a circle? I should think they would at least call you General Fritz?"

Standing at attention, Fritz thrust forward his muscular chest and strong, square chin and proudly announced, "I am a Fregattenkapitän Friedrich Joséf

Von Brandt, Commander of the Naval Airship Division."

Mimi continued to tease, "Oh, the navy! So, what do you command Fregattenkapitän? A rowboat?"

Fritz laughed. "You have a rather low opinion of me. I am a respected destroyer captain, who is the most experienced and skillful Zeppelin commander in the Naval Airship Division."

Mimi taunted the Commander, "Zeppelins? Oh, really? So, you fly balloons?"

"No, not balloons but dirigibles…airships. They're much larger than balloons."

"How big are these balloons that you fly?" Mimi asked and flashed coquettish eyes at Fritz.

With an air of self-importance, he explained, "These so-called balloons are 128 meters long."

Nicky returned with Mimi's champagne. Without a glance at Nicky, she exchanged her empty glass for the full one Nicky offered her.

"Hmmm, 128 meters long did you say?" Mimi gave Fritz a sly smile and said, "I'd like to see that."

Fritz smiled, "I would be delighted to show it to you. Can you come, say…tomorrow?"

Agitated, Nicky's asked, "What are you talking about?"

"Fritz is telling me about his big balloon."

"Herr Von Reichen, forgive my rudeness. I was explaining to Fraulein—"

"Call me Mimi!"

"Pardon, I was describing the airship I command and I offered to show it to her."

Without hesitation, Mimi said, "Tomorrow, yes! I would love to see your big balloon tomorrow."

With pleading eyes, Nicky looked at Mimi. "Darling, these ships can be dangerous. They're filled with highly explosive hydrogen…and I'm sure the commander is busy…besides, we are expected at Herr Zinzendorf's tomorrow."

Turning to Nicky, Fritz said, "If tomorrow is not possible—"

Mimi responded, "Tomorrow is absolutely fine!"

Fritz regarded Nicky, "I will be most proud to give you both a flight in my Zeppelin."

"Nicky couldn't possibly come." Mimi gave Nicky a hard stare. "He must go the Zinzendorf's tomorrow for important business, but I most certainly will be there."

Fritz peered at Nicky with a puzzled expression. "But for a woman to be unaccompanied, surely that will not be—"

"Nicky won't mind. Being unaccompanied only heightens the excitement, don't you think?"

Fritz hesitated, "Well, ah…"

Mimi turned to Nicky. With an insincere smile said, "Schatzi, of course, you won't mind, isn't that so?"

Dejected, he acquiesced, "She may go with you."

Fritz looked serious, "Are you sure? This is very unusual."

Mimi chimed in, "Fritzy, I think you may already know that I am an unusual woman."

Fritz smiled charmingly, "So! With your permission then, Herr Von Reichen, I will be delighted. We take off at sunrise. Be sure to dress warm, the air gets cold at 300 meters."

That evening, as they undressed for bed, Nicky pleaded, "Please don't go tomorrow. I fear for you. Zeppelins are dangerous. You can be seriously injured."

"Oh, Nicky, stop your pleading, you know it just irritates me. You say Zeppelin's are dangerous, so what? That makes it all the more exciting. Don't you ever want to do anything exciting? You're such a scared little rabbit. Afraid of your father. Afraid of your mother. Afraid of me. Will you never take risks?"

"Risks?" He ran his fingers through his hair. In a strident voice, he said, "Does it make sense for you to risk your life?"

"That's the thing! The pounding of my heart as the blood surges through my body. The quickness of my breath as danger approaches. The intensity of heat in my loins as they become inflamed with passion when I'm on the razor's edge. That's what makes me feel alive. Don't you want to feel alive?"

Nicky grabbed Mimi in his arms. His feverish lips sought hers.

Mimi laughed and pushed him away. "You're like a little boy. Learn to be a man. Do something dangerous. Live life on the edge! Maybe then, I will consider giving myself to you again."

"I've never seen anything so big in my life!" Mimi announced through the open window of her limousine.

Fritz opened the car door and took her hand as she exited. "*Guten Tag*, Mimi."

Mimi surprised Fritz by kissing him on both cheeks. She could see in his eyes he beheld her with admiration, or at least, lust.

403

Ravishing in her long white ermine coat and matching hat, she smiled impishly and said, "Surely, it's too big to fit."

With a puzzled visage, Fritz followed Mimi's eyes. "Oh, you're speaking of the Zeppelin. It may appear that the airship won't fit through the hanger doors but," Fritz smiled smugly, "we Germans believe in precision, you know. Yes, it is big, but I assure you it will fit. Come, you'll see."

She put her arm in his and they entered the gigantic hanger. Walking the breadth of the shiny, silver, cigar-shaped Zeppelin, Mimi said, "It's the biggest balloon I've ever seen!"

Fritz frowned, "Perhaps after you've had a flight in this magnificent machine, you'll think of it by its rightful name."

Mimi eyed the men inside the hangar. There were hundreds of them preparing the ship for flight. "So, you need all of these men to help you get your balloon up?"

Fritz looked uncomfortable. He cleared his throat. "These men are my ground crew." He pointed, "You see the sandbags? They hold the ship down. When they're removed, the ship will rise about seven meters, which places a strain on the ropes. To bring her through the hangar doors it takes a ground crew of 300 to hold the ropes."

Mimi's eyes grew wide, "Three hundred men, oh my!"

"Yes, they're necessary to keep the ship from floating. Once outside the hangar, seventeen hydrogen gas-filled cells keep the ship aloft. Once aloft, the ship's streamlined design allows it to flow smoothly, moving through the air much the same as a fish moves through water. The engines will drive the ship as we steer her with movable flaps and rudders."

"This is all very fascinating, but shouldn't we be getting started? I'd like to climb aboard."

"Of course." Fritz brought Mimi inside the gondola, the control room of the ship. "Please wait here while I get us underway." Mimi watched him jump from the gondola and walk beside the ship. His well-trained eyes observed every detail of the maneuver.

When he returned to the gondola, Fritz informed Mimi, "I don't want to frighten you but my main concern is a sudden, unexpected gust of wind that could smash the frail hull against the hangar door."

"Oh, Fritzy, a little collision doesn't frighten me."

He gave her a peculiar look, then watched the ship move smoothly through the hanger doors. Once they were out on the field, Fritz shouted the command: "Up Ship!"

The lines were released and the ground handlers heaved on the handrails attached to the control car. Like a giant bubble, the ship began to rise. The next moment, the engines came to life with a roar and the Zeppelin climbed to cruising altitude.

Fritz explained, "We will stay at cruising altitude so you can enjoy the view. You'll be able to see Germany as if you were flying like a bird."

As the ship slipped gracefully through the cold morning sky, they stood together looking out the open window. He pointed out the sights as Mimi leaned seductively against him. Although he treated her courteously, she sensed his arousal. He surprised her when he excused himself to approach the crewmen. He remained with them a long while giving them instructions.

Hearing her call his name, Fritz turned to see Mimi's ermine coat on the floor. Except for her high-heeled, high-laced boots and her ermine hat, Mimi stood before him naked with arms akimbo.

Fritz's eyes popped when he saw her naked jaunty pose. "Frau Von Reichen!"

"I said, call me Mimi, everybody does."

"What are you doing? My crew—my crew can see you!"

"You're their Commander, are you not?"

"Yes."

"So, command them not to look!"

Fritz cleared his throat and bellowed, "Men! Eyes forward!"

Mimi crooned, "Ooooh, Commander...what a big Zeppelin you have!"

Chapter 55

Not many events excited Mimi, but when Nicky announced that His Imperial and Royal Majesty, the German Emperor and King of Prussia, Kaiser Willhelm II, had invited them to a court ball, excitement rippled through her body.

On the evening of the ball, they arrived at the magnificent Würzburg Residence. The main structure comprised a central rotunda with two side wings, each with two interior courts. Richly decorated, vases, trophies, and a large coat-of-arms covered the exterior façade.

The astounding 400-room residence had a formal reception area, considered a masterpiece of Baroque style construction, with a grandiose double staircase of immense proportions.

Above, one of the world's largest frescos exhibited four continents: Europe, America, Asia and Africa.

White painted walls with silvered moldings and a glistening parquet floor that displayed a crowned Prussian eagle added to the pomp and pageantry of the magnificent White Hall ballroom.

Wearing a formal starched white uniform ornamented with gold, Kaiser Wilhelm greeted his guests. The eldest grandchild of Queen Victoria, he appeared the embodiment of majesty and might. With his upturned W-shaped mustache, his erect carriage and finely chiseled features, he gave the impression of a self-confident leader and warlord of a great and prosperous nation. Admired and beloved by the German people, his subjects firmly believed God himself anointed the Kaiser with the right to rule.

Nicky's family had close ties with the Kaiser, as they had had with his deceased father, Friedrich III. When they approached the Kaiser, he greeted Nicky fondly and inquired about his parent's health.

Upon greeting her, a glimmer in the Kaiser's eyes belied his attraction to Mimi's beauty. Nevertheless, the Emperor received her with his typical stern expression. Born with a malformed left arm, he had developed an extremely powerful right arm. He enjoyed exploiting his power with a vice-like handshake, turning his ring inward to add to the pain of his grip.

Mimi had been forewarned by Nicky of Wilhelm's penchant for disarming those unaccustomed to his quirks. She devised her own surprise for the Kaiser with a ring specially made for the occasion. The ring's exquisite fire opal had concealed a sharp, needle-like point at the back of the ring. When the Kaiser squeezed Mimi's hand, he winced in pain. Watching the Kaiser's face flush with anger delighted Mimi. When he realized her joke, his anger turned to boisterous laughter. With a broad smile, he said, "Frau Von Reichen, never has a woman left such an impression upon me!"

Second in importance to the Emperor, Chief of Staff and Military Cabinet Chief, Alfred Von Großer Käse, stood beside the Kaiser. His eyes wandered from Mimi's face, along her graceful neck to an outrageously expensive marquise-shaped diamond necklace that nuzzled atop her fleshy cleavage.

He smiled wickedly. "Frau Von Reichen, you are a true original. You must join me for dinner tomorrow night so we can get to know each other better." With eyes on Mimi, he said to Nicky, "Oh, Herr Von Reichen, you will, of course, accompany your lovely wife."

Before Nicky had a chance to respond, Mimi said, "Thank you for the invitation, Herr Von Großer Käse, but Nicky's been ill of late and I think it would be best if he remained home tomorrow to catch up on some rest. "Don't you agree, Nicky?"

Nicky's face flashed with animus. His voice was taut. "I'm feeling quite well and would love to join you for dinner tomorrow evening."

"Oh Nicky, there's no need to be such a brave soldier. You must stay home and rest. As for me, Herr Von Großer Käse, I'm in perfect health and would love to join you."

They moved into the glittering ballroom to see over 200 uniformed men adorned by an overabundance of polished medals and by a similar number of women in dazzling gowns and sparkling jewels. Mimi was prepared to not be outdone by the grandeur. All heads turned to Mimi in her diaphanous, red silk gown that clung scandalously to her supple body. She glided through the hall like the snake in the Garden of Eden.

Soon the room opened for dancing. After several waltzes, Mimi ordered, "Nicky, bring them our sheet music."

"No, Mimi." Nicky hesitated. "This is not a good idea. These guests will not be amused and you will gain a bad reputation."

"Do you think I care about my reputation? I can't wait to see the look on their faces. Nicky go and give them the sheet music, now!"

Like an obedient puppy, Nicky gave the music to the conductor, who grumbled when he saw the name of the piece, but Nicky insisted. When he returned to Mimi, the orchestra played "La Canguela," The dance floor emptied as Nicky and Mimi danced a sexy Argentine Tango, shocking their audience. Even the Kaiser was taken aback. Her name on the lips of everyone in the crowded ballroom gave Mimi immense pleasure.

The following evening, Mimi's dinner with Von Großer Käse ended in his bedroom. As they lay naked on his bed, Mimi asked, "Alfy darling, can you use your influence to get me closer to the Kaiser?"

He laughed. "You're quite the ambitious vixen, my dear." Mimi squealed as he leaned over and bit her shoulder. "I'm sure I can arrange a private meeting between you and the Kaiser. But I must warn you he has a predilection for, how shall I say it? Extreme pleasures. More so than anything we've enjoyed, if you know what I mean."

"All the better. "She dug her nails into his arms and purred, "I think Willy and I will get along just fine."

Chapter 56

With a frown of consternation, Fritz knocked on the door of his commanding officer. *It is very unusual for Admiral Moser to ask for me,* he thought. *Am I in trouble?*

He heard the admiral permit him to enter. Inside the room, Fritz saluted and said, "You asked to see me, Admiral?"

Admiral Moser sat behind a large, well-worn desk. He wore a monocle in his right eye and smiled broadly, exposing a mouth of yellow teeth below a flamboyant gray mustache.

"Yes, yes, Commander Von Brandt." He waved to a chair. "Sit." Admiral Moser presented a cigar box. "Have a cigar. It's one of the new types in the shape of a Zeppelin. It's just a gimmick but they aren't bad."

"*Danke,* Admiral." Fritz took a cigar and leaned forward as the Admiral lit it.

"Commander, I have asked you here today to tell you how satisfied I've been with your performance...up to this time."

"Up to this time, Admiral?" Sweat formed on Fritz's upper lip. *Did Mimi or Nicky complain about our indiscretion on the airship?* "Have I displeased you, Admiral?"

Admiral Moser lit a cigar for himself, rose from his overstuffed leather chair and walked to a window. Standing with his back to Fritz, he remained silent as he gazed outside. Puffing on his

411

cigar with one hand, he rested his other hand in a balled fist against the small of his back.

Fritz swallowed hard.

Continuing to look out the window, the Admiral asked, "Commander, how much would you give for Germany?"

"Give for Germany? I'm a soldier. I would give my life without hesitation."

The Admiral turned abruptly and marched to his desk, leaned into Fritz's face, and with their noses almost touching, he snapped, "You would do anything Germany asked of you?"

Without hesitation, Fritz said, "I will always do my duty for my country."

"*Gut!* I have a special assignment for you. This assignment is of the utmost importance."

"*Danke*, Admiral for your faith in me. I will do anything you require."

The admiral gave a brief smile. His chair squeaked when he plopped into it. "I'm happy to hear that, Commander. It has come to our attention that you have had close relations with Frau Von Reichen."

Sweat dripped down the back of Fritz's neck. "Admiral, I—"

"Don't interrupt!" Admiral Moser shouted. He paused before he continued in a conversational tone, "My dear Commander, is it all right if I call you Fritz? Fritz, we are happy about your relationship with Frau Von Reichen. In fact, it will work perfectly in our plan."

Fritz squirmed in his chair, "Plan, sir?"

"Why yes, Fritz." The Admiral removed the monocle from his eye and cleaned it with his handkerchief. "Our beloved Emperor believes in peace, but the ambitions of other nations trouble him. Even as we speak, it's probable that England, Russia and France are plotting against us. After all, if the British were not preparing for war, why would they build their Dreadnoughts? They are larger, swifter and more heavily gunned than any battleship the world has seen, and they're building them by the dozens!"

"This is disheartening news, Admiral. I assume we are preparing to defend our country."

"Yes, of course. In self-defense, we've been expanding our navy and building our own Dreadnoughts." The admiral placed his handkerchief in his pocket and replaced the monocle to his eye. " However, German warships burn Welsh coal. If England stops the supply of coal to our fleet, Germany will be hopelessly crippled."

Fritz leaned forward in his chair. With furrowed eyebrows, he asked. "How can we prevent this from happening, Admiral?"

"The advantage for us is that the British fleet runs on oil purchased from Mexico. If Germany has access to this oil, we can control the spigot and bring the Royal Navy to its knees!"

"Ah, I knew you would have a plan!"

Admiral Moser pounded his desk.

Fritz flinched.

With a strident voice, the admiral said, " It's essential that we expand our foreign markets into Mexico and South America. However, the United States and their ridiculous Monroe Doctrine are standing in our way. The United States says they will go to war rather than let a country take possession of any territory in their hemisphere!"

Fritz's eyebrows shot up, "War with the United States, *mein Gott!*"

The Admiral's face grew stern. "We can't let them get away with this!" The admiral jumped from his seat. His face was red and puffed like an overblown balloon. "The United States has stolen land from Mexico and taken over the Panama Canal. Does the United States expect the world to believe they'd go through the trouble and expense to build a canal so far from their borders and not desire to possess the surrounding territories? Nonsense!"

Fritz nodded his head. "I agree. We cannot trust the United States."

Admiral Moser returned to his seat. In a calm, friendly voice, he said, "Now, Fritz, you're wondering what all this has to do with you and Frau Von Reichen, *ya?*"

Fritz cleared his throat.

"As you know, Herr Von Reichen owns the Tintenfisch Iron and Steel Company. He has factories with hundreds of employees in Mexico. Mexican peasants must be made to understand the danger they're in from the imperial ways of the United States. We must encourage them to stand up for their rights. To help them, we asked Herr Von Reichen to allow us to distribute pamphlets to his workers. However, he's been reluctant to cooperate with us."

Fritz cocked his head. "Reluctant? I would think he should be proud to assist Germany in this dire situation."

"Not all Germans understand the value of loyalty. However, the Emperor has had several opportunities to discuss our dilemma with Frau Von Reichen. She assures the Emperor that she will persuade her husband to allow us to distribute

414

pamphlets. But sadly, she has not agreed to help us to infiltrate our specially trained workers to join Von Reichen's company and convince the peasants to stand up for their rights. "Do you understand our dilemma?"

With knitted eyebrows, Fritz said hesitantly, "I think so."

"Listen carefully. If Mexico had a falling out with the United States, they might be willing to give their loyalty to a country that will provide them with protection and support. A country that would stabilize their economy and improve their lifestyle. What better country than Germany?"

The Commander sat erect and said, "These people should be honored to receive aid from Germany!"

"I believe that too. But Frau Von Reichen sees no benefit in involving herself. So, Commander, the Emperor has asked for your help in this matter."

Stunned, Fritz asked, "The Emperor asked for my help? But Admiral, I'm a soldier. I fly Zeppelins. Why does the Emperor want me for this project?"

"You can influence Frau Von Reichen to help us achieve our goal."

"Why me?" Fritz removed a handkerchief from his pocket and dabbed the sweat on the back of his neck. "I have no influence over her. I don't believe God himself has influence over her."

"So, we'll sweeten the pot, eh?" The admiral leaned into his chair, looked at his cigar and casually took a puff. "She has an affinity for power. If she helps us to gain economic influence in Mexico, the Emperor has informed me he will allow her to become President."

"President? Of Mexico?" Fritz thought for a moment. "But what about the existing President?"

"This is a time of great unrest in the world. Many leaders have been assassinated by disgruntled anarchists who believe their government does not work for the best interest of their people."

"But Admiral Moser, Frau Von Reichen, the President of Mexico? A woman?"

Admiral Moser shouted, "Do you question the Emperor's wisdom?"

Fritz squirmed, "I would never do that!"

"So, you may ask, Frau Von Reichen is not Mexican, the people don't know her. How is it possible for her to be elected?" Not waiting for an answer, the admiral continued, "Promise the people that you will satisfy their most immediate needs. Convince them they will have a better life and back it up with immediate relief. Desperate people will vote for anyone they believe will give them what they need."

"This is very interesting." Fritz nodded. "The Emperor is brilliant. But if I may ask, what makes him believe Frau Von Reichen is up to the task?"

The admiral looked to the window. "The Emperor is impressed with Frau Von Reichen. He realizes she is a smart and ruthless woman, and she has all the qualifications necessary to rule a land of dirty peasants." Whipping his head back to Fritz, the admiral's voice was firm. "Besides, we'll be in control. She can enjoy the title of President and do as she wishes, so long as she follows our rules.

"Fritz, you have carte blanche to accomplish this goal. Your funds are unlimited. You can take her to Paris or wherever you need to, but time is of the essence. We expect results soon. Get started immediately, Commander."

"You men are always playing with each other's territories, always trying to show off who has the biggest one." Mimi and Fritz lay in the bedroom of her Paris townhouse. They were relaxing between marathon sessions of sex when Fritz explained the Emperor's proposition.

Fritz kissed her neck and asked, "Would you like to be President of Mexico?"

"A woman president, hmm, well, there was Catherine the Great and Queen Victoria, why not Madame President Von Reichen, eh?" Mimi laughed. "I'm tempted, but my grand-père would have apoplexy if I worked for the German government. The Franco-Prussian war was more than thirty years ago. Yet, the French and Germans still hate each other. Grand-père keeps a ragged old picture showing a triumphant German soldier, in his spic-and-span uniform, on a highly groomed horse, single-handedly killing a dozen Frenchmen. He says a copy of it hangs on the walls of every German soldier's barracks."

Fritz nodded, "I am familiar with the picture, I've seen it many times. But that's just propaganda to bolster the courage of frightened recruits."

Mimi shook her head, "You should see his expression when he looks at it. He pulls out his handkerchief to wipe his runny nose and dry his wet eyes." Louder now and with more energy, she continued, "Do you have any idea how many times

I've heard about the German army parading victoriously through Arc de Triomphe de l'Étoile?"

Fritz ran the back of his finger along her cheek. "That was a long time ago. Germany and France are not at war now. Besides, France is no longer interested in Mexico or South America. This proposition will bring no harm to France." His voice softened. "Besides this could be revenge for Cinco de Mayo when the French lost their hold on Mexico. I think your grand-père would be proud of you if you were to become President of Mexico. And think of all those men you would have at your command." Fritz laughed and said, "You'd be the one commanding: Men, eyes forward!" They both laughed and went at it again.

Chapter 57

Although tempted, Mimi understood she'd be under the Kaiser's thumb and not allowed to make her own decisions. Besides, she took pleasure in keeping such a powerful man dangling as he awaited her decision.

In honor of the proposal, she threw a ball with Mexico as the theme.

Built to fit the massive ballroom of Nicky's Paris chateaux, a miniature Mexican village spilled outside onto the grounds. Designed to present an accurate version of a night in Mexico, the makeshift village included downsized haciendas, a small mission, adobe shops with tin roofs and Mexican artisans plying their various crafts.

Handlers walked among the attendees with indigenous animals such as ocelots, iguanas and rattlesnakes. Birds of every variety and color were free to fly throughout the grounds. Among the variety of flora were desert scrub, Agave cactus and in terracotta pots, fragrant and colorful flowers had been planted.

Mariachi bands provided the music for groups of hired dancers who performed the traditional *ballet folklórico* dressed in bright, colorful outfits.

Mexican chefs prepared food for the party attendees who mingled as they sipped tequila and ate burritos, enchiladas, tacos and tamales.

The chatter hushed to surprised whispers when the lights dimmed and large searchlights pointed to the landing atop an expansive staircase. Hearing the rhythmic blare of Mariachi trumpeters, all eyes looked upward.

The guests expelled murmurs and gasps as Mimi appeared in the traditional costume of a matador. Made with silver and gold sequins, the costume known as '*traje de luces*,' or the suit of lights, dazzled the audience.

Over one shoulder Mimi wore a silk promenading cape covered with intricate embroidery and adorned with gold, rubies, diamonds and other exquisite gemstones. Hair plaited in the traditional bun, a bullfighter's black Montera hat sat on her head. She wore a finely tapered tie and a short, close-fitting rigid jacket over a white silk shirt. On her feet were traditional ballerina-like slippers with silk stockings to the knee. An outstanding taleguilla, form-fitting pants, with an embroidered stripe rising from just below her knees to her waist, exposing every inch of her shapely outline, much to the delight of the men and the envy of the women.

Mimi removed her cape and twirled it in a spectacular manner. She spun it above her head, passed from hand to hand and whipped it down and around, to circle her waist. The cape's gold and gemstones shimmered as she moved with a dancer's grace.

Among the controversial guests, Madame Sophie Décharde, the most celebrated madam in Paris, attended with her lover, Apache.

Surprised and dismayed to see Sophie laughing and enjoying herself, Émile's jaw clenched. How he despised her. Painful memories flooded his brain as his mind flashed back to the day he had first met her.

How I hate this woman! The nerve she had to blackmail me for an outrageous sum of money and force me to accept my baby granddaughter, Mimi. So what if Sophie tells Mimi what I did? She will have much more to lose than I will. I've given Mimi everything. But Mimi is unpredictable and capable of anything. I hope Sophie takes no pleasure in revealing to Mimi that her mother committed suicide because of me.

When Émile saw Sophie approaching with a salacious smile, he gave her a monstrous glare and stormed away. He heard Sophie and her lover burst out laughing when they watched him scurry off.

Back from his travels, Charlie Sloan learned about Mimi's party and wangled an invitation. He hoped to see Lola and Mimi happily together. Arriving late, he missed Mimi's performance. Searching the crowd for Lola, he bumped into Sophie. He was surprised to see Sophie had been invited and assumed all the differences between she and Lola had been peacefully resolved.

Charlie approached. "Sophie, look at you! You've become quite the *grande dame* in your exquisite dress and jewels. You appear to be doing well." He jested, "I take it you're still in the business of pleasure."

"Yes, my life has taken a successful turn." With a grin, Sophie said, "It's so good to see you, Charlie, my old friend. You're as handsome as ever. It's been a very long time. Where have you been?"

"I've been traveling a great deal, mostly in Canada. I returned to Paris to attend the funeral of my grandmother."

Sophie offered her condolences and continued to catch up with their memories. As they chatted, Charlie turned to take a glass of tequila from a passing waiter. His eye caught sight of a dark-haired beauty approaching. He almost dropped his drink. "Lola!" He exclaimed. "I'm so happy to see you! I hoped you'd be here."

Mimi and Nicky were close by. When she heard her mother's name, she approached Charlie and offered him her hand and a charming smile. "I am Mimi Von Reichen. Everyone tells me I look like my mother."

"It's hard to believe you look so much alike. Is Lola here?"

Mimi looked at Charlie as if he was a fool. "Here?" She laughed. "Don't be ridiculous. My mother is dead! She died when I was born."

Charlie shook his head. "No, that's not true. Your mother was alive last time I saw her. It was several years ago."

Sophie screeched at Charlie, "Shut up, you fool!"

Mimi pushed Sophie away and stepped closer to Charlie. With narrowed eyes, she asked, "What are you talking about?"

Sophie whispered into Mimi's ear. "Don't listen to him. Everyone knows he's a crazy man!"

Mimi shouted, "Shut up, Sophie!" Then asked Charlie, "How do you know my mother?"

"Stay away from him," Sophie insisted. "He's a well-known trouble-maker!"

Mimi faced Sophie and grabbed her arm in a vice-like grip with one hand and Charlie's arm with the other. "You're both coming with me," she commanded. Mimi turned to Nicky and ordered, "Get my *grand-père* and bring him to the library at once!"

Sophie attempted to pull herself free from Mimi's grip. Mimi dug her nails into Sophie's arm. Sophie cried out in pain, "Let go of me! I demand to leave!"

Mimi's face turned to stone and with eyes like daggers, she glared at Sophie. "I warn you. You don't want to disobey me!"

Sophie's eyes searched the crowd for Apash. She yelled, "Apash, come help me!" Sophie's jaw dropped when she saw him hurry towards the exit.

About to enter the library, Émile stopped short in the doorway.

In an ominous voice, Mimi said, "Come in Grand-père. We have some things to discuss."

Émile removed his handkerchief from his pocket and wiped the perspiration from his face.

"Grand-père, this man tells me my mother is alive. What do you have to say?"

Blood drained from Émile's face. He stuttered, "Wh...What do you mean...alive?" Then his eyes narrowed and his head whipped towards Sophie, who cringed in the corner. With suspicion, he looked at Charlie. "Who are you to say Lola is alive?"

"My name is Charlie Sloane. I have been a close friend of Lola Dupin for several years but that was quite a while ago."

Sophie shouted. "You see! This man doesn't know what he's talking about. He has obviously mistaken Lola La Fontaine for someone named Lola Dupin. Don't listen to this madman!"

Charlie ignored Sophie and continued. "I don't know what's going on here but when I met Lola in the states—"

Émile gasped, "You met Lola in the United States?" He glared at Sophie. "How can that be possible? When did this happen?"

"DON'T LISTEN TO HIM, " Sophie screamed, "HE'S A LIAR!"

Mimi grabbed a letter opener from the desk. She charged to Sophie and pointed it at her throat. *"Imbécile, ta gueule!* Shut your face Sophie, or I swear I will ram this into you!"

With her mouth agape and popping eyes, Sophie squeezed further into the corner.

Continuing to eye Sophie, Mimi shouted. "I want to know EVERYTHING! Start from the beginning, Charlie."

"All right, Mimi. I met Lola in Paris many years ago and we had an affair. I had to leave for a while—"

"You had an affair with my mother!" Mimi snarled at Charlie. "Are you my father?"

Charlie looked straightforwardly into Mimi's eyes. "No, I swear to you I am not your father. I don't know who is, but maybe Sophie does."

With a face like a panther about to strike, Mimi turned to Sophie.

Sophie shook her head vehemently. "No, please, I don't know who your father is. I only know he is a German soldier."

Mimi slowly turned her face to Charlie, "Continue your story."

Charlie took a deep breath, "So, when I returned to Paris, Sophie came to me and told me that Lola had a miscarriage and was about to commit suicide.

She suggested I take Lola to America. "Sophie even accompanied us to the ship to bid us *bon voyage*"

He gave Sophie a dirty look. "I brought Lola to New Orleans but I had to leave soon after. We met up again in Rimrock Springs, Arizona, but once more I had to leave. I lost contact with her but when I returned to Rimrock Springs a few years later and met Lola by accident. She gave me this." Charlie reached into his breast pocket and pulled a picture from his wallet. "Look at this."

Mimi rushed to Charlie and grabbed the picture from his hand. Her eyes grew large as she stared at the photograph. It was as if she was looking at herself! "This is my mother? Who is the girl with her?"

Charlie responded. "That's Lola with her daughter, Rita. The picture was taken several years ago. I haven't seen her since."

Mimi thrust the picture at Émile's face. "What do you make of this?"

With his mouth agape, Émile stared at the photo. He turned the picture over and read the inscription:

To my dearest Charlie,
Wishing you good luck always.
Lola and Rita O'Reilly
August 20, 1895

"1895? This is Lola's handwriting." Émile looked at Sophie with anger. "Does this mean Lola is alive?"

Charlie said, "When Lola gave me the picture, she was very much alive and happy too. She's married to a rich miner. I can't remember his first name, but the little girl is Rita, Rita O'Reilly."

Mimi exclaimed, "My mother is alive? I have a sister? Charlie, where are they?"

"Last time I saw her, she lived in Rimrock Springs, Arizona. I told her I'd seen your picture in the newspaper several times and asked if she had visited you in Paris."

He looked at Mimi. "Your mother was shocked. Sophie told her you died in childbirth."

All heads turned to Sophie with anger in their eyes.

Charlie looked back at Mimi. "Lola never knew you were alive. She said she was coming to Paris to find you. I assumed she did."

"My mother never knew about me? She was coming to Paris to find me?" Mimi marched to Sophie and put her face close. She sneered, "This is all your fault. I will make you will pay for this!"

Her head shaking in fear, Sophie's mouth opened to speak but no words came.

Mimi looked at Nicky, "I must find my mother and my sister. "Nicky, make arrangements to leave for Arizona immediately!"

Charlie shook his head. "I'm sorry, you won't find them in Rimrock Springs."

Mimi raised an eyebrow. "And why is that?"

"Last year, I went there for the annual poker tournament. I hadn't been there in many years and I was surprised to find that town no longer exists. The entire town is a copper mining operation. There's nothing there but a huge hole in the ground."

"*Merde!* I must find them. If not there, where can they be?"

"I'm sorry Mimi, but they could be anywhere in Arizona or any other place. The United States is very

large and the name O'Reilly is common. I wouldn't
have any idea about how you can find them."

"Oh, I will find them, Mimi declared. "I swear I
will. Somehow, someday, no matter what it takes, I
will find them!"

The End. . . of this story...

Acknowledgements

I am grateful to everyone who helped me bring this long overdue book to life. To my friends Jackie and Dennis Kaperick, who, although I'd given up my dream to publish this book, encouraged me to persevere. To the Cuenca Writer's Collective led by Franny Hogg Lochow, whose critiques educated and inspired me to become a better writer. To my beta readers: Claire Middleton, Suzanne Ward, Brenda Schanzer, Pat Simmons, Laura Austin and fellow author Curt Locklear, who provided me with brilliant insights. To my mentor, editor and friend, Carolyn Hamilton, who took me by the hand and helped me through the maze of marketing and publishing. My thanks to each of you, for without your help, this novel would continue to collect dust in my bottom desk drawer.

Ren'e Fedyna, born in New York City, developed a love for historical fiction at an early age. After graduating magna cum laude from Mercy College, she worked for six years as a copywriter at an advertising agency in Los Angeles and later studied Interior Design at UCLA. After 25 years as a self-employed Interior Designer she retired and achieved her dream to become a writer of historical fiction.

A personal request:

If you enjoyed reading *Dance with the Devil*, I would really appreciate it if you would go to Amazon, rate the book, and write a sentence or two about what you liked best.

Here's a link you can paste into your search bar to go straight to the review page:

http://www.amazon.com/review/create-review?&asin=B07Z1GQM8C

If you have questions about *Dance of the Devil* reach out me here:

Rene@renefedyna-author.com

Please visit my website at

www.renefedyna-author.com

If you'd like to be on my VIP list to be the first to learn about events and future books, please email me here: Rene@renefedyna-author.com

If you would like to know more about Lola's adventures and haven't already read it, check out the first book in this series, *Dance of the Restless Soul.*

Ren'e

Ren'e Fedyna